LOST
HORIZONS

LOST HORIZONS

THE DESCENDING WORLDS BOOK 2

JUSTIN S. LESLIE

Podium

Cover design by Alexandre Rito

ISBN: 978-1-0394-5027-1

Published in 2024 by Podium Publishing
www.podiumaudio.com

LOST HORIZONS

We are just an advanced breed of monkeys on a minor planet of a very average star. But we can understand the universe. That makes us something very special.

—Stephen Hawking

PROLOGUE

W hat's that?" Lieutenant Laura McAlister, also known as Mac, asked as she yawned awake. Her warm middle-of-the-night breath was quickly sucked back in not to offend her companion. Seeing that her night-time heater, Master Sergeant Walker, wasn't stirring, she tapped her index finger on his forehead, finally waking the sleeping giant.

A light breeze flowed over the powdery, soft white cotton sheets supplied by a group of local handweavers on Asher. A leg, arm, and tendrils of long flowing hair contrasted the otherwise pristine pillowy white bed set. The rustle of the fabric invited them both to go back to sleep and forget about whatever it was that had piqued Mac's interest.

"It's zero two hundred. Go back to sleep," Walker insisted just as the odd, green, rapidly flashing light strobed through the window again.

The cool, calm, dark night once filled with the sounds of the massive swaying trees had been quickly transformed by the trembling sounds of distant rumbling thunder. The supposedly unfamiliar couple both sat up in bed, quickly letting their military reflexes of getting the hell up take charge of their now familiar bodies.

"Is that bad?" Mac asked as Walker shrugged.

Running to the window, Walker realized he was letting it all hang out, quickly grabbing a pair of discarded boxers on the floor. "I don't know. We haven't been here long enough to know everything. Maybe it's just a bad storm."

What greeted both their eyes was something they could not explain. Unless Asher's moon or clouds sent massive beams of green photon lasers to its surface, the chances of the occurrence unfolding in front of them being a natural event immediately dropped to a butt-puckering zero percent chance of not being an attack.

The settlement of *Brightstar*'s leftover crew and several of Fourth Foot's remaining soldiers now called the Gulch home. It was a quickly developing fortification tucked neatly under the several dozen-story-tall trees that darted out of the countryside like protective shields. If they weren't on the very edge of one of the massive swaths of forest, they would not have witnessed the event.

Red lights started flashing as the two once dormant communicators started buzzing in a mix of chirps, beeps, and *oh shits* from someone trying to get one of the not-too-sneaky pair's attention. Walker grabbed his quickly, responding to the night watch.

"Go ahead."

"It's an attack," Petty Officer Miller's voice came over the comm. He had been one of the Fleet personnel assigned to the engineering team aboard the *Brightstar*.

"Where?" Mac asked out loud. The man—already knowing about the couple, unbeknownst to them—heard her comment.

"Working on that now. I already sent a message to Dax to see if he knows anything. Oh, and we all know about you two," Miller finished as they both blushed.

Dax was one of the leaders of Arcadia. The massive mining city several miles away from the Gulch was still in various stages of self-realization that everything they knew about their day-to-day lives was a lie. His sister, Vax, had opted to stay at the Gulch, enthralled with the newcomers from both Earth and Solaria.

Fifteen long, now caffeine-fueled minutes later, the leadership team was all piled into the small briefing pod salvaged from the *Brightstar*'s wreckage. Dax's face, pale as ever, flickered onto the primary monitor as Miller walked in, handing out several tablets with all the collected data on it.

"Dax, it appears that your scanners were able to triangulate the event," Walker started.

"Yes. I can confirm the blast took place four hundred miles to our east." Dax paused, letting that sink in.

"That would mean . . ." Miller trailed off, only to have Mac finish for him.

"That would mean that blast was large enough to destroy an entire city the size of Arcadia. I mean, we could see it from here."

The room stilled as Dax took back over. "I know we were planning on reaching out to the other cities as soon as we got Arcadia under control, but I have triangulated this blast to have hit our neighboring city, Canto. According to the database Albert unlocked, the city's main function was food production."

"Food that we received a shipment of two days ago," Vax added. She had taken on the mantel of overseeing Arcadia's and the Gulch's food and power situation.

"Shit," Walker huffed. "We need to do a full scan of sub- and outer orbit. The fact we haven't had another attack means they're either testing us or it's a single ship with a single photon weapon that's recharging. Lieutenant McAlister, we will need to get a few attack fighters in orbit to recon the situation."

Mac nodded, knowing she would personally take on the assigned task. Vax walked up to the monitor, turning to the group. "From what we have gathered, there are several cities like Canto that produce food and other perishables. We will need to send the preprogrammed message Albert put together out to the rest of the cities."

Walker nodded, no hesitation, just as a light tremor made its way through the floor and through the soles of everyone's feet. Dax looked stressed, turning to a group of citizens who had come forward after hearing the news supporting the change.

The truth was that several of the city's inhabitants were already involved in seeking out the truth. One such group had helped Mac when she first arrived on the planet, finding her in Totoks.

"It's another attack," Dax noted. "It looks like they attacked some type of substructure. No city."

"Hmph," Walker huffed, turning. "Send a message to Dailey. Tell him."

"Tell him what?" Miller followed up.

"Tell him we are under attack and need immediate assistance." Walker turned to see Mac already gone from the briefing room, heading to the makeshift fighter bay.

One of Fourth Foot's soldiers stepped forward. "We will send out a scouting party to evaluate and report back on the damage," Staff Sergeant Randell Grear noted. It wasn't a request. He was telling the group what he was going to do.

Just as the Nova Space Ranger turned to leave, the prerecorded message from Albert started blaring over every speaker and communication device in all of Asher, including the Gulch. As always, Albert had lived up to his promise.

"People of Asher, I am the great Albert the Almighty, super friendly AI, with a message of peace . . ." The message continued as planned after the exaggerated introduction.

Miller looked down at the communication panel, looking at the signal meter reading thirty percent. At that level, it would take decades for the message to reach the closest outpost or sensor relay. Luckily for Miller, before leaving, Bellman and Albert had devised a plan to send a one-time singular message blast that would be detectable by the crew of the USF *Murphy* after several weeks.

Lifting the small clear casing, Miller pressed the red button, clearly labeled DO NOT PUSH, sending the only message he could think of.

SOS.

CHAPTER 1

THE TIP OF THE ICEBERG

The blue glow of thrusters humming close to ground level sliced through the calm morning sun, reflecting off the blinding Antarctic snow. Grey rocks protruding from sharply angled mountains loomed on either side of the valley, looking as if they had melted into the flat, gleaming hardpack. In random spots, looking out of the cockpit, neon-blue chunks of glacier ice peaked out from random areas that had likely been a once upon a time landing place for the odd ship.

As of two hours ago, one of the Federation's private diplomatic transports had officially been reported stolen from the largest city now inhabiting the southernmost point of Earth, a city that had held more secrets and history than the world was willing to accept when first discovered.

After the Tectonic Wars, with the subsequent formation of the Federation and all the technological advancements, building cities in such harsh environments became within humankind's reach. Galbro was a massive city built half under the snowpack and half reaching the top of the surrounding Queen Maud Mountains, part of the Transantarctic range.

Dorax Flam had been held captive in the Federation's massive facility for the past ten years, only to finally have his chance to escape. After attacking an outpost on one of Saturn's moons, the Alurian, in an attempt to save his own life, had told a fantastical tale of wars fought galaxies away by beings that humans wouldn't be able to fathom. He had even warned of a possible attack on one of their major cities from outside parties.

The part of his tale that had given Dorax his chance to escape was also about to catch up to him.

"Definitely not a pilot. Must be an Alurian flight attendant or something. Would you like some peanuts?" Albert the AI proposed to Captain Ben Dailey.

As of three months prior, his rank of colonel and position as the acting commander of the Pathfinder Battalion had been thankfully sidelined.

The man had been given a simple choice: either keep the rank and title and be stationed within Fleet Headquarters, or revert to his previous command of Viper Company with its crew of Nova Space Rangers. The decision had been made before the offer could be rescinded by the good Senator Deborah Powell.

"You just keep the targeting system locked on his heat signature," Dailey instructed, sitting in the gunner seats of one of the USF *Murphy*'s Harpy drop ships.

"That's a class two Flowman transport. If he figures out how to engage the hyperthrusters, it will be hard to keep up," Lieutenant Jenny Brax, better known as Jen, informed the small group now within visual range of the sleek ship.

The ship was the size of a large car, able to hold two occupants and little to no cargo. The vessel was made to get whoever was inside to their destination in style.

Dailey turned after hearing the clacking of armor from Master Sergeant Don Grantham. "I'm good to go," he informed the group as Dailey turned back to the weapons panel in front of him.

"I'm not sure you'll be able to keep up with that ship planetside," Jen again pointed out as the thrusters on board the Harpy started humming louder.

"Albert!" Dailey barked, wishing Sparky hadn't been left onboard the orbiting *Murphy*. He would have simply asked the ham-crazed, self-proclaimed Alurian war hound leader of Asher to do that little disappearing trick directly onto the bridge of the runaway ship.

"Dailey!" Albert barked back. "Just kidding. Sup?"

Upon integrating into several of Earth's systems, the AI had gained an even more immense appreciation for the classics, including their vocabulary. "I'm guessing they're staying low to keep off the tracker sensors. It's going to take Fleet security too long to get here. I need a course to get us high enough to drop Grantham—"

Dailey didn't finish his sentence, his words lost to the roar of the orbital thrusters being engaged as the Harpy shot straight up at an angle and away from the blurring, snowy ground.

Jen lifted her hands as if riding an out-of-control roller coaster. Dailey was surprised by the grin on her face, considering the tongue-lashing he got the last time he took over the controls of a ship she was flying.

"Yee-haw!" Albert exclaimed as Jen slowly lowered her hands back onto the Harpy's controls; the ship leveled out as the curvature of the Earth came into view. Just as quickly as the AI let loose the old-school cowboy motto of champions, he refocused on the task at hand. "You are back in control. The reentry heading is loading in the nav computer. At five thousand feet, release the kraken."

Jen shrugged. Fortunately, and in some ways, unfortunately, on Solaria, krakens were a very real thing. "Don, you ready?" Jen shouted, focusing on the ground quickly approaching.

Dailey gave a thumbs-up, relaying the good to go from the back of the drop ship. The whistle of air cut through the humming silence as sharply as the arctic cold air now flooding into the Harpy.

Master Sergeant Don Grantham's face shield snapped closed as his voice came over the internal comms. "Dropping in thirty seconds. You say we want to keep the vehicle intact?"

"I would rather not destroy the senator's personal vehicle," Dailey relayed as Grantham chuffed. He was clearly going to do his very best to keep the time-honored tradition of destroying pretty much anything that Viper Company touched that involved a possible threat.

"Might I suggest we get along with it? I detect a change in the ship's thermal signature," Albert cut in.

"In English," Dailey replied.

Jen translated, "He's getting ready to engage the hyperthrusters."

On that note, Don engaged his jump pack, leaping out the cargo door of the Harpy in one fluid, well-practiced motion. Jen quickly closed the door, turning back in time to see Master Sergeant Grantham shot forward like a launched missile.

"I've always wanted to see this," Albert noted as Dailey shook his head.

"You didn't know we existed until a few months ago."

"Well, who's counting," Albert said, the Harpy leveling out just as the Nova Ranger latched onto the shiny, sleek main engine pod. "What's that he's doing?"

Dailey and Jen leaned forward as if it would help them see better. Doing the two a favor, Albert zoomed in on the ship, displaying the scene on the small readout in front of them.

Grantham pulled out a plasma rod, slamming it directly into the engine bay just as Dorax Flam pulled the yoke all the way to his stomach. The senator's ship launched upward at face-melting speed as Jen turned the Harpy just in time to avoid the thruster backwash.

"Damn, that thing's fast," Jen exclaimed, pulling the Harpy in a less graceful ascent into the water-blue sky.

Don's voice erupted over the comms. "My servos are locked up. It's going to be a minute or two."

"Albert, what's his status?" Dailey asked.

"According to his onboard diagnostics, the violent ascent, mixed with the subzero ball shriveling and the ungodly amount of g-forces he just got slapped in the face with, was pretty much the equivalent of hitting a frozen brick wall."

"Jesus, is he okay?" Dailey responded, trying not to sound aggravated.

"Plus, you don't know anything about shriveling," Jen cut in.

"Okay, guys, enough. Is he okay?"

"Oh, look, a direct question. My sensors do get cold, you know. Yes, he just regained full function of his suit and, as he enters lower orbit, will be able to finish whatever it is he is doing to the engine . . . Oh, that's what he's doing," Albert said, again focusing the cameras on the polished ship as the backdrop of space contrasted against the glow of the plasma rod once again activated.

The ship was spinning and lurching in several directions, working to shake off its newly attached appendage as both vessels entered the black of space. Several snapping sparks crackled off the back of the ship as its once brilliant-blue thrusters faltered.

"Is he launching a rocket pack into . . . ?" Jen trailed off as the entire back end of the senator's ship exploded in a flash of brilliant light. Grantham launched forward, pushing his armor suit to its limits as the power meter flashed red on his HUD. The past five minutes had pushed the system to its maximum operating parameters, adjusting for the ascent into orbit.

The explosion was bright enough to activate the light-dampening shields on the cockpit view panels, making its two occupants wince. The pair froze as Albert started whistling. "We got company."

Several dozen Federation patrol ships floated in a horseshow pattern just as Grantham came over the comms.

"I think we're good to go. Ship, not so much."

Dailey leaned forward. "How about Dorax Flam?"

"He's still in the cockpit; I just popped the thruster pod. It makes a hell of a show, but from what I can tell, this ship is made to protect the pilot. We in trouble?"

Dailey leaned back, knowing that Grantham absolutely hadn't taken that into consideration when launching the rocket into the ship's engine bay. "With these goons? No. With the senator? We will see."

"Viper Six, disengage thrusters and stand down," the voice of a young man came over the radio. It was clear they knew who was in the Harpy. Grantham pulsed his thrusters forward, pulling behind him the now detached cockpit of the destroyed ship.

Albert took this as an opportunity to start randomly playing slow jazz through the entire squad's internal comms systems.

"You know, they're going to lock you in a cage if you keep that shit up," Dailey grinned as Jen winked at Dailey.

"Well, at least we know who isn't winning any shuttle races in the near future. Those slowpokes were as slow as molasses in January. Good thing we didn't have a real problem on our hands," Albert chided as Jen glanced at Dailey.

"That's yet to be seen," Dailey replied. He followed this by opening the rear bay, a *whoosh* of air escaping the once pressurized cargo area in the back of the drop ship.

CHAPTER 2

NEW HORIZONS

Senator Deborah Powell side-eyed Captain Dailey while Jen and Grantham sat at the end of the dining table. After getting cleaned up and putting Dorax back in his respective cage, the team finally refocused on the task at hand.

Massive wood beams, carefully carved and preserved, arched over the large table, clearly made to host diplomatic parties. Along the longer sides of the table, fireplaces massive enough to walk inside burned and crackled.

While still a classic fireplace, as with many things, technology had improved not only its output but safety as well. Moshan crackle coals were the latest thing when it came to the classic burning fireplace, something that, in all reality, was rare to see. Not only would they light at a moment's notice with the simple introduction of fire, but they would also go out with a simple wet flick of one's hand and a few droplets. Even better, one set could, if taken care of, last ten years.

Intricate plates and glasses finished off the low, yellowish ambiance of the room. Cozy, inviting, and regal were the immediate thoughts that flowed through visitors' minds.

Dailey and the group, including a now fully automated and up-and-walking Albert, settled down to hear the Alurian's story. After several modifications to avoid everyone freaking out over an Alurian battle mech walking around with an AI that had been floating around in deep space for thousands of years, Science Officer Bellman had devised a visually less threatening droid.

While still lethal if needed, Bellman had removed most of the aggressive edges and, more importantly, the generally off-putting spiked tail. Instead of the Alurian sensor pod once mounted on the battle droid like a head, Bellman had opted to replace it with a general service droid's input array to give Albert an overall familiar look.

Dailey had insisted that if Albert ever got out of line, it would be replaced with a toaster, a threat that Albert had deemed to be at an acceptable level of risk in case he wanted to do something that would get him in trouble. It wasn't a matter of *if* that happened, but when.

Albert was proud of his new mechanized body. He could not only maneuver on his own but also be quickly taken out of the armor if needed. Back on Asher, his next project was the substantially larger mech Sparky had hitched a ride on.

The senator's compound was several miles south of Galbro, built into the side of a snow-covered mountain. Encased deep within the mountain were several high-profile prisoners, as well as top secret tech projects all working in tandem to help ensure the future of the human race.

"And destroying my ship was the only way to get Dorax back?" the senator asked as Dailey shrugged.

"I mean . . ." he stammered before Jen filled in the gap.

"He was about to activate the hyperdrive. We couldn't keep up, and Fleet security hadn't shown up yet."

Satisfied with the answer, Albert added, "You should totally let Sparky and I talk with this guy alone."

"I don't think that will be necessary this time," the senator replied while Albert did the robot equivalent of an evil grin. "Albert, to be fair, the only reason we are here is so you can walk around. Sparky might be pushing it, from what I understand."

Dailey leaned forward, grabbing his drink. "We plan on bringing him down, but we need certain assurances first."

"Such as?"

"Such as no one's going to want to poke and prod him. He doesn't take kindly to that kind of stuff. We've—Well," Dailey corrected himself, "Albert has already agreed to let your team run a diagnostic scan of his systems. Not to mention the ship, which I understand you don't want to broadcast out to the world just yet."

"Perceptive and naive," Deborah replied, making Jen nervously shift in her seat as Grantham chuckled. The senator was one of the few humans—or hell, anything—that could make a comment like this to Captain Dailey without him sticking them in an airlock until they reconsidered the statement.

"I guess you still remember what you used to say to me back at the academy," Dailey said, clinking her glass still sitting on the table as the senator grinned.

"That's what makes you dangerous. I see it as the driving force for often misguided bravery."

Grantham spoke up, also having known the senator for years. "That's why you're a senator and those other washouts are still teaching at the academy."

"An academy we very much need. Tell me again, Master Sergeant, how you launched a rocket into the drive of my personal ship?"

Grantham lightly blushed, something the man rarely, if ever, did. "It's a little foggy, ma'am."

With the pleasantries and general round of practiced jabs at each other out of the way, the senator cleared her throat, standing up as a holo-chart of the Earth erupted in the middle of the table.

"Albert, tell me about the pyramids."

"I mean, you did—well, someone did make a TV show about the star gates. Back in my day," Albert started to a round of groans from the phrase he loved using when about to dive into an overly complicated explanation. And dive he did, before finally summing up the entire hour's worth of overexplaining in one simple thought:

"All you had to do was activate your tracking beacon, and the larger pyramids, as you are calling them, would initiate a star gate above them. Each one goes to a different point in the cosmos. Plus, they used to throw hella good parties at night in the surrounding support cities," Albert finally concluded.

"I know this is going to come as a shock to some of you, but history as we teach it is often not completely accurate," Deborah started as Albert blew a raspberry.

"*Thpppt*, not even in the ballpark. Dailey and his team of misfits already know something strange is afoot at the Circle K." Again, only Dailey fully understood the throwback, the senator only rolling her eyes.

"As I was saying. There is a reason the old governments didn't release certain information. It was much easier to tell a story over time as history. If the general population knew the truth and that we had found actual gates, not to mention certain tech, things could have gotten complicated."

"You mean hard to control," Dailey replied. She nodded in affirmation. "The funny thing is, I get it. What I don't get is why everyone is not letting all this information out."

"Yes. To be completely transparent, if there is such a thing, we didn't truly understand what we were looking at until the war. It changed everything once we found markings in the Alurian ships that matched the tech we had found long since buried on Earth.

"Think about it. People already know to a point. They just don't know all the details," she added as Dailey finally took a bite of the sandwich sitting in front of him.

Jen walked over, manipulating the holographic globe, zooming in on the portion of Antarctica they were now sitting in, noticing the restricted markings on the holographic map. "Why not tell everyone the truth, then?"

Deborah grinned. "Yes, that is one of the things I am advocating for. With the Solarians here, not to mention everything else that has happened, we don't think this will be nearly as shocking as it would have been in the past. That being said, it's all about politics, not to mention there are still gaps that can't be filled in. We're hoping Albert here can fill some of those gaps."

Dailey cut in. "You mean the bottom line. There's money to be made, and it's all about who's going to make it. Why is this area marked restricted?" the *Murphy*'s captain followed up, seeing the same thing Jen had picked up on.

"Why don't I show you," she stated as Albert guffawed this time.

"This is going to be a good one. You want me to spill the tea?" Albert asked the senator.

"Let me guess: we never asked, so you never told us," Dailey added as Albert's mechanical body clicked and whirled as he stood up.

"Pretty much. Unless you want me to walk around rambling out random facts."

"No, we're good. Let's see it," Dailey insisted as the group made their way to a lift leading into the heart of the deceptively large compound.

While the facility had struck Dailey as odd, recent events had maxed out his you-won't-believe-this-shit meter. After several minutes of traveling under the Antarctic surface, the temperature change became quickly apparent as the doors to the lift slid open. Humid, moist air greeted the group as the senator motioned everyone into the massive corridor.

"Why is it so hot?" Jen asked as the senator smiled, punching in a code.

Albert stepped forward, waiting for the sound of gears turning and groaning, which sounded out of place in the high-tech facility, to stop. "Hope you got your tin foil hats ready, everyone," the AI added as Deborah shook her head, knowing the truth of what they were about to see.

"Grantham, remember that one guy in First Foot who was reassigned? We used to call him tin foil head," Dailey pondered.

"Yeah, he believed in all kinds of crazy conspiracies. The moon landing and all kinds of crazy stuff." Grantham looked up, finally remembering his name. "Rosco. Staff Sergeant Rosco. He was reassigned for some reason."

Just as the door opened, Senator Powell turned. "Lieutenant Rosco is now stationed in this facility. I don't think he was all that crazy if you ask me."

Her words were lost as the gravity and breadth of the scene in front of them unfolded. Warm, tropical air greeted them as the reason for the groaning gears came into view.

Massive, dull metal doors covered in vines looking older than time itself supported the newer, sleeker systems opening up into a breathtaking chasm. Giant trees, much like the ones on Asher, and buildings surrounded by the loving embrace of Mother Nature sat resolute in what could only be described as an underground lost ancient city.

Dotting the large buildings, dim lights hummed at odd intervals as Dailey and the others finally honed in on the source of the cavern's light. Massive crystals jutting from the roof gave the entire area a bright ambient glow. Low-hanging clouds formed their own ecosystems covering the far end of the chasm.

A waterfall flowed directly beside the opening, giving the area a dull, droning soundtrack.

"Well, shit," Dailey breathed out. Jen and Grantham stood with their mouths hanging open.

Albert was the first to break the silence, explaining the current situation. "Yup, that is the city of Atlantis. At least part of it. Hang on a sec. Let me scan the files I just pulled from the facility's subsystems." This garnered a glare from the senator. "What? It's what I do."

"This place is, as Albert just stated, the not-so-lost city of Atlantis," Deborah confirmed, stepping forward.

"Oh, we're going into the city?" Jen asked, hesitating.

"So, interesting stuff," Albert cut in as the group walked down several flights of stairs etched into the bedrock. "Seems like a few years after I left, a major event caused the city to be buried under what is now called the South Pole. I would bet my left servo that an Alurian ship or that one thing I can't seem to remember launched a few thermo nukes, and *walla!* Buried super city."

"There wasn't snow back then?" Jen asked. The senator likely already knew the answer.

"No. I was kind of wondering why the place you call the United States wasn't covered in ice anymore." This statement caused Deborah to stop just as they reached the bottom of several tall buildings.

"How old are you, exactly?"

"Well, from what I can tell, really, *really* old. I was created before I came to Earth; I am sure by now everyone fully understands the implications there. The one thing I have to work through is the gap in my memory banks, your data banks, and what actually happened. I think there is a good five to ten thousand years of me taking educated guesses. Good, no more questions,"

Albert paused before starting back up. "I see you don't have those records either, or any that go too far back. Some of this you have moderately figured out, though. So . . . points Gryffindor. What I can tell you is my data banks get a little fuzzy the further back I try to access them. Yes, this place was called the city of Atlantis, but you should understand it was just one of many, all of which likely no longer exist. A name is just a name. It simply carries the weight given to it."

The wisdom of Albert's take on the situation was refreshing, telling Dailey the AI was, in fact, starting to grasp basic concepts outside of his primary functions. What Albert wasn't telling them was just how important the city was in the planet's history.

"Yes," the senator started. "Earth was once a thriving civilization capable of interstellar travel, but from what we can tell, it was reset."

"*Reset* like completely wiped out and started from scratch?" Grantham asked as the one and only Rosco walked out of the closest building with a tablet tucked neatly under his arm.

"Precisely that." Rosco beamed, happy to see the familiar faces.

"I always said you were crazy. Can I take that back?" Dailey asked as Rosco let the genuine smile on his face reach his forehead.

"Depends on how much Albert here can tell us," Rosco said, handing the tablet to Jen. "It's a map of the usable parts of the city. A good portion of it was crushed and destroyed or is unstable."

"And I agree with Albert here," Rosco continued, taking in the absurdity of the droid. "We name our cities. They aren't always some magically manifested place."

"Whatever," Albert scoffed as Rosco motioned the group toward one of the one-story buildings pulsing with life. It resembled a biomechanical art piece due to Mother Nature's grasp on the site.

The senator walked forward. The entire speech seemed rehearsed in many ways, meaning they had had this exact conversation on multiple occasions. "They say we can learn much from children. I tend to agree."

Rosco turned on a recently installed light, showing a clearly once upon a time learning center. "It's a school. More specifically, preteenager, from what we gathered."

"You gathered correctly. These symbols are all meant for youngsters. Oh, looky here," Albert noted, walking to a dim panel as it flashed to life.

The senator and Rosco smiled, knowing what the group was about to learn. "Brought to you by the one and only Ateris Mining Company. Or as we like to call them now, syndicates," Rosco added as the familiar symbol flowed onto the touchscreen.

"You got to be kidding me," Jen huffed. "The mining company? Didn't they start after the war?"

Albert stepped forward, punching a few more panels on the screen. "Ah, just as I suspected. Look familiar?" Albert asked Dailey as he walked up to the star chart. "And yes, it's at a third-grade level."

Depicted on the screen was a simple schematic of the Shade Belt and a system the group immediately recognized, which included Asher. "What did you suspect?"

"That the Syndicate, as you all keep calling them now instead of companies, mining Asher was and is the Ateris Mining Company. Hope you aren't a shareholder. Things are about to get nasty."

The senator walked over, shutting off the screen. "Now you see why certain things are best kept in the shadows. At least for now."

"Yeah, no shit," Dailey blurted, holding his hands up. "The syndicates fund the Federation. You're telling me the mining companies have been around for thousands of years, doing what? Supplying both sides of a conflict or whatever this turns out to be

"No, it makes sense. Remember when I said I wouldn't be surprised if one of the syndicates was already in the system when we arrived? It's sort of a pilot thing. One of those unwritten rules. We all know they are doing whatever they want in the Void."

Rosco stepped forward. "And everyone conveniently turns a blind eye. We've known for several years now about their involvement with the

Alurians. After retrieving several of their crashed ships after the war, and more importantly, a few intact, our team quickly identified the connection."

"You make it seem like we fell into it. No, we found Ateris Syndicate employees on one of the ships. One of the ships where we also found our guest," Deborah added.

"Sounds like this is moderately new intel. I get why you don't want people poking around down here. Still, the mining syndicates are farming occupied planets. I can assure you, as you have witnessed from the video feed, they do not have our best interests," Dailey pondered as Albert continued to scan the room.

"Hate to interrupt, but do you all know there's a communications hub directly under this room?" Albert asked, leaning against the wall, trying to look smooth.

This caught the two hosts off guard. "Please continue," the senator requested.

Albert glanced at Dailey.

"For Christ's sake. Please," Dailey grumbled.

"In that case, sure thing. Will I get deactivated or threatened to be turned into a chili warmer if I pop a small hole in the floor?" Albert asked as Deborah nodded for him to continue.

The quick facade of an innocent droid was quickly dispelled when Albert reconfigured his arm into a hypercharged sledgehammer, thundering it down and through the floor. "It's hammer time!"

"Is he always like this?" Rosco asked. Grantham shrugged.

"Depends. I think he's showing off. It means he likes you."

"I can hear you, and yes, these two are acceptable," Albert's voice echoed out of the dark hole.

"I figured there was a reason you brought us down here," Dailey noted as Rosco's lips flattened.

"This is important, and if we are right, Albert might just be the key to keeping the scales from tipping."

Several bangs and clanks echoed from the hole in the floor before Albert leaped up, his footlike claws digging into the hard floor. "That should about do it. Now, where is the actual communications room? It appears you have eighty-two thousand four hundred and twenty-two new voicemails."

"What's there?" Rosco asked, dropping a small sensor pod into the hole.

"Well, it looks like someone unplugged the phone from the wall to keep whoever was at the other end of the line from using caller ID. You get the drift."

Jen shook her head. Out of the group, she was not nearly as interested in centuries-old pop culture.

To be fair, it had been making a comeback after several late-2000s serves were recovered after being projected as lost during the war. This, unfortunately, had been Albert's primary focus when uploading gigabytes of data. When asked, he'd simply responded, "*Priorities. I was really bored for a really long time.*"

After another hour of walking through the underground city, the overall museum vibe had taken no time to set in. The senator finally opened the door leading into the main communications room. Rosco had taken the group on a tour of the remaining living quarters, several labs, and a section still being excavated that Albert insisted was an orbital weapons storage compound. This piqued Deborah's interest, making several notes to focus on the area.

Rosco tapped his tablet as several lights and subsystems started humming to life. Albert finally stepped forward in the unmolested room, pausing as if trying to pull up a long since faded memory.

The group stayed back as the AI approached the main panel, plugging into the primary system. Lights that Rosco and the senator had never observed sprang to life, and the room shook lightly.

"Albert, what's up?" Dailey asked.

"Everyone stand back. I'm going to activate the main gate transceiver."

The word swirled around Dailey's thoughts as he quickly realized this was more than an everyday comm relay station. The realization was only amplified as the center section of the floor parted, revealing a round console with a floating, large, greenish-red glowing globe.

"Okay, everyone, should be safe. It would not be wise to fall into that gate transceiver," Albert noted, now focused on the dusty console. While age had taken its toll on the device, it had also been completely sealed in its previously undisturbed grave, only allowing for a light layer of dust.

"You said gate transceiver. Is that like the gate drive?" Dailey asked as the light on Albert's sensor-pod head blinked green.

"It absolutely does. This device allows messages to be sent and received through set locations. Before you ask, I have no idea how this place is powered. I am too busy going through your unbelievable amount of voice mail. Let me tell you, some of these are a doozy." Albert paused. The light on his sensor pod turned a shade of orange. "Oh-oh . . ." He trailed off, standing up.

"What? The double *Oh*'s are never good," Dailey spoke up, having heard Albert do this before.

"It, uh, is a message from the survivors of this planet and my home world, trying to talk with each other. I think I just filled one of those gaps."

"We know something bad happened here. Hell, something bad happened everywhere. We can go through these later," Dailey insisted. Rosco looked at them as if he should be making that decision, only to get a telling glare from his former commander.

"I'll just skip to the end. Wait one minute," Albert said, working through the data.

Rosco took the opportunity to walk up to the panel. "I think we need to get these reviewed as soon as possible."

Albert interrupted the man, taping his elongated metal finger on Rosco's tablet. "There you go. Have fun with that."

"Something got his attention," Jen noted as Albert sprang to attention.

"Good News, Bad News protocol initiated," Albert's modulated voice came out, only to be taken over by his usual cadence.

Senator Powell glanced at Dailey, who was now laser focused on the AI. "Send it."

"This station has been receiving messages the entire time. It's still receiving messages directed toward Earth. It will take some time to explain, but it captured your entire transmission from Asher in real time. If someone had been here, they could have just picked up the phone instead of all that synergistic synergies or whatever you had to do."

"Alright, point taken. The bad news?" Dailey shifted.

"Anything from Asher is being amplified and sent here through some other relay station, likely in the Shade Belt."

"Did someone hit the big red button you and Bellman set up?" Dailey asked. Albert's sensor pod affirmed the statement.

"Two days ago, a distress signal was sent from the team at the Gulch. It is an SOS, and yes, someone hit the big red button. If not, we would not be getting this message for a very long time."

Senator Powell walked to the entrance they had come through. "I'm not going to ask about the details of how that works or this communications system. What I am going to do is ask you to talk to Dorax and," she drawled out, "I'm either going to get in a lot of trouble or save more people on that planet."

Dailey, Grantham, Jen, and Albert all looked at each other curtly, nodding in affirmation. After everything they had been through, the crew of the *Murphy* had formed an odd type of democracy when it came to breaking the rules. The senator knew damn well the Federation, not to mention the Fleet, wanted to dismantle the *Murphy*, as well as Albert, for their tech.

"Yes, ma'am. Albert here will ensure you all get this system set up before we leave," Dailey replied as Albert once again tapped his metal middle finger on Rosco's tablet.

"Done. Oh, and Senator, if you are ever lonely and need—" Albert started, only to be cut off by every other sentient being in the room.

"Thank you, Albert. I'll keep that in mind," the senator winked back. Albert's sensor readout turned a blushing red.

The crew would be hearing about this later. Especially Sparky. The two had a damn near soap-operatic weekly review of the *Murphy*'s love triangles.

CHAPTER 3

STAR KILLER THIRTEEN

J ust me and Albert," Dailey insisted as Grantham and Jen headed toward the Harpy to debrief the rest of the crew after a quick pit stop. Senator Powell, knowing she was about to generate a shitstorm, had insisted on restocking the *Murphy* from her own facilities' provisions, which upon further inspection, were meant for dignitaries and leadership alike. Newly promoted Master Chief Thron would be significantly stepping up their galley's menu.

The one item that wasn't up for debate nor readily available in the Antarctic diplomatic facility was ham. Grantham and Jen would stop by the closest city and pick up enough to keep Sparky from taking over the *Murphy* and flying it back to Earth.

Dorax Flam sat with his hands and feet cuffed to a metal chair attached to the floor. After his jailbreak, security wasn't taking any more chances. True to form, the Alurian's skin was an off-putting shade of greyish green, looking like the mix between an oversize human and a lizard of some random pissed-off type with a flat face.

Dorax looked slightly different, though, leaning more toward the human end of the spectrum. To top it all off were several tattoos, not inked but instead etched into his skin like a brand.

The dull grey stone surrounding the Alurian gave off a depressing vibe of solitude and hopelessness, as if sitting on death row waiting for one's inevitable demise. Off-putting white light with a tint of blue added to the sterile vibe, casting lighter than usual shadows under the flat stone bed and toilet tucked away in the corner. The Alurian's glowing green eyes locked onto Dailey's as he let out a low rumbling hiss.

"Alright, calm down. We got all the fun stuff out of the way. I'm Captain Ben Dailey, and this is Albert." He pointed at the AI, who casually stood like a menacing instrument of death—or comedy, depending on his mood.

"That mutt has parts of an Alurian battle droid in it," Dorax hissed with a slight growl at the end.

Without asking for permission, Albert walked over and clipped open all of Dorax's restraints in four simple swipes of his clawed hand, followed by several supporting clanks of metal rods forming from Albert's arm, swiftly picking Dorax up several feet into the air.

"Satisfactory?" Albert asked in a Southern drawl.

"You'll have to excuse him. He gets a little sensitive when you talk about his Alurian bits," Dailey said as Dorax grinned.

"The great Captain Dailey. I know of you. Brave, bold, and reckless. Even your own people are afraid of you."

Dailey motioned for Albert to set the Alurian down, letting a flat grin spread across his face. "Well, that means I don't have to dazzle you with bullshit."

"No hard feelings," Dorax said, clearing his throat. "I like a good, gutsy droid."

Albert nodded, lowering his posture a few inches, likely reading the Alurian's vitals telling him he was no longer a threat. "And I like a good chase," Albert finished. Dailey was keeping the AI's comment about Dorax being a flight attendant to himself.

With the first dance of prisoner versus interrogator complete, Dailey sat on the small round stool placed in the room for him. "What do you want?" the *Murphy*'s commander asked.

"What do I want?" Dorax reflected. "Nothing you can give me, but since you're asking, I want to go home."

Dailey reflected on the statement as Albert chimed in. "Where's home?"

"That's the big question. Some would say here. Some would say Solaria."

"Why not Aluria?" Dailey asked.

Dorax laughed at the sentiment. "If there is such a place. Do you think a mutt like me has ever stepped foot on Aluria? If so, you humans are truly a lost cause."

"Fair enough," Dailey replied. "I'll make you a promise." This got the Alurian's attention, forcing him to sit up straight. Even in other civilizations, military honor and living up to one's word as an officer meant something. "You tell your story to Albert here, and I'll get you off this rock. I'm not saying in style, but I'll drop you off as close to wherever home is as I can. You bullshit us . . . I'll just let Albert here figure a way to convince you."

"Fair enough. Just know this, human: just because I believe something to be true doesn't mean it is."

Dailey and Albert nodded, understanding the statement clearly after being on Asher and realizing the quickly changing landscape of Earth's history. Dorax leaned back as the Alurian started at the beginning of his raider career, which had occurred three systems away.

The start was just as important as the beginning. Dailey slowly let the tension flow out of his body. The senator had been correct to describe his story as fantastical.

Dorax had been born and raised on a ship on the opposite side of the galaxy in a fleet of Alurian transport ships. By the time Dorax had explained why the transport ships were floating through space, Dailey had finally realized just how insignificant humankind was in the grand scheme of things. At least compared to how the civilization had developed after the war.

Much to Dailey's surprise, the Alurian had been born, raised, and put to work in the dark, lonely vacuum of space. After years of harassing Federation outposts and transporting materials to and from unknown parties, Dorax and a handful of other associates had chosen to flee after being left for dead, only to gain access to a treasure trove of information.

With no true identity, the Alurian had simply done as he was raised to do while not questioning his orders. While fully aware of an Alurian home world, there was more to Dorax's story that genuinely gained Dailey's attention.

According to the Alurian, their job was to keep the outer colonies in line and capable of supplying able bodies to support their home world's expansion efforts. Albert was quick to point out this boiled down to their aggressive expansion efforts, often overtaking simple civilizations to further support their goals.

This opened up one of Albert's dormant memory caches in the middle of the conversation, bringing up one foreboding term that made Dorax pause: The Creare Overlords.

From what the group gathered, the Alurians had poked the wrong ancient hornets' nest in a faraway galaxy several thousands of years ago. This, in turn, had put the Alurians on the defensive just as they started expanding into other systems, which included Earth and Solaria.

From there, it was a simple long game of gathering resources and building an army capable of taking on the Creare Overlords when the inevitable reunion occurred. While both Albert and Dorax had limited information on the race, it was clear the Alurians would not take no for an answer or accept defeat. This was the same attitude that pushed them to enslave entire civilizations while keeping the facade of everyday life.

At one point in Earth's history, humankind started to push back, taking part in what was called the Great Awakening. This was the reason for the Tectonic Wars and constant monitoring of the system. What the Alurians hadn't expected was how quickly humankind adapted and turned from a meek planet supplying labor to a threat.

If Dailey and Albert were to believe what Dorax was telling them, the Alurian himself would have to honestly believe his own story. The entire situation had put the Alurians on a war footing on two fronts until they could handle the Federation's dominion of planets, which was rapidly growing.

The crux of the entire situation was that Dailey had become painfully aware of just how much of his own planet's history had been a lie. This put into question Dorax's own understanding of the situation, being so far removed from everything.

Ultimately, Dailey was satisfied with the Alurian's explanation of things and how he knew them. It was also clear he skirted around the mining syndicate conversation. After asking several other odd questions, Albert, in an attempt to unlock other memory nodes, nodded at Dailey as his sensor screen turned green.

"What's next?" Dorax asked, genuinely happy to have told his story.

"For what it's worth, I believe you. At least, I believe what you believe you know. I'm going to keep my end of the bargain. While we're at it, why does *Creare* sound familiar?" Dailey asked as the security guard outside the room motioned for Albert to resecure Dorax.

"The word *Creare*, in what you call Latin, or the old tongue, stands for creator. So, the Creators." Albert let the phrase sink in like a rock in a pond.

"Albert, open the door. Dorax here is coming with us. He twitches, feel free to turn him into a smoothy or something for Sparky."

"Who's Sparky?" Dorax asked.

Albert chose to back up his partner in crime. "One of the nastiest, evilest planet-claiming Alurian war hounds you will ever lay eyes on."

Dorax grimaced. "I'm good. I'll not be an issue."

"Good boy," Albert proclaimed as the security guard started protesting, not opening the door, only to have Albert wave his hand and counteract the locking mechanism.

Dorax grinned, enjoying the interaction. The youthful security guard followed closely behind as tracking cameras whirled, following the group making their way back to the docking bay. Albert was not able to contain his opinion on the interaction, utterly tone-deaf to the fact that Dorax was directly behind him.

"Then I was all like bad cop coming in with one swipe of my retracto claw. Then you played it all smooth, acting like we aren't going to just shoot him out of an airlock as soon as we get into orbit," Albert professed as Dailey stopped in the ship's crew prep area.

"I'm not going to shoot him out of an airlock," Dailey huffed. The security guard was trying to melt into the surrounding wall due to the absurdity of the scene, already having called the senator.

"You were all Detective David Starsky, and I was the diviner, suave data port entry man Detective Ken 'Hutch' Hutchinson, of course. And if you insist, we won't shoot Dorax out of the airlock. I reviewed your Fleet files from the Army and computed an extremely high probability of you taking the airlock course of action."

Dailey was about to dive into the metaphysical conversation when Albert's viewscreen winked. Knowing Albert didn't leave much of anything to chance, Dailey nodded, returning to the Harpy drop ship.

"And no. I'm Hutch, and you're Starsky," Dailey noted as Albert opened the Harpy's cargo door.

"Who's been plugged in more recently?" Albert asked, effectively ending the conversation as Dorax let out a snicker. Dailey and Jen's sort of relationship was still on a first-base level, having been shelved after they left Asher.

"You think this is funny?" Dailey asked, turning on the heat.

Resetting himself, Dorax stood still. "I have never been around an AI like this. You said a lot. Where are you from?"

"*When* is the best way to look at it. To answer directly and keep you from asking twenty questions, first, I was here on Earth several thousand years before the war," Albert drawled out just as Senator Powell and Rosco marched into the bay. "Then I was lost in space . . . get it?"

"Well, I didn't see this coming or anything," Deborah stated flatly as Rosco walked to the security guard, likely trying to stay out of the senator's line of fire.

"I made a promise and got what I needed. Albert." Dailey motioned, and the AI walked over to Rosco again, tapping his middle finger on his tablet.

"I charted out the entire interview with Dorax and added my two cents' worth. Everything you wanted to discuss with me is in that file, including star charts of other planets, likely enough information to keep your people busy for say . . . the next decade or so. If you stick to the files that say read me first, however, you should be just fine. It includes all the gate drive information I knew you wanted from the communications I pulled from your tablet. Shitty security systems, by the way."

"I see. Well, you never disappoint." Deborah grinned, knowing Dailey understood what she needed. "Listen, I talked with the other diplomats and the Federation Security Committee. I convinced them to sanction you leaving."

This surprised Dailey, taking away the entire pirate rebel vibe of his quickly forming plan. "What's the catch?"

"You need to be back in sixty days. Rosco pulled the data files on the comms station Albert activated. We believe we can keep an open line of communication as long as nothing out of sorts happens."

"That's not the catch," Dailey noted. Deborah side-eyed Rosco.

"You will be taking a Federation representative along with you. This person is to be respected and treated with the dignity afforded their position."

"And that is?" Dailey drawled out.

"Chairman Roush will be accompanying you, from the Federation Intelligence Administration."

"You're sending a FIA chairman with us?" Dailey protested, only to be met with complete serenity from the senator. There would be no more questions asked about the subject.

The Federation Intelligence Administration was the future's version of the FBI. All previous law enforcement systems had gone out the door when the first alien species had landed on Earth, forcing the once upon a time warring countries to pull together.

The FIA spent most of its time collecting information and analyzing enemy threats, which led to their enforcement of certain Federation regulations by their contact teams when needed, something Dailey had little to no respect for after a handful of previous encounters. The main one being the FIA's failures leading up to the death of Stella, his wife.

The senator and Lieutenant Rosco spent another hour reviewing the ins and outs of the Federation's and Fleet's concerns with sending the *Murphy* and its much-needed tech back out. By the end of the briefing, Dailey was starting to feel more like a novelty than a combat commander.

The Harpy's lift thrusters flashed off the launchpad as Dailey, Dorax, and Albert streaked into the bitter cold of the Antarctic night. Dailey, satisfied that the ship was on autopilot, turned to Dorax.

"I'm going to need you to do me a favor. And I want to set a few ground rules."

Dorax nodded as Albert started talking with King over the comms.

"First, I'm going to have you working in the galley with Master Chief Thron. He's an ex-Solarian warlord, and I think you two will get along just fine."

Again, Dorax nodded, understanding just who Thron was but also what he was capable of doing. "Next, when this FIA officer shows up, I want you to take them on a tour of the ship."

"But I don't know my way around the ship."

"It doesn't matter. Albert, pull up a schematic of the area around the galley. Alright. You see that grey area by the trash shoot?"

"You mean the airlock?" Dorax asked skeptically.

"When this Roush guy or gal shows up, I'm going to need you to lock him in that airlock. That one has a shuttle pod. We will be passing by Fleet HQ in orbit before gating. We will make sure the pod makes it there."

"I knew it. My systems projected a ninety-nine percent chance that you were due for a disciplinary action because of some type of airlock evacuation!" Albert barked.

Dorax looked confused as Dailey spoke up. "I'm not going to the brig for shooting that assclown out the airlock. Dorax here is. Well, not to the brig, but we are dropping him off anyway. Would be a shame if we reported him lost."

Dorax's look of confusion turned to a wicked grin. He liked the man that had just given him a chance. "We on the same program, Dorax? I'm not saying you aren't going to have to get your hands dirty, but I am a man of my word, and I will take you wherever you want to go." Dailey paused. "Where is that, by the way?"

CHAPTER 4

A CONVENIENT TRUTH

Mac pressed the comms link on the control panel as Dax pulled up an orbital point of origin chart on the large viewscreen in the center of the room. While in orbit, a handful of attack fighters had deployed several sensor pods into the atmosphere as an early detection system tuned to the radiation produced by a gamma ray used to attack a planet's surface.

Staff Sergeant Randell Grear's face appeared on the secondary viewscreen, having just arrived at the outskirts of Canto, one of Arcadia's neighboring cities. The initial plan was to clear the skies above the city and then send out a scouting party.

A large windowpane overlooked the city, a layer of clouds creating a pillowy ground several stories under their current floor. Over that, grey clouds, looking as they did back home, hung unmoving in the sky, sprinkling the window with rain. The rest of the sidewall was covered in control stations and monitors.

The control room was strategically placed between two levels of atmosphere and clouds. Rain was a typical event in Arcadia, and as experienced, the sun rarely made its way down to the lower-level streets.

"We can see and hear you," Mac confirmed. Grear nodded. "What's the status?"

"I'm going to be blunt; I don't know what we're looking at. It's just a pile of rubble, and from what our meters read, putting off a ton of rad."

Miller stepped forward as Walker continued to watch the point-of-origin screen Dax was working on. "Any signs of life?"

"Negative. It's like this place was wiped off the planet's surface. We saw several crop fields that seemed to still be intact on our way here, but we didn't stop to check if they were radiated. We'll do that on the way back. From what we could see coming in, the city is roughly ten square miles; that includes some crops or livestock. This attack didn't come from any ship I know."

The red cross from the point of origin chart finally landed on its target, turning a deep shade of green. "It's because it didn't," Walker spoke, gaining everyone's attention.

The chart clearly identified Asher's primary moon as the source of the blast. Vax cocked her head, taking in all the information. "It was a surface-mining scraper."

"How do you know?" Mac asked as she punched several more buttons, bringing up a schematic of one of the inner planets' mining gamma rays.

"It's the only thing that makes sense. We received an odd update about gamma radiation surface scrapers several years ago. We thought it was for one of the other cities, but I think we know better now," Vax smartly replied, again showing her keen attention to detail.

"Is there a way to pull up mining charts from the planet? You know, to see how much is left?" Miller asked, using his engineering background.

"I never thought about it," Vax noted, motioning for Dax to enter the request.

Much like having a conversation with Albert, when you asked the system a direct question, you got a direct answer, and a red chart blinking *four percent* glared back at the group.

"What does that mean?" Mac asked as the already struggling frown drooped and slid further south on Vax's face.

"They were going to start strip-mining the surface. I didn't know what that fully meant, but I do now," Vax mumbled as Miller cleared his throat.

"They do that all the time on the nonpopulated moons and, in some cases, planets. It's like taking a big eraser to the surface, killing everything and making the planet uninhabitable. I don't know how that all works, but the mining companies usually have to grease some palms to get the permits to do it. Long story short, it's not common practice, and it's rather nasty,"

Miller huffed. "It still doesn't make any sense, though. If they were mining the planet's surface, they wouldn't be knocking cities out. They would be stripping the mountains, and I can assure you, they would have stopped destroying the cities. No, someone attacked us using a mining laser, likely a new addition to the system."

Miller paused, looking at a concerned Dax and Vax. "What is it?"

Vax typed a handful of commands into the console, and the screen went blank. This time, the regular mining shipment schedule appeared, followed by a chart of the planet showing several mining ships like the *Scarecrow* moving in and out of orbit.

"Seems like the other side of the planet isn't as concerned. I had a hunch something like this might be going on," Vax noted, honing in on one of the cargo ships. "The ships' nav system was updated a few weeks ago. They are going to a new location."

Mac, picking up on the inference, spoke up. "What does it mean?"

"It means," Dax started, taking a deep breath while talking, "someone or something is still controlling the planet's shipping and mining operations."

"Why not take back this portion of the operation?" Miller asked.

Mac responded without thinking. "We took their ship and, for lack of a better term, took the city offline. If I were somewhere else managing the operation, I would figure this place was offline. It might be good news they are ignoring us. Think about it. They hit the food-producing hub for this area. They probably think it's a wash here?"

The room pondered the conversation as Grear's voice returned over the radio. "It appears those security Alurian battle droids everyone keeps talking about are coming out of the ground. Send the QRF," Grear barked, asking for the quick reaction force to be deployed.

Mac ran out of the control room toward her attack fighter without a word. At the same time, several alarms started sounding in the room, and to further confuse the situation, Albert's voice erupted from the speakers, making everyone turn to hear the message.

"Hey, everyone! Albert and your homies here. We are heading your way. Hang tight and keep the lights on for us."

While the message was clear, it was also a one-way transmission. Albert would calibrate their comms system once they arrived, allowing to quickly talk back with Earth, the senator, and their companions.

Grear activated his suit's HUD as several targets erupted in a long list. "Team One, Team Two, stay on the ground. Let the drop ships move out of the area. We don't want them destroyed. Rally point on me. Coleman, get the targeting drone in the air," he instructed, activating his jump pack.

Within a minute, the entire group that had been scouting the area had consolidated behind a large wall that, at one time, had been no less than twenty stories high. After the blast, the outer city wall was now only two stories in height.

"What's the game plan, Sarge?" the one and only, now Specialist Woody asked.

"Lieutenant Mac has a squad of attack fighters en route. Once they get here, we clear the place by sector. Until then, we hold. They're not attacking yet, but as soon as they get their bearings, I promise they sure as shit will."

Grear was correct. Before leaving, Albert had reviewed the Alurian security droids' protocol in case they ran into any of the blenders of death while back on Earth. According to Albert, the droids had been dormant so long that any change in environment or action would result in the systems having to recalibrate. Meaning if the droids weren't engaging, according to Albert, *"They would be trying to figure out if they were in a bad part of town or not."*

When asked how they would know when they were calibrated, the answer had been fairly straightforward: they would start shooting or be figuring out a way to kill you. The droid's programming was simple yet effective: destroy anything that was, could, or would interfere with mining operations. Other than that, things would be addressed as needed.

Sergeant Coleman, also known as Coolio, the driver from Fourth Foot who had driven the team on their first surface mission on Asher, appeared from around the massive wall.

"Sarge, I launched a targeting drone. We should have a signal in five, four, three . . ." Coolio counted down as the previously identified target started taking shape on Grear's HUD.

Once a random list of possible threats, the drone had finally confirmed the size of the issue at hand. The group of Alurian security droids, which in all reality were battle droids, had split into two groups, moving outwardly.

"Halo Six, this is Scout One. Just sent targeting data. The group has split in half on either side of us. How copy?" the staff sergeant asked. Mac's stressed yet calm voice replied; she had been hauling ass to get in the air.

"Scout One, this is Halo Six. Good copy. Five mikes out."

Grear looked at the fully armored Nova Space Rangers sitting poised to strike.

"We are securing our position. You are weapons free outside the fifty-meter radius on my marker."

With a curt "Roger," Mac hammered down her suborbital thrusters as the four other attack fighters left Asher, screaming to life like a parade of angry banshees.

The first signs of encroaching violence started with a light rumble on the ground making its way through the boots of the Nova Ranger's armor.

"Sarge," Woody came over the comms. "There're about thirty of them running at us. What do you need us to do?"

"I swear to God that space-spider thingy must have poisoned your brain," Grear huffed, launching forward with a quick jolt of his thruster pack.

Once at the edge of the massive wall, Grear saw the tsunami of nonthinking death heading their way. "We fight," Grear finally replied, switching his HUD to an aerial view from the drone, only to see it now showing offline. At the same time, a streak of smoking fire darted toward the ground. They had lost their eyes in the sky.

Seeing the predicament they were about to be in, Grear launched an entire pod of mini seeker rockets from the sleek magazine he had activated from his pack, rising up and over his shoulder before firing.

Dailey himself kept a much smaller version of this on his forearm for closer-than-wanted encounters. The initial point detonation setting activated in a crackle of smoke and sparks as the group hesitated. The explosion's concussion did more damage to their sensors than the droids themselves. Grear was just buying time.

"Weapons hot!' he followed, letting loose a stream of glowing rounds from his Solarian Sauder rifle.

Now fully understanding the task, Woody pulled up his roto-grenade launcher, pounding into the group Grear had just slowed down. This time, the effects were more dramatic as the plasma grenade scrambled several of the droids, only to have the ones in the rear jump over the group, leaping forward while opening fire.

It was a mix of working weapons systems and semifunctioning lasers from decades, if not centuries, ago. Regardless of age, the wall of insectlike droids were rapidly gaining ground.

Seeing this, Grear motioned for the second fire team to take position on the right side of the wall. They immediately opened fire, several chunks of wall peppering the Rangers' hardened armor.

Coolio, wanting to get into the fight, activated his primary weapons system, creating a glowing hum on the ground behind him. Attached to his jump pack, Coolio's drone launcher also had the ability to fire one of two large, specialized munitions. For this trip, he had loaded an EMP cluster rocket.

The weapon was simple but effective. According to Albert, who had thoroughly reviewed the Nova Ranger's weapons, more straightforward was oftentimes better when fighting machines.

As its name suggested, the rocket would launch, reaching a set height and distance, only to release its payload of hundreds of mini EMP grenades. From there, each grenade would activate at a determined height, forming a web of electronic soul-crushing kiss my ass. At least, that's how Coolio explained it.

The munition activated in a flash of vibrant blue as the first dozen droids reached the three-hundred-meter mark away from the wall, immediately dropping them to the ground like chunks of useless metal. While the effect was drastic and effective, it was temporary against Alurian tech. The nanotechnology onboard was already working to recalibrate and synch the droid's power systems as if they had blood pumping through their carbon-reinforced nanohydraulic veins.

"Sarge!" Coolio said. "I've always wanted to fire one of those."

"Shut up and fire," Grear redirected. In reality, he was impressed by the weapon's effects, immediately wanting one for every team member.

As the droids approached, laser blasts started taking chunks out of the protective wall. The one issue with laser blasters was that the gravity-shackled distance on a planet's surface had a drastic effect on the weapon, unlike in space. The farther the intended target, the more the power from the blast would dissipate.

From the sky, all Mac could see was a chaotic kaleidoscope of laser fire, as if the two opposing forces were standing in front of each other. "Scout One, this is Halo Six. We are engaging, but we can't tell who is who."

Grear knew this was coming. Lurching back several meters, he activated his jump pack. "Danger close! Scouts out! On me!" he ordered as the well-oiled scouts of the now defunct Fourth Foot followed his lead without hesitation.

"Confirmed. Halo elements, danger close. Fire on target visual," Mac said. The pilots immediately dropped elevation, waiting until the last possible moment to fire upon the droids, who were now starting to recompute the situation.

What happened next was a display of the true awesomeness of human-kind. The initial strafing run lasted five short seconds as the Rangers took one more leap out of harm's way. The mix of old-school kinetic machine gun fire and plasma cannons ripped into the droids like they were brittle toys.

Dark grey smoke and several fires created a haze that covered the entire area. Not satisfied with their initial run, Mac directed the attack fighters to come in from a different angle, now that several green crosses showing the squad's location had finally appeared in the pilot's targeting displays, ensuring a clean field of fire.

The Nova Rangers stood with rifles in hand, pumping their fists as Mac unloaded on the already devastated patch of land.

"Scout One, this is Halo Six. The area is clear. We're going to continue patrolling the area. I recommend exfilling back to the Gulch."

Grear took stock of his soldiers, seeing nothing more than a handful of new pitting scars from close-range laser blasts. "Coolio, call the drop ships. We're going home."

"I wish, Sarge," Coolio replied, calling their taxi.

Grear took in the apocalyptic scene, seeing the mix of carnage and his team as one of the attack fighters zipped overhead, clearing the light haze around the unit.

"Me to, Coolio . . . Me too," Grear replied as the drop ships appeared on the horizon.

CHAPTER 5

AUF WIEDERSEHEN, MAYBE

Are you sure this is smart?" Master Chief Thron asked as Dailey, accompanied by Dorax and Albert, stood in front of the airlock's small, round viewport.

The off-putting man on the other side of the glass pounded his fists into the cushioned door, which didn't allow any noise to seep through. Dorax had spent the time it took to walk to the airlock trying to figure out if the man had literally poured a can of oil in his hair to give it that light-reflecting sheen.

"Dorax?" Dailey said as the absolute verbal assault FIA Chairman Roush was taking part in was lost behind the airlock's door. "You're telling me you waited till his ship came in and walked him straight to the airlock? Do not pass go, any of that bullshit?"

Dorax stared through the viewport with a flat expression. "He was being a dick, as you say. That is pretty much how it happened. Rather gullible if you ask me. It's not lost on me that I'm an Alurian."

"Huh," Dailey huffed. "You might just fit in here, after all. Guy's a politician and didn't find it odd an Alurian, which there are like a handful in protective custody, was showing him around the ship?"

Thron grinned.

Tapping feet echoed around the corner before Sparky stepped into view. Dorax took several steps back while Sparky plopped over on his hind legs, giving the assembled crew a view of his two moons. This was followed by the tilt of his head, seeing Dorax.

While the two hadn't met yet, they had both been briefed on the situation.

"He's dangerous. A small one, but dangerous. Is this the one you said took over a world?" Dorax asked as Albert turned to Dailey.

"Boss, I believe there is room for one more in that airlock." Albert recommended as Sparky chuffed. The dynamic duo was back together.

"We can put ham in the pod," Sparky added, his voice coming out through the newly devised universal translator mounted on his harness, which now proclaimed him as Captain Sparky. It was accompanied by the presidential seal Albert had helped him create for his self-appointed title as Lord Overlord President of Asher and the Ham Republic. The round patch depicted Asher with a moon resembling a ham in orbit.

"Nah. I have to keep our stores stocked enough to keep you out of trouble," Thron replied. Sparky nodded, standing back up and walking over to sniff Dorax.

"Albert, let's chat with Chairman Roush," Dailey instructed as the AI activated the pod's comms system.

"You will be court-martialed for this!" the man proclaimed as spittle launched from his mouth.

"Oh, I've been court-martialed before, and I'm sure it won't be the last. Tell you what. You tell me your prime directive in coming with us, and I might just let you stay onboard."

Albert cut off the comms. "I don't believe you. I just did a scan of all your UCMJ violations." The Uniform Code of Military Justice had probably kept Dailey from already being in charge of the Fleet at this point.

"You're not supposed to. He is. Stop goofing around," Dailey huffed as Roush's tirade of surprisingly new curse words started back up. Sparky plopped back down on the hard deck while Dorax continued to stare at the Alurian war hound.

"You will let me out of this pod now," Roush barked.

"Did you pay any attention to the Alurian raider here who locked you inside that airlock?"

Roush paused, taking in Dorax. Realization set it. The truth was that man's ego was large enough to have its own gravitational pull. He hadn't even looked the Alurian in the face.

"Oh God. What's happening here?" Roush protested as the color started draining from his face.

"Well, it looks like our prisoner here has locked you inside that airlock pod, and now, I have two problems to deal with. I might just have to put him in there with you," Dailey said.

Thron shrugged, with Albert mimicking the gesture.

"Captain Sparky here showed up just in the nick of time to protect us," Dailey insisted. Dorax, hearing this, started to reconsider his current situation. Seeing this, Dailey continued.

"But I'm not going to do that. We have four hours till we're ready to gate out of here, and I'd like to fully understand why *you*, specifically, were sent."

Roush started calming down, walking directly up to the small round viewport. "I'm here to make sure you bring this ship back to the Fleet command, and that you, and whatever this is"—he pointed to Sparky, Albert, and Dorax—"have the best interests of the Federation."

"Well, shit, why didn't you say so. Let me get you out of there," Dailey proclaimed, hitting the red button. Several flashing lights started beeping in rhythm with the alarm going off in the corridor. "Dammit, I screwed that up. Albert, can you override that so we can let Chairman Roush out?"

"Sorry, boss. Busy securing this super nasty bad Alurian," Albert replied while Roush started smacking on the viewport. "Up against the wall, you. Book 'em, Sparky." Albert gestured toward Dorax. Meanwhile, Dailey was acting as if he were pressing buttons, only slamming his fingers on a blank part of the wall out of eyeshot of Chairman Roush.

Dailey mouthed *sorry* as he put up the international sign for *call me* to his ear. After a *whoosh* of air, the escape pod launched into space, followed by a sprinkling of debris.

"Albert, shut the alarm off," Dailey said. Everyone except Dorax acted as if nothing had happened. "Also, make sure he gets to Fleet command. It should only take him a few hours."

"On it, boss," Albert replied as Sparky stood up.

"We go now to my planet and save the others?"

"Yup. I lied about the timeline. According to Bellman and Hontz, we can be out of here in twenty minutes. Which is probably long enough for someone to figure out we launched Chairman Roush out of the airlock. Well, Dorax here really did it, but who's keeping score," Dailey added.

"Why are you doing this?" Dorax asked as Thron motioned him toward the galley.

"For starters, *you* did that. You're totally taking the blame for that one. Second, according to the Fleet report we will eventually file, you were lost due to some situation that occurs at some point. I am keeping my promise to you, but I'm going to need you to be part of the crew for the time being. That man would not have allowed that to happen. Poetic, right?"

"I don't understand, but I feel this was just. He was, as Albert said, an asshat?" Dorax suggested as Albert nodded. "Yes, that is how I correctly described him after reviewing his files. Slippery fella. We already knew his directive was to secure and deactivate me, all while putting the ship under the control of a secondary AI that he would upload. At least he was being half honest."

Albert explained as Dailey sighed. "We all know the deal. The Federation, and hell, the Fleet, doesn't like the situation and is scrambling to get the new gen of ships online so they can head toward Asher. The senator thinks if we can salvage the gate drives from the other mining ships, it would be a game changer. She's not wrong," Dailey informed the group as Becket's voice sprang to life.

"Hey, sir. If you're done ruining your and my aspirations for future political careers, we can gate at any time. Oh, and the senator would like to know how our guest is doing."

Ignoring that last part, Dailey turned one last time to the group.

"Dorax, what I need from you is to be you. Be an Alurian. Minus all that bullshit you throw at the Fleet. You already did a data dump with the senator, so that's a start to help things balance out. We may very well come face-to-face with a group of Alurians, and it couldn't hurt to have you there to help talk when the time comes."

CHAPTER 6

HERE WE GO AGAIN

P earl, status report," Dailey requested as the *Murphy*'s Solarian executive and navigation officer stood up from the con.

"Good to see you, sir. The last provisions ship just docked. Lieutenant Brax also confirmed all attack fighters are in their respective bays. We are ready to get underway."

Lieutenant Jen Brax had taken a trip for a handful of specific, critical provisions.

Dailey scanned the bridge, seeing the rest of his crew looking refreshed and ready to go. The time on Earth had been good for everyone, including him.

The activity on the grey, glowing bridge of the *Murphy* was in full swing as crew members shuffled into their stations while the central command reviewed various tablets in preparation to leave. At the front of the group was the main viewport as well as several screens, including a primary, able to retract into the metal deck.

"Good. Send the senator a message. Let her know we are leaving early, and we will contact her as soon as we reach Asher. We need to keep her up to date. She knows the fact we are sending her a message means we are going to keep things in check.

"King." Dailey turned. "Albert just uploaded communications protocol Echo. That should get us real-time comms with the senator back on Earth. It also means we might be able to communicate with the Gulch."

King turned, having just activated the update. "Interesting. The ship's using the gate drive as a transceiver."

"That seems to be the point. Albert said he would be up here—" Albert cut him off.

"I'm synched again with the *Murphy*'s comms system. As promised, nothing else . . . Well, maybe a few things, but that's all tied to the drive and navigation system," Albert rattled out.

Pearl smirked. "So that's every system except for what? The entertainment and what, the septic system?"

"I would never take on a shitty job like that," Albert replied, pausing for the punch line to sink in. As usual, his take on a Solarian's sense of humor fell flat with Pearl. Dailey grinned.

Walking in, Becket handed the ship's commander a steaming cup of fresh coffee. "Everything's set. Bellman is working with Albert on setting up that direct link with Asher."

Dailey nodded, understanding that everyone was ready to leave. The journey itself would take three separate trips through the same gates they'd used during their initial trip.

According to Albert, the gate drive taken from the now infamous *Scarecrow* had been in another ship at one point. To celebrate Sparky's first and only command, a framed picture of the *Scarecrow* taken from one of the *Murphy*'s security cameras was now mounted in the officers' mess.

This meant it was loaded with several star charts and travel routes that would not have to be computed. According to Albert, manually calculating accurate gate trajectories could take several years. What they had was the result of thousands of years of travel.

"King, put me on the intercom," Dailey requested. The ship's announcement system crackled lightly, finally settling into a hum. "This is Captain Dailey. As many of you are now aware, we are leaving in short order to return to Asher. From what we have gathered, it is under some form of attack. Everyone should be well rested and ready for whatever lies ahead."

Becket glanced at his long-term military partner, nodding his approval.

"We don't know what will happen, but I promise things will only get tougher. We made a choice not to bring along any additional ships or forces other than the few replacement attack fighters." Dailey knew he was bullshitting, not truly telling everyone the full capability of the gate drive.

"We have three very distinct missions. First, we are to secure our brothers and sisters on Asher. This includes the indigenous population. Second, and what the Fleet would consider most important, we are to secure the additional mining ships and, with that, their gate drives. Last, and more than likely moving up in the list of importance, is to find and violently engage whoever attacked Asher. We don't know what the situation is there, but we need to be ready for anything.

"Albert, engage the gate drive," Dailey instructed with the intercom still engaged. The dark-spotted ripple of space shimmered in front of the *Murphy*. At the same time, several transmissions of Fleet Headquarters started flashing on the viewscreen. Their guest had made it to their final destination.

In reality, Albert had turned on a one-way communications link between the fuming pod's occupant and Fleet docking control.

The familiar vibration of passing through the event horizon still flowed through Dailey's nerves as the ship pulled itself into the tranquil calm of the gate.

"All clear," Albert chirped, cutting off the intercom. The crew, including their fearless leader, held their breath every time they entered a gate after not only witnessing what could happen but also Albert's colorful description of what transpired when things went wrong.

"Alright, time hack till we exit?" Dailey asked while Pearl set a timer on the main display screen. This was the longest leg of the journey, taking a mind-numbing forty-six hours to complete. From what Albert and the others could figure, the gate route to Earth went almost entirely around the galaxy for some unknown reason.

"Everyone knows the deal. We take this time to get back in Fleet mode. I want full status reports and a command huddle at twenty hundred. I'm going to talk with Bellman and Albert after stopping by my quarters. It shouldn't take long for the new communications protocol to work. I want to be talking with Asher before our meeting," Dailey spoke in general to everyone on the bridge before heading to his quarters.

The calming, familiar stillness of Dailey's small yet cozy quarters greeted him like an old friend while familiar smells filled his senses. After being surfaceside for several weeks, it felt oddly soothing to the man.

Pictures sat staring back at him as Dailey glanced at the flashing red beacon informing him he had a message. Walking over, he clicked it off, sitting in the familiar cushioned chair beside his desk.

Dark nothingness glared back at him from the viewport just as the gentle rap of knuckles made him flinch. "Who is it?"

"It's me," Jen's voice replied. Dailey stood up and opened the door.

Without asking for permission, the fighter wing's fearless leader entered the ship's captain's quarters. The last time they had been alone was before the trip home. Several things had been left undiscussed, including a moment between the two.

"And to what do I owe the pleasure?" Dailey asked.

"Oh, you think this is about pleasure?" She smirked.

Letting out a breath, Dailey walked over to his small collection of Earth liquor, holding up two glasses, which she quickly approved. They both understood times like this would not present themselves for much longer.

After pouring two glasses of whiskey on the rocks, Dailey motioned for Jen to sit in the chair he had once occupied. "What's up?"

"While you were talking with the senator, I was called into Space Force command, as you are aware." Jen took a sip, letting the smooth bite ripple through her body. "They want us to return to the ship depot and recover any remaining ships."

Dailey pondered the statement, still sitting on his bed. The man figured he would need more chairs in his quarters at some point, with people making it a habit of stopping by.

"Yeah, figured as much. They—not meaning the senator—sent a Federation plant onboard to take over the ship if we didn't fall in line. I think they would have either way."

"Sounds like all the fingers on the hand want something."

"That they do. In the past, neither the Federation nor the Fleet, take your pick, would have let us head back out like this. It means they fear what's coming; even more, what they don't know. Listen, all of the politicians, Fleet admirals, Army generals—everyone has had this dead wrong, from what we can tell. They're scrambling, but in my opinion, things aren't going to get back to normal until they can get the gate-drive tech figured out and more of the new class hyperships online. These people aren't dumb. They're just in a form of fixable denial."

"What's that mean?" Jen asked, taking another light sip, making her body warm.

"It means they mostly already knew about our planet's history. It's the direction they were focused on building up our defensive and offensive capabilities that's wrong. Even the Solarians got it wrong."

"Did they?" Jen pondered. The woman's wisdom didn't match her, at times, distracting looks. The same could be said about Dailey's ability to switch from an easygoing goof-off to an all-out decisive, intelligent, and at times brutal combat leader.

"Shit, I guess you're right. We didn't see Ran coming. I mean, all our previous efforts could have been driven by misinformation. It wouldn't be the first time. The senator and our new commander seem to think they have a pretty good idea of what to look for. It's going to come out eventually about the mining companies. The Fleet and Federation already know; at least the people who aren't propped up by their funding."

Jen leaned back, unzipping her flight suit and exposing her flushed upper chest. Dailey glanced back out of the dead viewport, trying not to be distracted. Smiling, she pulled the zipper down enough to show the curves of her body while holding in a grin.

"Looks like we might be at war with more than the Alurians by the time it's all over. We better enjoy ourselves while we can," she noted, grinning as Dailey couldn't resist taking her in. She was doing it on purpose, and as they looked at each other, he realized she was right.

Clothes were discarded as months of built-up tension flowed through their bodies. Both Jen and Dailey continued pushing each other harder as they finally found a much needed and wanted cadence of breathing and touching.

"Oh my God, you're bumping uglies!" Albert bellowed over the intercom, spoiling the cadence the two had found with each other. "This is much less appealing when it's someone you know. My God, boss, would you like me to measure your blood pressure or recommend a better position to get started?"

"Albert. I swear to all that is holy"—Dailey's voice cut—"I'm going to replace your sensors with a hydrotoilet splash system."

Albert, sensing the very real possibility, immediately winked off the comms as Dailey threw his shirt over the viewscreen on his desk. Jen giggled, and Dailey felt it through his body.

She pulled his face back to hers. "I'll help you mount that on him later. I think the toaster would be more poetic. But now's not the time. Now is *my* time."

Dailey let the tension flow out of his body once again, letting go.

CHAPTER 7

CONVERGENCE

The generic face of Mister Toaster himself in all his middle-aged mustached glory stared back as Pearl glared at Albert, now standing on the bridge. After some sleek maneuvering and the activation of an internal dampening field, Jen, Bellman, and Dailey had blown off some steam, replacing Albert's generic sensor array with the Viewsonic toaster two thousand.

Acting like a face, the touch screen was now showing the absolute eat-shit-and-die glare Albert was giving everyone. In many ways, it made him look more relatable. Once they entered the final gate, they would switch the new appendage back to the well-known head of a standard service droid.

Specialist Kline swiveled his seat around, pushing it forward on the rail system out of the small weapons targeting cubby tucked neatly away in the back of the bridge. "We are ready to transition the targeting sensors back online once we clear the gate. We will be at eighty percent."

The one issue the *Murphy* ran into was its use of the forward deflector shields to activate the gate in front of the ship, and the amount of energy needed to do so. This was energy fed from equal parts of the ship's systems, not taking too much from any singularly necessary capability. The easy go-to was the targeting sensor array on the nose of the vessel.

Once through, or as Albert put it, "You don't really go through it. You kind of slip and slide your way across the cosmos," and depending on the time between and duration of the gate jumps, the ship's primary targeting system and deflector shields would need to be recharged. The crew had determined a seventy-five percent power feed would be an acceptable risk. The main issue was the lack of any ability to scan the area in the location they would arrive at.

"Albert, on your order," Dailey instructed as the AI turned. The light *ding* of the toast-complete sensors made the scowl on his face distort. The whirl of gears and Alurian micro-nanohydraulics lightly hissed as Albert's arm reached for the navigation panel's green button.

"Does that mean we're done?" Dailey asked.

Albert groaned. "I have a mind to evaporate us all in an endless loop of innerspace. Sound good? Or do you want your toast?" Albert asked, not fully realizing an actual piece of toast was now protruding from his head.

Knowing it would be too much for the proud AI to take, Dailey simply nodded. "I'll get that turned off and your normal sensor pod back on when we get into the next gate."

Albert's eyes squinted. In many ways, the crew enjoyed seeing the actual emotion the AI was now displaying. "Okay."

Within seconds, the ship lurched, vibrating lightly as the rocking pull of the gate dissolved into space. Unfortunately for everyone trying not to laugh at the toast now bobbing up and down as Albert moved, the massive swarm of ships they had just gated next to immediately set off every bell and whistle onboard, including the toaster's toast-complete alarm due to Albert being hooked up to the ship's main alert systems.

"Shit," Dailey huffed as the crew went into motion.

Pearl immediately flared the ship's reverse thrusters, keeping its main plasma cannons pointing into the heart of the swarm in front of them.

"Shields at eighty-five percent," Kline barked, the display screen switching to targeting mode.

Albert's viewscreen went black as he started computing the operational capacity of an additional gate jump. "We need five minutes before reactivating the gate drive." His matter-of-fact statement lacked any of his usual bravado, which meant things were serious.

"Kline, what are we looking at?" Dailey asked as Jen came over the comms.

"QRF is ready. We are standing up the rest of the attack wing," Jen noted, not expecting a response. The QRF stayed ready to go at all times via a rotation of Nova Rangers and a handful of attack fighters.

"Sir," Kline started. "They have a dampening field activated, keeping our targeting sensors from locking on."

While close, the ship and crew were still too far away to get a positive visual ID. "Sir," Communications Officer King interjected. "Incoming message."

This meant one of two things. Either they knew the Fleet frequencies, which was one hell of a coincidence, or the *Murphy* was about to be given an ultimatum by an unknown entity who had first figured out who they were.

Dailey stood up, walking forward as the rest of the crew continued working on various tasks related to getting them out of their current situation. It was evident by the glow of thrusters they were significantly outmatched. Albert chirped another toast-is-done alert, pointing at the green gate drive button while holding up three mechanical fingers, signaling three minutes till they were clear to gate.

The screen crackled as the well-known symbol of the Ocess Mining Company morphed into Director Prescott's overly thin, familiar face. At least familiar to Pearl and Dailey, who shot each other glances.

"Director Prescott," Dailey said, letting the man set the tone for pleasantries.

"Captain Ben Dailey. How interesting," Prescott drawled out. The man's annoyingly grey suit looked like it was made of stone.

"I was about to say the same thing," Dailey retorted, seeing the conversation hadn't opened with a veiled threat. The man either wanted something or absolutely knew they would be there.

"Yes, well, you are in our outer rim territory. It has been some time, if ever, that the Fleet has sent a ship out here into the void of space. To what do we owe the pleasure?"

The man had been born in the outer reaches of space, never having set foot on Earth; his pale skin reinforced this known fact. Dailey, Becket, and Pearl had had the distinct honor of meeting the man during a mission several years back involving a supposedly rogue mining team that had attacked an outer rim outpost.

"I would be remiss not to state they didn't exactly send us here," Dailey noted, erring on the truth. He knew the man could smell bullshit. Albert tapped his finger out of view to a now green glowing button. They could leave if they wanted.

Dailey motioned to stand down, knowing there was a very good reason for both of them to be at this exact place at this exact time.

Prescott lifted a hand, motioning someone off-screen. "So I've heard. I'm glad we are being upfront about things. With that, I would like to have an audience. Nothing official; more of an exchange of information."

While the ship could gate away, Dailey was also aware that the quickly programmed jump would not be heading toward Asher. The ship's captain was also cognizant that Prescott's motion was likely standing down his attack force. "We need to get to a group of our stranded crew. This means we are short on time."

Prescott paused. "Ah yes, I hear you have a contingent on one of the Ateris Syndicates mining experiments."

This got everyone on the bridge's attention as Dailey shifted slightly. He was calling them a Syndicate, something not previously heard coming from one of the big mining companies. "Then you know we are short on time."

"Yes," Prescott replied. "I am heading your way. We will be docking in five minutes."

Dailey nodded. "It might be best if we meet you halfway." The screen winked out once again, showing the viewports dotted with the large mass of distant ships.

"Kline?" Dailey asked as the man pointed at the monitor without turning around. "They're sending a small personal transport vessel. Seems to be lightly armed."

"This guy is a lot of things, but he's not one to be out here without a reason," Pearl noted. The *Murphy*'s captain nodded.

"Agreed. More mining-syndicate nonsense. I liked them better when they were companies. We have bigger fish to fry," Dailey stated flatly as Albert walked toward the captain's chair.

"Do we? Seems to me we have two fish to fry," Albert stated as Dailey walked over, finally taking the piece of toast out of the small horizontal pocket.

"If Sparky sees that, he's going to go crazy."

The Ocess Mining Syndicate, according to Albert's initial debriefing, was created after he had left Earth.

"What's the play?" Pearl asked while Dailey keyed his personal comms system.

"Go ahead," Becket's voice responded, the sound of Sparky's translated voice muffled in the background.

"I'm sure you were monitoring that from the drop bay. We have about five—"

"Four," Albert corrected.

"I need you to get the new transport pod ready to leave in two," Dailey finished, walking off the bridge and motioning for Albert to join him.

During their time back on Earth, the Fleet had mounted a midsize transport ship to the hull of the *Murphy*. Only capable of space travel, the sleek vessel could carry a small contingent of personnel or equipment for a limited range in space. It was a clear attempt by the senator to help speed up the process of supporting the upcoming operations on Asher. Once in orbit, Dailey could leave the ship in space to intercept the mining vessels.

There had been a few other provisions and modifications done to the *Murphy* while it was docked, including the addition of two Orion ion cannon pods. The weapon system had both offensive and defensive capabilities. Through the use of micro fission particle accelerators, the ion cannons could not only disrupt enemy shields but also offset incoming enemy fire at an alarming rate. It did this primarily by scrambling the tech onboard all the way to, as Albert described it, "*Confusing the hell out of a deflector shield or a plasma blast.*"

When used as an offensive weapon, the effects were just as brutal, allowing the ion blast to electrically break down whatever ship or material it was fired at. It was described as being able to disable a smaller ship without any structural damage while at the same time also capable of ripping a ship apart depending on proximity and distance.

When used on a larger vessel, a direct hit—minus any deflector shield interference—could result in things such as shutting down a ship's thrusters, all the way to taking out its weapons or targeting systems without damaging the bones of the ship beyond repair.

In all his moderately infinite wisdom, Dailey had concluded that Fleet command wanted every Alurian ship within reason to be captured. Disabling them, tagging the ships with beacons, then leaving them to be picked up and assimilated at a later date. The team couldn't argue the logic.

Within five minutes, Dailey, Albert, Bellman, and Becket had boarded the small transport ship piloted by the one and only Jen. Sparky was staying onboard, and according to him, "*Taking charge of the con.*" The bridge of the small transport ship had six cockpit-like stations sitting under a large blast shield.

"Boss, what's the play here?" Becket asked, finally getting situated as the sleeker Ocess ship came into view.

"It's clear they already know some of what's going on. We need to find out just how much these guys hate Ateris. Let me handle the upfront stuff," Dailey said, looking at the comical mustached face on Albert's toaster viewscreen. "Can you change that to something more uninviting?"

The monitor started blinking as several different cartoonish characters flipped through the viewscreen. Becket and Jen glared at the spectacle before Albert finally landed on a generic pumpkin-like face void of any features other than the greenish-blue dots representing his eyes and the mouth that moved as he spoke.

"Jesus, that's creepy," Becket proclaimed as Jen grimaced.

"Yeah, I say we can go back to the OG face after this meeting. I don't feel like having nightmares after this," Dailey agreed as a goofy evil grin spread across the AI's face screen. "To answer your questions," Dailey continued. "I think we can use this to our advantage. The Ocess Syndicate doesn't like Ateris, and we don't like either. On top of that, we have the Alurians. I'm not sold on this bunch being tied in with them, but if they are, we need to know."

Albert cut in. "Do you want me to scan all their systems? Due to their dampening field, I couldn't, but I should be able to once we are onboard or connected to their ship."

"That's why you're here, sunshine," Dailey joked.

"You mean it's not because of my bubbling personality?"

Dailey sighed. "I just need the rest of you to stay calm."

"Shit," Becket huffed.

Jen turned, looking at the group behind her. "Am I missing something?"

"Plausible deniability, ma'am." Becket grinned.

"What's that supposed to mean?" she asked at the same time that Albert let off another toast-is-done *ding* just as the ship in front of them pinged a docking navigation sequence. A simple shaking of hands between the two ships while they synched on autopilot.

"What that means," Albert started, "is that it can't seem like they are helping the Fleet or that they are involved. Mostly in case things don't go their way. Which, at this point, is highly SUS." Albert's viewscreen winked at the old video game reference.

"Just stay cool and let me do the talking. Stay here," Dailey added, talking to Jen. "I plan on getting out of here in a hurry."

After a few short seconds, Jen watched the sleek ship slide beside the airlock, attaching the two vessels at the hip with a light bump. After checking for a good connection, Jen released the airlock, as the hissing thump of the space being sucked out of the passageway filled the area with a light haze, only to be immediately sucked into several overhead vents.

Prescott stood on the other side of the airlock as Dailey, Becket, and Albert stared back at the man shouldered by two fully suited Ocess imperial security guards. This was no ordinary coincidence. The extra muscle told Dailey there were likely several other higher-ups in the mass of ships hovering in the distance like fireflies.

"Please, join us." Prescott motioned, finally getting a good view of Albert. The immediate recognition of Alurian tech caught him off-guard, only to be quickly masked by his emotionless thin face.

The guard to his right leaned slightly over as Prescott again glanced at Albert. "I would respectfully ask that the droid stays on your ship."

Without flinching, Dailey stepped into the airlock. "He's coming with us. He has information that may be of interest to you."

Prescott paused, computing his next move. "He is to stay with my guards at all times."

Dailey nodded, knowing he meant that he didn't want the droid to sneak off and hook up to one of the ship's systems. The thing the man didn't know was that Albert could use a radio signal or a simple scan to work his way into a ship's fancy brain. Within five seconds of the interaction, Albert had already integrated into every node and drive the boring AI had.

While using AIs was the norm for the mining syndicates, they were still very much like the one loaded on the *Brightstar*, only designed for a handful of specific functions. Albert was unique and able to not only think on his own but also act, knowing the likely consequences. Thus, the toaster, which Prescott kept glancing at.

The mining syndicates often used advanced systems, but still mainly relied on good old-fashioned personal decision making and interactions. The driving force behind this was the ability for others to corrupt AI systems, one of the main reasons the Fleet had been so hesitant for hundreds of years to integrate them.

"Understood. I'm sure you can see this is a unique droid," Dailey added as the group entered the surprisingly opulent smaller ship. Albert, by then, fully understood he needed to play dumb.

Upscale, steampunk-esque gold and dark lines filled the over-the-top luxury ship's interior, forgetting that it was actually a spaceship. Ambient yellow lighting added to the calming vibe of the whisper-quiet interior.

Much like suborbital vehicles, nicer spacecraft also had noise-dampening substructures that gave the ship an almost distracting quietness and lack of any vibration felt through one's feet. Even the *Murphy* let people know it was a frigate. The gentle hum of the vessel was always present and constantly pulsing throughout.

Slightly larger than the Harpys the drop teams from the *Murphy* used, the ship was large enough to have a small cockpit and three separate sections, which included a passenger section, a large briefing room, and a third section that was a mix of personnel transport and storage.

Between each section, a small group of personal pods and general-use areas, such as a separate crew quarters, gave the ship just enough space and accommodations to support a delegation of dignitaries in the posh vessel.

While the *Murphy* had a few areas just as nice, including the officer's mess, the transport ship now attached to the Ocess vessel was sparse by comparison.

The guards turned, opening the doors directly into the small yet just as opulent briefing room. Set up for maximum efficiency and to show off to guests, the space had a U-shaped table facing a monitor. In the middle of the *U* was a holo-table with view panels at each seat to manipulate whatever was displayed. On the wall next to the entrance door was a bar manned by a bar droid standing resolute, waiting for orders.

"Nice ship. All this just for us?" Dailey asked as Prescott motioned the two guards to stand by Albert.

"If memory serves, once upon a time before it went defunct, you set an entire Torat Syndicate's mothership on fire," Prescott recalled, taking a seat at the table, again glancing at Albert. It wasn't because of the intimidation factor of a seven-foot-tall hybrid battle droid being on their small ship, but the fact that he had finally figured out Albert had a toaster for a head.

"I see you find our droid interesting. You should meet his Alurian war hound partner in crime. And for the record, I didn't set anything on fire. That star just happened to be in the way when that ship's navigation systems went out," Dailey noted as Becket held back a chuckle, straightening his lips.

The truth was, he had been on a covert operation on a hijacked Torat Syndicate mothership. The only issue had been the syndicate itself had hijacked its own ship, using it as bait for an opposing mining corporation.

It hadn't ended as expected for the dying syndicate.

"I see your time on the other side of the Shade Belt has served you well, adapting to the changing landscape. Yes . . . I know about the Alurians. Me and everyone else, except for the general population of several planets. Hell, systems." Prescott let the statement sink in as Dailey started focusing on the task at hand.

"I'm not going to mix any words here. We need to understand what you know about the Ateris Syndicate and the Alurian ship depots."

Prescott leaned back in his seat, punching several commands into the console in front of him. The familiar outline of the Alurian depot formed in the middle of the table in the holo-projector as a diagram connecting several factions appeared on the viewscreen.

"I know enough. The Ocess Syndicate, as you are aware, is concerned about Ateris's growth outside of the normal channels. We have reason to believe they have ulterior motives with the Federation."

Dailey took in the chart linking several figures to the Ateris Syndicate, including General Ran. Truth be told, it was an exact duplicate of the chart Senator Powell had shown him after an extensive background check of other senior military officers and officials. Director Prescott was fishing with old information.

"Interesting. And what about the depot? What do you know about that?" Dailey asked as Becket centered himself, knowing what Dailey was about to do.

"We know there are no less than a dozen of them," Prescott deadpanned. While Dailey and the others knew there were probably more, this number was something even he was having trouble computing.

"Where?"

"That is what we don't fully know," Prescott answered while Dailey motioned for Albert to step closer.

"Then how did you know about this one? You see, I've looked at that chart before, and we supplied the same schematic of the depot we are looking at now. That tells me you know more than you are putting on or fishing for information," Dailey said as Albert stepped directly beside him. The light hum of the gears in his legs whirled in the posh setting.

Prescott snorted as his own guards postured beside the director. "Both."

"Albert, why don't you introduce yourself?"

Albert turned toward the console, punching in several commands at laserlike speed. Several navigation points and comms links erupted on the screen, showing the recent movement of the Ateris Syndicate's ships and leadership communications. This was followed by Albert changing his face to that of a skull as he stared directly at Prescott.

"Fascinating," was all the man said, standing up. "I see you have something I didn't know about."

"My name is Albert, and I'd prefer you calm down there, rock star," Albert insisted, pulling back his shoulders as the two guards flexed. "I sense your heart rates are elevated. I suggest relaxing or grabbing a drink."

"You're an AI. How interesting. Are you one of the new gen systems coming out of the Federation?"

Dailey cleared his throat. "He's probably the oldest thing within several parsecs."

That got the director's attention, cocking his head sideways. "Alright. Let's not delay what we are here to discuss, since it seems you have me at a slight disadvantage."

Dailey followed this by saying a simple command that Albert had preprogrammed in his subsystems. "Albert, Directive One."

Within seconds, Albert had secured both guards with one arm, quickly fusing their wrists together in a spray of Solarian web fiber, followed by him opening the palms of his hands while the familiar glow of sub-lasers hovered dangerously close to letting loose on the director.

Taking a deep breath, Prescott sat back in his chair. "Huh, probable deniability, I see. Fair enough, as I hear you often say."

"Something like that. So this is how it's going to go. Why are you here, and how did you know?"

The play was simple. Both men knew they couldn't freely give each other information, so they would do so under duress, a forced conversation in the eyes of the syndicate and the imperial guards present. The two seasoned men knew the game and how to play it in the ever-shifting world of politics.

"Yes, we tracked your passage through a gate in the sector. After talking with our contacts, we knew it would only be a matter of time before you passed back through." Prescott paused, knowing he would only answer the questions asked.

Dailey glanced back at the guards. "Do any of your ships have gate drives?"

"A few. I bet it stung to find out everything you knew was a lie. But yes, we do have access to gate drives. Not many, but enough to accomplish what is needed."

Becket leaned forward. "What's needed?"

"Ah, the million-credit question. By now, you have figured out the mining syndicates' roles in the general order of things. War is coming, and not just the normal kind where one side wins and the other loses. The kind where everyone loses, minus the massive wall of pain heading our way."

"Heading our way?" Dailey asked. Prescott shifted in his seat.

"You will find out soon enough. But know this: the day will come when you—hell, *we* will all need the Alurian Fleets. Up until a few months ago, your precious Federation thought the enemy was coming from the east when in reality, they were staring at them from the west. You get the picture.

We want Ateris out of the system where the rest of your crew is stranded. On Asher, I believe you are calling it."

"You talk of war but only ask for mining territory. It's always the same story. Let me tell you what I see. I see the Alurians getting ready to attack the Federation's territory, and from what we now know, whatever mining syndicate supports the effort more wins whatever prize is at the end of the rainbow."

"Very much so. But there is so much more at stake. Worlds you have no comprehension of and galaxies yet to be explored. Your Federation knows this, yet they turn a blind eye, more concerned about their own position and titles. No, what's coming cannot be stopped, and I can promise you, it does not care about titles or speed bumps such as the Federation. Let me ask you a question, droid."

"Albert. My name is Albert. And I have a particle-enhanced laser beam pointed directly at your skull. Which is rather pointy, by the way. You're not human."

That got Dailey's attention. "Let me guess. The Ocess Syndicate is not what we think, and you are from what? Another galaxy?"

Prescott didn't reply, answering the question. To put it into perspective, the galaxy was massive. Massive beyond normal comprehension. Only in the past several hundred years had humankind even been able to get out of their own solar system, improved through the use of both Alurian and Solarian technology after the war.

Only after returning to Earth had the true breadth of the distance traveled by the inhabitants of the *Murphy* set in. In many Federation and Fleet circles, they still didn't believe the crew had traveled to Andromeda. The circle who actually knew the truth was small and unable to release the information to the greater population.

Prescott cleared his throat. It was time to get to business. "If you find the Ateris Syndicate no longer controls the system, we will take over the operations and, with that, hold out a friendly hand to the Federation."

"And still support the Alurian effort. I don't think that's going to cut it. Tell you what, seeing how gracious of a host you have been. We will go on our way. We will let you know if we find the system or sector clear."

Prescott nodded his approval. Even though the two men could have simply had a more specific conversation, this was the Ocess Syndicate using the Fleet for a proxy war that had been apparently going on for hundreds if not thousands of years. As long as the syndicates didn't actively engage each other, neither would be at risk of losing large swaths of their territory and ships.

"I believe our time here is done," Dailey noted as Albert stepped back, de-energizing his lasers.

"I really want to fry this guy's face off, or at least introduce him to Captain Sparky," Albert said.

"Here." Prescott stood up, chucking a small transponder to Dailey. "When the time comes, our transmission codes are loaded on that." With that, the hiss of the airlock slid back into action, and Albert finally turned to go back to the comparably gloomy transportation ship.

Prescott opened the far-end door to the briefing room as two more guards stepped in, helping the others free their hands. "Do you want to message the council?"

Prescott grinned what little he could. "I'll let them know the situation. Activate the deflector shields, and as soon as we are decoupled, take us to Chancellor Evert's ship. We have done as asked. The rest is up to Captain Dailey, if that holds any weight."

Back onboard the transport ship, Dailey, Becket, and Albert quickly took their seats as the Ocess ship lurched way. "Open fire," Dailey instructed to a confused Jen.

"This ship only has a pulse laser. Enough to deflect enemy ships at best," Jen noted as Dailey turned to Albert.

Before he could say anything, she turned, still confused by the statement. "Okay, dammit. Whatever. If we get killed, I'm going to be so pissed."

"Technically, if you're dead, you cannot really be pissed," Albert said as the light sounds of laser fire burped from the craft's short wings.

"You want that toaster removed?"

Albert shut up, finally reverting to the mustached face.

Onboard the Ocess transport ship, Prescott stared at the system monitor as the weak laser fire dissipated in the deflector shields without affecting their energy levels.

The crew was back aboard the *Murphy* within ten minutes, with Jen following a nearly running Dailey back to the bridge. "Stop," she barked before arriving at the bridge's blast doors.

Dailey stopped, turning as Jen's hands found purchase on her hips. "What the hell was that? We just threw banana peels at a damn near armada."

"Yup, ships that are about to attack us if we don't get out of here. I'll give you the details later, but the Ocess Syndicate wants us to help them fight their proxy war against Ateris, and they're a merry group of assholes. I'm starting to think that's who's giving the team on Asher a hard time."

"What does that have to do with what just happened?" Jen asked, frustrated. Dailey grinned just as Albert clanked up behind them.

"This is all theater in case someone's watching. This may save your life one day. Albert, we have maybe five minutes at most," Dailey stated while Jen shook her head. As the words left his mouth, the proximity alarms started, at the same time the sounds of light laser fire thumped off the deflector shields. "Albert, make it two. Lieutenant, we will fill you in once we get through the next gate."

Dailey was failing to mention the dozen or so Alurian depots, as well as the other threats Director Prescott had mentioned. He also knew Albert had had plenty of time to scour the ship's data banks and would be getting an information dump soon enough.

CHAPTER 8

NIGHT LIGHT

Mac paced the Gulch's repurposed command pod as Petty Officer Miller checked the signal again. Ten minutes prior, they had received several messages from not only Earth but the *Murphy* as well.

The cool, shaded afternoon air, accompanied by the earthy smell of the massive forest, breezed by Mac's senses as the entrance door whooshed shut. The Gulch was neatly tucked away under a section of the gigantic trees that adorned Asher's surface. Trees large enough to reach into the clouds in some instances. Here, on the outskirts of a sizable forest leading into a valley, the tree canopy stood at a respectable ten stories before giving way to foliage.

After several weeks—and months of rearranging and digging in several remaining sections of the *Brightstar*—the Gulch had taken on its own personality. The locals knew it was alien, but in many ways, so was the rest of Asher.

"I don't know how, but we have the *Murphy* on comms." Miller shrugged as Communications Officer King's familiar face phased into life on the viewscreen.

"Asher, this is the *Murphy*. How copy?" King asked again.

"Loud and freaking clear!" Miller exclaimed as Master Sergeant Walker marched into the room. Smiles erupted on everyone's faces as the sound of familiar voices echoed over the loudspeaker. Familiar faces they had called for help, adding to the excitement.

King's face morphed into a general view of the bridge and a smiling Dailey. "Good to see you all in one piece. We've been worried."

Mac glanced at Walker, letting him speak for the group in case the signal was lost. "How are we talking? We didn't think you'd gotten our message," Walker said as Albert stepped forward, taking the group at the Gulch off guard.

"That's an easy one, gang," Albert started as Mac whispered to the room, "Is that a toaster?"

"When we went back to Earth, we found an ancient comms station that was linked to the outer rim and several of the old mining colonies. After a little dancing with the Ocess Syndicate, which Dailey will surely brag to you about, we finally calibrated the *Murphy*'s gate drive to the relay communications array. You know, simple stuff. Just took some time. Anywho . . . with that done, we can use the gate drive as a type of hypertransmitter."

Miller nodded, not having a clue what Albert was saying. Mac cleared her throat.

"Dumb it down for us. How can we use the system? We are only using our equipment."

"Are you? I could have sworn I synched you into the communication hub in the city. That place is really, really old. Oh, and your commander and ham chief would like to say a word," Albert relayed as Sparky, having stayed relatively out of trouble over the past several months, stood up.

"Is my planet safe?" Sparky asked. Knowing they all had the same question, Dailey let the Alurian battle hound talk. He was also giving the war hound some space after the threat of spilling the literal beans about his love life, something he and Albert spent most of their free time gossiping about.

Mac grinned. "Almighty commander. I regret to report it's not." Mac's mood shifted as she motioned for Walker to take over the conversation, seeing that Sparky had plopped back on his hind legs.

"I don't know how to say this, but we have been attacked. When I mean attacked, I mean entire cities wiped out."

The words landed like a bomb on the *Murphy*'s crew as Dailey stood up. "By whom?"

"That's what we don't know. We are guessing someone from the Ateris Mining Syndicate. Ben, they used gamma surface-scraping lasers to wipe out one of our closest food sources. Every day or two, they fire that damn thing again."

Dailey paused, taking in the information as Sparky looked up, pulling his floppy tongue in his mouth. They were both concerned.

"We figured something was going on with Ateris. We had a little run-in with the Ocess Syndicate. I'll fill you in later, but you need to understand we have marching orders from the Federation and the Fleet," Dailey said, working to communicate as much information as possible.

"Figured as much," Walker replied as the viewscreen blipped. "We're not sending any attack fighters into orbit in case it's a fade. How long 'till you're here?"

Albert spoke up. "We have one more gate to complete. By my calculations, we will be there in a little under twenty-four hours."

The news was a much-needed relief. Walker nodded. "When you get into the sector, I'll have Miller send you the triangulation coordinates of the gamma laser. It appears to be on the moon or close to it."

Dailey nodded. At the same time, Pearl was already entering targeting data into the nav computer in reference to Asher's main orbiting moon. "We . . . see . . ." Static took over the conversation as someone was now either jamming or interrupting the signal, trying to intercept it.

The inconvenient truth was Ran and the Ateris leftovers on the moon, while unable to determine the contents of the communication, were blasting the signal with ionic radon, working on decrypting it. Luckily for the inhabitants of the Gulch and the *Murphy*, Albert had integrated a somewhat archaic yet effective security protocol for all communications coming into and out of their network.

In reality, the AI had uploaded a classic two-player video game set to play each other when a line of communication was opened. If you didn't have the programming and online-synching ability, you wouldn't be part of either the game or the conversation.

As Albert described it: "*I literally uploaded* Call of Duty 2150 *on both systems, and when we are communicating, we are literally in a game lobby talking. Those bozos will never figure that little ditty out.*" He had even enacted the protocol on the Gulch and Arcadia before leaving Asher. When talking to other locations on the planet's surface, the system would revert back to standard network parameters.

Mac patted Walker on the shoulder. The man had barely slept over the past week. "When does the delegation from Kodas arrive?"

"Five hours," Miller noted as Grear walked into the room.

"Good," Mac started. "Let's get Dax and Vax up to speed and wrap up this meeting with the Kodas delegation. From the message we received from the senator, we will be busy once the *Murphy* arrives. I wish they had given us more to go from other than tracking the cargo ships."

"They want the ships," Grear spoke up, drawing the room's attention. "Think about it. They took one of the fancy drive things from one of them, and the *Murphy* can now travel damn near anywhere."

"Shit," Mac huffed. "You're right. I bet that means they will need pilots."

Walker sipped a fresh cup of go juice, bringing up a tracking map of the incoming delegation. "There're a whole lot of assumptions in that, but I wouldn't doubt it. Dax is already tracking all the cargo ship traffic; let's just make sure he doesn't stop. We need to make it through the next twenty-four hours. There hasn't been an attack in a day and a half."

The man knocked on the wooden table carved from one of the massive trees providing a shaded cover for the mini base.

General Ran stood poised with his hands behind his back, watching the massive viewscreen in the moon's command center. Derrisa Monvet's—one of the Ateris Syndicate's human finance administrators—shoes clacked on the sleek black floor as she entered the room.

"I see you got word of the transmission," Ran stated flatly without turning around to face her. "It appears things are going as planned."

"Are they? Lashet," Derrisa said as the indifferent Alurian shifted his gaze from the viewscreen now showing a remote feed of Asher. "Replay the transmission."

Lashet huffed. "There is no transmission to replay. It was encrypted with some new type of tech. I can tell you it was sent via a gate transponder that appears to match the gate drive the USF *Murphy* used."

"That could mean a plethora of things," Derrisa chided in her usual cadence.

General Ran turned to face the rest of the occupants in the room. "Captain Dailey is on his way here as we speak. We all know that somebody on the surface called for help. Since we were able to get operations back up and running, I have been talking with Vice Admiral Tammar. At the first sign of the *Murphy*, or any other Fleet ship, he has agreed to send a rather sizable force into the sector."

Derrisa's eyebrows rose as she smirked. "So you're now talking to vice admirals without my knowledge." She walked closer to Ran. "I see. So you plan to take out Captain Dailey and get the Alurians to address the planet-side situation."

She wasn't asking a question but rather making a statement of understanding.

"That would be a correct assessment of the situation, Derrisa. Might I also add that Vice Admiral Tammar has agreed to supply us with a star cruiser from the Eighth Alurian Fleet."

This was good news for the group, which was mostly stuck on the moon for the time being. Derrisa nodded in approval. "What's the catch?"

"The admiral takes all the credit for solving the issue in the sector. It will also buy us favor with him; favor we are very much going to need in the near future if we plan on expanding our empire."

"You mean to start a war," Derrisa noted quickly.

"Don't we all? Only the strong are going to survive what's coming. The Alurians are too busy focusing on the issues growing in Orion's Arm with Earth and its neighbors, the Solarians, in Alpha Centauri. Soon enough, the Ateris Syndicate will be their main partner on both fronts."

Derrisa pulled her shoulders back, standing up straighter. "Yes, when the Creare Overlords make their move, it will be wise to be positioned well. Other than Ocess, the other syndicates have been all but taken off the playing field."

With that, Derrisa walked up, standing beside Ran, pondering the remote view of Asher.

CHAPTER 9

KNOCK KNOCK

The clink of dishes, surrounded by the hum of low conversation, filled the officer's mess and chow hall of the *Murphy*. With only two hours left on their journey back to Asher, Master Chief Thron had put together a meal fit for a king.

Large screens positioned at the corners of the space displayed current and relatively recent news feeds from a mix of Solarian and Earth sources. Still front and center of most people's minds back home was the attack on Orlando. Memorial services and speeches clogged the news cycle, only to give way to more pressing items such as recent syndicate agreements for newly found planets' rights.

Dorax had been invited to join the command team after finishing his duties in the galley. In many ways, it had been refreshing for the rogue Alurian to have focus and purpose.

Sparky sat on the elevated pillow nestled in the corner of the command staff bench, sitting beside Dailey, slurping a bowl of soup with none other than a ham bone floating in the middle.

The one rule Thron had been insistent on was no droids in the chow hall. This meant Albert had to remote into the conversation, which he did through Sparky's translator.

"You think we will run into any trouble planetside?" Lieutenant Brian Cardinali asked Albert.

The heavy-weapons platoon leader of Second Foot had been assigned to go planetside as soon as they reached orbit. Lieutenant Ponce and Master Sergeant Don Grantham from First Foot would be on standby to head toward the moon. This left Master Sergeant Janix, the sole leader of Third Foot, to stay with the ship.

"Oh yeah, for sure," Albert replied as Dailey rolled his eyes.

"He meant to ask if you think we are going to run into any trouble when we arrived at Asher. Not fifty years down the road," the ship's commander clarified.

"Well, in that case, very likely. Or maybe not."

Sparky let out a slight snicker, knowing the AI was giving the group a hard time. Truth be told, they had no clue what they were about to encounter. As soon as they reached the system, they would engage the hyperdrive and be in orbit within thirty minutes.

This would give them a minimal amount of time to receive any updates or adjust the plan. Fortunately for the Nova Rangers and other Fleet personnel, the plan was so basic that they all fully expected it to go to hell as soon as they reached orbit.

"We're going to take the new transport ship to the moon as soon as the area is secured," Grantham noted, cramming a handful of Solarian wheat honks into his mouth. Bellman would be proud of the display of unflinchingly rude eating. "I'm not buying that this might not be a trap."

Wheat honks just happened to be one of Grantham's favorite Solarian side dishes. Now that things were about to get hectic, Thron had tried to sprinkle a little bit of everyone's favorites into the mix.

Dailey snickered. "Of course it's a trap. I mean, why not? Best-case scenario, we get in and out before the enemy can dispatch enough ships to take us on. After our last handful of encounters, they will be more cautious."

Becket chimed in, grabbing one of the fluffy honks. "What the boss here is saying is that cautious means an entire armada or fleet. We need to get the moon secured and set as a priority target. No change to the briefing and order of precedence. We have backup plans for most of the triggers if something goes wrong, but I don't see us getting out of there without a fight."

Albert cut in as Dailey smacked Sparky, who had decided to start grooming himself at the table. "We will have three main gate options available as soon as we hit orbit. Oh, and if anyone is interested, I'm doing a showing of the *Solarian Couples Movian* dating show, seeing that I will be hanging out while awaiting the shit, as you say, to hit the fan. Great stuff. Sparky and I are excited to see how things pan out."

The *Solarian Couples Movian* dating show was probably some of the worst reality entertainment Solaria had to offer. The premise was simple but devastatingly annoying. The show would put people in controlled near-death experiences in an attempt to see if they would find true love through the significant emotional event. As one would assume, this often got out of hand and, in some cases, caused people to lose all control of themselves. The more popular outtakes involved the couples that would say things like, "Hey, let's make out since this might be our last few moments alive."

Unfortunately for the show, during its fifth season, an unknowing couple, seeing no way out of a burning building, decided to hold hands and jump to their deaths instead of being cooked alive. The fire had been staged and completely controlled. Solarian humor and their take on things were, at times, hard to comprehend to humans.

"That's going to be a no from me," Dailey replied, dropping the transponder Prescott from the Ocess Syndicate had given him. "We get outnumbered, we call for backup."

"Hate to interrupt this mind-alteringly interesting conversation, but it appears we are ready to exit the gate."

Dailey set his fork down, placing his napkin over his plate. "Hit it."

Albert, on command, activated the *Murphy*'s call to battle stations. Red flashing lights strobed, making the officer's mess resemble a house of horrors. Smiles vanished as everyone moved with a practiced purpose.

Thron watched, grimacing as half-eaten plates of skillfully prepared food sat unfinished. Dorax walked to the door, turning off the alert for the mess hall.

"Well, I guess we get this cleaned up. Listen, Alurian," Thron scoffed, "you've done alright by me so far, but I can promise you things are about to get tough. I know the captain, and I can tell you he is absolutely picking a fight no matter what everyone else thinks or says."

"How do you know that?" Dorax asked as several commands came over the intercom.

"He asked for Solarian fluffy honks. Every time he's done that, we've had a fight coming." Dorax stared at the man as if he didn't understand.

Thron cleared his throat, helping Dorax stack plates. "Let's just say, when I cook honks, it's usually the last time I do so onboard that ship. You get the picture."

The galley's master chief glanced at the small table and picture of Lieutenant Dasher sitting in the corner of the room as a makeshift shrine to their lost companion, a companion Dorax would never meet.

The familiar vibration of the *Murphy* crossing the gate rippled through the bridge. Space rippled around the viewport, and the primary monitor lit up with familiar star charts, including the planet they had proudly labeled as Asher, a name still up for debate with Sparky.

Everyone was still, in a calm, trancelike state, waiting for enemy ships to appear on the radar. "Kline?" Dailey broke the silence.

"Nothing, sir."

Albert chimed in, "We have a direct line of communication with the Gulch. I recommend updating them before we activate thrusters."

Dailey nodded, just as the comms channel sprang to life. He stood up, walking to the navigation station beside Pearl. "Gulch, this is the *Murphy*. We are en route. Awaiting guidance."

Mac's voice came over the comms. "Good to hear your voice. All scans are clear here. Welcome back."

Dailey took a calming breath. "Pearl, engage thrusters."

After several days of debate, the decision had been made for Albert to station himself in front and to the left of Dailey's command station. Once assigned to a weapons specialist, the station had been modified to accept Albert, removing the chair and replacing it with an odd toiletlike charging station of his own design.

Petty Officer Kramer, one of the Fleet's finest yet unpolished weapons specialists, had been shifted to the secondary targeting station. Ultimately, even Kline preferred his new station due to the additional targeting screens and the possibility to not have everyone within touching distance.

"If I may," Albert interjected. "I was monitoring that last communication, and it appears someone has tracked the transmission."

Dailey leaned forward, expecting a significantly more emotional event than getting their signal intercepted. "Did they hear us?"

"Ha," Albert scoffed. "Not unless they have a Play Solarian Station 82 and the secret war cabinet addition."

"What are you babbling about?" Dailey asked. Albert's head, still a toaster, turned while his body stayed still.

"I'm not giving away the farm in case they have Scaralac mindworms."

"What?" Dailey huffed back.

"A worm from a planet that is clearly no longer in existence that you have no clue about. Those nasty little worms could be used to crack someone's thoughts. I take it there are no *Wrath of Khan* fans in here? No? Bueller? Anywho, someone's watching the incoming and outgoing signals, and that's all they got."

The star field in front of the *Murphy* shifted as Pearl engaged the hyperthrusters for the final leg of the journey. "Did they intercept our signals when we reached out before?"

"Possibly. We were sending them through a gate. With that, the signal could be coming from anywhere in the galaxy or next. No, if they are paying attention and have at least two cups of coffee in them, they are fully aware this signal came from within the sector."

Pearl turned to join the conversation, having set the coordinates without Albert's help. "Sir, do you think we are heading into an ambush?"

Dailey smiled the wicked grin he often did, knowing a fight was coming. "As Albert would say . . . yeah, sure. It's the *when* that I'm more concerned about. I mentioned it during our briefing. Who or whatever is out there could have acted more directly against our team by now. This is someone buying time for backup; something else."

"You don't think they know what we are capable of?" Pearl asked as Dailey made an incorrect assumption that would haunt him over the course of the next several days and weeks.

"I mean, Ran is likely floating around in a latrine pod somewhere. At this point, it might be some mining cleanup operations. We already know this wasn't a critical operation for the Alurians or the Ateris Syndicate anymore." Dailey paused. "I'm not assuming anything, but somebody, somewhere, is absolutely waiting for us to show back up."

CHAPTER 10

WHO'S THERE?

The *Murphy* hummed in orbit above Asher as several attack fighters buzzed around the area, shooting down several newly placed satellites. Light reflected off the moon from the local sun, making the light sheen of moisture glisten while it slowly faded from the ship's main thruster ventilation grids.

"I don't want to fully execute our plan until we figure out where all these damn things came from," Dailey instructed as the teams stood ready to execute the initial plan. As with all plans, they knew the likelihood of them actually going as directed was slim to none in the outer reaches of the galaxy.

Albert shifted, turning to look back at the rest of the bridge crew, pushing Mister Toaster to wink. "I have triangulated the tracking signal's origin, and as suspected, it is coming from the moon. Might I suggest we destroy it?"

"Last time we took out a moon . . ." Dailey drawled out, not wanting to admit the aftereffects on the hosting, unpopulated planet. "Let's get the ground forces engaged. I want to wait till the surface team is set before heading to the moon. I promise they already know we're here."

Within minutes, Second Foot was in motion, preparing to perform an orbital drop. From there, they would link up with the Gulch and then proceed to Arcadia, where a battery of orbital cannons had been found and activated, tucked away in one of the city's ivory towers.

Becket walked onto the bridge, strolling up to the navigation station, joining the others standing around the star chart like a group of kids glaring at something they'd just dropped on the floor, watching the icons representing the mining ships and satellites.

"Everyone's ready, sir. Waiting on you," Becket informed a nodding Dailey.

"They haven't fired the scraper since we hit orbit. According to Albert, the moon's orbit possibly kept it out of reach of the Gulch. It's a waiting game," Dailey responded.

It was clear he fully expected the onslaught of a revenge-seeking enemy, only to have the proximity alarms scream instead of chiming to life. There were incoming enemy vessels.

Dailey flattened his lips, nodding at Becket, knowing the moon mission would have to wait.

"Well, this wouldn't be the first time we didn't go to the moon," Albert scoffed, the joke only taking hold of the ship's direct command team, making Dailey and Becket shake their heads.

"Once this is over, we shift to the original plan. We stay in orbit while the other platoons head to the moon," Dailey instructed. Becket gave a light salute, heading back toward the drop bays.

Kline cocked his head over his shoulder, reporting on the incoming targeting data as the monitor erupted in red dots of all sizes. "We have two—no, three—no, five, ten . . . ah shit." That term was the measurement of a losing situation.

While the *Murphy*'s commander had thoroughly planned on some form of ambush, what he wasn't expecting was the entire fleet that had just gated into the sector. Instead of a head-to-head fight, they would have to go with plan B.

An Alurian dreadnaught, battlecruiser, and dozens of destroyers phased into existence as a literal swarm of fighters erupted from multiple ships like a shotgun blast.

"Oh shit," Albert said, the face on his viewscreen shifting to a flat digital set of eyes and a mouth. He was moving all his functional resources to computational systems.

Luckily for the *Murphy*'s commander, as well as the crew, Dailey, Pearl, and Albert had planned for such an occurrence. This was the worst-case scenario. While still concerned about the team planetside, they had set several gate navigation points to maneuver to if needed.

Pearl looked up, her expression stressed, understanding the genuine quandary they now found themselves in. "We can gate to point one at any time."

Dailey walked to the viewport, watching as the glow of plasma cannons heating up started shining like stars. "Execute now," he stated calmly, looking down at the planet. "Albert, send a message to the senator on our status. She already knows we're here."

Bodies shifted as space rippled in front of the *Murphy*. At the same time, the first pod of seeker missiles from the *Murphy*'s forward battery arose from their slumber, smacking several leading attack fighters before they realized what was happening.

"This is going to be close," Albert exclaimed, the literal oh-shit factor coming through in his voice.

Not realizing the *Murphy* was gating, several of the attack fighters shredded themselves in the event horizon the *Murphy* was already moving through. Throughout the trip, Albert, Bellman, and Pearl had spent some time working on ways to navigate the gate itself more efficiently.

For this trip, Albert had programmed a smaller event horizon, only allowing the *Murphy* through. The intent was to keep any unwanted guests from tagging along.

"Sir!" Kline barked. "We have incoming. Their destroyers are within direct fire range!"

The *Murphy* shuddered in a mix of passing through the gate and its tail end deflector shields getting hammered by several plasma cannons. A combination of chaos and brutal flashing lights surrounded the ship as it slipped into the gate, only to have the calming stillness of what they were calling innerspace take over.

A bead of sweat dripped from Dailey's forehead.

"What the hell was that?" Pearl spoke up first, smacking her hand on the navigation panel.

"That was an entire Alurian battle group," Albert replied.

Dailey looked at Albert, taking in a breath. "That was not what I expected to show up. Albert, keep signaling the team at the Gulch."

In most cases, signaling a team on a planet would place a massive target on them. Albert's ingenious plan was nearly impossible to triangulate. The only hedge at this point was that the gigantic dreadnaught had not simply evaporated the planet.

"This is Angel Two," Lieutenant Jim Novak from the Gulch's remaining attack wing's voice came over the comms, not waiting for an acknowledgment. "We are set and out of the air. Everyone is moving underground into the mines."

It was clear the inhabitants of Asher were also aware of the Alurian battle group taking position in orbit. As for the Kodas delegation, the team had lucked out when hearing from their closest remaining neighboring city. Kodas was a city filled with engineers and mechanics. While not nearly as sophisticated or connected to the overall management of the planet as Arcadia, Kodas's inhabitants managed and maintained all the planet's primary underground substructures, including the tram, mining ships, primary mining equipment, and even the gravity fields the *Murphy*'s team had encountered while hijacking the *Scarecrow*.

Another system they happened to control was the planet's inner defenses, including hundreds, if not thousands, of Alurian battle droids.

After the attacks had activated the storage warehouse of droids that the team from the Gulch had encountered, Kodas's primary leadership had quickly realized the entirety of the situation, shutting down the robots of death. In reality, they had known for some time that something was not aligned with the planet's operations after discovering several long-forgotten layers of the planet's previous iterations of unknowing workers.

Either way, the inhabitants of the Gulch and Arcadia had had a private VIP tour of the planet's substructures, lending to a place for them to safely disappear.

"We will report back soon. Stand by, and be safe," Dailey responded, walking to the targeting station. "Kline, how many ships?"

The pale shade of off-white told Dailey all he needed to know while Kline started methodically programming the targeting data into the primary monitor. "Dozens, sir."

Beside the schematic of Asher, several ships organized by size listed themselves on the left side of the screen. Stomachs dropped as the total size of the force came into focus.

The size of the Alurian force who had initially attacked Earth included five destroyers, two frigates, and one battlecruiser, with dozens of smaller vessels hanging off their bellies and in their bays. Within those assault ships had also been a mass of drone attack fighters.

What lay before the *Murphy* dwarfed that force threefold. The ship Dailey kept staring at was the massive behemoth labeled dreadnaught, a classification of craft that was a mix of space station and overbearing killing machine. The dreadnaught could fit one of the Alurian destroyers in its bays.

In contrast, even though called a frigate by Earth standards, the *Murphy* was just twice the size of the Alurian destroyers. In a toe-to-toe fight, it would only take the dreadnaught twenty or so batteries to take out the Fleet's now finest and most capable ship.

The *Brightstar* was the closest thing the Fleet had had to the monstrosity, and thanks to General Ran, it was now spread across the sector and moon surface in pieces.

Large layers resembling ships stacked on each other formed small mountains. If the weapons systems poking out from the dreadnaught's armored hide didn't kill you, its presence alone was enough to ward off any attacking force that Dailey could fathom.

As for the star cruiser, while still just as large, it was more focused on logistics and actual ground occupational forces. This was the part that was worrying Dailey the most. The whalelike ship was ginormous and wasn't thought to need endless layers of weapons systems. The sheer amount of attack fighters on board was enough to suffice, and if that didn't work, one of the ship's massive ion cannons would do the job.

"Albert, they'll be able to follow us, right?" Dailey asked, thinking the situation through. He had either miscalculated the threat or the importance of the sector.

In reality, he had miscalculated Ran, something he would not do twice.

"Oh yeah. Like an enlarged child leaving a candy shop with a hole in their pocket, there will be a trail leading them right to us. Good news, though: it's not like they will mess with us while in interspace, so we have that going for us. Oh, but they may have new-gen gate drives, so they may or may not beat us to our destination."

"Shit. Alright," Dailey started. "Someone get Dorax up here."

Dorax's chest heaved once he stood on the bridge. The stains on the apron he had slung over his neck smelled like soap and the rich tang of seared meat. Seeing this, the Alurian took the apron off, chucking it on an empty comms station. With Albert's automation of several systems, they had freed up some space on the bridge.

"We just gated out of the sector; I'm sure you get the idea. I'm even more sure they will follow us. How many ships will they send?" Dailey asked.

Dorax huffed. "You assume I know all this?"

"How many ships?" Dailey repeated. He pointed at the screen as Albert added several graphic arrows pointing at the bloated dreadnaught.

The Alurian's facial expression didn't change as he blurted out, "*Ruuuuuckish*," the Alurian version of dropping the F-bomb.

"Yeah, that's what everyone keeps saying," Albert added.

"Dorax." Dailey regained the Alurian's attention. "What will they do? I know you're not an Alurian fleet guy, but what is your gut telling you?"

"My gut's telling me we don't need to go back there. But . . . if that was me? I would send a handful of destroyers and maybe one of those interceptor ships. You know, the ones full of drone fighters. I doubt they'll send any of the M-class ships." The M-class ships referred to the larger cruiser-style vessels.

Dailey nodded, having the exact same thought. "Well, we've had good luck so far against their destroyers."

Pearl cleared her throat. "I believe you called them the B-team. I doubt this is the B-team."

She was right. Pearl was painfully correct in her assumption.

"Okay, Albert, where's this gate coming out?"

While they had a plan in place, some of the lighter details had been left out, since neither the crew, including Dailey, nor anyone else in the Fleet had ever been to any of the locations preprogrammed into the gate drive. Making matters even more interesting, Albert had informed them that the gate drive they had installed aboard the *Murphy* was a first-generation artifact.

The fact that he had used the word artifact told them all they needed to know about the necessity to upgrade the system at some point.

Doing his usual Albert spill, he started going into an explanation of how gates didn't really come out anywhere, only to be greeted with groans. "Okay then, smarty-pants. How about I just shut down and let you all burn some toast in my sensor pod instead of saving us all."

"We need to know if there is anything we can use to our advantage," Dailey followed as the smartass look on Mister Toaster's face morphed into a thoughtful glance.

"Maybe not here. But of course, it has been a few years—well, maybe a few thousand—since the gate drive nav points have been updated. We might be heading into something like an asteroid field . . . Oh shit."

Pearl turned. "Okay, so we are gating into a charted asteroid field. We can work with that."

Dailey contemplated the statement, looking at the timer counting down. There were thirty more minutes until they reached the other end of the gate. "Well, let's see if we can thin the herd some. I'm sure they have updated nav charts. I have an idea."

Five minutes later, the entire senior staff was huddled again around the navigation station, looking at the primary monitor. Becket held his hands down, silencing the loud group.

"Alright. I want to call this operation: plan C," Dailey spoke, chuckles and snorts echoing throughout the bridge.

"So creative," Albert chided as Dailey refocused.

"If the force we encounter is enough for us to handle, we take them head-on," Dailey said, to the nods of approval from the Nova Rangers and attack-wing senior pilots. The base Fleet personnel, on the other hand, shook their heads, knowing they had little say in the matter.

"Once we wrap that up, we take that trip to the depot early. Worst-case scenario, there's someone there cleaning up the mess. If not . . . we might be able to see what's left."

Jen stepped forward. "You're saying we hijack a bunch of ships and bring them back to Asher with us?"

"Two birds, one stone. Any other time, it wouldn't be an option."

Albert interjected. "You mean if it wasn't for me. And maybe just one or two big stones."

Dailey sighed, breathing out his nose. "For once, I agree with Mister Toaster here. We need to think outside our normal toolbox. I would like to see the look on those asshats' faces if we show up with a fleet of our own."

"Who's going to pilot those ships?" Jen asked, making a good point.

"One step at a time. I want everyone to be set to engage as soon as we exit the gate." Albert nodded his moderate approval while Dailey finished his idea. "I say we don't give them a second to react. We engage violently. Everything we got, without pushing her too hard. I'm going to lean on the attack wing here. Rangers, I want full engagement on the largest ships we encounter."

The platoon leaders all nodded in complete understanding as First Sergeant Becket started barking orders. Even though the Rangers knew what to do, the time-honored tradition of the senior-ranking, noncommissioned officer was not only expected but welcomed.

"Dorax," Dailey said, stopping the Alurian as he headed back toward the galley. "I want you up here."

"Why?"

"I want to get your take on the ships and what happens. I know you're not from any Alurian battle group, but you know how they think, and you know the outer rims. You'd be surprised. It's like the humans we met on Asher. We still have a feeling for things like that."

Dorax shrugged, setting his dirty apron back down on Pearl's station, only to get cut in half by her laserlike stare. "Okay," he grumbled, taking a seat. "You know what, Captain," Dorax started as the rest of the crew settled into their battle stations.

"Enlighten me, Dorax," Dailey replied, activating the weapons control on the panel he'd slid out of the arm of his seat.

"I get why Senior Chief Thron does what he does. He can stay in that galley and not have to put up with all this mess. I respect that in a man."

"I can tell you from experience he puts up with more than most and less than others. He is on his third galley in five years, but yeah, you're right. Look, you don't have to convince me you weren't one of those Alurians who attacked the Orlando spaceport."

Dorax scoffed. "You think the Alurians did that? Hah."

The rest of the bridge turned to the Alurian. "Oh shit, you all really think that was an Alurian attack."

"This is going to be good," Albert interjected.

"If you think the mining companies don't have their hands in that mess, you're lying to yourselves; keeping the war effort alive; keeping your precious Federation and Fleet buying their resources, making them richer and more powerful."

As the rest of the crew pondered the statement, the countdown meter on the primary viewscreen hit zero, and the familiar vibration of the *Murphy* exiting the gate rumbled through the ship.

CHAPTER 11

ASTEROID

The jumbled puzzle pieces of a massive asteroid field surrounding a gigantic gas planet filled the viewport while Pearl and Albert worked feverishly to avoid the moon-size space rock they had gated on top of. Chunks of random grey stone and even finer glinting particulates gave the entire area an eerie haze of foreboding caution.

As planned, the *Murphy* had gone into stealth mode, showing no exterior signs of light or function, including closing the ship's massive thruster dampeners.

"Kline? Anything showing on the radar?" Dailey asked as the ship lurched sideways. The asteroid was large enough to have a slight gravitational pull.

"Maybe?"

"What does that mean, Kline?"

Albert chimed in, already having run through the forward-sensor data. "Most of the asteroids are made of Gormanium. It's a rare alloy used to create gate drive cores."

"In English," Dailey followed.

"Super valuable materials that I am surprised are floating around without anybody scooping them up. Oh, it also means that our radars and sensor arrays will be a mess. The stuff is highly giga-radiated and, well, might provide us some cover. It will take me a few minutes to recompute the gate data to take us to the depot."

Dailey pressed the communicator on his wrist, reaching out to Becket. "Hey, I need you to get some eyes on the outside of the ship. The radar is likely degraded while we're here." Dailey paused. "That means we could have company and not know it."

"Sounds like that works both ways," Becket replied as the monitor noted one of the drop bays opening. Within a few seconds, four Nova Space Rangers in full armor, clearly from First Platoon, zoomed in front of the bridge, finally coming to a halt on top of the first battery of plasma cannons.

After a few seconds scanning the area, the Rangers coupled their mag boots to the ship's hull, visually inspecting the shifting areas between the massive asteroids dancing around the *Murphy*. Dailey honed in on the Ranger's patches, showing a golden foot adorned with a wing symbolizing Hermes.

"Kline, use a reverse polarization setting on the sensor array. It may help," Dailey instructed as Albert turned. "Congratulations. You have absolutely come up with a good idea. I didn't think of that. It might not get us to track what is here, but more what is not supposed to be here. I'll see if I can tweak a few settings."

Several years ago, Dailey and a team of other Rangers had been stuffed inside what appeared to be space junk in a scrapyard in orbit around a dead planet also putting out giga-radiation. The main point was to not give off any signals, all while being able to track possible ships in the area.

The lead science officer, which just so happened to be Bellman, had come up with the idea to prevent enemy ships from picking up their sensors by having them not scan for vessels. While theoretically simple, it also meant the sensors had to quickly chart the entire debris field. The ingenuity of the plan had stuck in Dailey's mind all these years and had been used on more than one occasion.

Grantham's voice cut through the comms. "Viper Six, this is Viper One. The team thinks something is happening behind that large greenish asteroid."

Without asking for details, Pearl, Albert, and Kline worked in tandem as the ship shifted lightly, pointing in the asteroid's general direction. Kline snapped his fingers, letting Albert know he was ready to send out a pulse to map the area.

Concentrating, Mister Toaster's viewscreen displayed the mustached figure's squinting eyes. The crew was starting to like the fact that they could see Albert's emotions through the toaster's AI personality generator. It had also been over forty-eight hours since he'd asked to have it swapped back out for good behavior.

The main viewscreen started forming outlines around the image projected from the ship's forward monitors. Within a minute, the area the *Murphy's* nose was pointing toward had been scanned and charted. Without Albert, this would have taken hours, if not days.

"There," Kline noted as a red cross shifted on the crest of the farthest asteroid.

Dailey stared at the display. "Viper One, Angel Six, how copy?"

"Loud and clear," both voices echoed back.

"I want one attack fighter and Ranger to go stealth to the facing side of that asteroid and get a visual on the following coordinates. Be aware, if someone's looking for us, they may have scouts out as well," Dailey instructed, continuing to stare at the screen.

"If I may," Albert started, not giving anyone a chance to answer. "You know, if we give one of those asteroids a little nudge or send out a probe in the opposite direction, we might be able to bamboozle them."

"Bamboozle?"

"We might be able to get the jump on them," Albert clarified.

"When this is all said and done, I need to know whose entertainment files you went through. That asteroid is farther than it looks. It's damn near a moon. All those small ones are keeping us looking like a floating rock. It will take the team a few minutes to get out there without drawing any attention to themselves."

Pearl hailed Bellman, having an idea. "Send it," he snapped back, obviously waiting for an update.

"How many of the communications sensor pods do we have left?" Pearl asked quickly.

"Three. They're the last ones we have. I was planning on dropping them around Asher."

"Can you set them to remotely detonate to cause a distraction if needed?" Dailey asked as Bellman begrudgingly replied with a yes.

Dailey nodded, approving Pearl's idea. With that, Bellman, with the help of the engineering team, had the sensor pods outside the ship by the time Jen was en route to the massive green asteroid that Albert was now lovingly calling the Pea.

"It's going to be a few minutes," Dailey said, walking up to Pearl, who was now feverishly working to triangulate their location. "Any idea where we are?"

"I'm not getting anything from our sensors," Pearl replied, switching to a visual image of the star field surrounding them. Swallowing her pride, she turned to Albert. "Any ideas?"

"Well, since you asked," Albert said. "Our best bet is to use the visual star tracker, since our sensors are a little hazy."

"Hmph," she huffed, remembering manual navigation classes from the academy. "It may take some time, but I can start immediately."

"Oh, no worries," Albert started in his matter-of-fact tone. "I did it while we were talking."

Pearl blushed, working not to scream at the AI. "Sounds like you have that covered then. Where are we?"

Dailey raised an eyebrow at Albert, also wanting to know.

"Well," Albert drawled out. "It's not that easy."

"If you don't know, just say it," Dailey offered.

"From what I can tell, we are somewhere in the Zona Galactica Incognita."

Pearl worked not to roll her eyes. "That's a mighty large area to be throwing Moshan darts. What he is saying," Pearl started, seeing the lack of understanding on Dailey's face of the term only used by hardened navigators, "is we're on the other side of the galactic core somewhere, in an uncharted region."

"Or," Albert interjected. "Smack-dab in the neighborhood of Sagittarius A."

Dailey and the rest of the crew knew this term. Sagittarius A was the black hole at the center of the galactic core, in an area deemed too unstable to explore. The truth of the matter was the Federation didn't have a ship capable of withstanding the journey.

Between the massive black holes, the galactic core had an overwhelming concentration of stars, many in their final stages of going supernova or too unstable to explore.

Pearl chewed her bottom lip, this time in contemplation and not frustration at the AI. Opening several star charts, the Solarian quickly pulled up an overlay that lined up twenty-five percent of the celestial bodies they could physically see out their main viewport.

"I believe Albert may be correct. After adding a few older projection overlays, twenty-five percent of the star field lines up."

"Twenty-five percent doesn't sound too sure to me," Dailey speculated, rubbing his stubbled chin.

Albert displayed a star chart of the night sky from Earth. He started with the stars visible to the naked eye, followed by him zooming into a dark patch of space showing hundreds if not thousands of distant stars. From there, Albert magnified the image once again, and galaxy clusters started to appear.

"We travel the cosmos with much less than twenty-five percent every time we hit that little green button to activate the gate drive. Just saying."

Sparky snorted, chuffed, then yipped, followed by another passage of gas. "Wise words. Maybe I can claim this system for the empire!"

"You might need to rethink that branding," Dailey pointed out. "Maybe something softer, like a republic. The whole empire thing never seems to work out."

Albert agreed as the servos on his neck lightly hissed.

Another yip followed. "So you're saying I can?"

"I'm not saying anything. I just don't think you want to go running around on a giga-radiated rock." Dailey stood up straight, pulling his shoulders back, dragging himself out of the quickly degrading conversation.

Pearl cleared her throat. "The average acceptable alignment for onboard Fleet navigation protocols is five percent. If I—" She corrected herself. "If we are right, we are likely in a moderately safe pocket within the galaxy core. No one will ever believe us." Pearl paused, looking at the ridiculous expression of Mister Toaster on Albert's face, realizing that no one would believe the past several months' escapades either way.

The main viewscreen flashed before Jen's face appeared. Lines of static flickered again, showing the signal was degraded from the local amount of radiation. "We have company. I'm going to go offline and see how close I can get. It looks like a destroyer and two assault ships, by the looks of them."

As expected, on the other side of the oversized pea, a single Alurian destroyer, accompanied by two smaller assault ships, loomed. The Alurians were also working through the best way to navigate the asteroid field and report back on their precious material find. Jen, realizing this, was floating aimlessly on the far side of the green mass, working to blend in with the thousands of other rocks she was praying would not ram into her ship.

Harvest Moon was the name Lieutenant Jenny Brax had given her command attack fighter. The ship was slightly larger and more robust than the other attack fighters, with the simple mission of staying alive and controlling the fight.

The plan was simple and already in motion by the time Dailey suited up in his armor and returned to the bridge minus his helmet. Elements of First and Third Foot were split into two groups. First Platoon was set to go under the large mass, while Third Platoon would close the gap by going over the Pea.

Within a few minutes, the teams were already using slang for peas. *Let's split the pea in half* and *making pea soup* were some of the front-runners. Of course, Specialist Jacob Perkins took the opportunity to ensure that everyone fully understood he hated peas. He followed this with a tirade about hating steamed carrots and green beans mixed with peas even more.

Of course, that would be the first thing the platoon served if they, in fact, accomplished their mission despite the complaining specialist.

The communications sensors started pinging the far end of the asteroid out of sight of the Alurian destroyer. It didn't take long for the ship to make itself known, firing several volleys from its forward plasma cannons. With the help of what Albert called his magic touch, King and Kline were able to form a rendering of the enemy ships and area on the far side of the Pea before maneuvering toward their suspecting prey.

Planned as a distraction, one of the sensors overheated, creating a small explosion, taking the Alurian's focus off the incoming swarm of death. "It's go time," Dailey instructed as the swarm of angry Nova Rangers attached to their corresponding attack fighter poured over the asteroid's surface.

While Lady Luck had dealt them a good hand, she hadn't fully folded, as the two assault ships remained focused on the Pea. The blue glow from the ass of the destroyer faced away, and the two escorting assault ships pulled security, ready to act if needed.

Seconds after the initial push, the forward laser cannons of the much smaller assault ships started blindly ripping into the incoming onslaught. The attack fighters were significantly more agile, only allowing a few glancing whiffs from the laser fire, as if playing a game.

Jen, now in formation, held back, watching over the scene, transmitting visuals to the crew onboard the *Murphy*, which was in motion, heading toward the far-right side of the Pea to close the gap, hopefully overwhelming their Alurian pursuers.

"Yup, not the B-team," Dailey noted, seeing the assault ships opening fire as the destroyer started maneuvering forward to turn once out of range of the attack fighters.

It became immediately apparent why the main destroyer had so much faith in the two small assault ships. Pods of the same drones they had encountered when first discovering the *Asher-5* peeled off from the ship's frame, leaving the nearly skeletal automated craft.

The assault ships consisted of four simple things: a main thruster, a forward laser, an automated AI system of some type, and the drones themselves. Once they deployed, it left the ship almost looking like a whale skeleton with its head and tail still attached.

Dailey and the others listened to Jen as she doled out orders. "All elements drop here. We will carry on to the destroyer."

She intended to let the Nova Rangers deal with the drones while the attack wing focused on the destroyer. The *Murphy* would round the corner and support the Nova Rangers while also engaging the main ship with its ranged plasma cannons and kinetic missile systems.

Master Sergeant Don Grantham was the first to launch forward, his attack fighter speeding off after firing a ripping burst of laser fire into the middle of the oncoming drones. The entire action resembled a group of angry teenagers meeting in the middle of a mosh pit at a heavy metal concert. Something the man had very much indulged in during his youth.

Pulling up his Sauder rifle, Grantham started cutting into the closest drone as it realized it was in a one-on-one fight with a Nova Ranger. As Albert explained, AI often had one function and one function only. For these assault drones, their programming was simple: to assault whatever they were pointed at.

As luck would have it, one of the attack fighter's laser blasts clipped the drone just before it targeted Grantham, giving him that extra second needed to take the proverbial high ground. It was quickly replaced by another that, in turn, fired pencil-size charged darts directly at Grantham, who activated his thruster pack a second too late.

The charged round clipped the back of Grantham's pack just as he turned to engage. Holding his rifle up, it absorbed the four additional rounds about to slam directly into his chest plate. Their purpose was to disable small to midsize electric systems.

Without time to think, Grantham activated his pulse shield while pulling out what could only be described as a laser axe. The Moshan blade was a favorite among the hand-to-hand combat weapons of the Nova Rangers, lovingly called a ripper.

While the blade itself was made from Moshan steel, the edge was rectified with a laser beam to be able to cut into most armor. If used on flesh, it would simply sever the appendage without a second thought.

The drones all started sprouting octopus-like appendages, doubling in size. The appendage's intent was immediately made clear by the glowing blue fission cutters at the end surrounding the laser turret sticking out one side of the round drone.

Grantham pressed forward using his mag boots stabilizer thruster, spinning while several of the closest drones' cutting tentacles slashed overhead. The ground and the sky all mixed into a confusing slurry of Nova Rangers and drones flying in random directions above and below the *Murphy*'s drop leader.

Reaching up to block, a tentacle slammed into Grantham's pulse shield, shuttering the blue light and sending sparks flying. Two more drones' whipping arms started drilling toward the man as he held up his ripper, slicing the tip off one as the other slammed into his side like a sledgehammer with a rocket tied to it.

In a last-ditch effort to save not only himself but his stubborn pride, Grantham gripped the bottom of his ripper, pressing the small button above the grip ring and aiming directly at the drone's main sensor. In a flash of brilliant light, the bottom of the ripper opened, exposing a mini thruster.

The last-ditch feature of the ripper was twofold. First, to be used as Grantham was doing: to kill whatever had just killed you or pissed you off enough to want to launch your last weapon into them. Second, it could be used as a backup thruster in zero-gravity environments.

Grantham squinted as the spark and light pop of a drone failing flashed across his HUD, followed by a spatter of static. The drone had hit Grantham hard enough to force his skull against the helmet's stabilizers.

Shaking it off, space again blurred in front of the man as the loud *thunk* of a hypercharged magnet wrenched Grantham directly up and into less active space. Sergeant Taylor Raine's voice called Grantham's direct channel, blocking out a platoon's usual noise in the heat of combat.

"You looked like you needed a ride, Master Sergeant." Raine chuckled as the sound and trace of his Sauder rifle drew a straight line below them, slicing directly through a spinning drone heading toward them.

Grantham focused on the HUD's readout. While equipped with an onboard automated system, it wasn't as intuitive as Albert's. Bellman and the AI had actually been working on an upgrade on a few of the Nova Ranger's armored suits.

"I'm going to be another two minutes before my pack recharges." Just as the words left his mouth, the proximity alarm alerted of another large ship entering the fight. The *Murphy* was cresting the asteroid.

A smile pushed Grantham's cheeks into his HUD as the rest of the problem entered the playing field. The attack fighters had finally made it to the destroyer, which was, in turn, firing its secondary close-range weapons systems.

HUDs and readouts on the fighters alerted that the *Murphy* was about to fire several midrange hounder missiles at the destroyer without repositioning. Dailey had directed Albert, who was now fully entrusted with the weapons systems, to fire as soon as the ship was within line of sight.

The missiles were nicknamed hounders due to their ability to think, or as Albert stated, *"Choose their own ending out of a handful, like a Which Way book,"* while making contact with its target. If the ship moved, the missile would follow. If its target activated shields right before impact, the missile would switch over to an EMP pulse, then send its full payload through the affected area and detonate.

Grantham's thruster pack kicked back on as the rocking flash of four hounders streaked by, pulling the attention of the attacking drone. Raine handed Grantham his matching laser blasters, nodding as he dove back into the fight, already having picked out a drone.

"Viper Six, this is Grantham, over."

Dailey's voice echoed back just as the destroyer repositioned itself enough to engage its forward cannons. "Go ahead."

"The two assault ships are automated, and it looks like they have been reassigned as missiles. They just broke off and are heading your way."

Kline immediately shifted the main targeting array away from the blur of drone and Nova Rangers, honing in on the two assault ships, quickly picking up speed.

"Albert, any chance you could plug into those two assault ships?" Dailey asked, focusing on the destroyer now facing them just out of direct firing range.

"Possibly. Worst-case scenario, you won't owe Grantham any of that money you lost to him several years back that you've never repaid. Don't shoot the messenger," Albert scoffed.

"For the love of God, please stop looking at people's personal files before I take Lieutenant Brax up on her recommendation of replacing that toaster with the toilet seat," Dailey grumbled back, standing up and walking over to the main viewscreen.

"Sir," Pearl interrupted. "Five more seconds and our missiles will be within their targeting range. After that, they will go hypersonic."

The statement was short-lived as the Alurian destroyer pushed its aft thrusters into overdrive, moving the ship even closer toward the *Murphy*. "Damn, A-team," Dailey mumbled under his breath.

Both ships opened fire simultaneously, with ion and plasma cannons thumping in both directions. The saving grace in this situation was the nagging of the *Murphy*'s attack fighters bearing down on the destroyer, and the hounder missiles keeping its crew occupied on several fronts, the close assault and the full weight of the *Murphy* about to bear down on them.

Maneuvering to address the missiles head-on, the destroyer activated what the Fleet called a mesh countermeasure. Simply put, the system worked to confuse any guided munitions such as hounder or seeker missiles. While the display of a laser grid in front of the ship was very intimidating, it was, in reality, a reasonably simple concept.

The ship maneuvered directly toward the missile, working to confuse and/or make the projectile readjust its heading and speed. On top of this, the mesh system was nearly undetectable, unlike deflector shields. The system itself would launch out of whatever side it was needed, and as soon as it was clear of the ship's hull, would quickly break apart and expand into a massive, electrified laser net with four thrusters at each corner to stay in synch with the moving vessel for a limited amount of time.

Expensive and usually reserved for command ships, the fact that the Alurians were using such a defensive countermeasure that had been, in fact, designed on Earth added more fuel to the already burning fire.

The bright flash of the missiles coincided with the whooshing sound of the *Murphy's* deflector shields being hit by the destroyer's forward cannons.

Pearl zoomed in on the vessel's hull as Dorax spoke up.

"*Dark Root,*" the Alurian drawled out under his breath, reading the ship's name. "I've never heard of this ship before, and I know of most of the Alurian destroyers in the galaxy, if even just through stories."

"Well, I'm betting that one's not from around here. Albert?" Dailey prompted as Mister Toaster's face showed a strained concentration that made the AI look as if he needed to relieve himself of some oil.

"Right, we are good to go. They finally scanned us, and I used that as my in. I convinced them we are the destroyer, and they are the super Fleet bad guys," Albert replied as another volley of ranged plasma fire dug into the *Murphy's* deflector shields.

"Sir," Kline spoke up. "The drones are heading toward the destroyer alongside the assault ships. It looks like they are tethered together."

"Duh," Albert scoffed. "Listen, we have about two minutes before whoever is commanding that ship figures this all out, including the fact that I deactivated the drones' targeting sensors."

Knowing the need to take out the destroyer, Dailey set his jaw. "Angel Six." He was using her rank and title, keeping it professional.

"Go ahead," Jen replied, the sound of her forward lasers zipping in the background.

"Disengage at close range and fall back to support the Rangers. We got this from here."

"That's a good copy."

After a few seconds, the attack wing had stopped its patterned strafing runs of the destroyer's deck, splitting up into two columns before heading back to secure the Nova Ranges, who had just gotten a friendly message in their HUDs from Albert informing them that the assault ships and drones were now batting for the home team.

As the ships disengaged, one of the attack fighters shot out of formation, the crackle of its main thruster fizzling in a sparking arch, only to quickly wink out. The pilot, pending them not being incinerated in the cockpit, would don their light-series space suit and wait for rescue.

"It appears they are confused about the assault ships and are being very digitally aggressive with them," Albert noted as the two commandeered ships started moving faster.

"Incoming!" Kline barked as a red proximity alarm sounded.

The *Murphy* rocked as an Alurian stealth missile whipped into the ship's forward-sensor array. The very array they used to activate their gate drive.

"We don't have time for this. Albert, do your worst."

Mister Toaster's lips curled into a smile, a creepy face that could very well be the main character in a cheap horror film that took itself too seriously. The crew paused, waiting for Albert to shift into motion as "For Whom the Bell Tolls" by Metallica started blaring through the bridge's intercom.

While many bands had been lost in the sands of time, the classic metal band from years long since passed had continued to be a staple among Army soldiers. Albert had picked up on the love of the head-moving music from the rank and file Nova Rangers.

"Pearl," Albert started. "Please maneuver us to the coordinates on your display."

In order to make his initial idea work, he had convinced the onboard systems to overdrive the forward deflector shields of the hijacked ships. Long story short, a Nova Ranger could take the ships out of the fight with a Sauder rifle from the rear.

"Specialist Kline," Albert continued. "Please target the tail end of the ship."

Kline turned. "What about the forward cannons?"

"Three, two, and check out the monitors, kiddoes," Albert instructed as the first crunching riff of the song started.

The assault ships split off in two directions as the amount of close-range fire coming from the Alurian destroyer created a glow around the vessel.

While everyone was watching the scene, they didn't hear Albert instruct the Nova Rangers to disengage and regroup with the attack fighters, pulling the drones away from the former Alurian assault ships.

Three distinct motions happened on the battlefield as the destroyer once again fired several volleys toward the *Murphy*.

"You actually going to do anything?" Dailey asked when Albert started nodding to the music. As the words left his mouth, one of the assault ships began glowing on the targeting screen from being overcharged. Sparky had joined the fight.

"Patience, young grasshopper. Patience," Albert said, tapping out a flurry of commands on the control panel.

CHAPTER 12

DARK ROOT

Commanding Officer Voray Calabasas leaned forward, watching as his two assault ships approached, no longer under their control. Unlike the *Murphy*, the *Dark Root*'s bridge's primary focus was combat operations. Four separate weapons stations sat in two rows, facing a large viewport overlayed with graphics.

The haze of deep space hung in the humid air like a steamy shower. The Alurian bridge was not a large space, not allowing for people to congregate. It was simple and to the point. This also meant it was in pretty tight quarters, and the lighting, as well as other creature comforts, took a back row. The glow of consoles lit up the crew's faces, adding to the overall feel of the ship.

The Alurian ship and crew had spent the majority of their initial time after tracing the gate resonance of the *Murphy* gathering data on the material makeup of the giant asteroid that had kept them hidden from their prey.

"What do you mean we have lost control?" Voray asked as the assault ships started shifting course. At the same time, several of the swarming

Nova Rangers jetted off in different directions, like a teenage party getting broken up by Federation enforcers, formally known as cops.

"Their systems are no longer taking inputs," the gruff Alurian sitting beside the ship's commander huffed. "They appear to be trying to dock, but their forward deflector shields are hypercharged. They have been somehow compromised."

"Human trash," Voray barked. "Open fire with the main guns."

The choice to shift fire from the *Murphy*, unbeknownst to the Alurian command crew, likely saved what was left of the *Murphy*'s forward arrays that allowed it to gate.

The thump of the main cannons started rocking the actuators on the guns, not letting up for several seconds. "How are the ships maneuvering?" Voray again barked, not knowing Albert had programmed a simple logic program in the ships.

"Sir, they're heading directly for our cannon batteries. They will be too close to fire at soon," a young weapons specialist stated loudly.

Voray, knowing his time was becoming limited, took control of the helm from the small panel in front of him, and the ship lurched its nose down, activating its full thrusters. While the assault ships were moving fast, the destroyer, under full thrust, was quickly maneuvering away and out of position while the *Murphy* stood resolute, not firing.

"Why aren't they firing," the weapons specialist asked as the ship started turning.

"They are keeping us occupied while targeting the ship. Prepare the gate drive," Voray ordered as the ship's system readouts showed an acceptable shade of yellowish green.

Unlike other vessels in the Alurian battle group, the *Dark Root* depended on the assault ships and attack droids for its mid- to long-range fighting and protection. Living up to its name, the *Dark Root*'s bays were full to the brim with various munitions and orbit-to-surface bombs. The kind that could wipe out entire cities while not radiating the area.

The main reason the ship had been sent to pursue the *Murphy* was the experienced team aboard. A crew that Dailey and the others, including a jailbroken AI, were putting to the test.

"This Dailey is living up to his reputation. But I feel he has overplayed his hand. We will reposition and attack from the far end of the asteroid field. If we can't fight them head-on, we will detonate that asteroid."

Voray knew the precious material that made up the asteroid was extremely volatile. So much so that he was surprised it had not already started reacting to all the electrostatic being slung around it. In reality, if he were to detonate the asteroid, it would take out the entire sector, likely causing a chain reaction.

The experienced crew aboard the *Dark Root*, not having the area loaded on their star charts, had spent the entirety of their time, including the fight they were currently in, charting out the sector. With the data they had used to follow the *Murphy* and the work they had completed, gating would be a relatively safe option.

"Gate activated," a taller-than-average Alurian noted from the back of the bridge.

In front of the ship, a massive wave rippled through space as quickly as it winked out. "What's the problem?" Voray barked as several proximity alarms rang on the bridge.

"There seems to have been a dampening field activated just as we slowed down to go through the gate."

"*BORGOSH!*" Voray screamed. The word was the Alurian version of *Oh shit, I think we have a problem*, all summed up in one simple agitated word.

The *Dark Root* again shifted as its thrusters screamed to life. The one problem now facing them was the asteroid field being too dense to go into hyperdrive. The ship's cannons started firing again as several small missiles erupted from several sections of the vessel in a last-ditch effort to take out the assault ships.

One of the assault ships shuddered under the stress of its deflector shields when a smaller seeker missile found purchase, going around to the rear thrusters, igniting the craft in a rage of fire. Voray grinned at the victory, feeling he was back in the fight just as the other assault ship's deflector shields lightly dropped, pushing all of its power to its rear thrusters.

Bleak realization set in, forcing the Alurian's grin into a grimace.

Just as the assault ship screeched to a halt, its fission power cells were flung directly into the *Dark Root*'s rear thrusters in a chorus of mayhem. The gate in front of the ship shimmered to life as the destroyer's commander, in a last-ditch effort to save the vessel, tried to gate out of the fight to lick their wounds elsewhere.

By the time the destroyer started to enter the gate, its orbital stabilizers were in control of the ship, keeping it from rolling ass over tea kettle through space, but they were offset by the four seeker missiles that slammed directly into the ship's ass end, pushing away the assault ship while also vaporizing it. At the same time, the entrance to the gate sliced the craft in half after sucking what it could through.

The last thing Commanding Officer Voray Calabasas saw before detaching the ship's command section was an image of Mister Toaster's face winking at him through the viewscreen while Metallica played in the background.

CHAPTER 13

AFTERGLOW

Dorax glared at Albert as the music shut off. On the other side of the see-through carbon viewport, the Nova Rangers were finishing off what was left of the automated drones. The doors opened as Becket entered, still in his armor, a light vapor coming off his shoulders from the change in environment.

"What happened to them?" Dorax asked, looking down at his still grimy fingernails from his work in the galley. While Alurians were generally different to humans and Solarians, they still had the typical amount of fingers and toes.

"Whelp," Albert started. "I . . . *we*," the AI corrected himself, "shut down the two assault ships' deflector shields and pushed all the ships' remaining energy into a dampening field. When they took one out, well . . . let's just say that didn't go as planned but still met the goal."

Dailey walked over to the main viewscreen. "I'm with Dorax here. What happened as the gate opened and shut?"

"From what I can tell, they, being the ship's commander, jettisoned the command section. I believe after reviewing your files, they designed this ship with the same ability," Albert concluded.

"So they're able to gate back to the battle group?" Dailey followed up as Albert paused.

"No. They lost their gate drive. When you said do your worst, I very well might have. The remaining section of the ship is caught in innerspace. The gate is a management system for what you call a wormhole. This means they lost the systems managing their passage through and have no way to control what or where they are. Maybe even when. Who knows," Albert concluded.

Pearl cleared her throat.

"All systems are at eighty-two percent. We are able to gate out of the sector at any time," she notified the bridge as Dailey glanced at Becket.

"I want to be at a hundred before we leave. Top, can you get a team to check out the remains of that destroyer? We might find something Albert here can use. Kline, I want you to send out a few probes and see what else is in the area. The targeting systems were putting up some weird readings on the screen," Dailey doled out, standing up.

"Sir," Becket started as Dorax also stood up, grabbing his apron. "He didn't want anyone to tell you, but Sparky is in that dead assault ship. I have a feeling someone's keeping that radio traffic out of earshot."

"Albert, I get you want to protect your gossiping partner in crime, but if he's floating in one of those ships, I need to know," Dailey instructed.

"Sure thing. He did take charge of the assault ships, but that's not what we will talk about. I'm sure it will be about the attack fighter that he fried while getting aboard one of the ships," Albert huffed, already playing defense for Sparky.

"Just get him back here. If he helped, good. If he fried an attack fighter, then we may only ration his ham," Dailey insisted as Sparky's voice came over the comms, having heard the conversation.

"I would like to report we won the battle. You can prepare the celebratory feast upon my arrival. I also have a new ship." Sparky's voice echoed around the room, garnering smiles.

"I'm sure the Nova Rangers and Albert had nothing to do with the victory. Well, president and grand commander of the ham fleet, we need you back onboard," Dailey replied.

"We agree. I will be back for body refurbishments in ten mikes," Sparky concluded.

"I'm going back to the galley," Dorax interrupted. "I don't think you need me here."

Dailey stood up, walking behind the Alurian, the smell of cooked food still lingering around him. "I want a few minutes of your time." Dorax nodded, knowing he didn't truly have an option.

The dull grey lighting of the main corridor leading to Dailey's quarters flickered lightly as the engineering team worked on the damaged forward-sensor array. The two men stopped just outside the main lift.

"I'm not sure what you want from me, but I don't know if I have anything to give," Dorax insisted, sounding mildly annoyed. The Alurian truly just wanted to go back to the galley.

"Listen, I know Albert busted your chops about not being a good, or hell, even an okay pilot, but the fact that you hijacked the senator's personal shuttle and gave us a run for our money is enough for me," Dailey pointed out as the ends of the Alurian's mouth perked in a wry, mischievous grin.

"You want me to pilot an Alurian ship if we find one," Dorax asked in the form of a statement.

"You said *we*. So, it's settled, then."

"Nothing is settled. I don't know what or who you think I am, but I'm not a ship commander. I'm just trying to get home, wherever the hell that ends up being."

Dailey smiled, holding out his hand to shake. "You have a home. You just don't know it yet."

The *Murphy*'s commander was doing the one thing he did best: building a team. There was something about the Alurian that convinced Dailey there was more to his story. It wasn't that Dorax was running from something; rather, he was looking for something. Something he couldn't even figure out. Dailey knew the type from years in the military, not to mention deep space.

Dailey almost activated his blade when he entered his quarters and saw Sparky sprawled out in his armor on the bed, licking himself.

"Boundaries, Sparky. Boundaries."

"It was a long day. I needed to get myself situated. Plus, you threatened to cut off the ham. Let the ham flow . . ." Sparky drawled out, having watched *Dune* with Albert.

Dailey clicked the release button on his suit of armor, which started clanking open. In the current configuration, it resembled a half-opened metal skeleton, allowing the ship's commander to step down, still in his formfitting flight suit.

"You're my main man, Sparky; you're my dog . . . literally," Dailey started. "I just like to know when the ancient AI onboard and the Alurian war hound with some kind of magical powers scheme something in the middle of a fight."

Sparky sat up straight, stretching. The odd smell of burning plastic permeating his fur wafted through the small cabin. "I am part of the team."

"Yes, you're part of the team. Hey, let me ask you about that little trick you keep doing. Is that something you can teach me or show me?"

Sparky pondered the statement. "Maybe, maybe not."

"I get it. It just happens. We never really talked about your family back on Terra Minor Three. If we get time, do you want to go back there? We need to check up on the colonization team we left there."

Sparky's mood shifted as excitement took over his face. "Yes, please. I can tell them all about ham, then show them the moving pictures, then tell them about all the sexy time onboard the ship."

Dailey held up his finger, cutting Sparky off before he got overly detailed. "Point taken. Thanks for the help. I'll let Thron know he can resume your ham rations."

Sparky chuffed, standing up. A fresh slice of ham sat nestled under his arm, previously out of sight. "Of course," Dailey huffed as the Alurian battle hound left Dailey's personal space.

Getting changed into his regular-duty uniform, Dailey put a message together to be sent to the senator once they gated to their following location. He also recorded a brief message for the team on Asher. With a longing breath, the man stared at the framed picture of Stella, his wife.

The *Murphy's* commander looked down at his hand, noticing for the first time he could remember his hand lightly trembling. It wasn't the battle that had his nerves on edge, but the odds of a Fleet frigate taking out the amount of Alurian ships it had. The math wasn't adding up, and the battle-hardened man knew it.

Ben Dailey contemplated the thought as visions of Mister Toaster's face came front and center, followed by the ham overlord himself. What he wasn't thinking about was his own contribution to the fight.

What kept nagging at the back of Dailey's thoughts was just how much of an advantage Albert was, and even more concerning the likelihood of there being many more just like him in the cosmos.

The reflective moment was interrupted when Pearl's voice cut through the silence. "Sir, you might want to come to the bridge and see this."

The man stood up, making the short walk to the bridge.

Jen and Becket had already made their way onboard, and the entirety of the bridge's crew stood around the main viewscreen. "Okay, what do we have?" Dailey asked as Albert clicked several buttons in rapid succession, switching to one of the probe's cameras.

On the other side of the asteroid, a massive figure as large as a star cruiser floated in space, outlined by a distant star. Covered in dark patches of pitted strikes from not only weapons but debris, the massive figure appeared to be hundreds if not thousands of years old.

Arms resembling not only massive cannons but landing bays stretched as if yawning lazily while massive legs bent at what appeared to be knees, locked in place by giant round gears. Sitting like a head between two towerlike structures, a massive, heavily fortified command module stared back at the camera as if posing for a macabre picture depicting its final breath.

"Albert, please tell me you know what that is," Dailey breathed out.

Albert's face morphed from Mister Toaster's once again to the flat analog screen that appeared when the AI was accessing its data banks. "In the immortal words of Randy Jackson, that's going to be a no from me, dog."

The only person who picked up on the reference was Becket, who clearly had old reruns of *American Idol* on his entertainment drive.

"King, send a copy of this image to Dorax and Thron in the galley. See if either of them knows what the hell that is," Dailey ordered, shifting to Specialist Kline. "How big is that thing?"

"Well, sir . . . according to the probe, about the size of the Federation's main space station in orbit around Earth. Maybe bigger."

"Perfect. A floating ancient space titan," Dailey said. In reality, the same thoughts he'd had while in his quarters about the unknown and awe-inspiring advantage Albert was giving them were front and center in his mind as the team leaned in to get a better view.

There was more to the universe than he or, as he was betting, even the most secretive Federation organization knew. What was floating on the other side of the asteroid could take out Earth in a matter of minutes.

"I'm starting to think this has something to do with the Creators Dorax and you mentioned," Dailey said, speaking directly to Albert.

"Hmph, why didn't I think of that," Albert scoffed. "Hang on."

Again, Albert focused his internal memory banks on searching through the massive amount of data stored within the AI's central processor core. One thing the crew had learned after Bellman's report was that Albert had a case of suggested recollection. If he didn't know what he was searching for internally, the AI would not think to access specific files.

"Well, shit," Albert let out.

"We don't like *well-shits* onboard this ship, Albert," Dailey stated as Albert leaned back.

"I believe we are looking at a Creare megatitan. You were close there, boss. All I have are records of them being described. According to legend—mind you, this was all reported way before I was a wee little processing board—the Creare sent for these out into the various galaxies in a last-ditch effort to thwart the Alurians."

Dailey digested the oddness of the statement. "You know what I find funny? This was a preprogrammed waypoint from the old gate drive we have. That means somebody somewhere, at some point, was here."

Pearl tapped her index finger on her bottom lip, a habit she had when deep in thought. "Maybe someone did know about this place. The fact that we haven't run into any sensors or probes tells me this place was hidden away from prying eyes. I bet one of the mining syndicates found out about it and might not have made it back to tell the tale."

Jen, not wanting to be outdone, chimed in. "Or they very well know about it and are saving it for a rainy day."

Dailey glanced at Becket, seeing the light shaking of his head. They both had other things to focus on and worry about. There would be time to follow up on this later. "All right," the *Murphy*'s commander said. "We need to focus on getting back to Asher. Bellman, how's the gate drive looking?"

"The forward-sensor array was damaged, but not enough to take us out of commission. Don't get me wrong, it will need to be fully fixed, but from what we can tell and what Albert has analyzed, we should be good for now. I would just highly recommend us not doing any more damage to the ship."

What Bellman wasn't fully stating was the fact that they could very well be lost in space, unable to return home. Without the use of the gate drive, it could take years to get back to Asher from their current location, a possibility that Dailey had briefed the entire crew on before leaving.

CHAPTER 14

DREADNAUGHT

The trip back to the Andromeda depot was surprisingly lackluster but brought a much-needed refit. After the dust had settled, the battle with the Alurian destroyer had taken two attack fighters out of operation, injuring not only its pilots but two Nova Rangers as well. But there was also one new addition to the *Murphy*: the assault ship Sparky had commandeered.

While unable to secure an active link, Dailey had been able to exchange several messages with the senator and an update from Asher. On Earth, the Fleet was gearing up the manufacturing of the three sister ships to the *Brightstar*, *Asher-5*, and the *Murphy*. With a firm understanding of the situation on Asher, the Federation as a whole was starting to shift focus away from what they had previously believed were the front lines of defense against the Alurians.

The team on Asher had rightfully sent an update before going underground. According to their new partnership with the engineers from Kodas, sending messages from the planet's substructure would require enough power to draw attention. Receiving the message, Dailey understood that Lieutenant Laura McAlister and the dynamic duo from Arcadia would only respond once the *Murphy* was back in the sector and able to support the team.

Unlike their last trip to the depot, there were no outdated destroyers or other mining cargo ships buzzing through space. Taking their place were massive chunks of the once upon a time depot. The crew never saw the aftereffects of their handiwork, proving they had indeed accomplished their mission.

On the radar, small pockets of constructo bots appeared to still be active but no longer controlled by the depot. After a scan for organic material, only a few faint wisps remained on a handful of the larger chunks of station, floating randomly.

Being the size of a large moon, the chunk that still appeared to be powered caught the crew's attention. A group of ships was still attached to the remnants of the depot. Making this even more interesting was the viewscreen displaying a similar build to the dreadnaught-class starship now in orbit around Asher.

"Jackpot, boys," Albert gushed.

"I want to send in a few attack fighters to see if we catch anyone's attention first. Lieutenant Brax," Dailey called over the intercom. "Report to the bridge."

By the time Jen made her way through the ship, Specialist Kline had identified three other smaller vessels in seemingly operational condition. Until Albert could synch with the main dreadnaught, they wouldn't be able to fully tell if the death machine was usable.

"Sir," Jen greeted, seeing the viewscreen. "Looks like we might get lucky for once."

Now sitting beside Albert, Sparky turned as his translator sprang to life. "There are plenty of people onboard getting lucky."

Albert lowered his hand as Sparky deposited a paw in a low-key fist bump.

"Alright, alright, we get it. I know everyone's excited," Dailey started as Sparky chuffed, forcing the ship's commander to rethink his phrasing. "I need you to send a fighter out for a recon run. We need to ensure this graveyard is as dead as it seems. The rest of the command team needs to meet in the briefing room in five minutes."

Saluting, Jen exited the bridge as the primary crew started shuffling toward the briefing room. Dailey raised a finger. "Sparky. A word, please. You know what, both of you hang tight," Dailey said, referring to Albert as well.

"You need us to get that ship?" Sparky chuffed while Albert shrugged.

"Yeah, I think so. I'm not sure if that ship even has power cells, and if so, what condition they may be in. I need you both to promise me no funny business. We need to get back to Asher."

"Scouts honor," Albert proclaimed.

Dailey shook his head. "You know I can see your fingers through your exoskeleton."

Sparky chuffed again as Mister Toaster's face drooped slightly. "Okay, have it your way. No funny business."

"This is the important stuff. We all need to be tracking. If you see something or think of something, say something," Dailey finished before they made their way to the briefing room.

"Settle down," Becket yelled. A still, whispered hush overtook the room. While en route to the depot, the team had only gotten together once for an after-action review, better known as an AAR. "Sir."

"Thanks, everyone," Dailey started, clicking the holo-table to show a 3D rendering of the dreadnaught-class starship attached to the floating chunk of depot. "We have some good news for once. It appears we completed our primary objective last time we were here. We have also identified a ship that might be able to help us with the situation back on Asher."

This garnered approving grunts of acknowledgment as the comms link in the room flashed. "Go ahead," Dailey said, as Jen's voice came over the intercom.

"We've done three passes in the general area around the ship. No one and nothing is tracking our movement. Forwarding some close shots of the ship. It looks to be fully intact." With that, Jen cut off.

"That means we are a go. Master Sergeant Janix, I want Third Foot to join our team boarding the ship. Myself, Albert, Sparky, Pearl, Bellman, Dorax, and Lieutenant Brax will lead the mission. We need to clear the vessel and then get the thing moving. Hopefully, it has a gate drive. Once we get that established, we can plan our next steps."

Janix raised his hand. The Solarian platoon sergeant of Third Foot had been entrusted with complete control of the team, not needing an officer. In all reality, this was also due to the functionality of his team. They were the utility platoon who did as instructed without hesitation. True grunts.

"That ship looks massive. It might take a few days," Janix noted. Dailey nodded in understanding.

"Good point, and one I have been chewing over. Albert hasn't been able to synch with the ship's systems, as it's dormant. Top, remember that transportation ship we acquired at the start of the Scourge Rebellion?"

Becket nodded, as well as some of the other leaders in the room, remembering the situation. "Yes, sir," Becket replied as a fond memory flashed through his thoughts. "The ship was so damn big we sealed most of it off and only left a portion of it habitable. If memory serves, when you reversed the airlocks outside of the life-support zone, we surprisingly shot about two dozen hiding Scourge fighters out of the docking bay."

Grantham snorted, remembering the exchange of pleasantries as the fighters floated in front of the viewport before drifting into the dark, infinite night of space.

"Albert?" Dailey nudged. The AI turned to the group.

"No problem. We can even set up a way to turn sections of the ship on and off. If there're security droids onboard, we can try to keep them shut down, or . . ." Albert drawled out, "convince them to join the A-team."

"I prefer to keep them turned off, and preferably not on the ship. We don't know what kind of tech we will run into when we return to Asher," Dailey added.

"If"—Bellman stood up, walking to the front of the briefing room—"the forward-sensor array is working, but we need to be careful. I am suggesting we take the engineering team and maybe First Foot to see if we can salvage anything else. We might get lucky."

"Makes sense," Dailey replied, nodding at Lieutenant Ponce and Master Sergeant Grantham.

"Might I suggest sending out the probes and starting a scan? I can program a few tasty things to look for," Albert spoke, already working on the calibration.

"Alright, it's settled. I want us to make moves in twenty-four hours or less. Before anyone asks, I'm well aware that we may have another Alurian headache show up. If I were in charge of that battle group, this would be one of my primary targets. They know we've been here before. Once we figure this out, we will focus on returning to Asher."

Becket stepped forward. "Alright, ladies. What that means is the rest of you are to be on full alert and ready to get back to work. First and Second Foot, you, as well as the remaining attack wing, are on QRF. At the first sign of trouble, we do what we do best: violently engage the threat. Pearl." Becket motioned for her to step forward.

"We are taking the *Murphy* as close to the dreadnaught as possible. A debris field surrounds the area, so we will use the forward laser batteries to thin it out. We want to hug that chunk of rock. The longer we are here, the closer we should be able to get. The gate drive will be fully charged and set in ten hours. That gives us a window of time to work from," Pearl informed the team as heads nodded.

The sheer size of the dreadnaught surprised even Dailey, who stared out the cockpit of the drop ship. Jen looked back, nodding. The cramped quarters of the smaller vessel felt oddly comforting to the team.

Sleek, untarnished metal surface flowed over the massive vessel, giving way to large sections designed for various reasons. Alurian ships, while similar in design, kept functionality as the key principle. If a vessel was designated for combat, it was ninety-nine percent built around the task, not affording the usual creature comforts, such as an entertainment section.

The *Murphy*, in contrast, had both, including an officer's bar. The truth of the matter was the crew had been so busy trying to stay alive over the past several months that R&R had been the last thing on the majority of the crew's minds.

Large rectifier cannons cast a shadow on the small Harpy drop ships as even the gears on Albert's head whirled. The massive weapons of war were poking out the side of the dreadnaught like an out-of-place, violent appendage.

"This close up, it's much larger than I thought," Dailey stated.

Albert chuckled. "That's what she said."

"Okay, game faces. This isn't the time for jokes. I mean, this ship is massive. We could almost fit the *Murphy* inside that bay," Dailey noted just as the side of the ship yawned open.

The offset for the massive door shaded the drop ship while Jen veered it into a gap in the ship's outer hull. "Albert," she started as the second Harpy swerved out of the trench. "Where do we need to sit down?"

"Well, from what I can tell, there is an access hatch on the far end of the main bay. It looks to be a small airlock for ships about this size. Sparky should be able to charge up one of those doors enough to let us in and go from there."

Sparky, strapped in the command tracking station, snorted. "I have my armor. Do I need to save the day again?" The Alurian war hound had been gifted armor by his distant relatives on Asher, and as luck would have it, it was designed to handle the cold, dark hands of space for short amounts of time.

Private Anthony Lamb, also known as Lambert, chimed in. "He just wants to justify getting more ham after this is all done. You know, some of us like ham as well."

Sparky chuffed again. "You have to brush your teeth first."

Ohs and *ahs*, as well as armored elbows, smacked into Lambert as Sparky let out a full-on guffaw. The famed bad breath of Private Lamb was a thing of mood- and conversation-killing legend.

"There," Jen interjected, cutting the conversation short.

A small landing pad sat at the far end of the massive bay doors, leading into a much smaller set of doors. Two glass panels resembled eyes where security personnel would be overlooking the area, making an effort to stay awake, as smaller cargo was dropped off.

"There's a gravity field, if I can get that stupid knobby thing to try and scan us," Albert stated as the pop of ozone flickered and wafted through the ship. Sparky, in his gleaming Alurian battle hound armor, walked out of a shadow on the far end of the landing pad. "Oh, look at that. How convenient," Albert said flatly as Dailey smirked.

A spidering crackle of electricity spread across the wall, leading up to the scanning sensor like flowing water. Blue light flickered in the control room as the sensor panel in front of the cockpit dinged, notifying the crew something or someone was scanning the ship.

"And . . . winner, winner, chicken dinner," Albert blurted out, smiling. Lights flickered in the security room. "We have enough power, according to the bay transducers, to turn on the gravity field. It appears the bay is sealed. This might be a prisoner-exchange point."

Dailey unhooked from his seat, grabbing his helmet. "Master Sergeant Janix. Clear the bay, and let's get this party started."

The Solarian master chief and leader of Third Foot saluted, turning toward the back of the ship in a flurry of barking orders. "Primary fire status hot. There are no traces of organic matter aboard the ship, meaning anything we encounter will likely be droids. I want all initial loads to be EMP-charged rounds. Team leaders, you know that means to actually check."

Thumbs-up were given as the blue glow of EMP rounds registered on several of the team's rifles. The four squads of the platoon were made up just like the standard Army units from years past. Two three-person fire teams led by a sergeant made up each squad. Since Third Foot was a standard Nova Ranger Infantry Platoon, the group carried limited heavy or specialized weapons.

Each squad carried at least two Solarian Sauder rifles, while the rest used the XR-20 adjustable rifle. The XR-20 was standard issue for special units within the Army, as well as the Fleet. Each gun was capable of firing laser and kinetic rounds.

The rifle's ammunition was straightforward and to the point. Once loaded, a small glowing indicator on the side communicated what type of magazine was loaded. Each Nova Ranger usually carried two of the four styles available for the weapon. Blue stood for the EMP round, which, like its name, would temporarily, if not permanently, disable electronics, including battle droids. Red represented incendiary rounds. These rarely used rounds were more of a deterrent in a tight spot. Orange stood for a light HE, or high-explosive-tipped round, used against light armor and often in space combat. Last, green was for the standard titanium-tipped anti-armor round, the meat and potatoes of the infantry on all Federation planets.

The laser setting was for soft targets and often meant the fight was already over if the Rangers were downgrading to lasers or they wanted to limit collateral damage. Accurate and simple to adjust, the laser was activated by inserting a mini fission clip that lit the indicators in a dull white. Most Rangers adjusted the setting down enough to not entirely kill the target at the other end, only cooking them to an acceptable medium rare.

As with every platoon, there was an unofficial fifth squad consisting of the group's leaders and support personnel composed of five to eight persons of various specialties.

The vibration of the Harpy settling on the landing pad gave the Rangers the signal to stand, everyone inside either putting on their helmet or lowering sleek oxygen shields. Air hissed like an angry snake being sucked into space as Janix, followed closely by Dailey, exited the drop ship.

Within seconds, the two squads onboard had fanned out, securing the opening as well as the bay door to the control room. Dailey looked at the second Harpy, signaling it to land. Onboard the second ship, Bellman, Becket, and the others would follow behind after the initial entry to the dreadnaught was secured.

Sparky and Albert were the last two to walk off the drop ship, strolling up to the control panel as if taking a leisurely Sunday stroll.

"You can move with a purpose, you know," Dailey protested.

Albert raised an eyebrow on his viewscreen. "You can't rush excellence," the AI replied as Janix walked forward, the clunking of his mag boots ominous.

"That's what these EMP rounds are for. Rushing excellence to be excellent."

Sparky looked up at his partner in crime as Albert grinned, pointing at the two-barreled mini Gatling lasers wrapped around his shoulders, which he had mounted before leaving the *Murphy*. "You need a bigger gun to talk to a droid like that." Albert winked.

"Enough," Becket cut in, having heard the interaction over the comms. "It's time to get to work; we can play slap ass later."

"Jeeesus, all work and no play makes Albert and Sparky dull boys. Sparky, you're up, my man."

Sparky walked forward, doing the Sparkiest thing ever. "I claim this ship and all who inhabits it for the Ham Empire."

Before he could mark his territory, Dailey reminded him they were still in the vacuum of space. Sparky chuffed, jumping up onto the panel as if greeting his owner after a long day at work.

Instead of the usual crackle of electricity, a smooth flow of glowing blue wisps pulsed on the panel's surface. "Big ship. Needs more juice," Sparky informed the group as Albert opened the front panel of his armor, exposing the familiar cube that housed the AI.

After scanning the panel, Albert identified the connector needed to interface with the door. "I'm ready to go. It appears we will need to activate the internal sensor subsystem before I can go poking around. They have likely never been activated."

This was Albert's back door into just about everything. If he couldn't see or touch it, chances were, he would not be able to interface with the system. When whatever system scanned Albert or the ship he was occupying, that event was enough for him to hijack the signal and start taking over the vessel.

Luckily for the team, almost everything in every ship scanned for something. Living conditions, gravity, proximity sensors, targeting, communications, and the list went on.

Sparky dropped down as Albert plugged the cable now stretching from his chest neatly into the auxiliary panel he'd wrenched open. After several seconds of computing algorithms, the doors slowly parted.

The sucking *whoosh* of air told the team the ship was at least oxygenated, one of their main concerns. This would allow Albert to activate the gravity systems, if they were able to turn it on.

Rotating Mister Toaster's face around, Albert gave the group a thumbs-up. With a swipe of his hand, Janix motioned the platoon into the open bay.

Wrapped crates and equipment appeared untouched, likely waiting to be installed. The organized stacks hugged round walls, looking as if they had just been dropped off, awaiting workers. Several lights flickered under the power Sparky poured into the bay's systems. At the same time, Albert stood fully upright, dwarfing the other Nova Rangers, heading toward the control room.

CHAPTER 15

THE UNDERGROUND

Lights sputtered to life as Bringum Flint, the lead engineer from Kodas, spoke up while Dax and Vax also turned to Lieutenant Laura McAlister. "This is one of four main primary control rooms on the planet. This one has been inactive longer than I've been alive."

Moisture and humidity from the planet's inner core gave the entire underground area a tropical feel, only offset by the gloomy darkness of being so far underground. Mac took in a lungful of the damp air, focusing on the man.

Bringum Flint was as much an engineer as ever lived. Thin, always poised, and slightly oblivious to the outside world, the man was enough to give the often-flippant Lieutenant Commander Bellman a run for his money.

An odd feature of the man was his bizarre mix of traits. The engineer had clearly come from a half Solarian, half human family. Wearing bland clothes and speaking in an overly assured yet held back tone, it was clear why the man had been open to meeting with the others. Curiosity shone from his eyes like hungry lasers looking for a target.

Master Sergeant Walker walked to the main control panel, tapping a group of dusty buttons as the room started buzzing with electronic life. "I'll give whoever made this place credit. They knew how to make things that last."

Mac nodded as Dax sat on one of the old chairs, releasing what sounded like a lifetime's worth of groans. "We should be able to dial into the main system in Arcadia, which in turn is tied into the Gulch, from here," Dax suggested, motioning Vax to join him in working to get the control room online.

Several Nova Rangers from Fourth Foot, followed by Petty Officer Miller, filed into the room, looking over the adjoining area. Sergeant Coleman, also known as Coolio, released the latch from his helmet, sitting on one of the planning tables in the middle of the space.

"Just got a sitrep from Staff Sergeant Grear. Everyone from the Gulch, Arcadia, and Kodas are in the substructure. It should take another twenty-four hours before he believes they're deep enough to avoid any surfaceside orbital attacks."

Walker nodded, dusting off one of the prominent seats in the middle of the room. "I'm pretty sure once a handful of ships from that battle group get into low orbit, within eyeshot of the other cities, we will start getting more responses."

"Or when they decide to start firing on cities again," Mac added, winking at Walker when no one was paying attention. "Bringum, tell me again about this place and how you know about it?"

"Sure, I don't think I left much out. There really isn't much for us to tell. This place was abandoned centuries ago by the Overwatchers. In reality, we aren't supposed to know about its existence. We, as you know, are—" Mac cut him off.

"Were."

"We're in charge of the tram systems upkeep all over the planet. No one from Arcadia ever saw us, and that's how it was supposed to be. Directly under this facility is an access tunnel we eventually found to house a tram system unlike anything else we worked on or designed. It can take you almost anywhere on the planet. At least on this side of it, from what we can tell. The team had to repair an underground auger worm and found the tunnel had opened into a cavern supporting this hidden system."

Walker scratched his sandpaper-rough face. "I'm with Mac here. It's more the why."

"Well, we think it was used until an event occurred. Much like the one that happens every hundred years or so, as you all noted. But, to your point, your guess is as good as mine."

"That's what's got me worried," Miller chimed in, sitting down at the communications station and bringing it to life. "What if this was put here in case something like this happened, and those yahoos in space have a way to get down here."

Bringum gave what could only be described as a guess-we-will-find-out fake grin while Vax turned around from the console. "I think it was once manned by whoever had control of the planet, and was no longer needed over time. I mean, up until recently, we all played our part."

Vax's wisdom, as always, was closer to the truth. The underground facility had been manned by Alurian and mining syndicate members alike. Over the years, the controlling syndicate might have changed, but the overall Alurian control hadn't. Well over one hundred stories underground, the facility was a fortress of both solitaire and safety.

"I have direct control of all the mining ships from here. All of them! Status reports, everything!" Dax excitedly barked as dust vibrated from the ceiling. The man sat back down, feeling that his burst of excitement had caused the brief jolt.

"Shit," Miller huffed. "It looks like they are bombing the area directly overhead. Does anyone know what's up there?"

Bringum walked in front of the panel, jabbing in a set of instructions before a 3D rendering of the surface above them popped into the main screen. Everyone squinted as several large round structures the size of mountains disintegrated from the planet's surface. "It appears to be one of the main planetside power distribution depots. Our cities are likely without power now."

"What about down here?" Mac asked while the man nodded.

"Geothermal. Completely disconnected from the surface by design," Bringum stated, motioning for two of his counterparts to enter the room. "Get with the power distribution team. Make sure all power is transferred to the geothermal grid. Our people might be in the dark as we speak."

Grear's voice came over the comms no sooner than the man had given out the instructions. "Who turned off the lights?"

"Just keep everyone calm. It looks like it's being addressed," Walker replied as the engineers left just as quickly as they had entered the control room.

"They're taking out strategic topside targets. My guess is they are planning on sending an occupying ground force down," Mac threw out to the group. The sheer amount of nods proved everyone was thinking the same thing.

"Perfect," Walker blew out. "What about the cargo ships?"

Bringum shrugged, wiping his hand on his bland grey utility jacket. "It appears the probes you put into orbit are still functioning. Since Dax has control of their launch protocols from here, we can do almost anything since they're automated."

Walker pondered the statement as if about to ask out a girl, not knowing if she would say yes. "We talked about this earlier. Consolidating them would not be a good idea, but I want to ensure they're secured. How many are not under the water launch bays?"

"Fifteen," Dax noted, having a planetwide diagram showing their locations.

"And all of them are showing they have a gate drive?" Walker followed up. Up until now, they hadn't had a complete idea of the status of the rest of the ships, only having a limited view, and mostly from their surrounding area.

"It appears so," Dax replied.

Walker took a commanding position in front of the room, getting everyone's attention just as another light vibration shook the room. Overhead, on Asher's surface, it was easy to understand that the landscape was being changed by the bombardment.

"I want to know how many souls we can fit on each cargo ship. Even better, let's see if these systems can tell us how many people are on this planet. I want everything ready for when the *Murphy* gets back. It will only take Albert a few minutes to get things moving."

In prior discussions, the number of the planet's general population had been up for significant debate, being anywhere from the low millions to the tens of millions. Ultimately, it wasn't that Walker was trying to relocate the planet's inhabitants; he simply wanted an understanding of the possible fighting force and risk he and the others were dealing with.

Two Nova Rangers walked into the control room, returning from the long corridor leading off into another section of the compound.

"This place is stockpiled with everything from rations to weapons," Specialist Tim Banks, also known as Banksy, reported. "It also looks like there's some type of ship bay at the far end. The door's sealed shut, but I would think there may be a way to get a ship in and out of here."

Walker nodded. "See if the rations are still usable." The man paused, thinking through his instructions to the often obnoxious Rangers. The last thing the man needed was a bunch of drunk Nova Rangers flying into orbit, taking on the battle group. "If you happen to find booze, don't touch it." Drooping faces confirmed they had indeed found libations. "Also, get the weapons out and get them working. If they are, see if we can round up some able bodies from Arcadia and Kodas. Grear will let you know."

Dax, Vax, and Bringum nodded their approval while the two Rangers returned to work. As luck would have it, they had found one of the two main control hubs on the planet, both capable of supporting life for years, if not decades.

Dax again excitedly turned to the group. "I think I found something else useful."

Now displayed on the screen were the schematics of a suborbital ground-to-air plasma missile targeting system and launcher, followed by several more pinging on the global map also displaying the cargo ships.

"Fuck . . . me," Walker blew out as the entire room stared at the screen.

CHAPTER 16

POWER HOUR

Captain Dailey pulled the power cable from the Harpy's mini fission reactor as the lights in the cargo bay glowed brighter. After taking stock of their situation and listening to Sparky and Albert debate who would first have a smoking-hot make-out session onboard the dreadnaught, the AI started working through their next steps.

Much like ships designed on Earth, the Alurian dreadnaught was also partitioned, each section capable of sustaining itself in case of the catastrophic failure of another. Albert and the rest of the team weren't expecting most of the massive ship to be so self-contained.

Each primary section was supported by its own mini power core. There was a mix of fission power cores and an odder type that even Albert could not fully explain. As always, it was simply related to magic.

What Albert called the dry dock bay was used, according to the computer subsystems, for transporting organic material such as food, general personal items, and, most likely, prisoners.

While one of their ships would stay in the bay, the other would park on the landing pad once the cargo doors were closed. According to Albert, hooking up the ship's power module would, in most cases, do nothing. Here, with a little push from Sparky, the Harpy's power source would be able to slowly charge the ship's section after a kickstart. From there, Albert would contain the power output to ensure it didn't spill over into other sections of the vessel until needed.

The one saving grace of the module they were currently in was that each cargo bay had its own gravitational offset and life-support systems. The rest of the main ship shared one of four such systems, each backing the other in case of damage during combat.

Metal walls adorned with various controls reached the cavernous ceilings, adding to their understanding of the ship's size. When the dreadnaught split into modules, each became a vessel in its own right.

"Stick it in the hole there, hero," Albert instructed. Sparky could be heard snickering under his helmet.

Dailey shook his head as the small coupling Albert had quickly fashioned slinked into the magnetic port. Lights stopped stuttering as stable power started flowing into the cargo bay.

"What will we have powered up?" Dailey asked the AI while the door into the control room opened the rest of the way.

"The cargo bay and the control room. After that, there is a set of rooms that appear to be prisoner cells. After that, a set of open bay rooms and likely planning rooms. It appears there are also quarters for the officer in charge. Simple and to the point."

Dailey turned, Bellman, Pearl, and Dorax following him into the control room. The light space suit Dorax wore made him look like part of Bellman's engineering team. Even though the Alurian was present, he was working to stay out of the way. In many ways, Dorax still wasn't entirely convinced he wasn't about to be shot out of an airlock.

"How long till you get the life support up and running?" Dailey asked as Albert shut the door to the control room.

"According to this readout—which has zero personality, mind you— right about . . . now," Albert proclaimed just as a *whoosh* of pressurized air hissed thought the room and several once floating objects dropped to the hard deck.

Both the gravity stabilizers and life-support systems rose from the grave, making the lights flicker as the gentle hum of the system regulated into a synchronous drone. Various colors started speckling the walls and control panel, giving Bellman the go-ahead to test the air.

The familiar sticklike probe beeped before the small tablet attached to the science officer's wrist flashed green. Not waiting another minute to get out of the skintight leisure suit, as he called it, Bellman slapped the full-face shield up in a quick snap of the side button. Holding his breath for a short minute, he finally took in a lungful of air, followed by a flurry of coughs. "New . . . air . . . huck . . . Should be fine . . . huck, now."

Albert stood straight, sticking up his finger as a sensor pinged. "Yup, good to. It appears the air scrubbers in this section had never been activated. All the work had been automated. It will smell like burning plastic for a while."

Dailey slid his visor open and the others followed suit, including Sparky. Everyone repeated Bellman's initial reaction. At the same time, the outer bay doors closed after two thumbs-up from both pilots.

"That should do it." Albert grinned, Mister Toaster's mustache shuffling. "All you in the bay," Albert's voice crackled. "Oxygen levels are acceptable, as well as gravity for now. Just avoid touching that corridor leading out of the bay. That would be a no-no. Bad day type of stuff."

"Point taken. What else can you tell us?" Dailey asked as Becket saluted from inside the bay.

The rest of the group stood by, waiting on the initial report. By the time the AI had unplugged from the control panel, Jen had made her way into the control room, stretching her legs and rocking onto her toes.

"Well, it's kind of a mixed bag," Albert started, in serious mode. His voice was thoughtful. "The ship is in a type of calibration or testing mode. While it's making it a little hard to work through all the systems, it also means I may be able to integrate into the ship's mainframe and AI systems at boot up."

"English or Solarian, just dumb it down a little bit for us," Dailey cut in as Pearl snorted, her Solarian humor coming through. In her mind, Dailey had just called himself stupid; in Pearl's eyes, he wasn't talking in general about the group. Janix and a few other Solarians had been around humans long enough, or even been raised on Earth to a point where they could manage the absurd number of poorly timed dad jokes flowing from them.

"Okay. If you remember the HAM we uploaded on the *Scarecrow*, it was a similar concept. The cargo ships didn't have an AI system, so I sort of created and uploaded it into the ship. That meant no preloaded issues. Or are we all forgetting the *Asher-5*?"

"So, you're saying you can program the entire ship?" Bellman asked while Pearl sat down at a readout, mapping out the closer sections of the ship.

"Possibly. What I think is important is that we can probably daisy-chain power into a few other sections of the ship. I don't see us fully powering everything. The station would have taken several days to do that alone. The one bit of good news is that the gate drive doesn't need charging. It just needs power to operate."

"Thrusters and weapons systems?" Dorax asked.

"That will take some time, but I would say the thrusters are very similar to human design. We just need to kickstart the reactors. You know, turn the switch on."

Dailey sat down, taking in the situation. "How much time?"

"Oh, I don't know. Ten hours," Albert replied. Dailey rolled his eyes. "We could also charge the bridge."

Pearl spoke up at that. "It looks like you could damn near run the ship from here. Albert's right. The ship is in some type of calibration mode. This thing was about to go into its final checks within days, by the looks of it. That would allow us to program the stations as we deem fit."

"Albert, pull up a schematic of the bridge and its proximity to this bay," Dailey requested. One of the large screens on the wall facing away from the viewports snapped due to the static of turning on for the first time. "Not that entire section of the ship, just the bridge," Dailey added as Albert smirked.

"That is the bridge, my man. All fifty-six battle stations and accompanying four levels."

Pearl shook her head as Dailey blew out a lungful of air. "Jesus, they were not joking around," Dailey said. "All I need is this ship to get from point A to point B, be able to fire its main weapons system, and maybe transport people. Meanwhile, that little bay right there can shoot a drop ship out as fast as a crap after Solarian taco night."

"Well, then you can do all that from here; not to mention the bridge is roughly a mile away, and that's straight-line distance. The bridge is a ship on its own. It might be worth looking at, but from what I can see, there is also a pod of assault ships and drones in various stages of loadout in this beast's belly."

"Hmph," Becket grunted. "That can wait. I'm with the boss here. That sounds like a bunch of free chicken, but we need to crack a few eggs first. What about the shields," the wise First Sergeant brought up, thinking about the safety of his soldiers and the crew.

Albert turned, plugging his finger back into the control panel and looking up. "Neat. Oh, the shields will likely be at fifty percent; maybe slightly less. It appears that was one of the last things scheduled to be done by the constructo bots. Only half of them have been loaded. If we had time, I would say we tried to scavenge a few more out of the debris field."

"Fifty percent is a risk I'm willing to take. We just need to shoot first," Dailey noted as Becket let out a full-on snort. "Dorax."

Dailey started as the Alurian turned. "Present, I believe you humans say," Dorax joked.

"I want you to help get this ship from point A to point B. If you can do that, I will make sure you get a ship. If this is it, so be it," Dailey promised, garnering a nod from the Alurian.

Sparky chuffed. "I have not approved this action." The hound flopped onto his two hind legs in thought.

"Spark, Lord Ham Overlord the Third. With your approval, and with the understanding you claimed the ship, however, didn't mark it in time, you have half ownership. Pirate salvage rules."

Sparky contemplated the statement. "Acceptable. But I name the ship, and it flies under the flag of the Ham Empire."

He and Albert had been working on this new Empire in their spare time when not charting out the crew's love lives. "A planet, now a ship," Dailey sighed. "Alright. I agree to your terms. In the event the ship is not claimed by the Federation or unfortunately lost to Dorax here, I accept."

Sparky nodded, opening his leg armor, allowing for a behind-the-ear scratch, sealing the deal. He followed by standing up and licking Dailey's boot. The *Murphy*'s captain didn't want to know. All the Alurian war hound's little quirks changed on a daily basis, likely driven by a new bit of information or a movie Albert had watched.

"I swear to God, no ceremony—" Just as the words left his lips, Jen came over the comms.

"Does anyone know why there is a ham in the back of the Harpy?"

Rolling his eyes, Dailey refocused, getting the formalities out of the way. "Dorax, I'm going to leave you with a crew. I'm not saying to keep an eye on you, but to support this effort and be able to fly that Harpy out of here if needed."

"I can fly that ship," Dorax stated as Albert let out a raspberry.

"*Pfft* . . . You do know we saw you fly, right?"

"Alright, game faces, folks. I want Lieutenant Ponce and Master Sargeant Grantham to lead a team onboard the . . ." Dailey trailed off as Sparky chimed in.

"The *Crow*."

The group let the word roll off their tongues, hushed whispers mumbling the name. Even Dorax found himself doing it. Naming a ship was a big deal, and something that would give the vessel a personality. The *Scarecrow*, a once upon a time mining cargo ship turned famous, would lend its name and lineage to the massive dreadnaught.

"Well, that sounds—" Albert cut Dailey off.

"Already done and loaded into the subsystem, into which, by the way, I'm loading what I would like to call the HAM 2." HAM, standing for the Humanlike Autonomous Machine, according to Albert, was a mini program that the AI could overlay onto a ship's mainframe, giving it a set of parameters it had to adhere to. Things like "Don't get the humans killed" were on top of that list.

Not having time to jump into a deep conversation over the topic, Dailey shifted gears. "How much will the subsystem be able to run? I didn't even think about that."

"Guess that's one of my brilliant ideas, but never worry, it will ensure things don't go too far off the rails. I am uploading our gate drive nav data as we speak. In reality, we could fly this ship from the *Murphy*," the AI voiced. Dailey pondered the idea.

"We will if needed. All right, let's get this party started." Dailey hailed the team from First Foot over the comms Pearl now had functioning.

"Here, sir," Ponce replied.

"I need you, Grantham, and two squads to prepare and shift to the *Crow*, as we are calling it. There is no change to our initial plans. We are only keeping a small section of the ship powered on, so we only want to bring over enough people to get back off in a hurry if needed."

"Roger, sir," Ponce replied, already putting his platoon in motion.

Bellman turned to Dailey, nodding. "I'll leave two of the engineers on the *Crow*, as well as myself. Ensign Barthelo is enough of a meathead to make up for a dozen other engineers."

Captain Dailey nodded his approval, also having planned on needing and leaving more engineering personnel. What he hadn't planned on was the absolute pristine working condition of the *Crow*, a ship that was loaded not only with a massive assortment of the Alurian's newest weapons tech but, according to Albert, an entire droid ground assault force.

The man huffed, looking back at Pearl, Dorax, and a grinning Mister Toaster. "I was planning on leaving Albert and Pearl here, but if we can control the ship from the *Murphy*, it might be easier to consolidate the main command element."

Dailey wasn't making a statement, instead looking for advice. Pearl spoke up first. "I'm second in command of the *Murphy* and will stay on the *Crow*. We will keep whatever drop ship pilot stays behind on weapons control and two of the engineers. Between Bellman and I, we can manage as long as Albert can dial in if needed."

"If needed. That's what I'm worried about. I don't need anyone going all Sparky on us here." Dailey paused as the Alurian war hound let out a raspberry, followed by an unexpected passage of gas. "We are for sure taking this ship into that battle group and starting a fight. I'm still thinking they sent several ships out looking for us and have probably found what we left behind by this point."

"That's a damn fine point, sir," Becket started, setting his helmet on the console. "That battle group had one of these too, and on top of that, they know how to use it."

"Excuse me. I never said I didn't know how to use this oversize tin can," Albert interjected.

Dailey let his eyes wander around the hard edges and purposeful layout of the space. Truth be told, the AI had, in just under forty-five minutes, figured out a way to control an entire dreadnaught from a simple docking bay.

"Hell, we didn't know if we'd make it this far. Albert, didn't you say something about the *Murphy* being able to fit in this thing's main drop bay?"

"More like tucked under its arm. I might have exaggerated slightly."

Dorax pushed himself into the wall. "It's what we call a docking stall. I'm not sure if you have ever been around an Alurian ship this big to see one. Where I come from, there are, not ships like this, but big enough to have a docking stall. They're also known as stables."

The Alurian went on to explain the principle. Instead of docking a larger vessel in its immense bay, it would open several massive retractable panels under the ship. After that, the main ship would, in effect, hug the other like a newborn, shielding it not only from attack but also from prying eyes and radar.

Even Bellman was impressed by how something so simple could be so useful. It was unassuming enough that humankind wouldn't even give the concept a fleeting thought.

"Well shit," Dailey exclaimed, using a western drawl for no reason. "That might just come in handy."

Becket walked to the main console. "This is in English," he observed as Albert's digital face let a smile sweep across it.

"Yeah, well. I don't think Dorax here could even translate all the Alurian readouts. Some of it might be a little bland, but you will get the point. I even added symbols for the super confusing ones."

Pearl clicked her tongue on the top of her mouth. "Albert, could we use our gate drive while using this stable?"

"Huh. Give me a sec."

While he computed the question, Dailey nodded at Jen, who was looking inside the control room from the main bay. Using the universal sign to wrap it up by twirling his armored finger in the air, Jen turned, barking out several orders. Becket, also seeing this, walked out.

"Well," Albert started. "I think we can. The only issue I can see is the need to have the *Murphy* activate the event horizon, then the *Crow* scoop it up, so to speak, while both enter the gate. Yeah, sure. No worries."

"No worries?" Dailey asked. Albert just hmphed.

After a few minutes of going over last-minute plans with Pearl, Dailey clicked his helmet back in place. The *Murphy*'s executive and navigation officer would command the skeleton crew out of the debris field, allowing Albert time to work through the rest of the gate details.

Albert pointed out they would need to draw power from the dreadnaught to create a large enough event. From there, they would gate to a secondary position before finally returning to Asher.

There were two options on the table, and some much-needed time to send and receive whatever messages they could to the good senator, as well as the team on Asher. The initially discussed course of action was to engage in a game of cat and mouse with the battle group, using the planet and the moon as cover. While likely leading to a negative outcome, they would have the element of surprise.

With this option, Albert would be working on a solution to remotely activate and control the assault ships jammed full of drones and suborbital droids.

As for option number two, this was more of a subversion plan, trying to convince the Alurian battle group they were one of their own while flying a fully overcharged dreadnaught directly into the center of the mass of ships. This option was highly problematic and would likely cause the most issues; issues being the lack of life by the end of the plan for the *Murphy* and its crew.

CHAPTER 17

THINNING THE HERD

Massive chunks of the remaining depot broke further apart as the *Crow* detached itself from its only known home. Several flashing pops signaled the claws jutting out from the structure, like an eagle's claws that had just lost their prize fish, fully letting the dreadnaught loose into the wild.

Dailey leaned back, watching the view of the *Crow*'s bridge from a remote camera pointing at Sparky and Pearl sitting in front of the main control panel. While not usually used as a bridge, the area was more than sufficient, with several monitors and singular stations able to run whatever systems the ship had activated.

After two days of reprogramming and activating more of the dreadnaught, it had been a welcomed surprise to discover that most of the energy cells and reactors were fully charged. Albert insisted it was as close to pulling the plastic off a new car's seats after removing the window sticker as they would get. This was, as usual, lost on the younger crew members, forcing Becket into fully explaining the old ritual known as buying a car, seeing how spaceships generally didn't have window stickers.

With more power than initially expected, the team onboard had activated a quarter of the ship, which included the main docking bay, additional living quarters, one of three medical bays, several assault-ship compartments and droids, and finally, the lift leading to the ship's main bridge, which had yet to be explored.

Having the rest of the ship's power diverted to the shields and weapons systems meant the rest of the *Crow* would have to wait. The lack of a gate drive onboard opened up several arguments as to the reasoning behind the absence of a navigational system. Either the ship was set to be a local asset, or according to Albert, something more nefarious could be at play.

When asked to clarify, Albert had suggested the presence of a new type of gate tech that even he couldn't detect or had yet to be installed. Either way, the ship still boggled Captain Dailey's mind as he studied the dreadnaught, knowing they would soon engage with a similar-style vessel.

While the ship's interior had a dark military feel, the design was simplistic enough to afford the *Crow* a personality. This was summed up by Albert proclaiming that the person who designed the ship had probably also built space stations at one time, laying out the interior like several small individual communities all serving a different purpose. This reminded Dailey and the others of the various cities on Asher.

Pearl, keeping her eye on the proximity monitor in front of her, started talking to an attentive Sparky, who was staring at one of the battle mechs they had managed to bring into the hangar bay. "You think we can use those things?"

Sparky chuffed, having ridden a constructo bot all the way back to Asher through a heavily questionable gate. "If we do, I will claim it for our crew. Albert promised to make it work."

"You and Albert. Well, if we do, then I say go for it. The pilots don't want anything to do with those things."

Sparky situated himself in the seat, flopping his legs in the other direction. "For the Glory of Hamica."

Pearl breathed out, knowing the hound was laser focused on claiming the mech. While closely resembling one of the constructo bots, the mech was significantly more fortified. From larger blast shields to massive arms covered in various weapon systems, it included a cannon on one side and a gigantic blaster of some type on the other.

Topping this off were two rocket pods in the normal place where a person's pectoral muscles would be, and in the center, a cockpit large enough to hold one pilot sat inconspicuously nestled in place of its heart.

"What's that?" Dorax asked, pointing at a red blip on the screen in front of him. Lines traced various areas around the debris field, showing their current trajectory.

"*Murphy*, you seeing this?" Pearl asked over the comms. Dailey looked at the monitor onboard the bridge of the *Murphy*, also showing not only one but now two distinct signals.

"Kline?" Dailey asked as the mood on both bridges quickly shifted.

"Two ships. They're just outside of the depot's debris field."

"Shit," Dailey huffed, turning toward Albert. "What are we looking at?" It wasn't that he didn't trust Specialist Kline. It was just the very real fact that the young man didn't have a veritable encyclopedia of alien ships stuffed into his brains.

"Good news or bad news?" Albert snapped back like a teacher scolding a rowdy student during class.

"Not the time for this. We talked about this."

"Okay, bad news, team," Albert started, launching into a flurry of tapping on his console. "Those are two rather nasty D-class imperial attack cruisers."

"English," Dailey interrupted.

"Smaller than a dreadnaught and nastier than the Alurian destroyers, we have been somehow lucky enough to have me onboard to handle. I'm sending over the sensor data to the *Crow* now."

Dailey clicked the comms button, talking back to the newly minted crew aboard the *Crow*. "Don't change course. If they're just sitting still, there's a good chance all this wreckage is throwing off their sensors."

"Oh poo," Albert noted, cutting into the comms between the two ships. "They just launched several sensor drones in our general direction. Before you ask, we already knew what was outside the field, so that's how we saw them first. Oh, and I do have good news. Want to hear it?"

Pearl, not in the mood, spoke up. "For the love of the Solarian moon gods, get to the point."

"Whelp, since you put it so graciously. I have several transponder codes the Alurians have—well, *had* uploaded into the depot before my main man, Sparky got a hold of it. Might I suggest we dock the *Murphy* as mentioned and try to . . . you know . . . talk our way out of it, and then go *BAM*, right in the kisser."

Dailey was getting used to sifting through the AI's slang. "Make them think we are a leftover ship and then attack," Dailey stated, almost asking a question.

"Something like that. I'll get to the point. The only thing we have is the element of surprise . . . Nope, that's gone," Albert noted as another set of alarms chimed, notifying the crew one or several of the sensor pods had scanned the ship.

"Just do it," Dailey barked, while both ships went into full battle stations.

Lights flashed as the already highly alerted crews postured for an inevitable fight. While the monitors all shifted to targeting screens, Albert started sending out several messages simultaneously. In an effort to keep the peace, he was also translating them into both English and Solarian on the main viewscreens for both crews to see. The message was simple.

We engaged a Federation ship trying to hide and cannot maneuver due to previously acquired damage to our systems. Their ship is damaged but still functional. Please advise status.

Initially, there was silence, then a follow-on bounce back on the ship's transponder codes. Several lights flashed green, which no one had any clue what they meant as Albert continued to feverishly hammer the console in front of him.

"You're doing a lot of work for not much output," Dailey noted, turning to Becket, who had just walked onto the bridge.

Albert didn't respond as the once green light started flickering red, joining the rest of the flashing red alerts. The first sign that the Alurians fully understood that the transponder codes Albert had sent were for a garbage transport and not a full-on dreadnaught was the glowing horizon of the previous wreckage forming a wall of blue and flaming blood-red explosions.

"Shit," Dailey and Pearl breathed out simultaneously, seeing the awe-inspiring sight.

The Alurians had fired several massive pulse missiles into the wreckage directly in front of them. Missiles that were used to destroy entire cities or significant threats when needed. During space combat, large weapons like this were often not used due to their size and the possibility of being intercepted prior to reaching their desired target.

"Permission to take over weapons systems," Albert asked both ships at the same time.

"Granted," Dailey replied, knowing Pearl, seeing this, was in agreement.

"Everyone, calm down. We have something they don't," Albert noted. Dailey shook his head, glancing at Becket, who was giving a thumbs-up, letting him know the Nova Rangers were ready to go.

"Albert!" Dailey exclaimed as every laser and plasma cannon from both ships streaked toward the slowly dying blue-and-red flame from the assault, chipping away at the debris field.

"ME!" the AI screeched as he stood up, holding his hands to the bridge's ceiling, sounding like Doctor Frankenstein himself. "Rise, my minions! Rise and kill! *Wohahah.*"

Following the streaking, singular volley from both the *Crow* and the *Murphy*, hundreds if not thousands of the small floating pieces of wreckage started flashing and blinking at random intervals.

Dailey pondered the absurdity of the scene unfolding in front of him. The man was missing some good old, straight-up fist fighting at this point, not fully understanding Albert's plan until the first dozen or so constructo bots zipped in front of the main viewport. Some were missing legs and others arms, while glowing white plasma cutters and welders left comet like streaks behind them.

"You son of a bitch. You were sitting there programming the constructo bots that are left." Dailey grinned, sitting back, quickly shifting his mood back to the fight at hand.

"Every last one. Sparky will be so impressed," Albert noted, turning to Dailey as Mister Toaster's eyes slanted into the rest of an evil grin.

The truth of the matter was Sparky had already activated his armor and was slowly trotting toward the battle mech in the main bay. Glancing over, the war hound could see the streaking thrusters roaring by, some even sputtering out as a handful of constructo bots dropped out of the fight before they could get into it.

Dailey refocused on maneuvering out of the area instead of taking the two Alurian ships head-on. "Engage route two," Dailey ordered as Albert held up a finger.

Route two was another way out of the massive wreckage field, being the second least congested path away from the depot.

"Might I recommend we see how this works first?" Albert asked.

Dailey, this time not wanting to take the chance, shook his head to a now frowning Mister Toaster. Both ships started shifting course, firing rapidly to clear a path.

"You take all the fun out of things. I totally wanted to watch," Albert replied in time for the first crackle of something happening on the other side of the debris field.

The command crew of the *Starfire Reaper* stared at the targeting screen, notifying Captain Vergosh of their options. They could fire another volley of missiles toward their prey as if slowly digging a hole, working to get to the buried treasure below.

As the glow from the missile barrage started to fade like a setting sun, the Alurian ships' automated proximity alarms shifted into high gear. The perfectly timed wall of laser and plasma fire slammed into both ships' forward shields.

Unlike the destroyers, these ships were more automated, able to detect the oncoming threat and adjust accordingly. Captain Vergosh remained unflinching as he raised his greenish, lightly scaled chin.

While impressive to witness, the shots flashed on the forward deflector shields, creating a Fourth of July display of sparking fireworks. Put into perspective, the attack had been the equivalent of a horse swatting off a fly.

Vergosh didn't smile or grin, knowing something was likely not correct. Looking down at the control screen in front of him, it became immediately clear from the large blotch of white-and-red sensor data that something was wrong.

"Reverse thrusters!" Vergosh commanded when the first wave of constructo bots slammed into the ship's forward-sensor array.

Both the ships, seeing they were being swarmed, started firing with short-range laser cannons, picking off the seemingly endless swarm of angry glowing bees now swarming them. The second Alurian vessel was a fast-moving escort ship designed to support the larger war machine doing most of the heavy lifting.

The smaller ship's name was loosely translated as the *Nebula Fury*. Letting loose a flurry of small hounder missiles, the *Fury*, as it was called by the crew, covered for its bigger brother, the *Starfire Reaper*, while it turned away from the swarm.

Massive port thrusters roared like an angry river, working to take the *Starfire Reaper* to safety, when no less than two dozen constructo bots committed the ultimate sacrifice. While ending their singular existence, the uninvited party guests slammed directly into the thruster's intake ports, feeding the angry, raging blue glow.

At first, the blue undulating thrusters lightly shuddered, stating it would take more than a punch on the chin to take them out. Unfortunately for the repositioning *Starfire Reaper*, the next dozen or so constructo bots flew directly into the belly of the beast, causing several popping explosions and making the once raging thrusters go dormant.

Vergosh's eyes hardened as the bridge's primary navigation engineer turned, not wanting to look his Alurian captain in the face. "Sir, we must eject the main bottom-hull thrusters."

Red lights found a way to flash an even angrier shade of scarlet as rage rippled across Vergosh's face. He knew the implications of this. There would be no gating out of the system. Both the hyper and gate drive were attached and powered by the massive thrusters on the ship's bottom.

While the *Starfire Reaper*'s main rear engines could propel the ship at blazing, face-melting speeds, the thrusters mounted on the belly of the vessel, allowing it to drop into lower planetary orbit, meaning a massive amount of power was directed toward the system.

"Proceed," Vergosh snarled through clenched, pointed teeth. "Activate the fission field."

The fission field caused a massive drain of the ship's main reactors, which left them defenseless for several hours but shut down any threats or drones outside the thin electromagnetic field hugging the rugged exterior. But it also meant possibly shutting down the *Nebula Fury*. Still, the crew of the *Starfire Reaper* was not the type to question the direct orders of their leaders.

Within seconds, the alarms and sounds of fighting winked out like a house during a brownout, losing enough power to dim the lights and shut down most major appliances only to have them slowly come back on.

Out the forward viewport, the *Nebula Fury* floated momentarily without purpose, covered with constructo bots, as its lights flickered into a dull, yellowish glow. Vergosh had been gracious enough to send a quick message for the *Fury* to raise its harmonic shields, a system used when in close proximity to an electromagnetic field producing munition.

CHAPTER 18

NINE LIVES

The familiar vibration of entering a gate had increased to the point of rattling out teeth as the massive, combined behemoth of the *Murphy* now attached to the *Crow*'s docking stall slowly poked its nose through the shimmering anomaly in space. After several hours of calculating the risks, the decision had been made to test the boundaries of their small gate drive, proving once again how powerful the tech was.

"See, I told you so. No problem. I'll have an oil change and lube by the time those other ships are able to flush a toilet. Which, by the way, when Alurians go number two, they—" Albert droned on before Dailey cut him off.

"We can talk about this after we get through this gate," Dailey said, seeing a bead of sweat dripping from Becket's forehead. The Nova Ranger's First Sergeant had vocally made his opinion of gating known. For the man who had been in more significant emotionally violent events than the devil himself, it was the little things that got to him. Most notable were things and events out of his control, such as gating.

As for the two Alurian ships, Albert had pulled off what could only be called a stroke of genius. Seeing that the *Crow* had not been thoroughly tested and Dailey's general disinterest in getting stuck at the far edges of another galaxy, the AI had caused as much chaos as possible.

After witnessing the *Starfire Reaper*'s capabilities of destroying large chunks of the remaining depot to get to the prize, it was a simple stall and redirect tactic. Albert had fired all the ship's primary laser and plasma systems, knowing from the output readings of the Alurian vessels they would do little more than produce a chaotic laser light show.

While calculating each individual laser's targeting through the mess of wrecked hulls and the depot itself, Albert had spent the rest of his time reprogramming the constructo bots to engage and disassemble the two ships in an attempt to self-salvage themselves. In doing so, Vergosh had ordered the *Starfire Reaper* and the *Nebula Fury* to eject any damaged parts of the ship.

One significant and not wholly planned outcome was the disabling of the ship's gating abilities, leaving them stuck in the system and also hampering their ability to communicate over vast distances, a trick Dailey and the others had quickly learned to exploit.

After another hour of pulling constructo bots off the Alurian hulls like ticks, the *Murphy* and crew had made their way safely out of the debris field. It would take weeks, if not months, to get the two Alurian ships back into some semblance of functioning vessels. The only risk Dailey could see was the graveyard of ships and spare parts floating around them.

Pearl cut in over the comms while the last of the vibrations wrinkled through the ship. "It appears we are clear of the gate entrance. All systems are showing stable, and as of ten seconds ago, Sparky decided to take a nap beside the mech."

Dailey nodded, turning off the battle station's alert. Flashing lights and alarms started winding down as the *Murphy*'s crew sighed in relief. They had once again done the impossible, and all thanks to Albert. It wasn't lost on Dailey that nothing this good ever lasted, like most if not all things in life.

Unlike the old Earth saying about a cat having nine lives, on Solaria, they only allowed their feline-type animal five. Dailey was quickly working through the math in his head of just how many times they would be able to utilize Albert, or even worse, if something happened to him and his subsystems.

Dailey nodded at Becket, standing up. "I'd like to regroup in the briefing room in an hour. It will take us four to get to our first stop. We can pull the others into the meeting. I'd also like to send a message to Asher and try to talk with the senator." He was talking to no one and everyone on the bridge at the same time, like a politician. "We said we would wait till we got out of there to put a plan together. It's time."

The rest of the bridge nodded as Becket motioned his command partner to join him for a much-needed drink. Specialist Kline stood up, walking toward the departing captain.

"Sir, the sensor pod we sent ahead is already sending back information. I believe it will work, giving us a set of eyes around Asher once we are one gate away."

"Of course it will work," Albert guffawed. "The only problem we may encounter is the sensor pod getting intercepted. I have come up with a few ideas. Having that other ship will give us some options."

Dailey sighed. "Whatever it is, I'm sure it will be brilliant. That was great, what you did back there. Tell you what, want me to change that toaster back to your original head?"

Albert pondered the question as the grin on Mister Toasters' face widened. "You know, it's kind of growing on me. Plus, these Induce Corp products are second to none. This thing's tougher than that old football of a head. Not to mention, I understand everything there is to know about toast and/or toasting protocols. Oh, and you should see how the ship's main subsystem keeps letting me plug into it." Mister Toaster's raised eyebrows were enough to end the conversation.

"Fair enough," Dailey said, walking off the bridge with Becket, making their way to the officers' club before getting the entire team together. A bar for officers and, on occasion, the senior noncommissioned officers onboard, Thron always made sure the tradition was followed.

The officers' club felt eclectic, much like the mess hall, thanks to Master Chief Thron and the time he took honoring long-held military traditions of both worlds. Pictures from old wars and friends long since passed joined the patrons of the small but functional area from beyond time.

Solarian warlords holding massive decorative swords sat beside photos of Patton standing in front of the American flag, followed by Stormin' Norman Schwarzkopf in desert fatigues walking through a unit's station in the dunes of Iraq before it was incorporated into the Middle Eastern Federation, also known as the MEF, a group led by the Saudis that had, over time, brought peace to the region after oil lost the majority of its value.

Surprisingly, the room was one of the least used gathering areas on the *Murphy*, considering it was a cozy getaway. They preferred to socialize in the officers' mess, only having a limited amount of officers onboard, but it was an area Dailey had promised to start using more. Thron insisted on having one of his staff wait on the officers when in the club, often taking away from the operation of the ship's galley. This was another reason Dailey didn't often tap into the space.

Within ten minutes, the two men were sipping a glass of Moshan mead. While similar to wine on Earth, the Moshans used a version of honey cultivated and harvested from a bramble in the frozen tundras of their planet's Southern Hemisphere.

Unlike Earth, Mosha had two distinct hemispheres. The northern, subtropical section of the planet, including its North Pole, was covered entirely in jungle-wrapped mountains. As for the southern part of the planet, its bottom half had massive, rocky planes of snow, ice-covered mountains, and frozen ocean.

The bramble was a flowering fruit best described as the outcome of a banana and a blackberry making a baby that stayed soft when in subfreezing temperatures wrapped in a protective vanilla husk, allowing the exotic fruit to be used as ice, a trademark of Moshan cocktails.

Most of the planet's population lived in the small strip of land separating the two regions. Simplistically called the Belt, the area was a perfect mix of the two regions, providing a pleasant year-round living experience.

The two other extremes of the planet were peppered with precious mineral mining operations. To date, it was one of the only planets in the sector that none of the other mining syndicates had a grip on.

Becket removed his last armor piece, downing his glass in one violent gulp. "What's on your mind, boss?"

"It's this thing about the moon and then the Alurian's showing up. Think about it. Someone was on that moon firing down on the planet with highly targeted and effective fires," Dailey started, finishing his glass, not to be outdone.

"I'm still trying to compute that we're hanging off the belly of an Alurian dreadnaught, something I never thought I would live to see. The boys back home are never going to believe this shit," Becket joked as they both chuckled lightly. "All kidding aside, boss, I was talking with the other platoons, and they all seem to think Ran is the one up there doing all this."

While Dailey pondered the same scenario, hearing it out loud from someone he respected and trusted to the ends of the galaxy started solidifying the idea. "Yeah, that's what I keep thinking. I thought he bugged out at first, but the more I think about it, why would he? Shit, from what we can figure, the Alurians and some, if not all, of the mining syndicates are tied together. I feel like one of the tin-foil-hat conspiracy theorists we always read about in the history books."

"You mean the ones who said Atlantis was real?" Becket joked, knowing they had, in fact, stepped inside the city. "Back then, they were called crazies. Yeah, everyone is a conspiracy theorist until the shit is sitting right in front of you asking for a drink."

"I feel like this entire thing has been happening on a loop for thousands of years before we even thought about space flight. As for Ran, I'm starting to think if we can find and take out that moon base, it might give us the upper hand."

"Take it over? The way I see it, a big-ass laser is sitting on it somewhere, powerful enough to take out a city."

This caught Dailey's attention, some semblance of an actual plan starting to form. Again, this was the entire point of the two men having a moment away from the noise and distraction of command, including their close friends.

Dailey leaned over, pouring a smaller portion of Moshan mead. "We have a much larger footprint than we did before. What about the forces on Asher? They have an entire platoon, not to mention some of the planet's security forces. Walker and McAlister said they were capable."

"Capable and able to execute are two different things," Becket said, starting to think through the rapidly forming plan.

"Maybe we could gate in, just the *Murphy*, and pull a few more ships away. Cause a distraction long enough for them to get a team on the moon, then we haul ass to pick up the *Crow*."

Both men pondered the scenario, running it through their minds at lightning-fast speeds, something both men, as well as the rest of the *Murphy*'s crew, were getting used to.

"That's a lot of moving pieces, boss," Becket contemplated.

"Agreed. I would usually not entertain something like this, but with Albert and, hell, Sparky, it seems like we've been able to pull off the impossible lately."

"The key word is *lately*," Becket followed up.

Nodding, Dailey smacked his tablet on the old knotted wooden bar top. The sign hanging above, declaring it used to be part of the Officers' Club at Fort Benning, Georgia, the once upon a time home of the United States Armor and Infantry. This Army post had been a primary target and was all but destroyed during the first forty-eight hours of the Alurian war.

"What about one of the ships on the *Crow*? Dorax and Bellman have a couple of assault ships working. Or maybe we focus on that mech. I'm glad we haven't seen one of those in action yet."

"Yet?" Becket asked, screwing up his face.

"I'm just saying. Maybe we can gate in the *Murphy*, cause a little distraction, then get them to follow us again. They are, what . . . like three for three on that shit plan. Well . . ." Dailey trailed off. "Shit for them. Maybe we gate somewhere close, where we can get back faster. Set up a trap. Take those ships or ship out of commission, then once we confirm the moon is secured, we hit them with the dreadnaught. Maybe even use the old Trojan horse game plan," Dailey proposed as Becket scraped his fingers across his stubbled chin.

"That's a mouthful, but it's something. Boss, I'm going to say something we're both thinking. Either our luck with Albert is eventually going to run out, or we run into his equal and we get sniffed out. I wouldn't doubt they have something like him on that star cruiser. There's a whole hell of a lotta what-ifs in this plan."

Dailey nodded, agreeing. His communicator started beeping, and Jen's name flashed.

Becket shook his head. "You know there'll be time for all that later," Becket suggested as Dailey simply nodded.

"It's not what you think."

"It's not? You do know that all Albert and Sparky do is put damn dating and hook-up charts together. I think they even place bets with some of the rank and file. Plus, you can't bullshit me, sir. I know you like her. Just remember. When it's time to make the hard decisions, we can't let them be made for us."

The battle-hardened first sergeant was right. Being emotionally involved with other team or crew members could sway tactical decisions, a lesson both men had learned at a young age, and one that had put the scar that adorned Becket's face from his hairline down to his hardened chin.

Dailey clicked on his communicator. "Go ahead." He didn't mute the conversation or send it to the earpiece tucked in his pocket.

"You in the shower or something?" Jen asked as Dailey rolled his eyes and Becket grinned.

"No, but I probably need to at some point. What's up?"

"Everyone's set in the drop bays. I—" She hesitated. "I just wanted to check in with you and see how things are going. I've been jammed in that attack fighter for hours."

There was an invitation in her voice that Dailey hadn't heard since their last encounter in his quarters. Taking a steadying breath, the *Murphy*'s captain picked up his tablet, looking at the jumble of written notes shifting under the powerful recognition software loaded on the device. Not only had it turned their voice and written notes into a list but the table had also put together a proposed timeline. He would need to delete the later part of the conversation, only having shut the voice function off halfway through.

"Just working through the next part of this clown show," Dailey replied.

"Well, if you need any help, let me know. I'll be in the briefing room in twenty," Jen said, signing off.

"You totally got a girlfriend," Becket accused, followed up by a quick, "Sir."

"I don't have a . . ." Dailey breathed, stopping midsentence. "Shit. I'll shelf whatever it is till later. No distractions." Standing up, Dailey dropped a handful of credits into the empty tip jar at the end of the bar.

Unlike their previous planning meeting, the briefing room was packed like an overzealous clown car. Besides the standby pilots assigned to the bay, every person certified to fly an attack fighter lined the walls, joined by their Nova Ranger counterparts.

Dorax, Bellman, Sparky, and the rest of the temporary crew of the *Crow* sat in the front row. Squinting, Dailey noticed the outline of an ominous, hastily added crow on their uniforms. Thanks to the sizable airlock and the nanotech included aboard both ships, Albert and Bellman had been able to create a connection between the two vessels, including the ability of the *Crow* to generate an electromagnetic atmosphere bubble, allowing for a small cargo hauler to maneuver between the two spacecrafts via a ramp.

Before he could ask, Albert decided to kick the meeting off.

"Hello, ladies and gentlemen." Albert paused, glancing at Lambert, before correcting himself. "Ladies and whatever he is." The young private had made a name for himself. A name that was synonymous with his ability to offend most of his teammates and, much to his surprise, generally anything or anyone who breathed.

The funny thing about it was his fellow Rangers egging him on for the sheer enjoyment of watching other people outside their tribe being offended by the young man.

Albert started back up. "We are gathered here today—" Dailey cut him off.

"Alright, no speeches today, Albert. Maybe next time we can get some entrance music," Dailey joked before realizing he had likely made a mistake that he would pay for later with the recommendation.

Becket walked in a few seconds later, having stopped to talk to one of the *Murphy*'s weapon technicians. "Alright, everyone. Sit the hell down and shut the hell up. That is, unless you outrank me. Then carry on."

The man knew how to set the mood, and as was tradition in the Army, even the officers respected the senior-most enlisted soldier on their team.

Dailey laid out the plan for the next thirty minutes, generating only minimal questions. Even Becket was shocked by the amount of buy-in the team was giving him. In all fairness, they also fully understood the advantage Albert gave them in a fight. That, and the Alurian dreadnaught, fresh off the lot it had been latched onto like a newborn to its mother.

The next major step in the operation was to reach out and talk with the senator and the team on Asher. Once they arrived at their next stop, they would stage the force and make the call.

Once stopped, they would relay the plan and timeline to the Gulch via a small gate and wait for a sign that confirmed they were tracking and able to support the plan. If not, Dailey and the crew would resort to their favorite pastime: justified violence.

Jen leaned against the wall beside the command team with Sparky leaning on her foot while Albert adjusted the holo-table's 3D rendering of the battle plan to match the timeline. Dailey caught himself glancing at her on and off, trying not to be obvious but only making her realize what he was doing, generating a sly grin gently resting on her face.

With no more questions, the plan was set. They would get the team on Asher to partake in a covert mission to secure the laser on the moon while Dailey and the others took on the Alurian battle group.

From there, the team would reconsolidate and either send the dreadnaught directly into the middle of the Alurian fleet, self-detonating it, or they would use every tool at their disposal to sneak into their ranks like a Trojan horse and start the fight from inside their hive right next to the queen bee. This also included figuring out how to fire the planet-scraping laser directly into the mass of ships while doing so as another form of distraction.

CHAPTER 19

HOW TIME FLIES

H e wants us to do what?" Mac asked, walking up to Master Sergeant Walker. The rest of the newly formed alliance on Asher glared at the main screen like kids from old movies huddling around the family TV on a Saturday morning.

A layout of the timeline Dailey and the others had put together flashed, followed by a set of instructions. In the corner, a pulsing banner instructed its reader to hit the *X* button to enter the lobby. It was Albert's unbelievably simplistic yet effective way of encrypting messages using old multiplayer video games.

"Send them a signal we are good with the plan. Once we do that, the clock starts," Walker replied, winking at Mac.

Petty Officer Miller walked up to the two appointed leaders of the Gulch with Vax close behind. "I just talked with the Sergeants Grear and Coolio. They're ready to send a drone up. If everything goes without a hitch, we can send them a full-on reply, as well as our sensor data from the battle group parked overhead."

Dax cleared his throat. "Might I suggest we find a way to get into orbit without being vaporized?" The man had a way of sucking all the energy out of a room, but he had just made a good point while doing so. Vax walked over to the control panel, punching in several commands, making the still active mining cargo ships appear on the display map of Asher.

"If Dailey says he will cause a distraction, I believe him. We only need to focus on getting off-planet. Sergeant Grear, am I correct in stating your armor's thrusters can take you to the Parif?" She was saying the name by which the planet's inhabitants called the moon lingering in the night sky above Asher.

"Time's the issue." Walker layered onto her comment like a thick coat of paint. "Once we send that relay probe into orbit, we must be ready to move." The man stared at the floating cargo ships Vax had populated the screen with. "Are you proposing we load up on a cargo ship?"

Vax smiled. The pale white skin stretched to her eyes. After spending time aboard the *Murphy*, she was proud to contribute to the operation. "Yes. I think we could get a jump start. I'm unsure how connected that battle group is to Parif."

"Well, at least it's not a fleet up there. It looks like two of the four ships that gated haven't come back yet. I'm guessing they ran into the *Murphy*," Walker said, turning to the group. "Listen up. We send the relay drone and two fire teams from Fourth Foot into orbit simultaneously," Walker instructed, getting his head back in the game. He turned to Bringum Flint, one of the engineers from Kodas. "I need to know the fastest and safest way to get our teams to one of those cargo ships. Any ideas?"

Bringum, being the engineer he was, cocked his head, looking up into the dark vaulted ceiling. "We have already identified several high-speed trams in close proximity," the man started grumbling, pulling out a small tablet and punching in a flight-log request. "There is a cargo ship set to launch in ten hours. According to the timeline on the screen, that would meet the mission's timeline tolerance levels."

Walker nodded at Grear and Coolio, and both men headed toward the main staging area the rest of the remaining Nova Rangers from the once-upon-a-time, famed Fourth Foot called home for day-to-day operations. Mac, also knowing the drill, turned to the larger display, setting the rest of the timeline that had just been lightly put together with slow-drying glue.

Engineering Petty Officer Miller motioned for Walker to join him in front of the communications section. "How do you want to play this?" the man asked while the sounds of the rest of the group shuffled into various corners of the control room.

"According to the message, they want us to seize the mining laser and turn it on the battle group. Which means we'll likely need to take a few of these engineers from Kodas with us, and yourself, if you think it's needed."

Miller pondered the statement, wondering if they could control the laser from the planet's surface. That was the entire point of the control room. "Too much risk getting everything to line up. I'll take the trip and see if we can get a few of those pencil pushers to grow a pair."

Both men chuckled, only to stop after realizing that most of the engineers in the control room were built like athletes. Focused in body and mind, the engineers were the type that not only figured out problems but also executed them.

After several hours of planning and maneuvering forces, the team was set to execute phase one of their plan. Miller's message to the *Murphy* was straightforward, explaining they would likely already be on the moon by the time they started a distraction, something Dailey and the others would greatly appreciate, giving them some operational breathing room, as Becket called it.

One glaring issue making itself known was the battle group shifting orbit, moving toward the far end of the planet, away from Arcadia. This was likely due to the massive weapons the Alurians were very much aware of.

With the outer portions of Arcadia in flames, the newly formed planetary alliance on Asher understood they had to succeed. After a few short seconds of transmitting, which had been all that was needed, the relay drone had been destroyed.

Staff Sergeant Grear shuffled in his seat as a bead of unwanted sweat was quickly evaporated by his helmet's internal-environment control systems, or as the Nova Rangers lovingly called it, the ASAS. Better known as: the anti–swamp ass system.

Instead of cramming into the cargo ship's bridge, they had opted to stow the Rangers away in the actual cargo bay, void of a proper atmosphere. Two Kodas engineers, including Petty Officer Miller, were situated on the small bridge in regular space suits.

The dull metal of the craft's interior looked rusted in the ambient light the ODA suits put off. Small droplets of water resembling a light sweat clung to its walls after being opened while in its underground home.

Unlike the Nova Rangers' prior trip underground, this one had been mostly uneventful, the main obstacle being the tram no longer servicing the area due to it being completely automated.

Coolio held up his tracking tablet, wiping off a layer of condensation before showing it to Grear in an effort to pass the nerve-racking gap in time from orbit to the literal dark side of the moon. From there, they had triangulated a valley that led into what appeared to be an access shaft they would briefly divert the ship toward.

"Ten minutes," Coolio breathed out, having counted down every annoying one. "They'll be here when the time comes." He worked to not only convince himself but also the others.

Grear nodded, also needing the affirmation. "If not, we will become official moon men."

Winters leaned forward. "Moon women? Anyone?" she joked.

Miller followed the two engineers into the cargo bay shaking his head.

"Moon *people.* You happy now?" Coolio grinned as she shook her head in return.

"Just making sure you guys know I'm not one of the boys," Winters replied. The banter, while commonplace between the team, seemed misplaced to the two from Kodas, who were taking it all in. They had never witnessed a military unit poking fun at each other in an attempt to calm their nerves before a fight.

Ringer, one of the additional Nova Rangers, cut in. "Oh yeah. She's a woman, alright."

Winters shook her head. "You wouldn't know a woman—" Grear cleared his throat, shutting down the exchange.

The cargo vessel was set to gate shortly after passing the moon and making a close flyby of the designated area, one of the many parameters Bringum had taken into consideration when picking a ride. With no true viewports, they were at the mercy of the small nav sensor attached to the hull.

"Five minutes!" Grear barked through his communicator, standing up. The whirl of servos and gears went back into motion, breaking the rest of the team's reflective silence. Activating his mag boots, the lack of gravity spread a plume of dust in front of his helmet's light, the dusty interior adding to the grimy vibe of the cargo ship.

Much to the man's surprise, instead of tagging along as excess baggage, the engineers, being who they were, were utterly mesmerized by the entire flying-through-space ordeal they were about to partake in. They had even bugged Miller to exhaustion when asking about all the space suits' capabilities. Dana, a young woman on the team, had done several manual calculations, verifying she would live, before agreeing to participate.

The hissing *whoosh* of a rusty airlock cracked like someone opening a canned soda as flecks of condensation showered the ship's interior. Parif slowly passed under the vessel's belly, blocking Asher's reflective light, now hiding the glow of thrusters from the Alurian battle group.

Grear held up his hand, being the first to activate the small thruster pack attached to the back of the two-piece automated laser turret strapped to his armor. Being one of two orbital drop leaders from the *Murphy*'s crew, Grear knew the routine inside and out.

Knowing that communicating with the planet would be equivalent to jumping into shark-infested waters with a freely bleeding wound, the team had switched to a single internal channel.

Coolio and two other Rangers walked to the engineers, connecting themselves via a nano-alloy tether. Jumping or, as was in most cases, floating out of a spaceship onto a planet below was the Nova Ranger's bread and butter. To put it into perspective, they loved that shit more than they enjoyed getting into a good fight. It was even better if the two were combined.

Miller was moderately used to the practice of tethering to a Ranger. The moderately part was him only doing it during training in deep space, which didn't include an actual surface landing. The man gulped, knowing once the Rangers went into motion, there would be no turning back.

The engineers were in full-on geek mode, analyzing and taking in the entire process. Grear cut over the radio, putting himself in the role of drop master, "Ten seconds. Five seconds between drops."

Finally seeing the designated landing location, Grear grabbed a thin rifle with a beacon on the end, floating lightly. Attaching it to the swiveling mount on his shoulder, he locked in the location through his HUD, firing the beacon. "Locations are locked on your onboard nav systems. Five, four, three, two, one!"

Grear watched as two of the single Nova Rangers plunged out of the airlock. Not having a gravity field around the vessel made the event less exciting than usual, as the engineers expected something more dramatic. They would, however, get their wish the closer they got to their target.

The entire team flowed through space for two minutes as their onboard nav systems directed their thrusters on autopilot. With a whip and a snap, the entire group turned, seeing the cargo ship wink out of existence after entering a gate.

CHAPTER 20

MOONRAKER

Coolio continued to scan the surrounding mid-sized glowing dull white mountain range on the atmosphere lacking massive rock. Remnants of the *Brightstar* lay strewn like a trail of breadcrumbs in several directions, all leading to the confirmation they needed.

On a ridge three kilometers away, several communications towers topped with caps resembling the planet's rocky surface jutted out of the desolate landscape. To the left of the array was a smaller collection of rocks that led into the now visible ground-level entrance. Resembling a cave, they engineerhad identified the entrance from the vents and airlocks leading into the larger mountain behind and a set of disappearing tire tracks leading directly inside.

The team had been split into two smaller groups. For this mission, they had assigned one group of Rangers to support the engineers. Or as Specialist Banksy put it: babysitting.

"Coolio, anything on the reverse scan?" Grear asked, magnifying the video feed in front of him. One cool feature of all the Ranger's armor was the ability to switch between a video feed through their HUD or a regular, enhanced, and usually preferred view from their helmets. Not seeing any movement, Grear switched off the zoomed-in video feed.

"It's clear."

Coolio lowered the small, reinforced tablet mounted on his forearm. "Nothing's scanning for us. I think we are good to go."

With that, the team, using small booster thrusters attached to their mag boots, pushed along in large, low-gravity leaps. Weapons at the ready, the group happily arrived under the shadowed cover of the entrance.

The two lead fire teams spread out on either side of the wall while Grear launched an illumination pod down the long, empty corridor. Unlike the illumination grenades the Rangers mostly used, this system was set for stealth operations.

The pod bathed the far end of the entrance in a specific infrared pulse synched with the Rangers' HUD, letting them see. It was old yet time-tested Earth tech that the Solarians didn't figure out until the Federation introduced it.

Miller motioned for his team to stay put, unable to see like the others, while Coolio slipped into the dark abyss. After several short, butt-puckering seconds, a dot of light appeared at the end of the opening. Grear's voice jolted Miller even though he was expecting it like a slow-motion slap to the face. "All clear. I opened the airlock. The security system appears to not be working. Stay frosty. The facility is damaged."

The truth of the matter was that the dying *Brightstar* had caused significant harm to the underground facility. Ran and his crew had focused all their efforts on repairing the external communications array to send and receive messages, but the inside of the hidden moon base was a different story. Several sections had been destroyed after a chunk of the *Brightstar* slammed into its primary ship bays, effectively stranding them on the rugged landscape. It also meant all the primary security systems in the area the Rangers had entered were fully offline. That was also why Ran had placed several Alurian battle droids throughout the moon base's damaged sections.

Gravity slowly poured over the team, but the environment didn't fully stabilize until they passed through another round of airlocks. The audible *thump* of the team's mag boots deactivating echoed lightly through the dimly lit storage area they had quickly secured.

Grear motioned for two Rangers to cover the far end of the bay while Miller pulled out a small box, setting it on the ground. "Recon drone," Miller said. Grear nodded. They were fully aware the team would show up on a radar or security scan sooner rather than later.

A buzzing, palm-sized, insectlike drone whirled to life, floating directly in front of both men. Miller tapped a few commands on the tablet secured to his forearm, and a small blue light flashed. "Hit your synch button, and you should have video feed."

Grear nodded, having used the smaller drones on several boarding missions. Once linked, he could even share the live feed with the rest of his team. After a quick snap of static, the laser-sharp image of Miller's hand came to life.

By this time, the engineering team was already sifting through several crates. One of the more vocal Kodas engineers, named Filman, raised a hand. "Is this normal?"

Banksy walked to the crate, seeing Fleet markings on several rocket pods. The Kodas team had quickly become familiar with the symbol. After opening several more containers, the sheer amount of Fleet equipment became overly concerning, and another problem to add to the growing list of issues.

"Catalog what you can. We need to keep track of this stuff. It might be useful," Grear instructed, thinking about the able hands that could wield the misplaced weapons.

Miller cleared his throat as the drone signal beeped. Not only had it mapped out a large section of the damaged structure, but it had also pinged movement. "Look sharp," Grear ordered as the map appeared in the Rangers' HUDs.

Coolio checked the charge on his automatic laser rifle, followed by the EMP pulse grenade launcher attached to the bottom. Specialist Stacy Winters followed this by activating her targeting module. The safety of the two small rocket pods mounted on her armor's shoulders clicked off. The red lights told everyone around Winters she was a walking porcupine of death, which meant not to step in front of her.

Miller and Grear walked to the blast doors at the far end of the large room. Clicking a button, he projected the facility's layout on a flat wall. In the bottom corner, the drone's live video feed slowly panned around the room it had made its way to, mapping out the shadows.

Filman walked in front of the group, almost blocking the projection. "This is a utility corridor. If we take this route"—the man pointed to the far left, just out of the currently scanned space—"we will end up near the scraper. And . . ." he dragged out, "if we go this way"—he shifted to the opposite side of the layout—"we will have a direct shot to the command center. If you keep going straight, all that other stuff is living quarters and life support."

The others couldn't see Grear raise his eyebrows behind his helmet's visor. "How do you know all this?"

"It's basic design. We used to study this layout in engineering school. That included studying some of the other communities on Asher," Filman replied, using the newly crowned name for the planet. The other two engineers grumbled in agreement.

The mood quickly shifted as the drone's live feed winked out. At the same time, a red light flashed on Miller's tablet. He looked up, giving the universal sign for it being destroyed, dragging his thumb across his throat.

Figuring their time was limited, Grear turned to the internal blast doors. "If they don't know we're here, they will soon enough. Weapons hot. We have no friends here."

Private Donald Berks, a younger man in his twenties from Dallas, Texas, and Specialist Winters, a strong-willed woman from what was left of Detroit, Michigan, immediately started opening the door using what the Fleet referred to as barrage kits. One Ranger would smack the devices in three separate locations, and once activated, the small, round pucks seeped nanoparticles into the crack.

Once seated, the user would activate the particles, creating a silent, popping rush of energy, opening the doors enough for the other Ranger to slide a reverse-response actuator. Simply put, it would energize the door enough to send a signal, forcing it to open of its own nonexplosive free will. The entire action took no more than ten seconds.

The engineers again marveled at the tech as the Rangers moved at lightning-fast speeds, shuffling into the dark corridor. Grear slung an illumination grenade with the full might of his suit's servos, lighting the entire space to the far end. Coolio motioned for Miller and the others to stay on the other side of the blast doors in time to probably save their lives.

As soon as the Ateris security droids had destroyed the drone, they'd traced its signal back to the bay, moving directly toward the threat, a simple yet effective programming protocol.

Armor-piercing, hypercharged rounds erupted as the illumination grenade clunked off the flat armor plate of one of the security droids. Dozens of glowing bullets smacked into the Rangers as their pulse shields snapped into place. While able to deflect laser fire, the kinetic rounds punched hard, making several ringing *dings* echo.

Without hesitation, Grear started unleashing a spray of EMP rounds, allowing the targeting crosshairs in his HUD to guide him. The system was straightforward: a laser mounted on the barrel of the rifle reflected the exact location the weapon was pointing through his heads-up display.

Winters ducked left, avoiding a direct hit by more than one of the droids, as the thrusters mounted on the calf portion of her armor hissed to life. While doing this, she let loose a flurry of rounds into the transforming mass of moving metal.

Not to be outdone, she paused behind Staff Sergeant Grear long enough to set the range on a handful of the now hesitating droids. Coolio and Berks were laying down a wall of fire to keep them from focusing.

Specialist Winters quickly launched four of the small rockets as Grear, seeing the chance, chucked a scrambler grenade in front of them, further confusing the security droids' sensors.

The mix of EMP rounds and the contained explosion of the mini rockets brought the entire fight to a screeching halt. Unlike the high-explosive mini rockets others like Dailey carried, these were specifically designed for close-quarters combat, allowing for a rapid explosion followed by the sucking pullback of an aftershock.

Berks and Winters held their weapons at the ready, moving forward, while the jumbled mass of robots twitched and sparked. Seeing one of the droids working to shake off the violence, Winters pulled out a small, flat EMP grenade, chucking it in the middle of the pile. A blue streak flowed through the doomed scrap heaps.

"Everyone good?" Grear asked, seeing green dots on the upper left of his HUD, showing all his Rangers were indeed intact. Thumbs-up were given as Miller stepped from behind the blast doors.

Turning, he saw the faces behind the engineers' face masks. All three of them stood there, taking in the overwhelming and immediate violence the Rangers had just displayed.

It wasn't that they didn't believe they were capable of such feats. Instead, it was the immediate flip of the switch from giving each other a hard time to displaying a laserlike attack on a group of security droids that would have likely ripped through dozens, if not hundreds, of regular people.

"Hey, Winters," Coolio called, stepping forward as she turned. "Leg," he pointed out. She glanced down as far as her armored helmet would allow.

Quickly running a system scan, she noticed the armor plating on her right shin had degraded by five percent. Coolio could see the eight to nine large pits, looking as if someone had poked their fingers into a container of fresh Play-Doh.

"You were just checking me out," Winters quickly replied as the two grinned, looking at the pile of security droids.

"Always," he replied as Grear motioned them to secure the access door they had come through.

"Clear," Coolio whispered over the comms, somehow forgetting they had just caused enough of a ruckus to raise the dead.

The group entered and quickly secured the secondary payload-transfer station. Swiftly scanning the area, the team realized the significantly improved condition of the large room.

"You think they know we're here now?" Miller asked, pulling up a small scanning sensor. If there were cameras in the area, he would be able to detect them.

Grear stood resolute, listening through the enhanced hearing device he had just activated. While nothing out of a spy novel, the device would allow a simple amplification of the immediate area around the suit's wearer. It mainly dampened ambient noise, allowing things such as machines or the clack of weapons to take center stage.

The squad leader shook his head. "No . . ." he drawled out, working through the team's next steps. "No, we are likely in an abandoned area they dumped a few security droids in. They would have set off some kind of alarm if they were being tracked."

Everyone nodded in agreeance, knowing the only other option was a trap. Dana, having been oddly silent since entering the facility, stepped forward after waving an energy spike sensor around the intersection of a few corridors.

"I can confirm the main weapon core is fully functional and to our left. I set the sensor inputs to match that of the security droids. There does not appear to be any more in the immediate area. I support Staff Sergeant Grear's hypothesis. I can also state I believe they are remotely firing the device from a command module. If this is a standard scraper, we should be able to control it from the manual overrides in the control room."

Grear glanced at Coolio, whose shoulders dropped. He knew what was coming next. "Coolio . . . Banksy. I need you to escort the engineers to the weapons station. I know it's not ideal, and I wish we had a full company to take this station over, but we don't. Miller, are we good?"

Miller pulled up his rifle, motioning the other engineers to do the same. They had been instructed to not engage or use their weapons until necessary. According to Grear, everything after their splitting up was weapons hot. "Roger, we got this. Just don't leave our asses hanging out too long."

The men had a mutual respect for each other, which only years of working together created. Miller was letting the Nova Ranger know he had limited faith in their ability to survive for long if attacked.

Dana, picking up on this, again spoke up. "If we can make it to the control room by the scraper, we should be able to secure ourselves. It is designed to withstand attack if adequately locked down."

"I suggest doing that," Grear said, turning to the rest of his team, motioning them to maneuver toward the command center.

CHAPTER 21

SILENT NIGHT

S ir, something's pinging the security droids in sector five," Lashet, the station's Alurian first officer, said as Ran and Derrisa stood in front of the main viewscreen showing the Alurian battle group.

"Something?" Ran asked, motioning to have the Alurian pull up the station's schematics.

"More of a lost signal about five minutes ago. The environment is stable. We lost the droids when they left the main corridor leading out of the secondary off-loading bay." Lashet paused, seeing Ran needed further explanation.

Sighing, Lashet started back. The green accent of his cheeks turned a darker shade, an emotional reaction Alurians had when they were getting annoyed, much like a human turning red. Most Alurians didn't like being second-guessed or questioned by a Syndicate human. "That means they left their assigned sector, where we could track them, due to a disturbance or issue in the damaged area."

"We don't have a video feed up yet in that sector. Send a squad of men to check it out. If the droids don't show back up in five minutes, put the base on lockdown protocol," Ran instructed.

While the man knew that Dailey was probably not around, he wasn't taking any chances, knowing the chaos even one platoon of Nova Rangers could create.

Derrisa huffed lightly. "I don't see any ships on the main radar display."

Ran smirked at the woman. "That's what's bothering me. If we do have a problem, it may be a real problem. There is a confirmed small group of Nova Rangers on Asher. Do not count them out."

"I'm sure we will be able to handle them when the time comes," Derrisa replied, walking off while activating her communicator.

Ran wasn't as convinced. Most of the Syndicate's security team had been lost when the *Brightstar* was destroyed. Between several stray munitions making their way to the moon's surface and a massive chunk of Ran's former ship slamming directly into the security team's staging area, the damage had almost been catastrophic to the station.

While he could probably convince the Alurian battle group to send a detail to the moon, he also knew he wanted as few Alurians as possible around his operation.

Ran walked to Lashet. "Any word from the security detail?"

"They are leaving the main command section as we speak. I would give them ten minutes to get to sector five." The Alurian flashed over to a camera overlooking at least two dozen men.

Even though they were called security, the team was, in reality, full of highly trained paramilitary shock troopers receiving paychecks from the Syndicate. However, only wearing light infantry assault armor and carrying an assortment of kinetic bullet-firing rifles, only one fully armored Nova Space Ranger was needed to give the small crowd a run for their money.

"Send a few drones out as well. I know we were saving them, but I would rather not take the chance," Ran replied, not using his regular cadence of assholeness with the Alurian.

Taken aback by this, Lashet nodded, following the instructions. "Done. We have two drones heading out. They will arrive a few minutes before the team."

Satisfied, Ran nodded. "While we're at it, also repurpose a team of security droids to this command center."

"Agreed," Derrisa added, overhearing the command as she placed her communicator in the small pocket inside her Syndicate uniform. She had not only changed but was starting to catch on to Ran's well-placed paranoia. "I just checked in with the battle group, since we are getting to know each other. We bounced the shipping schedule from the planet against their sensors."

"And?" Ran asked as she adjusted her belt, ensuring the others saw the blaster neatly affixed to her hip.

"No anomalies. Business as usual. You're a lot of things, General Ran," she started, using his old title for no reason other than to get his attention, letting the others know she was serious. "But wanting to be dead is not one of them."

"I suppose that is a compliment," Ran replied, as Derrisa nodded.

The woman walked over to a group of communications personnel, handing one of them a prerecorded message. "Perhaps. I agree things are too quiet. We are, in effect, just waiting for them to inevitably come to us. We know several pockets of the planet's population went underground. Firing the scraper will do nothing more than to drive more into the planet's substructure."

Ran also nodded with a mutual show of respect. "The message?"

"I am sending a report to the high office. We need them to check depot four-two. It's likely the *Murphy* is there, or at least used the area as a gate point. I am also sending a full status report."

Ran clearly disapproved, scowling as she motioned to let her explain. Derrisa clicked a few buttons as a fresh image of the Alurian battle group appeared on the main viewscreen, stretching from floor to ceiling.

"Between the battle group and the depot recently, I am concerned that the Ocess Syndicate may make a move. Since we already have the funding, it wouldn't hurt to have an Ateris military squadron to help support us at this station specifically."

"Agreed," Ran replied as they both watched the flurry of attack fighters flying in and out of the leading space cruiser. "We aren't scheduled to meet with the battle group commander till tomorrow. I want to get any issues here resolved before zero one hundred."

Lights and ambient noise continued to steadily grow brighter and louder as the small team of Rangers bypassed what appeared to be the final set of blast doors before reaching the main facility. Winters held up a small sensor pod, trying to get a reading on the other side of the massive doors with no luck.

"How long to bypass them?" Grear asked, starting to get operationally anxious. He didn't like standing around.

"Another couple of minutes," a concentrating Private Berks replied. Unlike the other blast doors, this set was on the main facility's power and control grid. This meant once they disabled these, they were in for a fight.

The light *clank* of something in the adjacent air duct froze the team as if staring into the eyes of Medusa. Weapons were focused as the unmistakable sound of a drone buzzing in the ductwork was amplified by the lack of anything else surrounding it to absorb the noise.

Grear, taking the lead, ripped into the tube-shaped air duct attached to the top of the angled wall as red lights and alarms shrieked into existence. By the time the Nova Rangers had identified the threat, it was too late.

The tiny drone, similar in design to the one Miller had used, had already mapped out the other side of the blast doors, transmitting the data to a now laser-focused Ran. Distracted by the alarms and the drone zipping out of a slit in one of the grill plates, the team was not paying attention when three of the Ateris shock troops blew out a panel on the side wall, which clearly had an access tunnel on the other side, several meters from where they had been moments ago.

As Winters and Grear turned to cover the team still working on the blast door, it immediately dawned on Grear that opening the door would likely introduce another shitstorm to the party. As the thought made its way to his lips, the door started opening, followed by an onslaught of bullets whipping through the gap.

"Shut it off!" Grear barked. Berks, seeing no alternative, gave the panel a much-needed middle finger as he pulled out his ripper. The Moshan blade was a favorite among the hand-to-hand combat weapons of the Nova Rangers. It was made of high-quality Moshan steel with a rectified edge, creating a laserlike blade able to cut into and through armor.

After two quick whack-a-mole blows, Berks smashed the panel in, using the servos in his armored hands, before depositing a small grenade directly in the blast door's controls.

After a hammering pop and ceremonial slinging of debris from the once usable panel, the blast doors came to a screeching halt. Looking back, Grear could make out the remaining gap, barely large enough to squeeze his fully armored team through.

Several bullets tinged off his helmet, forcing him to turn back to what he determined to be goons popping in and out of the hole in the corridor like a group of drunk prairie dogs taking turns. Grear refocused his efforts, activating his forward shield as the blue disk erupted from his forearm.

Noticing that the only thing being thrown at them so far were bullets, the man charged the hole in the wall, latching his Sauder rifle on his back and pulling up a sleek laser blaster incorporated into his armor.

Winters covered the man, firing directly at the gap with single-focused shots from her rifle. Neither she nor the team had switched to regular rounds from their loaded EMP ammunition. In all reality, the bullets still got the job done on soft targets, just not as effective.

The violence was quick and shocking to the three goons leaning against the wall. The last thing they all witnessed was a massively bulky Nova Ranger appearing in the opening through the haze. Grear's blue shield took several shots from the doomed crew before the Ranger let loose several precise spatters of fire from his blaster.

While typical lasers didn't create much in the way of blood, a blast at close range did. Even though the weapon still cauterized the wound, the initial punch was the equivalent of a shotgun smacking into their armored plates at point-blank range. Even more unlucky for the doomed Ateris goons was the precision with which Grear used his weapons. He didn't aim for the chest or the head, but instead, at close range, opted for soft spots such as the neck and underarms.

Blood spattered the access tunnel as lurching, final groans were lost to the sounds of gunfire from the corridor. Grear, quickly realizing his visor was sprinkled with blood, pulled down a small screen, wiping off the gore. The rest of his armor would have to wait till later.

Walking out of the opening like a victorious gladiator, Grear launched himself forward, activating the thrusters on his back calves. Joining the rest of the team, the growling pop of the grenade he threw in the tunnel slung debris and smoke into the corridor.

Ran looked up from the viewscreen, watching the chaos unfold from their side of the blast doors as several security droids marched into the room. "Lock down the station."

Lashet, not in the mood to meet a group of Nova Rangers, complied without hesitation before speaking up. "That team, or anyone else outside the inner perimeter, will not be able to get back in until we turn the lock-down protocols off."

Impenetrable blast doors protecting the command section erupted from the main corridor's substructure. Luckily for Miller and his team, they had already made their way to the inner control room of the scraper.

Derrisa chimed in, being her usually chipper self. "That's why they had death insurance. Unfortunately, they will not receive it if they are at the losing end of the battle or if Ateris property is damaged due to their negligence. Those men knew what they signed up for. There's a reason they're not in here controlling things."

She was reassuring the rest of the station's crew they would not be in the same situation, while also letting them know it was part of their contract with the Syndicate to fight to the death.

CHAPTER 22

THE LONG AND WINDING NAVIGATION POINT

Albert sat staring at the viewscreen beside Sparky in their secret lair onboard the *Murphy*. While everyone knew they had taken over a custodial closet, it was unclear what they did there. The only known mystery from the room was Albert's love-connection wall, which connected the team's romantic entanglements, as he liked to call them.

Lessons had been learned. The next time—if there was a next time—any civilization encountered an all-seeing, maybe all-knowing artificial intelligence, it would be highly recommended to not have one of the first things they scan be Solarian or human dating shows from the past hundred or so years.

"Can you believe Dorax has been talking to Pearl nonstop since they boarded the *Crow*? I swear I saw them making eyes," Albert professed. Sparky burped, shaking his head.

After a few snorts, Sparky finally let his opinion be known. "I smell the magic ham god."

"Hmm," Albert pondered. "You're saying Master Chief Thron and Pearl are rolling in the Solarian hay sprouts? That's scandalous!"

"If the pants fit, wear them," Sparky followed as Mister Toaster's face smirked.

"If the shoe fits . . . Never mind. You just smelled ham on her—" A loud knock interrupted the universe-altering conversation.

"You two decent in there?" Captain Ben Dailey asked loud enough to be heard through the metal door.

Without pausing, he hit the lock override before Albert could act. Albert and Sparky shuffled to drop the sheet they had set up to cover their love chart, only to have it fall on the Alurian war hound's head. Sparky tried running from under the sheet in a last-ditch effort to hide their predictions, only to pull it completely off.

The resulting scene was as expected. Albert sat on the ground with the sheet covering his shoulders as Sparky sat still like a ghost about to haunt an old house. A small grabber jutted from Albert's arm, quickly pulling the sheet off them as if sucked into a vacuum cleaner.

"You know . . ." Dailey started, shaking his head. "The two of you have destroyed, what? Three, four Alurian destroyers. Sparky, you blew up an Alurian depot by flying a cargo ship with a nuke in its bay into the belly of the beast. And you, Albert, don't get me started with you. I'm starting to think you built the damn pyramids."

Mister Toaster huffed with indifference. Dailey squinted his eyes while Albert followed suit, making the locking-his-lips-and-throwing-away-the-key motion before responding. "Saying it like that, you might just be right about how awesome we are."

"Well, if you two are done being awesome for now." Dailey shifted gears, seeing a picture of him and Jen connected with a string. Drawn above him with robotlike precision, several hearts represented Dailey's assumed feelings toward Lieutenant Jenny Brax. "Dorax and Pearl have asked to go to the bridge on the *Crow*. They think they can get more systems online."

Albert and Sparky looked at each other, glancing at the printed pictures of Dorax and Pearl beside each other. The fact that they weren't connected by a line stated they could not confirm the relationship but assumed one may likely be brewing.

"Sounds like the little bridge we set up isn't cozy enough. I can't fault their logic. I checked about thirty minutes ago: most of the *Crow* is habitable; it's just that most of the secondary systems are offline."

"Like what?" Dailey asked, inspecting the eyebrow-raising relationship layout before finally turning away.

"Oh, things like the medical bay, food and water processing plants, and last, a secondary drive system. I'm betting they have some super-secret drive onboard, but I'd have to be plugged directly into it to tell; security blocks, and all that jazz. And, last but not least, the mech bay. It's all in the report."

"What report?"

"The one I uploaded when we got back, duh."

Sparky chuffed. "Mine."

Dailey nodded, understanding that he should probably start reading Albert's annoying updates. The AI was ignoring the fact that he wrote and uploaded anywhere between thirty to forty reports an hour, including everything from essential system updates to who was taking a longer than needed break, and for how long.

"We should have enough time," Albert said as the clang of Sparky putting his armor on interrupted the conversation.

Dorax and Pearl met Albert, Sparky, Dailey, and a handful of engineers in front of the tram directly outside the secondary bay they had called home until now. Pearl nodded at the Alurian, shrugging.

The tram was a mix of an elevator and a transportation monorail, large enough to fit one of the dozen or so transport carts with a full load. Dorax stepped beside Albert. "We want to see more of the ship while we have time. There's nothing more we can do here. We all agree we need a quick exit route, and this bay may be our best option, but I want to see if it's close to the bridges on the older, similar ships I grew up around."

"Albert, can we get a video feed from here?" Dailey asked while the team loaded the tram.

"It's all in the report. But, since you're asking, while we have a layout of the ship from the security-data banks, since the ship is all compartmentalized, I would not be able to activate and access the bridge's video feed unless we turned it on. Simply put, the power cells will not be fully charged for some time. We have enough power to fire up the bridge, but it will take several more days to fully bring it online, not to mention all the programming, yada, yada, yada,"

The new elevator silently went into motion, instantly hitting its full running speed. A small viewport was the only thing letting its riders know they were actually in motion.

The rest of the short trip's conversation revolved around the plan once they arrived back on Asher, followed by several beeps from Dailey's communicator. He had sent a message to the senator to relay communications at a set time before exiting the gate.

Fifteen minutes later, including two unprogrammed stops, the team stood before the plated entrance doors as they slowly parted. The mix of smells, from fresh plastics to recently welded metals, greeted the group as Sparky trotted into the hazy bridge.

"Not this time," Pearl said, freezing the pup in his tracks. Pearl rarely used this voice. Dailey, not used to this, cocked his head when Sparky turned back, looking at the both of them. "There will be no further claiming or marking of this ship while Dorax and I are in command."

The oddity of the situation was her being deadpan serious. Albert's toast-is-done bell dinged as Sparky chuffed, bowing his head. "Of course, Commander."

Sparky was a lot of things, but dumb wasn't one of them, emphasizing the word *commander*, even pushing the translation speaker to let the word carry weight.

In general, Solarians were a profoundly proud race. According to Dailey, they took things such as leadership and command to an annoyingly serious level. This was one of the foundations of the Solarian military and why it was steeped in such rich, time-honored military tradition.

The top level of the bridge was more of a catwalk overlooking the other levels of the large room. Taking the lead, Albert activated several lights and a secondary platform lift that went from the top floor to the central command section like a spine.

Each floor of the bridge wrapped around the center, resembling ribs, furthering the almost organic layout of the space. On the bottom floor, a clear commander's thronelike station was offset by two other seats surrounded by blank panels and buttons in various thrown-up patterns.

Unlike most Fleet bridges, the *Crow's* was built into the body of the ship, with only its roof exposed to the outside. In front of the rib cage, a screen stretched from the bottom floor, almost reaching the ceiling, similar to the one that Ran had on Parif's moon base.

Using a touristy, commercial voice, Albert started giving a guided tour after plugging into a panel on the far end of the catwalk. "And to your left, you will see the viewscreen."

Dorax headed toward the lift as Dailey cut off Albert's likely four-hour-long overture on the structural flaws in the design of the bolts holding the railing together. "Get to the important stuff we need to know."

"Oh, right. The bridge consists of four levels. Each, as you can see, is consolidated into sections. Top level, ship logistics and primary systems.

Level three consists of space-aviation controls and stations. Level two, communications and intelligence. Last, the bottom level behind the lift is for targeting, shields, and droid control stations, which could probably activate the mechs. The two recessed sections, surrounded by another row of stations on the main level, are navigation on the left and weapons control on the right."

Dorax ran his hand along the commander's chair. He wasn't admiring the craftsmanship but rather connecting to a part of his species he had never seen. The Alurian raider had grown up in oversized, ancient transport ships and desolate outer-rim planets mined before humankind had invented the wheel.

"How many people would it take to run all this?" Dorax asked with a thoughtful voice.

"Well, considering I put most of the systems you need on autopilot, not many. But, say you wanted to use the entire ship to the best of its abilities without any help from yours truly, then I would say thirty. Ten to twenty with the crew of the *Murphy*, based on experience and the closeness of the crew."

Sparky snorted a dog version of a laugh, walking over to one of the command chairs and taking a seat. Dailey turned to Dorax and Pearl. "Tell you what. We don't blow this thing up in all this mess, and we'll staff it."

Dorax nodded, almost letting a slight smile slip from the edges of his mouth. To date, no one had seen the Alurian grin. Under the dark cover of night, however, the truth was he had, in fact, smiled while prepping Moshan mungles, an alien version of potatoes that resembled a banana in texture.

Often called a ground fruit, mungles were considered a treat on Earth due to their exotic status. On the outer rims, however, it was for the less fortunate. Able to grow in harsh conditions, it wasn't that it wasn't good, just overly abundant. Thron had even made a special dessert with it for the humans onboard, being left untouched by the other races.

Albert's toast-is-done bell chimed, echoing through the large chamber. The group turned to see the AI plugged into a panel on the con.

"I don't like interesting," Dailey repeated, checking the time. "We hit our final stop soon. Is this one of those interesting, super-cool things, or one of those interesting, I-think-we-have-a-problem kinda stuff?"

"Well, boss," Albert said, still chewing on whatever data he had intercepted. "I think I have an idea about the drive installed on the ship, and I must say, this one is something I didn't even think was possible."

Everyone stood still, waiting for him to continue. This was a thing he and Sparky both did. They explained it as pausing for dramatic effect, something they had learned from several of the movies and TV shows they had been watching.

"Okay, I'll spare you having to ask. It appears that once it's fully operational, the intent of this ship's navigation system is to be able to change gate locations while in . . . well, innerspace. This isn't a normal ship, if that makes it easier for everyone to understand."

"More planets to claim," Sparky chuffed as Dailey glanced at Pearl, motioning her over.

"Before you say it, yes, this may change my plans." Dailey paused, having both Albert and Sparky nod in approval of his use of dramatic effect. The *Murphy*'s commander didn't intend it as such, while he started thinking through the possible long-term uses of the ship.

Dorax spoke up, seeing the transaction. "You were going to use the ship as a feint and blow it up either way in the middle of the battle group, weren't you," the Alurian asked in the form of a statement.

Albert chimed in. "He totally was. President Sparky and I . . . well mostly I, computed an eighty-nine percent chance of him doing so."

"You're going to have to inform the senator," Pearl added. It wasn't to try and convince Dailey to do so but to state the gravity, or for lack of a better term, the *opportunity* the ship posed for the Fleet.

"I'll let the senator know. In the meantime, I want all the information I can on this supposed drive." Dailey walked to the panel Albert was plugged into as the AI turned on the display, showing several alien schematics. "I need you on this. When you're back on the *Murphy*, I want you working on this."

Sparky started walking to the lift in the bridge's spine as the proximity alarm to their final destination before finally gating to Asher pinged.

CHAPTER 23

UNDER PRESSURE

The deep void of space greeted the newly formed monstrosity the crew was now calling the *Murphy's Crow*, a mix of both ships working in tandem under the direction of Albert. A generally nondestructive AI system who had a rather odd obsession with Solarian dating shows that were, in all reality, several hundred years old.

Becket walked into the drop bay as a mix of platoons shuffled around like a hive of bees, prepping the drop ships. Dailey, still having thirty minutes left before having to send a message to Senator Deborah Powell, marched into the organized chaos.

Lieutenant Cardinali and Master Sergeant Grantham, from their respective platoons, stood on the far end, laughing at an unheard joke. "Grantham!" Dailey barked. "Where's your boss?" He was referring to Lieutenant Ponce, the sometimes fearless leader of First Platoon.

"Sir!" Ponce responded, breaking out of a private conversation.

"I'm going to send a message to the team on Asher. I want you to be there. I'm starting to think we may need to do an orbital drop on Parif," Dailey suggested, already working through keeping the *Crow* in one piece.

Grantham whistled in a manner that Ponce knew all too well. The man wasn't going to have the conversation without his platoon leader. Truth be told, Dailey trusted Ponce with his own life, but at times, had unintentionally left him out of important conversations.

Grantham, Viper Company's drop leader, had ensured his significantly younger officer-in-charge was no longer left out of conversations such as the one about to be had. While Ponce was as rock solid as they came, the *Murphy*'s commander had grown up with Grantham through the ranks, not to mention through more combat operations than he could remember.

"One of those?" Ponce chuckled, trotting up to the group.

"Pretty much," Dailey said, smiling at the group in front of him. "Listen, things might change on the fly, and while I know you guys have things under control, I need you to be ready."

"Sounds like a drop op," Ponce noted as Dailey nodded.

"Possibly. I'm starting to think the more havoc we can cause in various locations, the better. I'm radioing Asher either way. I want to see what their status is and go from there. Just have your drop kits ready."

With that, the team nodded, heading off in various directions as Becket stood beside the *Murphy*'s commander. "Boss, don't get any bright ideas. That whole blowing-ships-up thing is kinda your deal." The grizzled first sergeant took in the shuffling bay before continuing. "A deal that has kept both of us and a hell of a lotta our people alive."

Dailey nodded without responding. Jen cut through the reflective silence, walking toward the two men in her flight suit. He unthoughtfully caught himself taking her in as Becket quickly nudged him, already knowing the situation.

"The attack wing is ready to roll." Jen smiled, followed by a salute. "I have two teams set up. One for an attack force in case we get into a dogfight, and the other if we need to go planetside."

Dailey nodded, knowing his crew was doing their jobs on cruise control. "You must have read my mind. Or just watched us talking to First Foot." Jen beamed a smile, telling him she had done both.

"We are as ready as we can be," Jen replied as several pilots walked out of the small briefing room expressly set aside for the attack wing.

The plan was to have the entire crew of both ships combat-ready by the time they reached their staging area before their final gate to Asher. They would take that time to make any final adjustments, or as Albert put it, "To kick the tires."

Thirty minutes later, Albert and the rest of the group gathered by Dailey in the main briefing room as Senator Deborah Powell's voice echoed over the loudspeakers.

"Yes, I can hear you," the senator replied after Albert had sent out an initial synch message. While highly complex in theory, Albert was using hundreds if not thousands of small pulses through the gate to communicate with the station he'd found back on Earth.

The one trick to the entire link was the group actively using the gate was the only side able to initiate the conversation. Once the long-distance high five, as Albert put it, was done, they could talk with relative ease.

"Good. We have twenty minutes before we arrive at our next destination. I just sent you an intel-update package. You should be able to open it from the station Albert wrote 'the dumb-dumb machine' on."

"Yes, that went over well with the local chancellor. I can read it later. How's it going?" the senator asked, wanting to gauge Dailey's overall feel for the current status of the operation.

"Things keep changing. I can state we have something that may be more important than a bunch of old cargo ships."

Dailey could hear the senator's breath as she took in the statement. "I trust you. But I need to know you are taking the Fleet's priorities into consideration."

The room all nodded. The newer people in the group didn't know how much respect the two having the conversation had for each other, figuring Dailey was giving the Fleet one of his usual middle fingers. The look on Becket and Pearl's faces told the truth of the situation. This was an open and honest conversation.

"If it wasn't this important, I absolutely wouldn't, and you know that. This is something different."

The senator didn't respond immediately, conversing with someone in the room. That someone was Staff Sergeant Rosco, a person who had, in their own time, been under Dailey's command.

"Understood," Powell replied. "I thought you would like to know the third-generation ships are ahead of schedule. We are putting them online in two weeks."

Dailey and the rest of the group stared at the blank screen like a kid in the back of a school bus driving away from home for the first time. While not an immediate fix, this meant support would soon be en route.

"Understood, ma'am. Is there anything else?" Dailey asked, wanting to wrap the conversation up and send a message to Asher.

"I need you and your crew to stay focused—"

Becket interjected before she could continue. This was his department, and the man knew something wasn't good by her shift in tone. "With all due respect, I've heard that before. What happened?" Becket asked with all the gravity he could muster.

The senator's sigh followed his words. "There was a major attack. The outer-rim Alurians hit Solaria. It's not good."

Dorax licked his greenish lips in a nervous motion. Pearl cocked her head as Senior Chief Thron took a breath that pumped out his chest like a balloon.

Dailey looked around his team, seeing everyone focused on the screen. "Tell us. We are all adults here."

"They somehow hit Theta with a gamma missile."

In that moment, you could not only hear a pin drop but would likely not be able to take a full breath, as the air had been sucked out of the room by the statement.

"Any survivors?" Thron asked quickly.

Deborah paused without the dramatic fanfare of Albert or Sparky. "It's gone." Silence took hold, like a funeral for an unliked family.

Theta was one of Solaria's five main capitals. Acting as the planet's main industrial hub, the thriving, busy city was the center of mining operations for the surrounding system. This would be the second major attack on a Federation planet in a short amount of time.

Thoughts of Orlando flashed through Dailey's mind, landing like a glob of melting ice cream sliding off the edges of his nerves. Over the past several decades, most—if not all—attacks had been carried out on remote outposts and desolate mining planets.

"Are they connected?" Dailey asked, already knowing the answer. Even Albert shuffled as Mister Toaster's face went flat. Sparky, sharing his partner in crime's mood, lightly sat on his hind legs, unlike his usual plop down on the floor.

Deborah's voice came back over the comms, resolute and still as only a practiced politician's could. "Yes. It's not up for debate. I can state that our intel teams don't believe this was done by Alurian raiders." The statement gave Dorax some room to breathe, and he slightly relaxed. "Both cities were held by the Torat Syndicate. From what I understand, they are no longer operational."

Unlike the Ocess and Ateris Syndicates, the Torat Mining Corporation was a dying organization that had recently had most of its territory absorbed. The fact that the Federation and a good portion of the general public were starting to understand the syndicates sordid history had emboldened the organizations like never before. They were no longer corporations, but rather mob-like space gangs.

Dailey turned, talking to the room. "Looks like we might have more than one fight on our hands." He paused, seeing Master Chief Thron, the *Murphy*'s lead culinary specialist and former warlord, wring his hands before the man snapped off the culinary badge he proudly displayed on his chest, setting it calmly on the table.

If you weren't looking, you wouldn't have noticed the motion. The Solarian's entire family was from Theta. The only saving grace for the man was the fact that his family had died many moons ago, which had been a contributing factor to his new profession. That, and a promise he had once made to the gods of Solaria.

At that very moment in time and space, the man decided to break that vow.

Dailey clicked the comms back on. "Do we know which syndicate?"

"We are assuming it is connected to Ateris. They have gone black and removed all their delegates and main flagships from the system, as well as the outer rims. It's like they vanished."

Dailey nodded, knowing they likely had used hidden gate technology. "Understood. Thanks for the update. We are set to intercept the battle group. We'll keep you updated."

Albert took this moment to cut in. "Yes, Senator. I have been using this conversation to further calibrate the gate communication nodes. We will be able to send a live feed from the ship as soon as we arrive at Asher. Before you ask, yes, I'm awesome, and yes, I will continue to improve the link."

The mood slightly shifted at Albert's levity.

"Very well. I look forward to reviewing the data package you sent. Be safe, and Godspeed."

With that, the conversation was over. Being this far from home, in the deep void of space, at times caused a sort of disconnect from home, making the horrors of things like the attack on Solaria hard to fully digest.

Once they exited the gate and Albert had decoded all the other signals included in the back-and-forth with Earth, he would be able to post the prior day's Fleet news for the crew to watch.

Becket cleared his throat. "There's no need fretting about this now. We need to focus on the task at hand. Everyone, get back to work."

As the words left his mouth, the proximity alarms started chirping, informing the crew they were about to exit their final gate before heading to Asher.

CHAPTER 24

REVOLVER

S team from the access tunnel fogged Grear's visor as he pushed through a tighter than anticipated opening leading to a run of random pipes reaching twenty feet overhead. The tunnels were clearly made for smaller maintenance technicians and repair droids.

Scuff marks, dull lighting, and wheel tracks laid out the obvious path forward, overriding several other even narrower, claustrophobia-inducing trails spidering off into even darker tunnels.

Fourth Foot's black armor made the group almost invisible, minus the sleek, focused LED lights shining in front of them. Winters glanced to her right, seeing the famed symbol of the platoon on Grear's shoulder plate; a grim reaper with a skeletal finger held up to its shadowed face glared back as if telling her it was already too late.

It had indeed been too late for the speed bumps they had run into so far on the mission. After dispatching the security forces on the other side of the blast doors, they had only been greeted by more doors and random battle droids that had likely already been damaged before their arrival. It was clear the facility had been put on lockdown. With this knowledge, Grear instructed his team to go through the narrow access panel.

Specialist Stacy Winters huffed into her communicator as they turned into yet another narrow passage. "I bet this comes out in the reactor bays." .

"Nah," Private Donald Berks replied as Grear ignored the back-and-forth. "There's no cooling tubes."

Even Grear paused at the moderately intelligent observation from the younger private. While he was lethal in a fight, he hadn't proven to be the sharpest tool in the shed. As Dasher had once described him, he was delightfully dull.

"And you know this from what?" Winters replied as she activated her thermal sensors, reading the temperatures from the various pipes.

"I was talking to Miller earlier, and he said if I see a big tube with frost on it, it would be in my best interest not to shoot in its general direction."

Grear paused, seeing the path opening up in front of them. "That's good advice. I suggest we follow it. It looks like there's an access hatch up ahead."

Two of the Rangers walked around their fearless leaders, inspecting the opening as Winters continued to scan the corridor. "I don't see any security cameras around this area either."

They had been surprised no other soldiers had been sent after them after their previous engagement, confirming their suspicions that the remaining sections of the base were on lockdown.

Sparks flickered as the lead Nova Ranger blew out the access panel with hypercharged nanobot gel. After emptying the small tube around the hatch's edges, the nanobots became what was often described as super excited. Eventually, they dissolved the boundaries of the barrier in a quick pop of ozone. Only able to be used on thinner openings, such as panels, the gel was often a last-minute add to a Nova Ranger's kit. Grear was fully grasping that the enemy may just have given them a back door to the control room.

Red flashed in the other Nova Rangers' HUDs as Grear had them pause before exiting the access shaft. "Everyone, hang on a minute." The man lifted his arm, launching a small, round, marble-sized ball into the sleek, shiny black hallway.

A quick video feed popped up in the corner of his visor, showing the lack of security. The red light in the Nova Rangers' HUDs turned green before disappearing. The small camera only worked over a short distance, designed to perform this very task.

Seeing the shiny black flooring, the trained team immediately switched their mag boots to padded. Several hundred small rubber studs jutted out, making Grear's first step silent.

Quickly scanning the corridor, Grear noticed the life-support readings of the area. It was temperate, and the oxygen was luckily regulated, as well as the gravity. The group finally exited the access panel, taking up positions on either side, creating an effective field of fire in both directions.

Winters fired a quick, snapping laser blast into the security camera glaring directly at them while Grear glanced at his tablet. The base layout continued to match the engineer's description from earlier.

Grear breathed into his communicator. "It won't be long. If this layout is correct, we are close to the command module. Miller, you copy?"

Miller's voice came over the comms choppy and broken, only every other syllable understandable. Petty Officer Miller had stated that if they made it to the scraper's control room, they would likely lose signal due to the static radiation until they could tap in and use the base's comms. "We . . . secured . . . not long . . ." Miller's voice pushed.

Satisfied that Miller was telling them they would have comms up shortly and that they were, in fact, all still very much alive, Grear turned toward the blast doors at the far end of the corridor.

The relief of knowing the mission was still a go refocused both teams. At the same time, loud clanking started reverberating down the long, sleek hall.

"Winters, Berks, cover that door. Ringer, Parks," he continued, talking to the other Nova Rangers on his team, "see if you can locate any other access panels."

Parks and Ringer were what Grear and the other Rangers called the meat and potatoes. Their function wasn't specialized but relatively straightforward. Point, shoot, and engage when asked, told, or shot at first.

Both Grear and the inhabitants of the station had had an immediate, stark realization. The Nova Rangers were somehow behind the lockdown protocols and, within seconds, would be swarmed by battle droids.

Ran, seeing this, checked his private communicator, seeing the alert that his ride had indeed made its way to the station. In order to keep the ship from being noticed by the others, Ran had identified a specific location from where he would be able to access it without raising any suspicions. He had considered telling Derrisa or Lashet, but in the end, he also understood the time-honored tradition of having a scapegoat in case things didn't go as planned.

The truth of the situation was that things were going as planned, at least for Ran. With Derrisa and her perceived failure on Asher and the station out of the way, he was sure to gain the respect he quickly realized he had yet to receive. On paper, he was right. The man had carried through his part of the mission, destroying three state-of-the-art Fleet vessels.

Grear launched forward down the dark corridor, signaling Winters to open the blast doors. At the same time, he launched the rest of the small, high-explosive mini rockets from the pod attached to his armor toward the resolute barriers.

Streaks of light-grey smoke zoomed at the door as it slid open with an immediate rush of air, laser fire, and the standard kinetic ammunition being fired by one of the battle droids' rotary guns mounted on its shoulders, similar to the ones Albert used when needed.

The missiles beat the onslaught of droid fire as Grear and the others slammed themselves against the walls. The squad leader did so less gracefully, turning his thruster-fueled charge into more of a rolling stop.

For the second time, the entire team of Rangers unleashed a flurry of organized, practiced fire, only to be met with the almost surgical precision of the battle droids. Seeing her opportunity, Winters unloaded the larger rockets from one of the two pods sitting atop her shoulders, creating a storm of chaos while Grear and the others used the one unique feature their ODA suits afforded the platoon. Their orbital drop armor was equipped with a plasma shield capable of sustaining heavy close-range fire. While only able to do so for a limited amount of time due to the energy drain, it was more than enough to get the Nova Rangers of Fourth Foot through most of the sticky situations they encountered.

Four glowing blue shields sprang to life simultaneously as a mix of flying debris and bullets popped and snapped off the protective barriers. What the group wasn't expecting was the hiss of several electrified metal rods coming from the opposite direction, followed by a red flashing beacon on Grear's HUD as Parks's vitals flashed zero percent. Ringer, his battle buddy, turned, blindly firing his rifle into the dark. Grear nodded at Winters, who turned to join Ringer, leaving him and Berks to finish the task at hand.

Winter's attack had been fruitful as most of the accurate direct fire fizzled to a drip. Seeing an opportunity, Grear again activated the thrusters mounted on the calves of his armor, launching himself forward, leaving his shield up as the first thumping tang of a droid's torso stopped his forward motion.

The eyeless, bland, almost nightmare-inducing flat face of the battle droid cocked its head, computing a way to rip out its attacker's very soul like a demon looking for a soul to take. Grear hated droids. He especially hated combat droids, soulless machines of war that didn't have to spend years training and shedding real blood. All they needed was an upload and a few tweaks. He found fighting them boringly predictable. While they could be overwhelming in large numbers and accurate to a life-stealing fault, Grear had always agreed with Dailey's simple take on them.

The *Murphy*'s commander always told his Rangers how he felt about fighting the metal menaces. *"Droids don't have guts; they have programming. They could be in the middle of a life-ending last stand or fighting an inferior enemy, and they would still do the same thing. People don't work like that. We adjust to the threat, and when the threat gets to the point of no return, we don't have programming telling us what crazy shit we need to or not do next."*

This was, of course, why the man had destroyed his own ship and, on several occasions, entire space stations. A droid wouldn't do that. It would likely be programmed to prevent overreaching collateral damage, especially in its own facility, to avoid killing its patrons. On the other hand, Dailey and the Nova Rangers couldn't care less if they took the moon with them.

Grear slammed the barrel of his rifle directly into the flat face of the battle droid, ripping dozens of EMP rounds into and through its outer plating. At point-blank range, the weapon was a scalpel. The droid, no longer able to take sensor inputs, started its emergency protocol of wildly flailing its appendages in a final stand often referred to as the blender. Grear ripped several more rounds into the hole, using his armor's gloves to keep a firm grip on the machine. After a few more seconds, the EMP rounds punched the droid into its final bout of spasms.

The sound and flash of Berks charging by, following his leader's example, almost put a grin back on Grear's strained face as the man worked to ignore most of the flashing warnings in his HUD.

Crashing sounds echoed as Berks slammed into a group of droids in various stages of resetting their sensors after Winters's missile barrage. It was a pathetic, almost sad mix of droids working out a way to continue their mission while in shambles.

Berks, seeing his chance, pulled out his axe at the same time he started draining his magazine into the jumbled mess of droid parts. Several scrapes and light spatters of laser fire smacked into the Nova Ranger as the droids continued to wink out.

Grear stood fully up, honing in on the lack of fire coming from Winters and Ringer. Satisfied Berks was in control of the last few droids, he trotted forward to the horrifying scene in front of him. Unlike Woody, who had been injured to the point of convincing the others he was dead, only to find him very much painfully alive, there was no question about Specialist Parks's condition.

Dozens of metal rods protruded from the Nova Ranger's armor, making him resemble a porcupine. It was evident each and every one had broken through both levels of nanoarmor. Blood seeped from every spike, too much to consider somehow sucking it back into the man's body. While the ODA armor could do mild medical triage, this was beyond the system's abilities.

An angry scowl took hold of Grear's face. He could hear the tears coming from Winters as she sniffled lightly. Nova Rangers weren't supposed to cry, so they didn't; this was something different, something feral and boiling inside the woman's blood. She would sacrifice her own life avenging the death of her brother in arms.

Grear knew the outcome, as he felt the same heat churning out of his guts like an overly spicy dish, followed by a neck-wrenching case of heartburn. There would be a pound of flesh . . . no, two pounds of flesh taken for this transgression, and every single Ranger in that smoky, haze-covered hallway knew it. No words were needed as Winters and Ringer turned, all three nodding at the same time Berks finished clearing the far end of the hall.

They would willingly die here avenging their friend as long as they got to violently kill and destroy every single living piece of sentient life on the station.

CHAPTER 25

GREAR'S FINAL STAND

R an cleared his throat, walking out of the command room where they were watching the carnage unfold. Unlike them, he truly knew the capabilities of the Nova Rangers now stalking the corridors. The station would be a complete loss no matter the amount of droids and security personnel they threw at them.

"I'll be back," Ran noted while Lashet eyed the blast doors, heading to his quarters.

The one thing that Ran had ensured for himself was a path out of the station in case of any last-minute problems that would likely end in his death or imprisonment. Knowing his fate, he quickly entered his quarters, punching a code into the small access panel in his private closet.

Derrisa probably also had a pathway to safety, but what she didn't have was a personal Alurian ship to pick her up.

While she didn't have a golden parachute, she did have the station programmed to alert her of any internal locks being opened. The woman looked down, seeing the unfamiliar alert code and a red flashing dot strobing directly over Ran's living quarters.

"That son of a bitch," she hissed, getting Lashet's attention.

"What?" he asked, not using any official title or form of respect for her.

"There is an alert on Ran's quarters. He's up to something," she spit out, walking to her station and grabbing a blaster rifle.

"You're all up to something. Maybe it's nothing," Lashet suggested, feeling like he would know if Ran was leaving for safety or other reasons. But looking down, the Alurian knew the truth as Derrisa started barking orders.

"Send a message to the Syndicate and the battle group. Tell them we have a defector."

Nodding, Lashet started putting the message together, only to find several red lights blinking back at him. "It can't be," he huffed, anger cutting through the statement.

"What is it?"

"All the station's communication systems are offline, and it appears more than a slight fix," Lashet barked as he looked up, seeing the Nova Rangers blowing their way through another set of doors. The fact of the matter was that they were inside the lockdown protocol area, meaning the doors were not nearly as much of an obstacle as the ones they had circumvented via a lapse in design.

"You!" Derrisa pointed at the team operating the room's stations and the handful of armored battle droids. "Grab a rifle and follow me."

The group of reluctant but subservient participants did as told as Lashet continued to furiously hammer at his console.

It only took a few short minutes to realize the scope of the situation, as the door to Ran's quarters was sealed shut. Checking her scanner one last time, a launch notification, followed by a loud bang from inside Ran's quarters, confirmed he was indeed making an exit. Frustration washed over the woman like an ice-cold shower, stilling her nerves.

Turning with clenched teeth, Derrisa stormed back into the main control room, followed by the goon squad. Furthering her frustration was the group reracking their rifles before heading back to their respective workstations.

Ran smirked as he boarded the sleek dignitary ship adorned in plush leather and rich, shiny metals. Turning, he clicked a small remote, and the hallway he'd just come from slid together, making the passage useless unless drilled or blasted out.

After quickly confirming with the battle group that the station was a total loss and being overrun, the man promptly launched the small craft into space. Once onboard the leading battle group's command ship, he would direct them to destroy what remained of the moon base.

Ran initially requested to engage the base as soon as the moon shrunk behind him, but the Alurian commander had insisted it could wait due to several of his destroyers not reporting in. While it frustrated the former general, it would also be unwise to act desperate or otherwise motivated to complete the task, since the base was a complete wash according to him. Derrisa and the others would take the fall for everything they'd failed to do.

After all, the man had told them of the implications of having Nova Rangers on Parif, only to have the situation downplayed by the others. They would pay for this, and he knew. The only saving grace out of the entire Asher operation was Ran completing the singular mission he had been tasked with of destroying the Fleet vessels.

The whisper-quiet hum of the small ship's engines perked a smile on the disgraced general's face. Ran pinged the Parif moon base one last time, ensuring the communications hub was no long operable.

Grear's raiders finally made their way to the command section, blowing the final blast doors inward with every bit of major firepower they had left at their disposal, including Grear's backup mini fission core.

Lashet was ready, having watched the chaos unfolding on the monitors, firing several well-aimed blasts into the smoking opening in an effort to hit something while Derrisa motioned what was left of the security team back into the control room, taking up the rear.

Frustration radiated from the woman enough to make her glow like she had fallen into a reactor. The sounds of violence immediately took over, the unfamiliar sounds of thrusters and weapon cadences she was not familiar with overpowering the laser blasters her team carried, including the handful of battle droids leading the charge.

Seeing the violence-hungry reinforcements pushing through the far entrance, Ringer threw his last EMP grenade as if it was the final pitch in the World Series, landing perfectly in the group's center. The reflection of the blue pulse flickered off his angry eyes through his visor.

Seeing Lashet standing out from the group of basic-control operators, Grear activated his axe, also known as a ripper, turning on the mini thruster on the bottom. The Alurian, seeing the incoming threat, lurched sideways to duck behind another console, only to have Grear surgically remove his right arm with an insanely focused burst of rounds.

The snapping pop of bullets smacking the massive viewscreen created a strobing effect as large sections started malfunctioning. Greenish-red muck oozed from the Alurian's arm while his wild eyes worked to figure out why he was no longer able to pull the trigger.

Grear had given the Alurian enough time to come to terms with his own smug death as he dislodged his ripper from the console Lashet had been behind. Bullets and laser fire smacked the man's armor as he moved toward the injured Alurian like a wolf after its long-stalked prey.

Not one word had been uttered since the team had entered the control room. There was nothing left to say. No comments or commands to change the direction of the fight. They would either be victorious or die. The Rangers were in perfect synch with each other without any need for further guidance, as they let the violence of revenge drive their actions.

Derrisa watched from the shadowed veil of the corridor leading to Ran's quarters. Eyes wide, she watched as the massive, hulking Nova Ranger slammed the ripper directly into and through Lashet's no longer incorporated skull. Another layer of gore sloshing onto Grear's already tarnished armor added to the scene's horror.

Looking up, his motion detector sensed movement. Before Grear could act, Winters, already seeing this, cut into the darkness. The light-green outline of a body told him the exact location of Derrisa Monvet before the body crumpled over.

Ringer, Winters, Berks, and Grear all paused, seeing the results of the sheer carnage they had just rained down upon the group who had caused the *Murphy*'s crew and their platoon so much pain. The loss of their platoon leader, Dasher, as well as Parks, not to mention the wounded from the attack on the drop bay, had been burned into their minds.

"They're still alive," Winters said, cutting through the silence.

Grear didn't hesitate walking over to Derrisa, seeing her working to keep her guts from spilling onto the floor. Snapping the brackets on either side of the neck, Grear removed his helmet, clunking it on the console Lashet had once occupied.

The others followed his lead while Specialist Stacy Winters helped Grear pull the woman into the control room's main console. Grear shook his head, seeing the woman in pain. While he was a lot of things, he was not a monster, even if he had shown that side of him seconds earlier. In combat, faceless enemies were not the same.

Winters, not caring, pulled the woman up, whose color drained from her face. Derrisa swallowed a shriek resembling a child trying to get down an overly boiled vegetable. The only thing holding the woman together was her pride. "End this," she hissed as Winters glanced at Grear. The man nodded.

Winters tapped a small square on her hip; a container with several marble-sized metal balls. Quickly popping all of them out, she placed the small container back in its place. Every Nova Ranger carried four pain pods, small round spheres capable of relaxing the body and mind long enough for the person to make it to medical treatment. It would only take one to get the job done. Four would be enough to ensure you felt no pain while drifting off into one's own inner void.

Reaching down, she opened Derrisa's hand, depositing all four. Several medicine-giving spikes shot out from all sides of the small spheres. Without seeking further approval, Winters closed Derrisa's hand, leading to her immediately letting out a sigh of relief.

The group stared at her as a small grin perked the right side of her mouth. "I was a young, happy girl once. I saw the moons of Barron." She was staring at something not there.

Winters helped prop the woman up. "How do we communicate with the scraper facility?"

Derrisa let out a light gargling chuff, lifting a hand and pointing at the console Lashet had once occupied. "One, five, one, three," she said as Grear walked over, seeing the keypad in readable numbers. Punching in the code, a green light flashed, telling them they had a direct line of communication with the scraper control room.

Looking at Darissa's quickly hazing-over stare, Grear paused, realizing he had likely also activated some type of kill-switch protocol. One that Ran had deactivated in order to keep them from communicating with the Alurian battle group. Winters, seeing this, kneeled down in front of the woman.

"Hello?" Miller's voice echoed through the control room as Grear leaned over.

"Read you loud and clear. We have control of the station. Status report?"

Miller paused, talking to the two other engineers, ensuring they were all on the same page after having worked feverishly for the past thirty minutes trying to get the system online. "We are set, but we can't get the scraper to activate. It's remotely locked out. I'd give my left nut to have Albert here right now."

Winters leaned closer to Derrisa as she held her hand out, looking as if she was reaching out to touch someone's face. In her own mind, she was feeling the masculine skin of the love of her life. A love that was cut short by a Fleet operation.

"Tate . . ." she whispered into the air.

"How do we unlock the scraper?" Winters asked, situating herself closer as the woman's voice continued a low conversation with an unseen ghost.

"Power. You would have to shut down the rest of the power. One, three, one, three."

Grear tapped the numbers into the console, then several yellow lights started whirling on the ceiling.

"You know . . ." She gasped. "I was young once. And pretty. Very pretty. Everyone used to tell me."

Winters glanced back at the group. Miller's voice cut back through, interrupting the dying woman. "Control, we have control. Wait . . . what are you doing? There's a warning flashing on our screen."

Grear's raiders didn't immediately respond, still working through the situation.

"Yes, I'm sure you were," Winters replied, actually starting to feel bad as the adrenaline of the fight began wearing off. "What did we activate?"

"Promise me something first," Derrisa coughed.

Winters nodded, so the woman continued. "We overloaded the scraper two days ago." Derrisa paused, taking a gurgling breath as she let her other hand slip from her belly, no longer caring about holding herself together. "To power it now, you would have to overload this section's reactor. We planned on doing that when your main sh . . . sh . . . ship arrived," the dying woman stammered. "You know I was young once?"

Grear, realizing what she was saying, looked down at his tablet. The power meter flashed red from the effort of using his own mini reactor to blast their way into the control room. The truth of the matter was that they had all done so while making their way there.

The only thing they could do was set their suits to preservation mode in an effort to survive the initial jolt of power. If this had been an outpost, they could have easily hooked up to the station's power and charged their armor enough to figure something out.

"This section is going to overload. We are going to overload it when the time comes. The scraper is secured and separate from this facility. If the reactor here overloads, it will surge the scraper, but that means we will be overexposed, and the section may vaporize itself," Grear noted to the team in front of him, not holding down the comms button.

Everyone nodded in agreement. At this point, rank was no longer a thing. It was Nova Rangers being Nova Rangers. Brothers- and sisters-in-arms.

Grear cleared his throat, activating the comms. "Miller, when the time comes, we have a way to power the scraper, but we have to do it from here." Grear didn't mind telling a half truth to the man. "We have the targeting systems unlocked. It appears there are several damaged satellites, but there should be enough tracking to shift that thing directly into the middle of that battle group."

Derrisa gargled a breath. "Yes, kill Ran . . ."

Grear looked down at the woman, now covered in sweat and pale as winter snow. "I will promise you one thing. I . . ." Grear paused, agreeing with her final wish. "We will." Grear knew it might not be him, but Ran would meet his fate at the hands of a Nova Ranger.

"I was in love once . . ." Derrisa breathed out in one final breath. The last thing floating through her mind was true love lost on a wasted life of anger, pain, and profits for the Syndicate.

"We will stand by," Miller replied as the other Nova Rangers in the control room stared at the remaining section of the monitor, now showing the battle group hovering over Asher from a remote feed.

CHAPTER 26

TERRA MINOR FOUR

The blue glow of a water-covered planet lightly tinted the bridge while the *Murphy's* leadership team looked at the uncharted virgin world. Dailey glanced at Sparky and Albert, working to have a private conversation.

"You two care to share?" Dailey asked, walking to the viewport while the main screen retracted into the ceiling.

Albert shifted as Sparky raised his head. "New planet to claim."

"I see," Dailey followed. "Albert, what planet is this?"

Turning, Mister Toaster's face looked sheepish. "Well, I would say we can call this one Terra Minor Four. You know, because it's sort of next to Terra Minor Three."

Pearl pulled up the navigational charts from their time on Sparky's home planet. "It checks out. From what I can tell, we are—"

Albert cut her off. "Right around three billion miles, give or take. About the distance from Earth to Pluto. Did you know that once upon a time, they dropped Pluto's planetary status? Also—"

"Enough," Dailey stopped the long explanation before Albert could warm his data banks up. "What a coincidence. Anyways, you sure this system is untouched?"

"Well, as of the last time I was plugged into an updated database before my little cruise, and from what I can tell so far—yes. I do want to add this probably means it's that way for a reason," Albert replied, throwing a small drive at Pearl, who caught it without flinching.

"Thanks. I'll upload these nav charts into the *Crow*'s database," Pearl said, picking up a small bag and putting her tablet and a few other small items in. She was clearly planning on spending most of her time on the dreadnaught.

Albert's point was well taken. Terra Minor Three was a virtual paradise in the deep, dark reaches of space. The unexplored part of the galaxy, often called the Void, held secrets at every turn. New planets and civilizations in various stages of development were being found yearly with the amount of colonization ships the Federation was sending out into the Void. The *Murphy* was one of the few combat ships sent out on such a mission, and as Dailey and the others had learned, for a reason.

Sparky let out a few barks. "I want to go to my home."

Dailey nodded, seeing that Albert and the war hound were already scheming to accomplish this task. "Once this is all wrapped up, we will do just that. Remember, you're the one who hitched a ride."

Sparky chuffed. "The Ham Empire would be grateful."

"Of course," Dailey said, turning to Specialist Kline while glancing at the countdown for the timeline they had transmitted. "How long till we are at one hundred percent?"

"Sir, you already know this, but with us having to supercharge the gate drive to fit the *Crow*, it will take about five hours."

The plan was to fully charge the *Murphy*'s drives to allow as much flexibility as the ship could provide once they arrived back at Asher. According to Albert, there was little to no room for error against an Alurian battle group.

"That lines up with the timeline. Albert, any updates on those mechs onboard the *Crow*?" Dailey asked.

"Yes, about those little rascals. They are a hybrid model. Even the newer databases don't have much on them. They can be either automated or manned by a person. Too big to use for ship boarding, but likely devastating in space combat or ground maneuvers."

"Thanks for the lesson. Can you get them working?"

Albert paused in actual thought. "Define *working*?"

"Can we use them in the very likely probability of an upcoming fight?"

"Oh, yeah, for sure. I could load a limited-AI protocol onboard, based on yours truly, and we could probably get half of them to work."

"Half?" Dailey asked as Becket let out a light snort. He enjoyed watching his commander try to get a straight answer from Albert.

"While I'm super smart and all that, we don't know if the Alurians will have the ability to take control of them, and I would rather be able to mitigate that risk."

Admitting there may be more than one of Albert in the universe was a known yet unspoken taboo. Dailey and the others knew their good fortune would only last so long. In space combat, luck was a scarce commodity.

"I want to put a couple of them in our drop bay. You never know." Dailey typed out a message to Jen to get an update on the attack wing.

Albert nodded, returning to his console and getting to work on the request like a fat kid in a candy store. While Albert often sounded indifferent, he was strictly business when given a specific task. That is, unless he was given no real direction on accomplishing said task.

Dailey's communicator chimed with a response from Jen. *Your quarters. Ten minutes?* Trying and failing to hide his blushed reaction, Becket picked up on the shift in the captain's mood.

"Go ahead, boss; we got it up here."

Becket noted as Albert turned, likely already knowing the message.

"Yeah, boss, we got it up here. You got it down there?" Albert oozed to a room full of light chuckles. This was followed by a gurgling snort from Sparky.

Dailey stood by the small viewport in his private quarters, staring at the planet as Jen walked in. The smell of fresh grease and silicone from loading missile pods hung around her, reminding Dailey that the rest of the ship's crew was in full motion, like ants finding food on a hot day.

"Couldn't this wait till later?" Dailey asked before turning, seeing her outline in the reflective carbon glass.

"You assume a hell of a lot in that statement there, cowboy," Jen replied, sliding her arms around the man's waist from behind.

Dailey found himself petting her hands as she pulled back slightly, letting him turn around. "I think I'm right. But, if memory serves, we seem to be getting into this habit of whatever this is, right before the shit hits the fan."

Jen smiled, replying with a simple, "Yes, sir."

"Don't say that. It sounds weird like this. Listen," Dailey thoughtfully said, finding himself wrapping his arms around Jen. "What if we just call the Ocess Syndicate and make something up to get them here. Let them fight the fight."

Jen leaned back, looking up at the man's hardened chin. "The mighty Captain Dailey and his Nova Rangers not wanting to pick a fight with an Alurian battle group? The horror of it all."

This garnered a genuine smile from the man, reaching his forehead. "Yeah, you're right. Becket would be upset, and to be honest, no one here wants to see that. Trust me. No, I'm just saying"—Dailey pointed at the transponder he had received during his meeting with the syndicate—"we activate this thing, and they simply show up."

"What's that phrase?" Jen asked as Dailey paused, pointing at the speaker in the ceiling to see if Albert would chime in with the answer. After no smartass response was added from the AI, Dailey continued. "Plausible deniability."

Albert was indeed listening to the conversation, just as he was doing in several other sections of both vessels. He had learned his lesson, however, and after inspecting several of the toilet seats he believed were candidates for Jen or Dailey to replace as his head, he'd erred on not interrupting.

"Yeah, that. Kinda like us," Jen added, also enjoying the moment. "Whatever happens out there, it's our job. I sure as shit don't want to die, and you kinda suck at it so far. If anything, I'm more worried about the people on Asher. Did you know Master Chief Thron entered the drop bay in his duty uniform?"

This was far from the usual chef's jacket he donned in the galley, and something Dailey had only witnessed once in his ten-year relationship with the Solarian. "Shit. Does he want a ship?"

"Yup," she said again, having grown fond of the simple response.

"You going to give him one?" Dailey asked. She nodded. "You ever seen a Solarian warlord in combat?"

"No, but I did go to the academy, you know. We are giving him one of the larger recon fighters we picked up back home. He seemed to know how to fly the damn thing already."

Dailey shrugged, letting the tension flow from his body as his shoulders dropped. "I need you to be safe. If we can somehow pull this Trojan-horse bullshit off, we might not even need to send you guys out there."

"Oh, it's totally not going to work. That's why you are sitting here thinking about calling for backup from the Ocess Syndicate. You know I'm right. What'd Becket say?" She had quickly learned how the two men operated.

Dailey sighed, knowing she was right. The idea of them sneaking up, getting in the middle of an Alurian battle group—something humankind, as far as Dailey knew, had never encountered—sounded increasingly ludicrous as she said it aloud.

"Something like that." Dailey grinned lightly as Jen leaned forward, kissing the man for what felt like days. He started back up right where he'd left off after taking a much-needed breath. "You ever felt like you were in the middle of something historic and didn't even realize it?"

"You mean when we made it all the way to another galaxy? Maybe when we destroyed those Alurian ships? Or, no, maybe it's having a talking, magical dog? Nah, hadn't crossed my mind."

The two smiled at each other, looking outside the viewport. Jen cleared her throat. "What does the senator think? I mean, really think. You know her." She paused to see his response and just how well he knew her. This was misguided, as their relationship was one of respect.

"What are you getting at?" Dailey asked, not referring to the question but rather the statement.

"Busted."

"No, really. What is this?" Dailey asked as he quickly shuffled his eyes away from the picture of Stella judging him from the shelf. Truth be told, the woman had always told herself, as well as Ben, that if anything were to ever happen to her, he would need to move on with life. While it hurt often being separated for months, if not years at a time, she had come to terms with the volatility of their relationship due to the nature of Dailey's profession.

Jen let out a chuckle. "Easy. The answer is no if you're asking me to marry you."

Dailey felt a flood of relief mixed with the tingle of a youthful crush sweeping over his body. While he wasn't grossly older than Jen, he had a solid ten years on her. Which in the future was not saying much, since people lived significantly longer due to technology.

"Not that." Dailey blushed.

"I like you. It's clear you like me," she said, looking down. "I like this the way it is."

While still in place over the past several hundred years, well-known institutions, such as marriage, held a significantly different status. In the past, legal unions oftentimes held heavy ramifications for unhappy couples. Due to the rapid advances in technology and the overall changes in the universe, it was now more of a simple promise to each other. A commitment that, in some ways, meant more than it ever had before the eyes of whatever God was watching.

"Look, I'm not saying when we get back to Earth," Jen started before Dailey cut her off.

"*If* we get back," he emphasized.

Jen shuffled slightly, realizing she had her combat flight suit on and would probably be in a heated dogfight above Asher within four hours. "You sure do know how to set the mood, sir."

Dailey nodded his head, understanding the truth of her statement. "It is what it is."

Jen giggled quickly. "It is what it is?" she mirrored him, adding a little reflection at the end of the statement. For the next ten minutes, the pair discussed possible options if they were to call in another mining syndicate.

While this was a conversation often reserved for the first sergeant, Dailey was enjoying the outside perspective.

They both had noticed the amount of pride Pearl and Dorax had displayed since being put in charge of the *Crow*. They both had the underlying suspicion that neither would want to relinquish command of the ship, let alone scuttle it to take out the Alurian battle group.

Before leaving Dailey's quarters, Jen pinned her shoulders back, looking at the man, taking him in. "What's that look for?" Dailey asked as she let a grin perk her lips while she cocked her head.

"Let's do our best to bring everybody home. And to answer your question, just getting a good look at you before I leave."

Dailey pondered the statement as Jen swayed her hips, walking out of his quarters. She had also snapped to attention, saluting the man, letting him know she was fully focused on the upcoming fight. Dailey already knew it wasn't a good idea to be in any type of relationship with a member of his crew, let alone the head of an attached attack wing.

CHAPTER 27

INCONVENIENT TRUTHS

P icking up the transponder, Dailey let it rest in his hand, dropping like the weighing scales of justice. "Becket, you copy?"

"Go ahead, boss." You could hear the echoing voices of the Rangers in the background.

"I need you to meet me in my quarters in ten minutes."

Knowing Becket was already en route, he paused, talking to the empty room. "Albert." Dailey paused, waiting for the inevitable response.

"Hey, how's it going. You know, things are popping all over the ship. It's about showtime."

"Yeah, I get all that. Can you dial into my personal comms port? I have a call to make and want you in it."

"Right, the transponder you're holding . . ." Albert cut himself off.

Sighing, Dailey rolled his eyes to the ceiling. "After the lights dimmed when Lieutenant Brax walked in, I figured you were already watching, so you can cut the bullshit."

"My damn mood protocol. Sparky and I have been working on it. Never mind, dialing in now."

Mister Toaster's face erupted on the screen, making Dailey jump just as Becket opened the door. The *Murphy*'s first sergeant looked around the dimly lit room, getting a whiff of Jen's coconut shampoo, a distinctive smell that only followed her.

"What's up?" Becket asked, sitting in the chair beside Dailey in front of the monitor. Dailey held up the transponder. "I figured as much. What are you thinking?"

"About to find out. I have a feeling Director Prescott already has eyes on Asher. He already wants to play ball. I'm thinking the more confusion we cause, the better. Oh, and before you ask, we're still absolutely parking this bus right in the middle of the party."

Setting the transponder on the small pad in front of the two men, Albert immediately started linking the device to the gate drive, allowing several pulses to fire off, activating the live signal. Without the use of his new super-secret encryption system installed on the Ocess ship during their visit, he would send out the signal in microbursts instead of the usual thirty-second rotation of activating a needle-sized opening close to the receiver's location, only possible if the other party was in or near a charted gate location imprinted into the drive.

Dailey scrunched his eyes, looking at the now blank screen. "What's taking so long?"

"My goodness, you are impatient. You weren't so impatient a few minutes ago." Albert paused as the transponder blinked from red to green. "There you go. I had to sweep, you know . . . half the galaxy to find the transponder's location then find the nearest gate opening to send this signal through. They are remarkably close to a gate near Asher. I'm sure you could have figured that out in, say, two hundred years or so."

"You pick up anything from our team?"

"No, not per se, but there is a ton of traffic between the battle group and what they are hoping is their lost destroyers. Oh boy, someone is really pissed off about all that. If anyone asks. I wasn't involved."

Becket and Dailey shook their heads as Director Prescott's overly thin, familiar face popped onto the small screen, the Ocess Mining Syndicate's symbol of two wings surrounding a planet in the background.

From the smug look on the man's face, he had been expecting the message. It also went without saying the man always had a smug look. Seeing the voice button was still red, Dailey waited for him to queue it up, glancing at the camera Albert was obviously using to watch them.

"Why can we see him and not the others when we talk?"

"It's hit or miss, but I think they have some type of active gate tech. The station on Earth, as well as Asher, are passive. I just turned them on, so, like I said, it's hit or miss. Not to mention my encryption protocols."

Nodding, Dailey hit the red button, opening the call. "Director Prescott." He paused.

"You called me," Prescott snapped back.

"We will be gating into the Asher system soon. I'm proposing a joint effort. Your help to alleviate the system of Alurian presence would be greatly appreciated and noted."

Prescott knew this was coming. "Yes, I see," his nasal voice replied. The man clearly had his hands pinned behind his back. "We are already in the Void close to the system, having passed through the Shade Belt. We were considering sending the Federation an update."

"That would be a good sign of faith, especially with the recent events surrounding the Ateris Syndicate." Dailey was playing politics. Prescott nodded as the transponder flashed purple as the signal blurred, only to snap back in place.

"Oh my," Albert interrupted, talking directly to Prescott. "You just encrypted this message as soon as you got all that bullshit out of the way. Umm, how did you do that?"

Prescott, unfazed by the blazing face of Mister Toaster staring at him from the other side, nodded as Dailey and Becket reappeared in the main viewscreen.

"We figured you would reach back out. In case you haven't been in contact, one of your teams took control of the moon base on Parif." Dailey nodded at the good news. They were ahead of schedule.

"What else can you tell us?" Dailey asked as a random person handed Prescott a tablet.

"Apparently, someone has been busy. They are sending out scouting ships to get an updated status on a handful of Alurian destroyers missing in action. Do you know anything about that?"

Dailey shrugged, obviously knowing firsthand they were scattered across the cosmos. "Who knows. Things are getting crazy out here. What else?"

"Very well." Prescott understood the statement. "It appears we are both at a disadvantage on a few details, but I can tell you that Ran has made his way back to the battle group. He is currently onboard the star cruiser, if that helps."

The two men immediately started focusing on that one piece of information. Not only did they have a bone to pick, but they'd promised to chase the man down to the edges of the universe. Which they just happened to be at.

"We have an Alurian dreadnaught and are planning on bringing it to the fight."

This was the first thing that genuinely caught the man's attention. "A fully activated Alurian dreadnaught?" Prescott's head even cocked slightly at the news.

"Mostly," Dailey replied. The man nodded. "I want to hit them all at once."

"Define *hit them*?" Prescott asked.

Dailey quickly realized Prescott had no idea what he or the rest of his counterparts on Asher and Parif were planning. "Simple and to the point. We both show up from different vectors and say hello."

"You do know that is an Alurian battle group?" Prescott noted. Dailey smirked.

"With what, three—no, five fewer destroyers," Dailey added as Prescott shook his head, knowing Dailey and the crew of the *Murphy* had absolutely had something to do with them being gone.

Prescott pressed a flurry of buttons, sprouting a schematic of the battle group replacing the man's birdlike face. "While they are working to figure out where their destroyers are, it appears a ground-occupying force is being planned."

This meant a planetary attack with literal boots on the ground to the military minds, which meant the Alurians were planning on staying. This was detrimental to the others on Asher and, as Dailey already knew, also not aligned with the Ocess Syndicate's plans for the system, something the *Murphy*'s crew had yet to fully uncover.

Becket swallowed the remaining saliva in his mouth, chewing on the inside of his cheek. "Director Prescott," Becket spoke as the image dissolved to the man's unpleasant shade of grey. "Can you confirm if that force is made up of droids or Alurian Shock Troopers?"

Alurian Shock Troopers were their equivalent of the Nova Space Rangers. Also called the AST, this had been the leading group sent to the planet during the war with Earth. Over the years, humankind had kept up the time-honored tradition of allowing its civilian population to remain armed.

"Shock Troopers. There is a battalion of them stationed on the main star cruiser."

Dailey nodded. "That's our main objective."

Albert chimed in, making a recommendation. "Might I suggest we initiate the roshambo initiative?"

Dailey side-eyed the camera. "Please enlighten us."

"Well, you know the old game. Kick each other in the moons until one of us taps out of orbit."

Dailey, not caring Prescott was on the line, engaged the AI. "That's the whole point of space combat."

"Well, if you strip away all the fancy stuff. It simply means we kick them in the moons first and hope they don't kick back."

"Again," Dailey directed. "Same thing."

"For the love of the Solarian moon gods. I'm simply saying let's hit them all at once. Everything we got, right in the boys."

Prescott cleared his throat. "Ahem. Moons? Parif is the only moon surrounding Asher, as you are now calling it."

Albert took that time to slowly start piping Rick Astley through the comms. "What Albert is so eloquently trying to say is we all coordinate a directed initial attack on the star cruiser. Everything we got. That also means planetside and the force on the moon base."

"Yes, I see. What precisely is the team on the moon base going to do?" Prescott was pushing for more information as Rick Astley started getting louder. He was trying to Rickroll the Ocess director, something that had also withstood the test of time, specifically in the military. "It appears we are also getting interference on our end."

"Director Prescott, we are on a timeline. Albert will send you our transponder information, as well as the projected timeline." Dailey, while giving Prescott significantly more than he'd initially planned, would hold back certain pieces of their plan, such as the use of the scraper on Parif and just how many of their forces were planetside. Prescott had made it clear he was unaware of the situation on Asher. "If you agree, once we are in position, we will coordinate an attack on the star cruiser."

Prescott glanced at a group off-screen. "Agreed. In the event there are any issues, we will conduct business as usual under such circumstances."

With the conversation over, Dailey nodded. The director was stating that if things went wrong, they would go into self-preservation mode, even if that meant taking on the *Murphy*.

"See you all soon," Albert gushed. "Oh, and no funny business."

Prescott shook his head as Albert ended the link. "Well?" Dailey asked. Becket grunted.

"Better than nothing. We could use the extra horsepower. You heard the same thing I did. I would be more hesitant if they weren't planning on sending a full ground force in. That means they don't plan on leaving any time soon."

"Yet, they don't plan on leaving yet," Dailey agreed. Becket nodded. This was the captain he knew.

"Hey, folks, I thought I might mention a little something. I sorta kinda slipped a communications tracking log into their subsystems while we were chatting it up. That ship had a major case of not giving a shit, to be honest with everyone."

"And what is that supposed to mean?" Dailey asked, working through the fact that Albert had bugged not only Prescott's ship but probably the entire syndicate in doing so. It was quickly becoming apparent the AI had a flair for overreaching.

"One of those one-way programmed AI brains. It didn't think it was amusing when I started dumping the subroutine into their comms."

"So they know you did that?"

"Oh lord, no. I overlayed it with that music video you humans obsess about. Then apologized for the overbleed, stating it must be a ghost signal trying to latch onto the conversation."

"So you played Rick Astley to confuse their AI and convince them someone or something was trying to intercept the encrypted call while you hacked their comms?"

"Yup." Albert did his dramatic pause thing again. "Oh, and likely everything else by the time it's done. I can tell you I did pull some immediate data. It appears their intel is very surface-level stuff. They have a handful of cloaked satellites. Crazy good tech but nothing too intrusive. Smart, if you ask me, unlike that Fleet of yours that hits everything over the head with a hammer. No, they are trying to be sneaky and trading that for less-detailed intel."

"Crazy good tech," Dailey let the words roll around his mouth, tasting them. "It's game time, gentlemen."

A chuff came from the dark corners of Dailey's quarters, while Sparky walked to the door, leaving. "Albert, you need to talk to your boy. I didn't even know he was in here. Hey, just how long have you been in here?" Dailey insisted as Albert scoffed.

"He's the president overlord of Hamica. You try getting through that ego," Albert said, activating the *Murphy*'s call to battle stations.

CHAPTER 28

TIP OF THE SPEAR

Every living soul onboard the monstrosity that was the *Murphy's Crow* held their collective breaths as Albert feverishly smacked his console. The cable dangling from the open panel on his chest glowed, transferring zettabytes of data at mind-boggling speeds.

When asked how fast the ancient AI could transfer data, Albert had compared the human brain's ability to comprehend such speeds to an overly cooked grilled cheese sandwich. Once understood, it would turn the human mind into a perfectly melted goo in the middle, moderately protected by a burnt crust. He then clarified that every piece of digital data on Earth around the 2000s was roughly two zettabytes.

"Everyone can relax their sphincters. Any scan will show us as a returning mining ship, which aligns with the scheduled deliveries. That is unless whoever is manning their deep-field gate scanners runs a backtrace on the electromagnetic field displacement surrounding us."

As per the plan, the *Murphy* and the *Crow* would gate back into an area close to Parif at a set time, close enough to the actually planned cargo ship runs so as not to raise any eyebrows. This also meant they would pass by the moon before heading toward the battle group.

"What are the chances of that?" Dailey asked as Mister Toaster turned and winked.

"One in eight million, two hundred and thirty-five thousand, four hundred and let's say two."

The entire crew groaned, knowing it wouldn't be happening. "Okay, point to the smart box. We have comms with Asher or the team on Parif?"

"Thought you'd never ask. And . . . go," Albert said, switching to his serious voice, pointing toward the screen. He knew the clock was ticking after getting his ego pumped again. It confused Dailey why he needed such a boost in the first place.

Petty Officer Miller's voice was the first to come over the comms, sounding overly excited to hear from the *Murphy*. "*Murphy*, this is Miller. Go ahead."

Bellman was the first to speak, glad to see one of his closest friends and, on paper, subordinates alive and well. "How are you? How are the others?"

Dailey nodded, having the same question. Unlike most instances, Bellman was wearing his full officer's flight suit. Blue and encrusted with platinum designs, he was thoroughly planning on having to get his hands dirty. After stocking the *Crow* with a few barrels of his renowned rum, the man had spent most of his recent time studying the new ship. Once they were through the gate, he would go back onboard.

By this time, Grear had also engaged, a video feed from his helmet panning around the carnage of the once pristine Ateris control room.

"We're good here. We have control of the scraper," Miller replied. Hearing this, Bellman gave Dailey a light salute before turning and exiting the bridge.

"Grear?" Dailey asked, seeing the pile of bodies and droid parts intermingled with each other like a sick game of macabre twister was being played in the corner.

"Sir, we are set here. The base is secure. There are still a few security droids roaming around. I hate to inform you Ran got away, and we have a KIA."

KIA was military slang for killed in action. Dailey took a deep breath. "Who?"

"Parks."

The crew digested the news as Dailey let out the breath he was holding. "Do you have a way to get off the moon?"

Grear hesitated a moment too long as Becket glanced over at the *Murphy*'s captain.

Miller cut in. "We do. We have a mining cargo hauler a few kilometers out. We had to park in the nosebleeds to avoid being picked up on local scanners."

"Staff Sergeant Grear, send someone to get that ship prepped. We have one shot from that scraper before they turn that place into ash."

Grear nodded, having propped his helmet up to show the rest of his crew. "Roger, sir. It will take us about twenty minutes or so. We found an airlock that will save us the hassle of going back through the station."

"Let us know when you're set. Just make sure you don't do any sightseeing. There have been some changes to our initial plan." Dailey pressed the red button, turning to Albert. "Are the comms secure?"

Albert pointed at the screen as a video game lobby showing two characters dressed in medieval armor carrying plasma cannons looked back at the bridge, waiting to go into virtual combat. They were still using the video game chat channels. Squinting, Dailey could make out the Hamica patch proudly displayed on both characters.

"Sir?" Miller prompted as Grear sent Winters to secure the ship.

"The Ocess Syndicate is going to engage the battle group from the opposite side of the planet." Dailey let the words hang in the air before finishing. "That is, if they follow through. Albert has targeting data for the main Alurian star cruiser. When we are all set, I want you to fire that thing to set things off, then you need to haul ass off that moon."

Grear, overhearing the conversation, nodded. "Do you have comms with Walker and Mac?"

"Not yet. We figured we would get noticed as soon as we tried," Dailey replied just as Albert cleared his fake throat.

"Ahem. Might I make a recommendation?" Albert drawled out. "I can send a coded message with the return beacon for one of the cargo ships. I'm sure I can make it subtle enough to not raise any suspicions. Then we can do that whole texting thing I've read so much about. Super pumped about that one."

Sparky gave a yip in support, clanking his armor on Pearl's no longer occupied station. While the hound had stated his intent to stay onboard the *Crow* in honor of its predecessor, things like getting back on board were nothing more than a momentary afterthought.

"Good idea. Glad I thought of it," Dailey said as a flat expression washed over Albert's face.

"You, no, that was—" He was cut off by the ping of the ship's linked transponder. The Ocess Syndicate had just gated into the system. Fully understanding things were now in motion, Albert shifted back into work mode, punching out a message as his toast-is-done alarm chimed. "Sent. We can talk about the street cred later."

A message flashed on the main viewscreen. *Understood. Awaiting further instructions.*

"What did you say?" Communications Officer King piped up from the back of the bridge. The man had been left with little to do over the past couple of days other than sit back and hope the *Murphy* wasn't turned into cinders by the Alurians.

"Told them their team was safe and we're on schedule. I also noted we will have backup."

A red light pinged on the viewscreen, while Targeting Specialist Kline let out a flurry of cuss words under his breath before finally speaking up. "Looks like those scouting ships Grear mentioned are coming to check out the cargo ships that just gated in."

"Albert?" Dailey asked as a schematic of the battlefield came into view. Parif, Asher, the Alurian battle group, as well as the projected location of the Ocess forces and their own ship came into view in impressive detail. He had been working on this little trick with Kline and Pearl after receiving the hijacked satellite data from Director Prescott.

"It appears all the patrolling fighters have been put on high alert. I'm still trying to work my way into their main systems, but I don't have a way to link into them yet. They know someone else is here."

"I'm betting it's our partners in crime. Prepare the forward EMP pulse cannons. I don't want any explosions." Dailey nodded at Becket as the *Murphy*'s first sergeant left the bridge, heading toward the drop bay.

"Pearl, you hearing this?" Dailey asked as she and Dorax's faces appeared on the bottom corner of the viewscreen. Bellman could be seen in the background huffing for air. The man had run to the *Crow*'s makeshift bridge they were still using.

"Roger, sir. Albert has linked us directly to your viewscreen. We can see everything as planned."

Dailey nodded in approval. There very well may be a new sensor module in Albert's future, which might not include a mustached face.

"Bring us about. I don't want them to have time to react. Albert, could you use one of those fighters to synch with the battle group?" the *Murphy*'s captain asked, thinking through the logic.

"More than likely. It would involve some old-fashioned fisticuffs with the pilots. But if needed, we could open one of the *Crow*'s inactive bays and let them simply float in and shut the door behind them till we can figure . . . well, *I* can figure out what to do."

"Sounds like a job for our almighty ham overlord," Dailey noted as Sparky stood up, activating his armor's belly-protection plate. The pup often left it open to provide ample space for belly rubs from the crew.

"The pilots will succumb to our mighty cause!" Without the translator, the entire statement came across as a few snorts, a yip, and a light rattling bark.

Focusing on the two blips now showing on the realistic layout of the battle space, Pearl took the initiative, turning the *Crow* on a dime toward the moon's crest. While the *Murphy* was in control of both ships at the time due to Albert, the *Crow* was the main driving force.

"In three, two, and fire," Albert stated, uneventfully clicking his finger on the panel in front of him.

Now hovering over the crest, the two light-blue translucent flares from the EMP pulse cannons reached the two fighters' nanoseconds after they came within eyeshot of the *Crow*. The two signals flickered out as Dailey quickly hailed what would go down in history as Grear's Raiders. "Miller, Grear, that window of time we had just closed. Status?"

Grear, holding up his small tablet, nodded in mild annoyance. "Winters is at the ship. She's getting it started. We are five mikes out."

The small camera panned to Miller, who gave a quick thumbs-up.

"Very good. You have five minutes. Tops. King," Dailey huffed, shifting his focus. "Use the transponder to message Prescott. Tell him we are five minutes out."

"Too late, boss," Albert noted as the schematic of the battlefield started lighting up on the far end of Asher. "I think they've been found out."

"King?" Dailey said, repeating the man's name as Albert took control of the *Crow*, turning the ship as the two enemy fighters drifted into one of the open bays, like a whale about to swallow a mouthful of krill.

"Open channel. If they're looking, we may not have five minutes," King replied.

Dailey nodded.

"I'll keep an eye out," Albert said as his face switched to the emotionless, generic set of eyes and modulated mouth. After all this time, they knew it represented the toaster's programming mode.

"Captain Dailey, I see you are here as promised," Prescott's nasal voice grated at the edge of his nerves.

"Same to you. What's happening?"

"We sent out a probing force. It will draw their attention long enough for you to do whatever it is you are doing over there, which, if I am correct, is aiming the scraper dead center of the space cruise."

Dailey and the others were at a loss for words for a moment. "Yeah. Five minutes till the big show. We will be in direct contact in eight. Just make sure you aren't shooting our noses off."

Prescott shrugged. "Understood. We are not deploying attack fighters other than our larger assault ships. I have programmed their targeting signals into the transponder. Your friend there should know what to do with that."

The Ocess director's face thankfully winked off the viewscreen. "You thinking what I'm thinking?" Albert asked quickly.

"That it's amazing they actually showed up?"

"No," Albert huffed, aggravated by Dailey's lack of forethought. "They have an AI doing the same damn things I am. Maybe not as good, mind you, but they have somehow accessed at least two of our systems . . . Wait, no, four. It's the transponder. Once this is done, might I recommend you put it in one of those electrified rum-bucket things you threatened me with once upon a time?"

"For the love of God. What systems?"

"Main targeting, primary sensors, our navigation systems, and . . . they are trying to figure out what the hell I am. Meaning while they can't decode what we are saying entirely through our super-secret handshake, as long as the transponder is active, they can pick up what our scanners are sensing, which would be us scoping out the scraper and space station. They know we are talking to them down there."

Dailey fully understood Albert was doing the same to the Ocess Syndicate. He also correctly guessed Albert was pumping reruns of old Solarian dating shows into their AI. That or the mysteries of how the pyramids were built, something he'd promised to discuss over drinks and a lube when this was all said and done.

Three minutes later, another alert flashed on the screen before Grear's face sprang to life. "Our ride is here. We are manually diverting power to the scraper and exfilling."

Dailey nodded as Albert responded. "Sorry, old chap. I couldn't do that remotely. Some things you just have to pull the switch for."

What Albert didn't know was that Grear would have to hold the switch open and let it flood the system due to the current state of the panel.

Grear turned to his remaining platoon as he grabbed his helmet, turning off the comms signal. The others froze, hoping he had some last-ditch idea to get them all off the planet.

"Sarge?" Ringer asked, an odd innocence coming through in the question. He looked up to the man like a big brother.

"I'll be right behind you," Grear said. The others didn't move. "If you all don't get on that ship, I'm not doing a damn thing. Understood?"

It was past the time for orders to be followed and military courtesy to be honored. This was personal. People talking to people, and they all fully understood the situation.

Grear locked his helmet in place before the others could see the tears forming in his eyes. It wasn't fear of death but pride. "You all get moving. That's an order."

"Shit, Grear," Berks huffed, walking over to the man. "That crap went out the window when we got in here. You ain't dying alone." The man's slight Texan accent cut through the conversation.

Ringer pressed the small personal carry pod on his armor, revealing a handful of honest-to-God cigars. Not giving Grear time to respond, he quickly called Winters. "Hey there, good looking. Why don't you go get the nerds taken care of."

Winters paused, knowing what was happening below. Moon dust fluttered around the ship's thrusters. "You think I'm good looking?" she asked, and they both unknowingly grinned.

"Who don't there, sunshine," Ringer replied, lighting the first cigar and handing it to Grear, who was no longer making demands of his Rangers. This wasn't about life or death but brotherhood. Something no order or shit-headed officer could change.

"Tell you what." This time, Winters's words hitched in her throat before she composed herself. "I'll be back once I have the extra baggage in tow."

"You do that . . . Hey, I always wanted to tell you I thought you were a total babe. You know, the total package."

Even Grear grinned at the conversation as Ringer blew out a halo of smoke while the others lit their cigars.

"It's a date," Winters replied as the thrusters pressed against the moon's surface, pushing the ship toward the small landing pad by the scraper control room.

Ringer chuckled, turning to the group. "Can you believe I kissed her once? Mind you, we were wasted on Bellman's rum, but it did happen."

"That's some bullshit, Ringer," Grear retorted with a grin, occupied typing a message on his tablet. The man simply smirked.

"Man, if we just had that date, it could be true love," Ringer joked.

Miller's voice came over the primary comms. Grear finished typing then finally shuffled to the scraper's reactor panel.

"Crank her up and get out of there!" Miller exclaimed.

Grear didn't hesitate, pulling the switch while holding it open.

Having heard the entire conversation, Albert quickly computed the probability of the overall mission being a success if Dailey and the others were made aware of what the man and his team were about to sacrifice. The AI did, however, pipe the conversation to the one crew member he trusted onboard to address a situation such as this.

The hum of radioactive, superexcited particles rushed through the team's suits, electrifying every nerve ending in their bodies. At the same time, they watched as the camera overseeing the scraper started to glow green, shaking the facility.

CHAPTER 29

THE BATTLE GROUP

Vice Admiral Kluvnew stood with his dark-green hands pinned behind his back, looking thoughtfully out the large viewport, taking in Asher. Even darker-green tones accented the Alurian's body, culminating on his face.

According to Alurian tradition, the darker the hue of green, the more prestige was carried by the owner's bloodline. This was such a time-honored tradition that even the lowest-class Alurians born into servitude could find themselves living an unfathomably rich life if the green was deep and dark enough. In many ways, it was like an overcharged lighthouse pointing a finger directly at a royal-bloodline bastard child.

Ran stood several feet away, never having met the Alurian and working to read him.

"Ran, or should I say, General Ran," Kluvnew started as the man held back a smile. He had accomplished his goal. "Tell me again why we should fire on the moon base after it is already a complete loss?"

Ran composed himself after the brief injection of good news, deciding the truth would matter here, and that Kluvnew was the type of Alurian who could smell bullshit as far away as he could. "Insurance."

"Yes, you Syndicate types are concerned about the petty idea of ensuring things are covered or completely destroyed. We need the resources in this system."

Feeling more at ease with the vice admiral's use of rank, Ran decided to push, knowing it was only a matter of time before the Nova Rangers made another move. The move they were planning on making, however, was one he would not have thought possible.

Possible that is without the help of Albert.

"It's more my Fleet commander background, which I'm sure you understand." The man was using the one thing he himself had in excess: ego. "I would prefer there be no surprises. I have been very clear in everything we have done here. The Nova Rangers are not to be discounted."

"And that is why I asked you why you are standing here. Weapons commander," Kluvnew barked, as a slender Alurian woman snapped to attention.

"Sir," the clearly experienced Alurian woman's razor-sharp voice replied.

"Target the moon base's power sections. After that, pull a detachment of gunships with a company of battle mechs and secure the location for permanent occupation."

Alarms blared to life as the woman turned, caught off guard. A gruff Alurian voice from behind the vice admiral rumbled to life, the ship's executive officer immediately slamming the blast shields over the massive viewport shut. "We are being targeted from the moon base. There is an energy weapon being fired!"

Ran's face, already pale white from years in deep space, lost another shade. "That cannot be."

"Two seconds; we are firing thrusters." As the words left the executive officer's mouth, the green hue of the scraper slamming into the rear engine section of the star cruiser manifested an immediate oh-shit factor, dropping the vice admiral's smug demeanor.

The smell of burning metal and electronics flooded the ventilation systems as orange and red lights flickered on every available screen. Fortunately for the Alurian command team, they were not only spread out among the battle group, but the ship was also designed much like other larger combat vessels. It could separate itself when certain sections were no longer operational, a must in deep-space warship design, no matter the race.

"Initiate separation procedures. Deploy all forces!" Kluvnew ordered just as the first round of attack-wing fighters from the *Murphy* sliced through the dark of space.

Lasers erupted in a concert of light and confusion as the Ocess Syndicate's gunships started firing long-range missiles into the opposite side of the battle group. The vice admiral glared at Ran before slamming down in the command chair of the bridge.

The Ocess Syndicate's gunships were sleek fighters with round, manned turrets protruding from either side like an unwanted set of lethal love handles. An ion cannon stuck out from the front of the midsize ships like an angry stinger, while several automated laser cannons swiveled atop two slanted missile pods.

Able to carry a crew of ten, the small gunships were explicitly designed to take on a heavy-class starship head-on while swatting smaller attack fighters at the same time. It was all about economies and mass of force. The most bang for one's buck, and fully purchasable from the Ocess Syndicate's weapons division for the right price.

The grinding crack of several airlocks separating was followed by the hiss of the independent life-support systems coming online on the now separated command module. Debris and short-lived flames shot out of the *Nova Sentinel*'s significantly larger hull. Both Ran and Kluvnew were not only confused but in utter shock over the complete and total amount of destruction the scraper had dished out, but knew there would not be another shot.

The remaining section of the *Nova Sentinel* was roughly a quarter the size of the *Murphy* and focused more on survivability than anything. As was procedure, the command module would integrate with either one of the destroyers or be taken into the Alurian dreadnaught, appropriately called the *Void Reaper*, now turning toward Parif and the oncoming attack force.

This was a crapshoot due to the Ocess Syndicate's gunships now also bearing down on the battle group. Massive plasma cannons lurched to life on two of the destroyers still left, splitting the gunships as two of them exploded in magnificent balls of blue, glowing light.

The *Void Reaper*'s pitch-black exterior reflected no lights as it maneuvered through the debris of the star cruiser. Kluvnew's jaw tightened to the point of snapping at his unforeseen lack of preparedness.

Truth be told, his battle group had witnessed limited combat, only having had to take on what were considered mid-tier spacefaring planets. Fighting the Federation toe to toe was the very thing they had been preparing for, besides the Creare Overlords. The plan was simple: put the planets now under the Federation in line and make them understand they were now part of something they had little say in. Of course, this was done using pure, brute raw strength. Many centuries ago, the planets now making up the Federation had supplied the Alurian war effort with enslaved people and manual labor. Underestimating the human race had cost the Alurians dearly. Something they would not do again.

The plan had been straightforward: assemble ten whole battle groups and then engage Earth, effectively cutting the head off the snake. As was already understood, they had greatly underestimated Earth's and Solaria's population. The ass-end of the *Nova Sentinel* slowly started dropping into the outer atmosphere of Asher, further supporting this underestimation.

Ran and Kluvnew watched as the once brilliant blue thrusters were replaced by what looked like the angrily opened maw of a dragon about to rain down hell on a primitive village.

"This is imposible," Kluvnew hissed as the *Void Reaper* launched several battle mechs and missiles toward Parif.

Ran, seeing a chance to gain more favor and, in the process, make himself look all-knowing, cleared his throat. "Now you see why I wanted the moon base leveled."

The vice admiral took a deep breath as his dark-green face turned even darker, the human equivalent of being red faced when indeed pissed off. "I will take this into consideration."

The statement wasn't sitting well with Ran, but he knew the most likely outcome of the battle group making it out of this if Dailey was there. Even more so if he had support.

Between Albert, the Ocess Syndicate, and the *Crow*, Ran, while not fully understanding the situation, was truly underestimating the problem.

Battle mechs jetted by the command module as a sizable magnetic arm grabbed it with a slamming thud, pulling it into the belly of the *Void Reaper*.

CHAPTER 30

THE BALLAD OF ALBERT THE AI

The *Murphy* launched out of the *Crow's* stall like a bomb being dropped in a war-ending attempt to overwhelm its opponent. Albert quickly zoomed in on the ship speeding away from the moon base as Dailey leaned forward, zeroing in on the small vessel.

The comms channels were a mix of Jen and the attack wing doling out orders, and the Nova Rangers pouring out of the drop bays, many latched onto their respective fighters like a newborn to its mother.

"We are weapons hot, activating the primary deflector shields," Pearl cut through the chaos. They were using the *Crow's* massive forward shields to protect the attack wing until they could engage whatever enemy was undoubtedly heading their way.

Dorax, surprisingly, followed up with, "Initial long-range hounder missiles away."

Looking at the viewport, Dailey and the others stared at the angelic trail from the missiles, now well on their way to the battle group. Becket had voiced several concerns with Dorax about his potential issues with killing his own people. The Alurian had noted it was an issue, but had also added the fact that he genuinely was not part of the Alurian home world, something that Earth and Solaria needed to understand.

He was telling the truth. If the Federation stopped spending all its time chasing down the leftover Alurians in the sector, they would probably find they were nothing more than relatives of a long since dead generation, not to mention low-level workers working with and for the syndicates.

Dailey keyed up Becket. "How long till we go hot with the attack wing?"

Becket's voice came in broken. He was with the rest of the Nova Rangers. "Twenty minutes."

Nodding, Dailey looked down at his own half-activated armor, ready to go at a moment's notice.

"Hey, boss, I think it's safe to say we can hail the ground forces on Asher," Albert interjected as Dailey glanced around the bridge, looking for a clearly absent Sparky just as the *Murphy*'s automated antimissile systems sprang to life under Albert's surgical precision. "Oh, no worries about those. It looks like that dreadnaught is trying to take out the moon base. Easy-peasy."

"Asher, this is the *Murphy*. You copy?" Dailey asked into the air. Miller's significantly relieved voice responded.

"Loud and damn clear, sir!"

"Glad to hear you too. Status report?" Dailey asked, knowing they had probably been monitoring the situation until now.

"We are good here. Well, relatively," Miller replied as Mac joined the conversation.

"We were tracking the battle group, and it appears they have a ground force that was about to launch. We aren't sure what the status is now."

Dailey squinted his eyes, seeing laser fire and small, popping explosions dotting the far end of the planet. All literal hell was breaking loose, and the Ocess Syndicate was living up to their part of the bargain. If this kept up, Director Prescott would go from being a complete asshat to an acceptable and moderately reliable asshat. The *Murphy*'s commander would also ensure the man and his syndicate had one in the bank, something that Dailey and space commanders in general did not take lightly.

"Stay put for now; I know you're already preparing for a ground assault. Is there an immediate threat?" Dailey asked, ensuring he didn't need to divert a platoon to the planet before they engaged the wasp nest of mechs and fighters.

"Oh, how funny," Albert said, causing Dailey to turn.

"I don't like funny, Albert."

"Well, it appears they are confused as the dickens about the *Crow*. The lead destroyer reported reinforcements had arrived."

"And?"

"I started piping '9 to 5' by Dolly Parton through their comms. Really got that vice admiral guy super pissed off. Oh, and they are also trying to take over the *Crow* remotely as of five, four, three—and take that."

The bridge crew paused, looking around the dark metal room, seemingly filled with a light haze. "What did you do?"

"I let them know it's not very nice to try and take over another ship without at least taking them out for dinner and a lube first. The AI system they have on the dreadnaught is doing most of the heavy lifting. The scraper apparently scuttled their primary AI system on that super sexy star cruiser. Its name was the *Nova Sentinel*. Super cool name."

You could hear Miller and the others on Asher listening to the ridiculousness that was Albert. The truth of the matter was they'd missed the oftentimes flighty AI, and the banter had given them a much-needed puff of wind in their sails.

A proximity alarm sounded as the *Crow*'s thrusters growled a darker shade of blue. Several missiles slammed directly into the forward deflector shields of the ship as the attack wing, seeing it was their time to say goodbye, split up like the horns of a bull above and below the *Void Reaper*.

Pearl's voice came over the comms. "We can't engage with the forward deflector shields fully charged."

"Hold on one," Albert said as Mister Toaster's face morphed into the program-loading featureless readout. The AI was fully engaged in whatever he was doing. "You are clear to engage," Albert instructed as the entire forward battery of the *Crow* exploded to life with damn near every workable weapon on the massive ship.

"Jesus Christ, help us," Dailey murmured. The sheer amount of devastation being unleashed by the awe-inspiring ship was something that even the likes of the Nova Rangers hadn't witnessed before.

"Oh, he would if he was here," Albert blurted out, making the commander shake his head. There would be a round of questions about that one later.

"Kline, status?" Dailey asked.

"We are within range of their destroyers. They seemed to be focused on the Ocess Syndicate's gunships. They are letting the dreadnaught deal with us. Also, they have a few battleships, but they seem to be holding back."

"Great, those destroyers are what I want. Pearl can handle that dreadnaught,"

Dailey regretted his words as a massive explosion rocked the side of the *Crow*. In all the chaos, a missile had made its way through to one of the docking bays. Luckily, they quickly realized it was not the one the team was located in.

"What was that?" Dailey asked as Albert magnified several pods of missiles being launched from the *Void Reaper*.

"Angel Six," Dailey started, using Jen's call sign.

"Go ahead," she replied, the sounds of her fighter's blasters smacking in the background.

"Albert's going to send you some coordinates. I need you or one of your team to go in low and take out that dreadnaught's missile pods."

"Missiles are coming out of every shadow on that ship," her strained voice replied.

"These are specific. Sending the data now," Dailey stated, not wanting to get into a conversation. Now was the time for precise, targeted action. Looking down, Dailey grabbed his helmet, setting it on his lap. If needed, he would cut the damn things off the ship himself. Even while he thought this, he knew the best people humanly or otherwise possible were on the task.

Three vessel trackers from the battlefield screen showed Jen and two of her fighters peeling off just as the leading group engaged the Alurian fighters and mechs.

Kline barked louder than needed, drawing Dailey's attention away from the viewscreen. "The destroyer is targeting us."

Dailey paused. "So target them back. Engage thrusters and synch all weapons to its signature."

Both Kline and Albert went to work as the *Murphy*'s primary thrusters screamed to life, shooting the vessel toward the straying destroyer, who had decided to fire several of its plasma cannons directly to where they had been previously.

Seeing the gap, Albert, working in tandem with Kline, fired the *Murphy*'s forward plasma cannons, as well as an entire pod of missiles. Within a few seconds, the Alurian destroyer was firing back, and the fire from the *Murphy*'s plasma cannons slammed into its front deflector shields.

The *Murphy* shuddered, having one of the destroyer's plasma rounds slam into its hull. At the same time, the popcorning crackle of several direct hits from their missiles turned the destroyer into a bubbled mess as electricity skirted its hull, crackling in all directions. The ship listed, having lost its secondary thrusters.

"One in a million there, kiddo," Albert boasted as Kline felt himself blushing. He had targeted the ship's secondary thruster systems. These didn't push the destroyer through space, but instead, stabilized it during space combat. When firing missiles, the thrusters would counteract the motion created by the act, an important and often overlooked weak spot and crucial system.

"What are those battleships doing?" Dailey asked as they started moving toward the dreadnaught.

"No taste whatsoever."

"Albert!"

"Well, I thought, why not stick with the Dolly Parton theme. They don't like 'Jolene' so much. They are being ordered to support the dreadnaught. Whoever is the HMFIC is onboard that ship and not the star cruiser. I can sort that all out later, though. I sucked a ton of data in, but you know, boss—kind of busy."

Even Dailey didn't know the song Albert had mentioned. "Any signs of the ground force deploying or of them activating a gate?"

"Considering their primary gate is by Parif, no. They may have another way to do so. You know the deal; they may be able to gate from anywhere in the general area as long as they have the correct computational data for the other end. I do not see any signs of them . . . Wait, no. Maybe."

"Albert!" Dailey barked.

"The Ocess Syndicate gunships have taken out two more destroyers and a good portion of their backup fighters. They have tons more, of course, but are holding those in reserve. I think the battleships are coming to support the dreadnaught while it gates or jumps away. Just my two cents' worth."

Dailey nodded as Kline fired the killing volley of plasma blasts into the destroyer now dropping into Asher's orbit, joining the burning chunk of space cruiser.

"Shit," Kline hissed, with Dailey catching on at the same time.

"Master Sergeant Walker, you have a very large chunk of space cruiser heading through orbit. Sending coordinates. Keep your heads down."

Albert was already working on a projected-impact area, pointing toward the screen. "They should be fine. That being said, this is going to cause some serious issues down there, so they're not off scot-free. Just keep your heads down," Albert insisted, ensuring the group below heard him.

The familiar radio chatter of Nova Rangers in the middle of a fight started taking over the comms, as they were now close enough to engage at point-blank range. "Sir, the mining ship from Parif is requesting permission to dock. The *Crow* has too much heat on it," Kline said as Dailey shifted.

"We have room?"

"Yes," Albert quickly replied. "If we eject that silly extra ship they latched onto our hull, we can have them dock there. Same as the *Scarecrow*."

"Do it. We can always come get that thing later. If you can, set it on a cruising racetrack."

Albert nodded, having downloaded all of the Fleet's terminology. A cruising racetrack simply meant putting the ship on a course that would have it going in circles.

The chaos of a full-scale battle unfolded on the viewscreen, giving way to dashes of random colors and shimmering flashes. The larger vessels slowly turned, as if dancing in slow motion, to either expose their primary shielded sections or to fire their weapons with maximum efficiency.

One thing was abundantly clear, however. They had been taken by surprise, and while ready for one threat, the mix of Fleet and Ocess Syndicate had utterly thrown the Alurian leadership into a tailspin, muddling through defending themselves. Dailey, as well as any good combat leader, knew this was the worst possible position to be in.

Onboard the *Crow*, the massive ship lightly shuddered under a barrage of enormous plasma cannon fire slamming into its nose like a bully finally carrying through with a threat after not receiving their requested lunch money.

Pearl's hands hovered over the almost overly simplified navigation control panel. At the same time, Dorax and Bellman focused on both the weapons and deflector shield stations. Albert had set the control panels up in a manner that he described as hitting a cheat code. A straightforward command to fire the forward theta-watt laser cannons would activate the targeting, power transfer, and firing systems instead of a team doing so.

While hyperefficient, if there was one issue in the chain, the system would likely fail.

"Are you turning into that thing?" Dorax asked as Pearl nodded.

"That thing, as you call it, is just the same basic ship. The *Crow* should be capable of taking anything it can put out, if that makes sense," Pearl stated flatly while putting the massive dreadnaught on a direct course to its sister Alurian ship, now doing its best to not only swat off the attack wing but also stop the *Crow*'s forward motion while preparing to gate out and regroup.

Bellman turned, pulling up the *Crow*'s overall status report. Several shades of yellowing green and light orange were starting to rainbow next to symbols that even they didn't understand.

"We need to route all power to the forward deflector shields. The attack wing can keep the heat on that thing," Bellman insisted, followed by an approving nod from his counterparts.

Being the size it was, they couldn't even hear the forward batteries stop firing. What they could see was the silverish-blue haze of the fully charged deflector shields starting to have power poured into them.

The shields strobed, telling the crew that the front of the ship was probably getting rocked. To confirm this, Dorax activated the forward cameras, which had now turned into the battle. Dozens, if not hundreds of pinpricks shone on the viewscreen, some from stray fire, others from direct fire from the Alurian battle mechs now engaging the attack fighters.

Just when things couldn't get any more nerve-racking, music started piping through the empty halls of the *Crow*. Albert was now synching with the ship, using its forward sensors to track if and when the Alurians would gate out of the system.

"Me and my Sparky-ee-eeee," Albert's voice grew louder in some offshoot of a Janis Joplin song. Again, even Dailey was having trouble picking up the old music references he was now using.

The singing and clearly AI-generated music also started playing throughout the *Murphy*, causing Dailey to shake his head. The familiar fog of war had the man on full alert, every single one of his senses maxed out not to miss a thing.

"Sir," Kline interrupted. "The team from Parif just docked."

"Good. Have Master Sergeant Grear report to the bridge."

The blank expression on Kline's face pulled Dailey out of his almost superhumanly focused state. "Miller," Dailey barked over the direct comms link.

"Sir," Miller's more hardened than usual voice replied.

"Where's Grear and the others?"

The slight pause told the man there was immediate trouble. "They are still on Parif."

Dailey didn't need to read between the lines as he approached Albert. "What happened?" It wasn't the time to be aggressive but to know the situation on the ground and in orbit.

Albert somehow pulled off an honest-to-God sigh. "In order for the scraper to activate, power had to be diverted from the command module. Ran somehow rigged the station to shut down after he left for the battle group."

"Albert," Dailey cut him off. "Get to the point. Where is Grear, and what is his status?"

"He and the remaining portion of his team were in the control room when they had to manually divert the power to the scraper. There is too much radiation to get a signal to and from there at this point. The probability of them surviving is one percent."

Dailey paused, letting that sink in. Grear had known he was probably not coming back when he was talking to him. The *Murphy*'s captain refocused, knowing there were other souls at stake. "You know something, Albert? That one percent is what separates the *uses* from the *yous*."

Albert didn't take it as a slight, as it genuinely wasn't meant to be. Mister Toaster's eyes drooped slightly. "One percent," Albert echoed. Another arm shot out from his chest plate, working on another panel.

"What are you doing?" Dailey asked, knowing there would be time for this later.

"I have an extra one percent available, just in case." Albert's eyes lit up slightly as a direct hit from several small fighters shook the bridge. Following closely behind, the ship Jen had allocated for Master Chief Thron screamed in front of the viewport.

Sparks flew as Thron rammed one of the fighters, showing just how skilled the *Murphy*'s chef indeed was. The fighter turned on a dime, moving at twice the speed of the larger ship. Thron simply killed his thrusters, immediately stopping his ship and letting the fighter scream by to fire randomly at the hull of the *Murphy*.

It was over before the ship could pull out of its run to avoid the *Murphy*'s auto close-range defenses. Four surgical laser blasts peppered the blue, glowing engines of the fighter before it started tumbling into space, only to end with a snapping explosion.

"King, call Director Prescott. We need to know just how much more fight he has and is willing to use," Dailey instructed the young man. Several off-putting beeps chirped from the communications station.

"Sir, they're not responding. You want Albert to do that thing?"

"No, we don't have time to mess with whatever they have going on. Just keep an eye on them. Try again in a few minutes. If they don't answer, we may have another problem on our hands."

While the man had given his word, it would be easy for someone outranking the director to order the Ocess Syndicate's forces to continue fighting all the way to the *Murphy*.

While there was some truth to the thought, Director Prescott and his primary command ships had found themselves the target of most of the space mechs now bearing down on them.

Even though the machines of war were a substantial threat, the syndicate's gunships were cutting them down before they could get in direct contact with their larger ships. It also didn't help they had just been configured for a ground-occupying operation.

The comms flashed as an open line from Asher blinked on the primary viewscreen.

CHAPTER 31

ASHER'S GRACE

The newly formed leadership team stood around a large readout displaying the ground-to-orbit plasma missile they had found earlier, a massive defensive weapon there to protect the planet from rival mining syndicates in case all else failed.

Following a butt-puckering ten-minute wait for the section of the Alurian ship to fall through orbit, luck finally sided with the band of misfits for once. The star cruiser had already begun to break up before entering orbit, ensuring that what was left of the vessel would not create an asteroid-sized missile that would land directly on top of Walker, Mac, and the others.

After breaking further apart, the largest sections of the ship landed directly in the middle of Asher's process plains. In simple terms, this area was covered in ultrafine sand close to a mile deep, the by-product of inner planet mining. It also served as a large catcher's mitt, letting the big chunks softly seep into the planet while preventing further explosions. Aside from several large piles of smoking debris, most of the wreckage was already sinking into the nightmarish quicksand.

Another round of flashing red lights caused Vax to breathe out. "Still no way to ignite the reactor. Maybe we could overcharge the entire sector," she asked the group in the form of a statement.

"No," Bringum Flint, Kodas's leader, answered, having grown up and lived the life of an engineer. "It has to be easier than that. They would have never built a system like this without a way to fire it up, even after being dormant."

"Why would you say that?" Mac asked, also eyeing the screen showing the complete jigsaw puzzle of violence taking place in the skies above.

"Because I would never design something without a way. How about diverting the regional life-support grid to spark it up? We can easily get that back online," Flint threw out to the group, to answering grimaces.

"Possibly back online, or for sure?" Walker asked. Flint turned, walking to a group of engineers and huddling with them in front of one of the old monolithic workstations.

"Drives me crazy when they do that," Mac whispered to Walker.

"It's worked so far. We could see if Albert can dial into the system from the *Murphy*? There's no point in hiding now," Walker suggested. Agreeing, Mac immediately hailed the *Murphy*.

"Nothing going on up here or anything," Albert's voice rang over the intercom as Flint walked away from the buzzing group.

"Yes, Lieutenant McAlister," Dailey corrected. The sounds of weapons firing could be heard pounding in the background from the *Murphy*'s hungry cannons.

"We are working to get the orbital defense main weapons online. There is a rather large suborbital ground-to-air plasma missile targeting system and launcher. From what Flint says, it's large enough to take out any ship within its range."

Albert cut in. "And you want me to, what? Power that dusty old thing on, aim, and fire it for you all while I'm up here doing the Lord's work?"

Dailey screwed his face at the dated expression. "Fighting Alurians is not the Lord's . . . Never mind. LT, what's the issue?"

"Power. We can't power it on. Plus, I'm sure you know where this thing needs to go. We can push the big red button here if that helps," Mac replied.

"I see," Albert pondered. The scene on the bridge was tense as the *Murphy* rocked again, only to have Master Chief Thron swoop in and take out the now advancing battle mechs. "Tell you what. I'll divert all auxiliary tram power to kickstart the system. Once that's done, it will run on its own. Hold one; still scanning." Albert was digging into all the information he could find on the weapon.

"Must be a pretty big weapon," Kline chimed in.

"Well, he's only capable of doing a handful of things at one time. I'm sure we will pay for it at some point," Dailey groaned.

Walker's voice echoed in the background. "We have reactor activation!"

"All set. I also gave you a nice, juicy target. Two birds, one stone. Bye for now. Toodle-oo!"

Albert turned off the comms midresponse. "Busy here, sorry, guys." The rest of the team didn't argue as Albert refocused on the task at hand: staying alive and destroying the rapidly advancing *Void Reaper*.

While the *Crow* was holding its own, the fully manned and experienced Alurian dreadnaught was taking attack fighters out of the fight at an alarming rate. Luckily for the crew of the *Murphy*, it was a Nova Ranger's number one priority to retrieve and take their pilots back to safety.

"Two more," King said, referring to the bottom-left corner of the viewscreen showing a smoking Nova Ranger carefully dropping a rattled pilot before turning, flipping off the camera, and dropping back into space. That was the type of shit that made Dailey smile. He would give anything to be with his men, but he knew more was at stake.

Dailey had the utmost respect for Medical Officer Casey Franklin, the woman now sprinting to the pilot with a group of medics. He had worked with her for the better part of a decade and would not have it any other way.

"Hey, where's Sparky?" Dailey finally realized, followed by Albert's statement landing in his brain's runway. "And what do you mean by two birds, one stone?"

"Oh, you're not worried Director Dickface is going to take us out once the Alurian battle group is neutralized?"

"Be professional. We're in a fight here. It's Director Asshat," Dailey chuffed as even Albert's digital face let a slight grin slip, represented by a green pixel shifting upward.

"Well, I was just thinking. From what I can tell, that missile is some nasty business. Once it detonates, the real fun begins. The plasma blast that follows is tuned to a frequency that also acts like an EMP. If we fire at the far end of the battle group, we can take out not only the remaining battleships, destroyers, and whatever the hell else the dreadnaught poops out but also shut down all the Ocess Syndicate's gunships. I already did the math and will adjust the missile when fired. And boy, let me tell you, that thing is a doozy from back in my days. They don't make things like that anymore."

"Spare us the lecture. How long till it's ready to fire?" Dailey asked just as Pearl's distressed face popped onto the screen, having heard the entire conversation.

"Five minutes, plus fire and launch time to target—eight minutes."

Concentrated swaths of fire started pouring out of the *Void Reaper* like a kid with a bloody nose after a playground fight. "Pearl?" Dailey asked, making sure she was good.

"We can hang on. The shields are holding. Our only concern is not being able to take out that forward battery of plasma cannons."

Nodding, Dailey turned to Kline. "Target those cannons and set the navigation systems to intercept."

"You don't want me to do that?" Albert asked, confused.

"No, I don't. I don't want you coming up with some odd computation and changing my plan," Dailey reinforced.

"Well, I never. But I do have other things I could be doing."

"Precisely. Make sure we get there in one piece. This is going to get sketchy fast. I'm thinking as soon as they see another big-ass weapon shit all over the rest of their firepower, they'll have no choice but to haul ass. They still think they can take us on long enough to either get out of here or wear us down. And you know what, Albert? You're just the badass to make sure that doesn't happen. Can you do that?"

With Dailey pumping the AI's already inflated ego to new heights, the low hum of Dolly Parton quickly shifted to a classical rendition of the "Ride of the Valkyries" by Wagner.

"Hold on to your goodies!" Albert exclaimed, absolutely taking control of the navigation systems against Dailey's wishes. In reality, he knew exactly what he was doing in priming the AI.

Lights started glowing after centuries of lying dormant on the control panel back on Asher. While the controls were sophisticated, they were primarily analog, minus the low-resolution displays.

A random engineer spoke up from the dark depths of the control room. "The tram's offline." While not immediately necessary, the tram system was everyone's only way to and from the underground fortress.

Several stations, once dormant, started chirping and buzzing like bad halogen light bulbs. Reactor monitoring, targeting, and even what appeared to be a backup firing station all finally came to life before quickly being swarmed by several of Kodas's engineers.

"Well, looks like they have those covered." Walker grinned as Mac winked at the man.

"You know what still amazes me?" she asked as his grin morphed into something only a lover could pull off.

"Well, yeah," he responded with raised eyebrows.

Shaking her head, Mac snorted, garnering a few glances before the engineers returned to the newly activated stations.

"No, not that. The galaxy is massive. I mean, shit, it's so mind-bogglingly big, we still don't have the whole thing charted. Here we are, talking about other galaxies, and of all things, we run into a race of human engineers all the way out in the true Void. It makes you think."

"I was thinking about that the other day while talking to Vax. She seems to think that Earth isn't the initial birthplace of humankind. When we get back on the *Murphy*, we can actually test some of that theory; see how closely we are related," Walker pondered thoughtfully.

"Takes times like these to make you think," she confessed, letting her vulnerable side come through her now hardened facade. A facade she rarely, if ever, let down after her experience aboard the *Asher-5*.

Walker leaned forward, tapping his forehead against hers. "We got this."

Flint's loud voice interrupted the moment. The cat was out of the bag pertaining to their relationship. "Countdown's on the screen."

Sitting neatly beside the plasma missile's schematic, the countdown meter read four minutes till fully charged. "You think there's a possibility that thing may, you know, go off while it's coming out of the silo?" Walker asked.

Flint just shrugged, something even the—at times—smooth-brained Nova Rangers didn't like seeing an engineer do.

CHAPTER 32

WILL BREAKER

The immediate effect on a ship the size of the *Murphy* when the gravity is turned off is jarring and oftentimes messy. Food floated through the galley, slopping on the walls, while Dailey was forced to grab his now floating helmet before activating his mag boots with a commanding *thud*. Others, like Kline and Communications Officer King, quickly started their gravity braces, keeping their asses firmly planted in their stations.

More interesting, though, was the ship's ability to maneuver in ways that gravity stabilizers wouldn't allow it to. In many ways, having full gravity onboard a vessel gave it a grounded base in space. Ships all relied on a universally used cardinal set of directions to keep them in line and not upside down while maneuvering around each other, something attack fighters thrived on not doing.

Instead of tossing its crew around like in cheesy *Star Trek* reruns, the lack of gravity allowed for the immediate and abrasive maneuvering of the vessel. It was a state that Alurian frigates often stayed in while operating in hostile territory, supporting other more vulnerable classes of ships.

The viewport swirled and made the incoming and surrounding laser fire move in waves as Albert corkscrewed the ship directly toward the dreadnaught, releasing the remaining forward battery of seeker missiles.

Chief Engineering Officer, Junior Lieutenant Barry Hontz's Irish voice screamed to life over the intercom. "What the shite! The . . ." Sounds of crates slamming into something clanked in the background. "The gate drive reactor's going crazy!"

Albert clearly didn't want to hear anymore, shutting down the conversation. "Watch this," the AI said.

Zooming in on the *Void Reaper*, all the missiles split off, following their primary targeted function and Albert's apparently on-the-fly programming. "Lickety-split!" the AI exclaimed, cranking up Wagner to a crescendo as he guided each missile independently around the large ship, rocketing only feet above the hull. "Oh, before you ask, I'm guiding each one to soft spots in the deflector shields. There's one," he noted as an explosion rocked the massive ship. "And two . . ." he sang lightly.

Dailey couldn't help but hold back a grin while working to focus on the main viewscreen instead of the vomit-inducing vortex whirling through the viewport. Glancing down at his command console, the countdown Albert had initiated flashed two minutes.

Under full thrust, the *Murphy* was close enough to smell the *Void Reaper*'s massive exhaust ports. To their left, the *Crow* slowly ground its way forward under the heaviest of the *Reaper*'s massive front cannons.

The ship's commander, realizing a Fleet frigate was barreling toward it under full thrust, cocked his head before yelling at the top of his deep, gurgling lungs, "Ramming impact!"

Being the trained crew they were, the *Void Reaper* conducted evasive maneuvers, giving the *Crow* some much-needed relief from its forward cannons. At the same time, the dozens of surgically targeted seeker missiles set off another round of alarms. While not affecting any major systems, it was enough to garner the attention of the primary bridge's crew, and another much-needed distraction.

"Hold my beer!" Albert screamed loudly, having to speak over the rest of the *Murphy*'s crew, who were also yelling at him by this point.

"Stop!" Dailey exclaimed in a mix of excitement and all-out holy-shit mode. The sheer speed and aggressive acceleration toward the *Void Reaper* while under the control of Albert had been enough to make the *Murphy*'s captain pump the air brakes. Even Becket shouted some form of profanity over the comms from somewhere outside the ship.

Albert just let out an evil laugh while the ship lurched upward, its forward-sensor array feet away from the *Void Reaper*'s hull. Every laser and cannon opened fire at the exact time the ship rolled over.

Explosions and balls of blue light followed the *Murphy*'s path up the side of the dreadnaught. Albert had brought the ships so close together that the *Murphy*'s weapons systems were not inhibited by the *Void Reaper*'s deflector shields, which had subsequently been shifted to protect the vessel from midrange fire from the *Crow*. The ship's commander had rightfully not believed a close-range attack from the Nova Rangers was a threat. Albert, on the other hand, was another story.

Zeros flashed on the display on Dailey's and Asher's consoles just as Albert pulled the *Murphy* away at even faster, mind-melting speeds toward the *Crow*. Gravity was subsequently restored, causing even more drama around the ship as everything crashed back to the deck.

Hontz, in the engineering bay, still fuming from the previous episode, smacked his console, figuring Albert would somehow be affected by it, continuing his tirade.

Mac's voice cut through the silence as Dailey gawked at the aftermath of Albert's *hold my beer* moment. A visible line spewed flames and crackled like a trail of firecrackers being set off. Even though the *Void Reaper* was very much operational, its leadership had clearly taken a moment to rethink their current situation, amplified when the massive plasma missile, now also visible, shot out of Asher's atmosphere like an escaping convict running toward freedom.

"Incoming," was all she said, as the *Crow* and the *Murphy* had already engaged reverse thrusters by the time the countdown reached zero.

"Do you want me to give Director Asshat a heads-up?" Albert asked, seconds feeling like minutes.

"Nope, not this time around," Dailey confirmed as a shimmering gate sprang to life in front of the *Void Reaper*.

While heading in its general direction, the plasma missile was obviously more concerned with the battle group's remaining warships away from the dreadnaught. So in a display of unknown tech, the *Void Reaper* winked out of existence, as if the Void itself had swallowed her whole.

"Albert?" Dailey snapped as the two crew-served weapon brackets went up and down in the form of a shrug.

"They gated the entire ship. At one time. All at once, no questions asked. It's likely on the other side of the cosmos now. Wow." Albert followed up with a whistle.

"Least of our worries now," Dailey insisted as the plasma missile shed its outer skin like a dried-out snake, sending a massive concussive explosion in all directions, followed by the enormous plasma blast now hurdling through the rest of the battle group.

Albert worked to zoom in on the chaos, only to find the bright, blinding light of the blast washing out the viewscreen. Several of the *Murphy's* attack-wing fighters zoomed in front of them, chasing what was left of the smaller Alurian ships. The fight, as Dailey and the others saw it, was winding down.

The massive, streaking ball of plasma rocketed into deep space, as the carnage it had left behind came into view. Several Alurian battleships lay in tattered pieces, since Albert had chosen the most effective course for the beam after shedding its explosive housing.

Albert quickly focused on several Ocess Syndicate gunships, scanning them for life before tagging them green on the overall layout of the battle space.

"Sir, it's going to take a few minutes to sort through all this and get a BDA," Kline noted, referring to a battle damage assessment of all the parties involved in the fight over Asher.

"Don't be so dramatic," Albert scoffed. "The Alurians are at a two percent remaining force, and the Ocess Syndicate still has its larger ships in reserve. It appears they are a little concerned about what just happened, and . . ." Albert stopped as Director Prescott's birdlike face erupted on the screen.

"Explain!" the man barked, clearly taken back by the sheer amount of unknown firepower that had just been unleashed directly in front of them, close enough to singe the man's nose hairs dangling out of the cavern on his face.

"No clue. I was about to ask you the same thing," Dailey replied, stone-cold serious in his bullshit reply. "You sure that wasn't you?"

"Cut the showmanship. That was not fired by us nor by the Alurians."

Albert muted the man for a brief second. "They have identified the POO."

Kline let out a snicker. Even though this was a serious situation, it was tradition to snicker every time someone referred to the POO; that was, unless you were standing directly in the middle of the aforementioned point of origin. This term was often used for what used to be known in conventional artillery as fodder for direct counterbattery fire.

"Hold on for a minute. Let me check with the team planetside," Dailey insisted as Albert morphed Prescott's face into a literal asshat. Two cheeks slowly grew out of his own, starting to resemble a butt, just as a perfect rendition of a five-gallon cowboy hat winked into existence.

Mister Toaster's face went blank to avoid giving Albert's utter satisfaction with his creative art a chance to register with the director.

"Turn him back on," Dailey said as two butt cheeks, now in place of the director's face, parted as if passing wind. "They sent that thing up from the planet. Looks like there's a whole lot more where that came from. Lucky for us, they fired it off and not the Alurians."

Prescott paused indignantly. The man's direct leadership had planned on fighting Dailey and the *Murphy* once the Alurians had been handled. "I see. No more surprises?"

"You tell me, director," Dailey said, using every bit of bullshitting swagger he could muster.

Becket cut in on a separate channel. "Sir, the attack wing and Rangers are all set and/or accounted for. Awaiting further instructions." Dailey had let Prescott hear the conversation. This was followed by Jen confirming the same information.

"We will secure the sector closest to our ships for any prisoners. I'll send the cutoff coordinates. Also, what is that power surge coming from that moon base?"

"It's on our side of the fence. Once you get done sweeping the area and we are done here, I suggest we reconvene. We plan to pursue that dreadnaught."

Prescott's modified face winked out while the rest of the bridge's crew let out the gut-busting laugh they had been holding.

Dailey stood up, clearing his throat.

"Alright, everyone. This isn't over. Albert, see if you can trace their gate location. I don't want to let Ran get away this time, and I know that will take some time. Also, where the hell is Sparky!"

CHAPTER 33

SILENCE OF THE HAMS

Albert's aversion to the question led Dailey to fully believe the AI knew where Sparky was. His first incorrect assumption, however, was that he had done his disappearing trick and was now onboard the *Void Reaper*.

"I swear to God, if you say, 'the one percent' again, I'm going to lose my mind," Dailey breathed out, looking down at his command tablet and taking stock of the outcome of the battle. Three lost attack fighters, severe damage to the *Crow*'s forward deflector shields and secondary weapons cluster, one KIA from the attack wing, four Nova Rangers in critical condition, and Grear's raiders."

Miller had insisted he didn't know that Grear would sacrifice himself. Upon stepping back aboard the *Murphy*, Specialist Stacy Winters had found First Sergeant Becket and given him a handful of written letters and drives with recordings from Grear and the others who had stayed behind.

No words or disciplinary action was taken as Becket pulled the tearing woman into a clanking hug, followed by an understanding pat on her back. Rangers had been lost; now wasn't the time to discuss it.

Jen and Becket finally made their way to the briefing room just as Albert completed laying out the losses taken by the Alurians. Miller sat sprawled out on one of the oversize chairs facing the front of the space, trying not to laugh at Master Chief Thron's biblical rant about the condition of his galley after Albert had deactivated the gravity. Pearl, Dorax, and Bellman sat aboard the *Crow*, remoting into the meeting, waiting for Albert to start.

The AI turned to the group. "Well, that was exciting, wasn't it?"

Groans followed, as even Dailey found himself rolling his eyes. "Get to it."

"We will have the gate information for the *Void Reaper* in thirty minutes tops. It takes some time for our gate drive to process the residual event. But that's not what we're here for. We are here for that one percent, boss."

Dailey motioned for Albert to get to the point. He also noticed the ship was now under full thrust, heading toward Parif. "When Grear and his raiders, as I am hearing them be called, flipped that switch in the command center, they had to stay put in order to do so, with that, sacrificing themselves."

Dailey manipulated his index finger again, signaling Albert to get to it. "I don't want to get anyone's hopes up, and I'm beside myself for doing it, but I plugged Sparky into the internal comms of Grear's team. Next thing I know, *poof* . . . He's gone." Mister Toaster's face genuinely drooped. "He thought he could do something to save them. I haven't been able to reach him since."

Silence took hold of the room; not even Dailey had an intelligent reply. "Why are we heading to the moon base?"

"The one percent. It appears power is still flowing through the command area. Either the base is going to supernova in the near future, or . . ."

Dailey nodded in complete understanding. "The one percent. First sergeant."

"Sir?"

"I need you to go down to engineering, talk with Ensign Barthelo, and get a set of his reactor-worker suits. I'm going down there, and Albert, so are you. First Sergeant Becket will be in charge of the ship while we're out."

"Sir, might I recommend sending Specialist Winters? I know she just returned, but if we don't . . . You know what I'm saying."

Indeed, he did, understanding that if they went back down to see the fate of Grear's raiders and possibly save them without her, she would steal an attack fighter and go herself if she found out about her not being involved.

Coolio stepped forward, having been in the shadows in the back of the room. "Me too, sir."

"Make it three suits. Albert, what's the play?"

The AI cut right to the point. "There is a slight chance Sparky overloaded the system himself and the entire place is somehow cocooned in a reactor loop."

"Dumb it down," Dailey cut in.

"If the almighty Ham Overlord overpowered the reactor at the same time Grear was trying to activate it, they very well may not have needed to leave it open. They could be hunkered down in the command room as the reactor is phasing."

"Meaning, they could very well be alive. You're saying Sparky could have jump-started the scraper and then somehow protected the room?"

"Yes. I believe that would be the best way to put it. Any command or control center would undoubtedly be shielded. If they didn't actually continue to run the power directly through their location and Sparky somehow routed it away, I project a one percent chance of them surviving."

Bellman cleared his throat from the *Crow*. "The radiation levels will be through the roof. You sure about this?" He already knew the answer to his question even before Dailey stood up, heading toward the exit.

"Albert, pack up. Time to go. As for the rest of you, I want everyone and everything ready to gate out of here as soon as we return. Have the team on Asher get topside ASAP. Prescott knows they're underground by now."

Pearl quickly interjected. "We are already coordinating with the team on Asher. It looks like the Gulch is still in one piece. They are also sending five mining ships to gate them close to Earth."

Albert turned, pressing several buttons before finally unplugging himself from the console. "I'll do them one better. Tell that senator lady that I'll have them delivered to the coordinates I just sent over. Before you ask, I will do the rest as soon as we return. Just have the ships waiting. Chow!"

The live feed from the *Crow* winked out, while Pearl and the others onboard went to work, securing several of the gate drives before the Ocess Mining Syndicate could figure out what they were doing. When it was all said and done, every gate drive they could send back to Earth or Solaria meant one more ship they could bring to the fight, which also meant getting the tech into the hands of the Federation to integrate and upgrade if possible.

Dust bloomed around the group on the alien lunar surface, driven mainly by the Harpy and Dailey, Coolio, and Winters's ODA suits. Albert had simply been an afterthought, dropping to the ground without any thrust assistance.

Jen saluted Dailey through the cockpit, spinning the Harpy and launching back into space to provide cover and support until the team was ready to leave. That, and the ambient radiation was cutting off her comms from the ground, which had been one of the many reasons she'd insisted they do a light drop instead of her touching the craft down.

"Damn," Coolio huffed, pointing at the alarm display glowing in front of them. "That thing's lit up like a Christmas tree."

"I didn't know you were religious, Coolio," Winters said, activating a pole that extended into the air, followed by a round dish sprouting around the top. After a few seconds of pressing buttons, Winters shared the system readings through the group's HUDs.

"We can enter through the main port, which has the lowest surface radiation level concerning an entrance. Any reason we can't just bust through the exostructure?"

Albert stepped forward, grabbing the dish and plugging the sensor into his chest plate, ensuring the team's safety. Another factor they had to take into consideration was that while still able to maneuver, the additional weight of the radiation suits would slow the team's progress.

"The power was fed or transferred to the scraper through the exterior structure. It would fry us if we tried. Well, you, at least," Albert said, motioning the team to follow him. "And no, it would really mess my mojo up as well."

Looking down, familiar tracks from Grear's raiders' ODA boots stayed poised in the moon dust like relics from a lost civilization. Dailey motioned for the team to enter the initial round of airlocks as Albert took the lead, making quick work of the entrance.

Twenty minutes later, the team was gawking at the aftermath of the Nova Rangers' initial insertion before splitting off through the maintenance shafts. Albert stopped, plugging into one of the internal security panels, only to find it ultimately fried.

"Any luck?" Dailey asked as the radiation started hitting levels that pinged a red warning.

"No, everything's completely fried. And I mean everything," Albert said, sounding oddly upbeat.

"Why so happy?" Dailey quickly asked as Winters turned sideways to fit into the access tunnel.

Albert walked forward, the clank of his armored hooves echoing just before he pulled Winters out of the tight access tunnel. Without talking,

Albert stepped forward, extending his arms and legs, effectively doubling the size of the opening.

"No time to waste. Something's keeping the power flowing."

"Sparky," Dailey breathed out, following Albert as he started barreling his way through the small corridor like a blender.

The group spilled out into the shiny black hallway where the Rangers had taken out the last of the Ateris's defenses. Mangled bodies and contorted droids lay randomly, having met a violent end. Dailey turned, seeing Winters standing by one of her fallen teammates.

Dailey put his hand to her shoulder as she slowly turned. Glancing at the mangled body, Dailey bared witness to the dozens of rods protruding from Parks's body.

Albert made quick work of the blast doors, peeling them back like a tin can. Not only was the droid's body Albert had taken as his own strong, but the energy powering the ancient AI supercharged to a point that even he didn't fully comprehend.

Now standing like a stubborn child in front of them was the final set of blast doors to the command center. More bodies sat waiting for their ride to the afterlife as Albert slammed on the doors with all his might. Pausing, a significantly lighter knock answered back.

"Shit, someone's in there," Dailey huffed. The rads meter readout in his HUD was now a stable orange.

The main threat was outside the facility, and the main reason for the lack of comms.

"Albert, can you get those doors open?" Dailey asked as the AI turned to the left and started shredding a section of the paneled wall with his hands now in the form of claws.

Dailey tried again to use his communicator, but nothing besides static annoyingly greeted him back. By the time he was done checking, Albert had torn into the wall enough to find the pressurized hydraulic cylinder keeping the doors shut.

"What's the holdup?" Dailey asked as Albert walked back over to the door.

"I'm not sure what the conditions are like on the other side of that door. It's not fully pressurized out here, but it's enough to keep the gravity in place. I don't want them to get sucked out of the room and all that jazz."

Nodding, Coolio started to tap out a set of instructions to suit up. This was followed by an affirming acknowledgment that only another Nova Ranger would do.

After another five minutes, all that was left was for Albert to cut the hydraulic lines to fully open the doors. The rest of the time had been spent dismantling the large titanium cylinders that had sprung from the ground as part of the base's security protocol.

"Punch it," Dailey instructed. The main entrance doors parted like two out-of-control freight trains slamming into the side walls, ending any chance of them ever being used again. Hydraulic fluid spewed into the polished black entrance hall like bad special effects from an old, cheesy horror film where someone had just been decapitated by Freddy Krueger.

Lights pulsed from inside the command station, only to be washed out by the floodlights now beaming into the large space.

There, standing in the middle of the room like statues honoring long-forgotten heroes, were the remaining members of Grear's raiders.

"Sparky!" Albert bellowed as Dailey and the others poured into the room.

Lights continued to scan the room while Grear pointed at the primary command seat. Sitting on his hind legs with a cocked head was the Grand Ham Overlord himself.

Unlike the last time Sparky had saved the day, he was upright and clearly functioning. Albert, unable to contain himself, lurched forward, only to have Sparky let out several chuffing barks.

"Need to break the circuit first. And I am glad my work has saved everyone once again."

Albert pulled back, figuring this meant Sparky was somehow using his body to regulate the energy flow. "Eww," he added, realizing a slight haze covered the Alurian war hounds' armor.

"What's the score? I don't want to be here longer than needed," Dailey pressed while Grear pulled up the schematics of the facility on his tablet.

Dailey noted the high radiation levels still present. Grear's screen flickered from the interference. "Sir," Grear started in a washing mix of relieved focus. "The fastest way out of here is through the corridor to our left. We checked it out but couldn't go any farther due to the rads sensor going haywire. There is a set of quarters and a tunnel that leads to a private launchpad. From what we can tell, it was deliberately collapsed when Ran left, which means it can be deliberately reopened. We can work our way through it. Especially with him."

Grear motioned toward Albert, who was replaying a video on his facial display, making exaggerated hand gestures of the maneuver he'd pulled off with the *Murphy*, going inverted with the *Void Reaper*. Instead of figuring a way out of there, they were too busy telling each other how badass they had been. The truth of the matter was they *had* been, and Dailey would let them briefly enjoy their reunion while working out an exit plan.

"Hey, you two. Fun time's over; you can kiss and tell later. We have a way out of here, but it will take some work. It'll save us about ten minutes backtracking. If this thing is grounded, as you call it, will the radiation wash out like it does in space?"

"Oh, yes. We just need to plug me into that outlet, then let me discharge the Sparkster."

The group stood around glaring as Albert went into motion. Static continued to crackle through the comms while Dailey put a message out to Jen on a repeating loop. They would know when the time was right.

Opening his chest plate, Albert pulled out a clear triangle-shaped plug, slowly walking back toward Sparky. Much like a kid rubbing their sneakers on the carpet, knowing they were about to be shocked, Albert slowly lowered one of his thin clawlike digits on Sparky's head.

The effect was immediate: Albert and Sparky flew in opposite directions with a crackling snap, splitting the group's attention.

Smoke rose from both their bodies just as Jen pinged Dailey back, having received his message. "That's a good copy. I'm heading to the designated location. Is everyone safe?" she asked.

Before moving in dramatic fashion, Albert replied, "It's electrifying down here. You should have seen it. All I had to do was ground the reactor's main energy displacement and then shoot it all toward the scraper into one micro-pinpoint location . . . *Oh shit.*"

"I don't like *oh-shits*, Albert," Dailey groaned while Winters helped a wobbly-legged Sparky get up.

"I, uh, think we, uh, may have just made this thing have a meltdown, or you know, it may go supernova or cause a tiny chain reaction. Who knows. Didn't think about that last part."

Elbows and assholes flew down the corridor, as even Sparky forgot he was supposed to milk the display of brave electrocution just a little longer. When Albert said *Oh shit*, it was something you listened to and either left the immediate area or ducked under a desk for protection during what would most likely become a significant emotional event.

Busting through Ran's living quarters, bland uniforms and even blander furniture was quickly pushed aside in a flurry of discombobulated clanks and bangs. "Jen," Dailey barked. "Do you see a damaged passageway leading out to the landing pad?"

Albert had already started ripping the opening to shreds when Jen replied. "It looks like there's a small walkway that's been damaged from the outside. Do you want me to blast it?"

She slowed the Harpy down, hovering directly above the small private landing pad leading into the facility. Even though the outer hole of the building had been made to resemble moon rock, it was clearly part of a structure.

A bright snapping pop grabbed her attention as the rads meter on her display started bouncing like a drunk country girl during a line dance, something that had oddly made a comeback after centuries of being successfully buried by time.

The room shuddered as the rest of the group glanced around, also feeling the start of what was likely a chain reaction from the scraper's fusion reactor. "Albert?" Dailey asked while a combination of metal moon rock and dust flew out of the small opening Albert was dismantling with his claws. Pausing, Albert's Mister Toaster face turned. It was odd to see sweat literally beading on the brow of the artificial face of the mustache-wearing representative of the brand that had supplied the toaster now atop his head. "You good if Lieutenant Brax blasts this thing the rest of the way open?"

Instead of replying, Albert pushed the group of Nova Rangers out of the room in a flurry of motion, also taking control of the drop ship's forward turrets before automatically opening fire. Sparky, seeing this, let out a howl just as the first flecks of debris started slamming into the room like Napoleonic cannonballs.

A large chunk of the metal outer shielding spattered the room as Albert pushed the others into what appeared to be a solid black bathroom made of marble or some other smooth material, just like the hallways. Wherever the stone had come from, it sparkled, resembling a map of the universe itself.

"I can see light!" Jen exclaimed, forcing the Nova Rangers once again into motion while another shudder rippled through the facility as if a hydraulic press was crushing an empty beer can with little to no effort.

The immediate sucking *whoosh* of the vacuum of space pulling out the dust and debris forced everybody to quickly brace themselves. Even though they were expecting it, it was clearly one of the only exposed openings to the outer environment, quadrupling the vacuum effect.

Several seconds after all the environment had been pulled out into space, the room landed on a steely calm. Winters, Coolio, and the other remaining Rangers plowed through what was left of the opening while Jen, having regained control of the Harpy, laid the ship down with its ass end wide open, pointing toward the gap in the crumpled fake moon rocks.

Dailey stopped, being the last man in the room other than Sparky, looking down at Albert, who was trying unsuccessfully to get himself upright. Between the slick marble and the fact that one of his legs was lying on the opposite side of the room, it was clear Albert was going to be struggling to get moving.

Sparky instinctually grabbed one of his appendages, pulling on them with all the might the dog could muster in the low-gravity situation. "Stop, you're just going to wear yourself out. Albert, talk to me," Dailey pushed.

"It looks like I'm not going to be winning any jump rope competitions today," Albert joked. A thin hairline crack in Mister Toaster's screen started to show. "I really like this body, guys. If you can grab my leg and pull me out of this corner, I should be able to drag myself to the ship."

With the tremors rumbling through the facility every few seconds, it was clear time was not on their side. Sparky and Dailey immediately went to work, the man motioning for Sparky to grab Albert's leg while Dailey turned his back to the AI.

"Turn on whatever kind of magnetic clip you have on your hands and slap them on the side of my legs," Dailey instructed. An even stronger rumble convinced Albert not to argue the point.

Grear's head popped in through the hole, seeing the chaos of them working to get Albert out. "Can't you just pop out that box in his chest?"

"We're going to get him out of here. All of him," Dailey replied, turning to see Mister Toaster smile.

Not wanting to waste any more time, Dailey activated all his rear thrusters, including the ones on his calves, and pressed forward, forcing Grear out of the way. Within seconds, the dark ball of the Harpy came into view, as Sparky dropped Albert's leg on the back deck, hopping up and down for them both to hurry.

The *Murphy*'s captain didn't pause to see what was causing the brilliant flashes of light reflecting off not only Sparky's armor but the back of the Harpy after a damn near Oscar-worthy rescue. There had been more than one on this day.

"We gotta go. Now!" Jen's now hardened voice commanded.

Without skipping a beat, Dailey slammed into the rear of the cargo bay while Albert finally released the magnetic connectors on his hands, sliding to a halt right beside Coolio and the other Rangers. Grear slammed the button to retract the ramp, as Jen had already taken off.

Turning, Dailey could see the ground shuffling, looking as if it was waving, sending them off with a goodbye note. *Goodbye, come see us again real soon now, ya hear.*

Before the ramp completely sealed shut, a blinding white light erupted from the moon as if it was giving birth to its own sun. The Harpy shuddered under the initial wave of the explosion, only to smooth out after Jen continued to push the drop ship to its very limits.

Dailey pushed his way to the cockpit while the rest of the team settled in. Albert had effectively pulled himself into the crew command seat in front of the monitors directly behind Jen and the other three flight stations.

Seeing the rads meter was now within reason, Dailey clicked the sides of his helmet, finally taking it off, followed by the others. As soon as Grear did the same, the rads meter lightly spiked. They would be in decontamination for days, if not weeks. Sparky, on the other hand, had a way with things like radiation. He was now sitting with his belly armor pulled back, exposing his death stars while sitting on his butt with his legs flopped over.

"All I can tell you is that the whole place is about to blow," Jen huffed, murmuring into her comms, relaying their status to the *Murphy.*

"If you ask me," Albert interjected, "I think that scraper is going to fire one more time when that thing blows. I was trying to work my way through the subsystems once we—well, I rechanneled all that energy." Albert paused, reviewing the information as the toast-is-done pinged. "I believe it's set on firing again as soon as it is charged at the exact same coordinates. Luckily for us, no one's there anymore."

"King!" Dailey barked into the comms. "Give me a direct line to Director Prescott."

Not able to affect the image on the small viewscreen in the Harpy, Director Prescott's actual birdlike face came into view. Aggravation painted his lips while he squeezed them tight enough to break concrete. "What," was all the man said.

"Albert, send the initial firing coordinates to this channel. Director Prescott, that big, nasty laser is about the fire again, and there's not a damn thing I can do to stop it."

As the words slipped across his lips like a surfer who had planned the perfect wave, a blinding green flash of light, followed by a rocking explosion, echoed through the now calm aftermath of the battle. Prescott's eyes widened as his audio cut short; he was clearly screaming directions at somebody. Likely forgetting he was still on a live video feed, he turned to someone else, showing a nod of respect before quickly turning back to the viewscreen.

"Our ships are out of the way. I expect a full explanation," Prescott insisted as Albert blew an audible raspberry over the comms.

"Sure thing. I'll get the entire report together for you and send it over as soon as possible," Albert concluded before the viewscreen winked out and was replaced by the rear camera view of Parif.

A massive chunk of the moon was floating away, looking as if somebody had accidentally swallowed a handful of sand and was now spitting it out while being videotaped in slow motion.

"Jesus," Dailey grumbled. "Albert, when you said entire report, did you mean one of those things that would take about fifty years to put together and even longer to sort through?"

"Yup. I'll even put together a couple of petabytes of information on the wind velocity on Parif's surface as an opener. Real dripping stuff."

Pearl's voice interrupted the calm as the *Murphy*, reattached to the *Crow*, became larger and larger through the cockpit windows. "It appears the detonation has stabilized. Most of the energy from the explosion was dispelled in the final overcharged activation of the scraper; I thought you all would like to know. Also, we have the charting data on the *Void Reaper*. Once Albert returns, we should be able to triangulate its location and get moving."

"Triangulate, shmiangulate. I've already got all that mostly figured out. Road trip! Shotgun!" Albert exclaimed as Sparky howled, which roughly translated to him stating he would bring the ham along for the ride.

CHAPTER 34

AFTERGLOW

Bellman, Hontz, and Barthelo stood back from the large metal table while Albert articulated his newly attached leg. After returning to the *Murphy*, it hadn't taken them long to realize that the team needed to not only reconstitute and refit themselves but take an actual deep breath.

Albert had already computed how to track the *Void Reaper* through whatever gates its crew decided to use. The now-back-together AI was also confident that after the battle, the team could take time to pull themselves back together.

Sparky had remained by his best friend's side during the entire overly dramatic procedure, which had included taking out Albert's original main housing and setting it neatly on a table during the whole operation, as he was calling it.

After clearing up the remainder of the small Alurian fighters, the Ocess Syndicate had taken a defensive posture and orbit above Asher. While Dailey and the others were not thrilled about this, it aligned with their previous conversation; they would be staying in the system.

Dailey's voice came over the comms in the engineering section. "If you guys are done putting Humpty Dumpty back together again, I'd like him to meet us back on the bridge. Lieutenant McAlister and the rest of the team from Asher are flying up to see us."

Glancing down at his tablet, a message flashed from Senator Deborah Powell. Now that the Alurians were no longer a threat, at least for now, they could utilize the gate communication system freely.

Dailey answered the call, the senator's face popping onto the main viewscreen. Communications Officer King and Albert's preprogrammed communications protocol took over, sharpening the image.

"Captain Dailey," the senator started. Dailey found himself squinting his eyes, trying to figure out the detail in the image that wasn't making any sense. "We just received five mining cargo ships. From what I understand, they should not take long to integrate into the new ships."

The truth of the matter was, Albert had left a version of the HAM to do nothing more than run the communication system through the gate in Atlantis and also integrate any gate tech they may be able to send back to Earth. The HAM was a slight variation of the initial subroutine created for the *Scarecrow*.

"Senator Powell, it's good to see you," Dailey replied.

Deborah Powell cleared her throat, pointing up to her shoulders. "You can call me Admiral Powell, if you feel inclined or obligated to do so, Captain Dailey."

Pausing at the statement, the gears started to whirl through his thoughts. "Don't tell me you resigned your position on the senate and got your commission reinstated."

"Someone has to take charge of all this stuff and also make sure things are on the up and up. Before you say it, they would not let me go back into the Army as a general, saying they needed me as a Fleet admiral."

"I'm just saying, Fleet food is a hell of a lot better than Army chow. Why do you think I have a Fleet mess crew."

Admiral Powell grinned at the statement. "I think the next part might be just as interesting. Once our three flagships are integrated with the gate drives, I'm leading the mission to Asher."

Dailey scowled at the statement, knowing that the Ocess Syndicate would find it highly aggravating to have a significantly larger fleet presence appear out of nowhere with gate-drive technology, something he had absolutely not shared with Director Prescott.

Admiral Powell held up a hand in placation. "I already know Director Prescott helped. Albert is rather forthcoming in what he discusses at times, especially if you get him off topic. Considering his recent actions and those of his syndicate, we are prepared to work with Director Prescott. To be one hundred percent transparent, they're pretty much the only mining syndicate left that the Federation feels it can trust. If you can believe that shit."

Dailey would have to talk with Albert later about his passing of too much information. In reality, Albert had scanned the woman's background and not only trusted her but also projected it would be in Dailey's and the other's best interest for her to know this information.

"I'll let Prescott know the situation. We plan on pursuing Ran and whatever Alurian team was in control of that battle group." Dailey wasn't asking for permission, instead telling the admiral precisely what he and his ships were going to do.

"I figured as much and already authorized the operation, just in case you were wondering." The admiral paused a second too long before starting back up. "They want to take the fight to the Alurians."

Dailey reflected on the statement as if he knew he was about to get bad news from the doctor but was somehow already at peace with it. "According to the crew on Asher, we have eight more mining ships to send. After that, it might be worth a trip back to the depot we took out. Listen, the Fleet isn't used to being this far out. It's different; it's wild; it's untamed. The more and more I'm this far out, the more and more I'm convinced there is a whole hell of a lot we don't understand about our own galaxy's outer systems."

Admiral Powell nodded, agreeing with the statement. Her overly pressed uniform stayed still, incapable of budging even if a tornado kicked off right beside her. In his mind, Dailey could picture her walking around stiff armed and legged in the crisp new uniform like an old soldier for some dictator back on Earth centuries ago.

"One more thing. I want the forces that we have on Asher to stay put for now. We will replace them as soon as we get a couple of ships out there. We would like to still have their presence planetside."

The logic was sound. Keep the planet secured and under control until the calvary arrived. After addressing a few more housekeeping items, Admiral Powell signed off. Turning, he saw Becket was waiting by the entrance to escort the *Murphy*'s captain to the briefing room.

"Everyone's waiting. Mac's here, as well as Walker. The engineers we got from the moon base are heading back to Asher. They didn't bring any other representatives; we want to keep this conversation in-house."

Dailey agreed with his first sergeant as usual as the men entered a loud and crowded briefing room. Familiar faces, smiles, and the sound of cups being set on tables only to be picked back up filled the air, reminding him of days long since passed.

The bluish-grey lights gave the room an ambiance that wasn't surgically bright. As was the norm, when the room filled up with people, a light haze filled the space from the environmental control system acclimating to the significant amount of carbon dioxide that was now being pumped into the room.

Glancing to his right, he caught Albert and Sparky leaning in while talking to each other. They were clearly discussing someone on the ship's love life, as it was nearly impossible not to see where Albert was looking.

"Alright, everybody, bring it in," Dailey started as a low, rumbling hush filled the room. "First, I want to let everyone here know what an exceptional job they have done, not only today but over the past several days. Next, I need to unfortunately continue to inform you that we are far from completing this mission."

"So, we're really going after them?" Science Officer Bellman asked, chuckling, already knowing the answer.

"All of us. That includes that whale of a ship we're now latched onto like a needy child. Since you bring up the point, I'd also like to get all section leaders to free up a body or two to man the *Crow* properly. We'll have some time while gating, and I would like to use it to get more than just a handful of people familiar with the ship."

Pausing, Dailey looked over at Dorax and Pearl. "As promised, I'm going to get you about fifteen bodies to run that bridge."

Dorax smiled slightly. "Does that mean you're not going to blow up the ship?"

"Point of order," Albert spoke up. "According to legalities and all that mumbo-jumbo, Captain Dailey never put any time parameters on that statement."

Albert's logic once again crushed Dorax's attempt to fit in.

"I think we can say we are good for now. I would also like to talk with you before we head out." Dorax nodded. First Sergeant Becket stepped forward like he was cutting line at a concert.

"We still have a lot of work to do. I need a full inventory of all damaged items to send back to the admiral before they head this way for replacement. My understanding is they have a location set up at the Gulch for us to work out of while the mission progresses."

First Sergeant Becket was making a good point. One of the plans they had come up with shortly after returning from Parif was to have Albert program the gate drive to send them back to Asher in case of an emergency. This, of course, could involve gating to several other locations first to avoid being followed.

After another ten minutes of housekeeping items, including assigning volunteers to help situate the galley, the group dispersed, minus Dorax; the Alurian raider sat with his arms crossed. In many ways, the freedom that Dailey had afforded him was more unnerving than any threats of getting ejected out of an airlock.

Dailey pulled the communicator off his hip, slapping it on the table in front of Dorax, signaling an open conversation. This relatively recent tradition let the other participants know they were talking off the books.

"So. What do ya think?" Dailey asked, leaning back in the chair opposite of him.

Dorax uncrossed his arms. "That's a rather open-ended question."

"I like you more and more every day. And, if we're being honest here, so does Pearl. She sent me a quick report on your actions during the engagement."

"I am guessing my actions were satisfactory," Dorax replied, shuffling lightly in his seat.

"Hell, if you were actually a member of the Fleet, you would likely be getting a medal or some shit. No, what do you think about sticking around for a while and seeing this thing through?"

Dorax briefly licked his greenish lips, working to keep it from being off-putting. "If you mean killing Alurians, then no." The statement took Dailey aback, but Dorax lifted a finger to let him finish his thought. "If you mean righting a wrong and also addressing the syndicates, then yes."

Dailey leaned forward, squinting his eyes as if trying to read the man's soul. "What wrongs are you . . . are we righting?"

"That battle group was days, if not hours, away from sending in a ground force to wipe out whatever noncomplying people they could find. Which, in their eyes, probably meant everyone. You asked me to hang around and think like an Alurian. Use my gut, I think you said."

"That's right." Dailey motioned for him to continue.

"That battle group was bought and paid for. Rogue, if that makes more sense. A true Alurian battle group would not be out here helping get a mining operation under control. They would have simply destroyed it from a system away and not blinked an eye. I'm thinking this group may be on their own. If they were, there is no turning back now due to the number of ships they lost. No way to keep that clean."

Dailey nodded, taking in the logic. "So you think this has something to do with the syndicates and Asher?"

"It would make sense. From what Pearl told me about this General Ran, yes. Maybe I'm wrong about them not being part of an Alurian operation. All I can say is that out here, I'm surprised we didn't run into a group of raiders," Dorax explained thoughtfully.

"You know something Becket and I were discussing that I just can't get over?" Dailey leaned forward. "We ran into an entire planet-sized moon made out of Gormanium, something I didn't know much about till a couple of days ago. Then we have Asher. There's something about that planet that I just can't put my finger on."

"Maybe it's more about location?"

"It does seem to connect to a hell of a lot of other locations. At least that's what Albert says about the programming in the gate drive. Either way, I'm glad to hear you're sticking around."

"For now," Dorax added. While he had been at the mercy of Dailey and the others, he was still a proud Alurian raider.

"I'm not going to ask you to do anything you don't want to do, but I'll make you this promise again. As long as you're part of this crew, you are under my protection."

"I see, and I also see you have friends in high places. One last thing; everyone around here seems to think the Alurians are the ones pushing all the buttons. I'd make sure that's the actual case." He was referring to now Admiral Powell, and his belief that the syndicates had more blood on their hands than the Federation wanted to believe.

Dailey's comms link beeped, only to have Albert's voice pop up. "Hey, boys and girls. If you two are done playing patty-cakes, I may have, in my infinite wisdom, sent a probe through a mini gate into innerspace to trace any anomalies following the *Void Reaper*. Total success, if you're interested in all that."

Both men looked at Dailey's comms link sitting on the table.

"You ready?" the *Murphy*'s captain asked as Dorax nodded, standing up and extending a hand to shake.

CHAPTER 35

PARTING IS SUCH SWEET ADIEU

The bridge on the *Crow* was alive with activity while Dailey and the others stood in the middle of what had been dubbed the rib cage. Several stations still sat empty, a mix of personnel shuffling around, making last-minute preparations to pursue the *Void Reaper*.

A full two days had passed since the end of the mission, and Albert was continuously sending probes out to ensure the *Murphy* would not get too far behind. The Ocess Syndicate, after a call with Admiral Powell, had come to terms with the heavens above Asher becoming even busier.

Director Prescott had turned three shades darker than he probably had since birth. During the conversation, not only had he been confused by the speed in which the Fleet would be able to make it to Asher, but also the fact that Dailey had likely known this all along.

In the man's defense, he hadn't, and was only now playing the mysterious, I-have-a-secret card.

The massive central screen in front of the multilayered bridge had been calibrated for ease of use. Unlike most ships, where there were just one or two transmit cameras, the *Crow*'s entire exterior was covered in miniature video-feed transponders. While not 3D, the live feed was hyperrealistic, looking as if you were standing in front of a spotless window. The type of window birds would often slam into, unable to see.

When the ship turned, the view could be customized or stay on the current heading. Above this, a weapons-and-targeting readout section stretched all the way up to the top of the roof, only cut off by a dashed countdown timer programmed by Albert to track gate times.

Below this, several different views of the ship were represented in various shades of colors, or as Albert put it, "The status report for dummies."

Sparky, now sporting a fancy One Percent logo on the retracted back-plate of his armor, patrolled the area overlooking the recessed navigation stations. He had been sure to give the crew below a good view of his undercarriage while doing so.

Dailey sat in the command chair, giving it a light bounce, smiling at Pearl and Dorax, who had clearly had a follow-up conversation after the briefing. "What do you think?"

Pearl smiled, also donning an appropriate set of rank on her shoulders. While it was a temporary field promotion, in her eyes, it was a promotion, nonetheless. "I believe we will be more than adequate. Everything checks out, and before you came aboard, we were able to gain functional control of twenty-five percent more of the outer weapons systems. Which reminds me, we were able to dial into the onboard mechs."

"Those dusty old things?" Albert scoffed, hopping out of the navigation stations at ground level. "Just remember you can manually pilot those things from the inside. That combat system they have programmed was nasty business. I deleted it, of course. In the process, I figured out a few neat little tricks to take them out of a fight if we ever run up against any."

Remembering the sheer amount of the metal machines of war onboard jogged his initial thoughts on them. These were new combatants to the Nova Rangers, who had only had to deal with older versions during the war.

"We didn't really get the brunt of those things during the fight. How would one of my Rangers fare against one? Just the automated ones, not one driven by an Alurian," Dailey asked while Barthelo handed him an old-school clipboard, the type gym teachers used to keep scores on.

"One-on-one, no question the Nova Ranger wins." Albert paused, literally going through a combat scenario using the software he'd downloaded from one of the mechs. "Uhh, ninety-eight point three percent of the time."

"What is the other one-point-seven percent about?" Dailey asked.

Mister Toaster's face let a grin slip. "You know. The Ranger might have a bad case of gas, or there could be, say, two thousand of them. Then that chance goes down to a cool zero-point-five percent."

"Zero-point-five?"

"Yes, zero-point-five. They may figure out they are a god or something, or all their prayers finally pay off, which goes up a tidbit. Who knows. The mechs could have also fallen victim to a scorned-lover mechanic who was angry with his droid girlfriend and poisoned all the lubricators. Do you want me to keep going?"

The scary part about the conversation was the odds that Albert had pulled those situations from actual events from files or some Alurian database somewhere.

"Point taken," Dailey said, trying to visualize all of Albert's scenarios. "Tell us about the gate drives. You said we were ready to go earlier."

"One takeaway—the ship absolutely has some super sexy drive on it. For now, I've got it tuned to the *Murphy*'s. Nothing too crazy until we figure it out." He ended the sentence sounding like a stern mother warning her child not to eat any more cookies out of the jar on top of the refrigerator.

"Sounds like we can just keep the ships hooked together and gate without any problems," Dorax added.

"Right you are. Or we could even gate separately and still end up at the same location."

This garnered a round of approving nods. Sparky joined the group, having no clue what was being discussed. "Hey, Sparky. I saw someone from the galley bring aboard a couple of crates of some mysterious type of meat from Earth. Do you know anything about that?"

Three rounds of chuffs, quick barks, puffs, and what was likely the passage of gas later, Sparky's translator kicked in. "I will carry on the legacy of the *Scarecrow*. Plus, I need more space for all my bravery medals."

"Well, hot damn." Dailey chuckled. "Sounds like we're about to get in a hell of a lot more trouble if you plan on earning that many more medals."

"Perhaps. I would also like to declare I have saved the day once again," Sparky yipped. He was looking for someone to scratch behind his ears, so Albert obliged, shooting a pointy rod in the gap between the hound's skin and armor, directly behind his stubby neck.

"Albert, you ready to do this thing?" Dailey asked. With the two ships connected, Dailey had decided to ride out the initial gate utilizing the *Crow*'s drive.

In many ways, the ships felt as if they were one and the same. The main differing factor was the rigid and, at times, overly militarized Alurian architecture.

Pearl walked over to the communications station, going through several orders, including informing Director Prescott that they were now leaving the sector. This was followed up with the projected three-day lead time of Admiral Powell and the new starships arriving at Asher.

With the new gate-drive technology installed, Becket, in a stroke of genius, had given the new class of vessel their own designation. Earth ships modified with gate drives would be known as Void-class starships moving forward.

Within thirty minutes, both teams were on full alert and had crewed their respective battle stations. Dailey had put this protocol in place for any time the ship was to enter or exit a gate, no matter the circumstances.

Nodding, Albert pressed the red button now flashing, as a snapping wave immediately formed in front of the *Crow*. It was instantly evident that the gate-drive technology they had been using aboard the *Murphy* was akin to something that had been pulled out of the river after several hundred years and put back in service, only for it to die then be brought back to life by a cheap mechanic.

Even the pulsing vibration was lessened by the new tech as the massive hull of the dreadnaught started slipping through the event horizon into the gate. Just as Dailey was about to lean back in the executive officer's chair, which he had commandeered on the bridge of the *Crow*, several purple and red lights started flashing. This was followed by several burping beeps from every station onboard.

"Albert!" Dailey barked, seeing everyone scramble, unable to comprehend the sheer number of alarms and buttons beeping on the oversize bridge.

"I—It's . . . We," Albert stuttered as a whooping *thump* preceded the still calmness of innerspace.

"Albert," Dailey said in a calmer tone.

"I don't—The transponder, it—" Albert stammered again before finally getting his digital shit together. "This is all my fault."

"What's your fault?" Dailey quickly asked. Albert, for the first time since Dailey could remember, leaned back, uncoupling everything he had on his body either from the console or some random plug.

"We forgot to take the transponder that Director Prescott gave us off the *Murphy*."

"So?" Dailey asked, cocking his head sideways. He didn't like how that statement was sitting in his guts.

"I'm going to turn that thing into cinders, and then I'm going to flush it down the toilet after I get done with dropping a lube. The transponder came alive as soon as we activated the gate. There was some kind of preloaded AI that did something to the system."

Dailey was down to four- and five-word sentences, trying to get to the point. "Did what to the systems?"

"That's it. We won't know until we come out of the other side. I'm already prepping a probe to see where we come out. I don't know any other way to say this, but we may very well be lost in space. Before you ask, the AI system used what is called a randomizer. It rolled the dice on our destination, and somehow, our system took it and executed it."

"Nothing is ever easy," Dailey said, standing up. "I'm going to go ahead and take a wild guess that they know exactly where this thing comes out."

Albert just shook his head, walking toward the small lift in the back of the spinelike bridge. Dailey turned to join the now slumped-over AI. "Pearl, Dorax. I'll let you know what we find. Until then, stay on alert."

They both saluted as the two made their way back to the *Murphy*. Albert continued to belittle himself as they walked to Pearl's old navigation station, seeing the transponder. Within seconds, Albert picked up the smooth, round device, turning it into dust within his clawed hands. "I'm sort of hoping you actually downloaded whatever crap was in that thing before you did that."

"Yes. I'm going to need some time to go through everything. This will at least give us some sort of idea if this damn thing did anything else while we weren't looking. When *I* wasn't looking," Albert emphasized.

"We both missed this one. If we can, we need to send a message back. Listen, take your time. Find out how long we're going to be in innerspace first."

Albert sat back on his modified station as all the lights, including Mister Toaster's face, went blank. Albert was in what he called deep-thought mode.

First Sergeant Becket walked onto the bridge at a light trot, seeing the frustration pouring off Dailey's face like a glass of wine slung at someone during a date gone wrong. "How bad is it?"

"Don't know yet," Dailey grumbled.

"The crew heard the alarms going off. I'm not saying everyone's freaking out, but they're freaking out," Becket said, still trying to gauge Dailey's perspective on the situation, not having heard the previous conversation.

"Top, for once, I have no clue what kind of shit show we got ourselves into. Albert, as you can see, is trying to figure that all out. This is all uncharted territory."

Becket pondered the statement, then both men realized the quietness of the bridge. Everyone was listening to their conversation. Becket cleared his throat. "Everyone, get back to work. We aren't dead yet, which means we're on the clock."

A few groans and *rogers* came their way as Dailey glanced back at Albert. "I want to get some time exploring the rest of the *Crow*. It will give everyone something to do, and we might just find something helpful."

With a nodding salute, Becket turned, walking off the bridge. Dailey slowly headed to the main viewport, staring into the black, starless abyss of innerspace.

EPILOGUE

Ships darted with random purposes as the *Void Reaper* melted into the hundreds of other massive ships, all swarming the spaceport with separate goals. Dozens of large, round, floating columns resembling upside-down cones that thinned out as they connected in the middle with docking platforms in set intervals supporting various sizes of ships. The overall scale of the port would be staggering by Earth standards.

The planet below glowed a radiant blue and green, giving way to a tropical world with an atmosphere so clear it looked fake.

Kluvnew stepped forward, pinning his arms behind his back. "I hope you understand the ramifications of this failure."

"Failure?" Ran rebuked, continuing to scan the view of the planet below as the *Void Reaper* docked.

"The Ateris Syndicate's. You seem to be the only one capable of surviving or getting anything done in your assigned sector. You know the Prime Assembly will have questions that they will look to you to answer."

Ran held back the grin he so wanted to let out in the open. "I will need to coordinate with my leadership."

"That will not be necessary," Kluvnew reaffirmed. "You accomplished your mission and, with that, will be respected. This was, as you say, off the books. The ships we lost, while grave, were not part of the primary initiative. We will endure this tragic loss. The incompetence of Derrisa and the others will not be soon forgotten."

Ran again nodded. "You know the Ocess Syndicate was present, as well as that Alurian dreadnaught."

"That will be addressed in due time. I am aware that things are not as simple as we initially believed them to be. We must secure Asher, as I am being told is now called, and the prize it holds." Kluvnew turned to a chiseled Alurian officer handing him a tablet.

Video feed of the massive canyon the *Murphy* had etched into the side of the *Void Reaper* made the Alurian's frown solidify. Seeing this, the younger officer cleared his throat, letting it rasp in the back of his throat, as did most Alurians. A habit that disgusted Ran.

"Sir, the Ateris Syndicate is sending an envoy. They want to talk with the human," the Alurian officer added, referring to Ran.

Kluvnew turned to Ran for guidance.

"Yes, they will want a full report," Ran said, nodding at the others. If he was correct, he had played his hand perfectly.

"Yes. Three of the latest generation of Fleet ships were destroyed, and the Ocess Syndicate has shown who they will bed down with at night. You see a failure." Kluvnew paused before starting again as a star cruiser pulled into view. "I can see it in your eyes you have reservations. But I see a victory. All your time with the Fleet has made you forget the broader picture of things. The Alurian council would sacrifice several battle groups for this. No, you need to understand that war is coming, and I will be more than glad to be the one lighting the flame."

Purplish greys swirled on the planet below as Daile and the others watched the small probe they had just launched disappear into the alien atmosphere. Several charts and odd targets blipped on and off the viewscreen to their side while Albert continued to work through their location. Even after exploring hundreds of planets, they had yet to see one with the color spectrum dully glowing like a fading light bulb below.

Within seconds, the probe confirmed the planet did indeed have a surface and wasn't a gas giant.

Two moons, appearing close enough to enable one to jump from one to the other, slowly turned. Light from the distant sun cast shadows between them, almost making them appear connected.

"Ah, yes," Albert finally said. The others turned. Even Sparky looked up in anticipation.

"And?" Dailey asked.

Since being diverted, the *Murphy*'s captain had grown impatient, unable to communicate with Earth or the team on Asher. According to Albert, with no real idea of the route the gate had taken, it would be impossible to configure a way to send a message as they had prior.

"We're totally lost. But I can tell you is, where we aren't."

The collective sigh from the group was audible. Having left the *Crow* to join the command team accompanied by Dorax, Pearl stepped forward. As a Federation-trained navigation officer, she knew understanding where you weren't was often the first step in understanding just how lost you truly were.

"I take it we aren't in the Milky Way or Andromeda?" Pearl stated flatly, looking at the space-chart icons Albert had left on the viewscreen, tracing her fingers along one of the star clusters visible from their location.

"Perhaps," Albert drawled out again, giving no true answer. "I'd say definitely not in the Milky Way."

Pearl squinted her eyes, pulling up several large star charts from various outer-rim satellites. Swiping them out of the way, she directed the program to remove any nonrelevant charts. "There," she concluded as a "two percent" flashed over three random star charts.

"You might have something here," Albert said, taking over the controls while Pearl crossed her arms over her chest, giving the AI a smug look of satisfaction.

"Let me guess," Dailey started. "Same as last time. It lines up two percent, so we likely have a match."

"Close. The two percent here tells us the probability of our location being within these dark voids," Albert replied, pulling up several more star charts. Some even looked as if they were part of the first human book ever written, including drawings and even etchings of star charts.

"What about the gate-drive data or the transponder?" Bellman asked, sipping some of his ever-famous homemade rum.

"I am taking that into account now," Albert said as all the data he had pulled up started morphing together. "Yes, we are likely somewhere on the complete opposite side of Andromeda."

Whistles and huffs exploded as the gravity of their current situation sunk in before Dailey cleared his throat. "Can we use the data you pulled from the transponder to get back?"

"Yes," was all Albert replied.

Dailey, knowing this game, clarified his question. "How long will it take?"

"If I put all the processing data I and both the ships' systems have together . . . Let's say one to two years. I put some cushion in there in case my super big brain is needed elsewhere."

Becket stood straight, rolling his shoulders back as Sparky jumped into a nearby seat. After several chuffs and a bark, his translator kicked in. "Just find another magic box."

Everyone turned to the Alurian war hound while Albert tapped his elongated finger on his face's viewscreen. "Hmph. Yeah, why not. Humankind has explored a good portion of their galaxy. Why wouldn't the Alurians or syndicates be doing the same in this galaxy? I mean, it's a great idea if you ask me."

"If there are any around. We can't use the gate drive without it being calibrated to the system we're in," Dailey grumbled.

Just as the *Murphy*'s commander started to refocus on the task, Kline spoke up. "Hey, hey! Something is coming over the VHF range bands," he excitably proclaimed as Albert took two leaping strides to the communications stations.

VHF range frequency bands were something used by planetside hobbyists or as a backup for degraded communications. It was also something very specific to Earth.

"Well, look at that. The only reason it pinged the radar is due to a rather outdated, rusted satellite in orbit," Albert said, tuning in the message as a staticky feed started droning through the *Crow*'s bridge.

While Albert shuffled through the frequencies, Dailey swore he could hear light jazz or something with an old 1920s horn vibe skim his ears before being immediately overshadowed by the sounds of a young woman's voice in clear English.

"Hello, this is Captain Sarah Thorton. I am at the following coordinates." The woman's neutral voice continued to dole out numbers in the same manner one would on Earth. "We need help. The Shade is here."

The message went on to repeat itself, being on a continuous loop. Albert displayed the transcription on the main screen as Dailey turned to the group. "Am I the only one who finds it odd that someone on what is likely the opposite side of an opposing galaxy speaks English?"

ACKNOWLEDGMENTS

To all the fans of the *Murphy*'s crew and their antics, Albert and Sparky would like to say thanks. Thank you for joining us on this epic ride. I hope you are enjoying reading the journey as much as I did creating it. Thank you to all my friends and family. That includes you, the reader or listener; you're fam now.

For our audio listeners: thank you. Luke Daniels, you the man! You are a master of your craft and an amazing person.

This book is ultimately dedicated to all the brave men and women I served with and, in some cases, lost in dire times of hardship, and the friendships also shared.

In the distant future immortal words of Sparky . . .

CARPE HAM

ABOUT THE AUTHOR

Justin S. Leslie is the bestselling author of the Max Abaddon, Sinking Man, and Descending Worlds series, as well as a retired Army major who served several combat tours. When he isn't writing, playing music, or spending time with his family, Leslie can be found at his home in Doctors Inlet, Florida, immersed in his latest urban-fantasy or military sci-fi project or a well-made cocktail.

DISCOVER
STORIES UNBOUND

PodiumAudio.com

Printed in the USA
CPSIA information can be obtained
at www.ICGtesting.com
JSHW022221140824
68134JS00018B/1181

9 781039 450271